I0731562

Division One:
Mega Moth

by Stephanie Osborn

Chromosphere Press

Huntsville, AL

Table of Contents

Foreword

Most of the *Division One* books are very action-adventure oriented. This one has a lot of that, but also a good bit of character development and interaction. I felt that much of this was required, to realistically depict the Alpha One team's recovery from the events of recent books. In that respect, this is a two-plot novel: Echo's recovery from torture and loss of limb and Omega's slow recovery from PTSD, and the Mega Moth itself.

However, fans also clamored for a complete depiction of the Division One 'family' through the holidays—Thanksgiving, Christmas, and New Years, all three. So I've done my best to work that in, and give the fans what they wanted. I hope you enjoy it.

Chapter 1

On the day before a major holiday on the host world, a Kydeen family of four, looking like nothing so much as giant koalas—though their cuddly appearance belied their fierce natures, necessary for survival on their rugged, half-wild homeworld—debarked their Tentesse Spacelines craft into the gate at the concourse, towing their carry-on luggage, then proceeded toward the people-mover that would take them to baggage claim.

In short order, they obtained their luggage in the baggage claim area in Grand Central Station, whereupon they entered the convenient changing area, emerging in disguises which made them look like a family of somewhat portly humans, and headed for the main exit of Division One Agency Headquarters to summon a taxi.

* * *

The usual taxi drivers who serviced Headquarters were, themselves, offworlders, and understood the needs of the visitors, helping them whenever necessary; it did not do for the local civilians to become aware of their true nature, as an attempted invasion of Earth a few years back had demonstrated.

So Chunga Kergun got out of the car and assisted the disguised Kydeen in loading their luggage into the trunk. The elder child, who was trundling two small cases, gave both to Kergun, then climbed into the back seat with her younger brother and mother; the father would be riding in the front with the cab driver.

Within moments, they were off, en route to their hotel and an exciting school-break vacation on Earth.

* * *

Thanksgiving morning arrived only a very few days after Echo had been released from the medlab, so he was still considered incapacitated and in physical—and mental—therapy after his encounter with the Cortians and their torture expert. His newly-regenerated leg was nowhere near strong enough to walk on as yet, and as of his first day in therapy some days prior, could not even support his weight; he had, therefore, been given very specific orders not to try. So when he awoke alone in the big bed, with nature calling exceeding loudly, and the antigrav 'wheelchair' across the room rather than close to the bed and within reach, he bit his lip and looked around, surveying the room.

Light's not on in the bathroom, he observed. *Door's not even closed; she's probably not in there. Bedroom door's closed, too, but there's a sliver of light coming from the other side. She's up and about, probably getting ready for company, since today's...today IS Thanksgiving, isn't it?* He reached over and grabbed his cell phone from his nightstand and checked the date, noting as he did so that another cell phone lay on the matching nightstand on the other side of the bed. *Yup. And she doesn't have her cell phone with her, so texting ain't gonna work. Okay, this is one 'a those rare times when the fact that our quarters are soundproofed is gonna be NOT good. I hope she can hear me through the door, or I'm liable to have one hell of an embarrassing accident, here. What with not being allowed to bear weight on the regenerated hand either, I can't even crawl to the damn bathroom.*

"Hey, Meg?" he tried, then waited, listening intently. When there was no response, he raised his voice to a bellow, allowing the call to flow through their mental bond, as well. "HEY, MEG!"

Seconds later, the bedroom door opened, and his wife and partner, clad in off-duty black jeans and t-shirt, was framed in it.

"Ace!" Omega exclaimed. "What's up? I didn't expect you awake yet..."

"Chair," he pointed at the antigrav medical chair, "bathroom. NOW."

* * *

"Whu-oh," Omega said in immediate understanding. Without delay, she scurried to the medical mobility chair—the Agency's equivalent to a wheelchair, with antigrav units instead of wheels, and the ability of the occupant to 'drive'—and activated and unlocked it, shoving it up against Echo's side of the bed as he swung his legs off the side. Then she grabbed his shoulders and helped him ease his nude body into the chair, since he only had the full use of one leg and the opposite arm. Once he was reasonably well settled in the seat, she grabbed the handgrips on the back and pushed it as fast as she could in the direction of the big bathroom.

Once inside the bathroom proper, she turned and aimed the chair at the water closet door in the corner. Echo grabbed the doorknob and opened it, and she carefully steered the chair through the doorway into the tiny room containing the toilet and a small pedestal sink. One quick push adjusted the position of the chair within the water closet, and she asked, "You got this from here?"

"Yeah," Echo said, scooting forward in the chair as she eased the door closed to allow him some privacy. "I'm not even gonna try to stand, or get onto the toilet, or anything. Bladder's damn full; I'mma aim from here."

"Is the seat up?" she asked, standing just outside the door in case he needed help. A ceramic-sounding *klunk* met her ears.

"It is now. Whoo," came Echo's sigh of relief as the sound of water flowing drifted through the cracked door. "I'm glad you heard me, baby; that was about to become awfully damn embarrassing. Not to mention making extra work to clean up the mess." Moments later, she heard the sound of flushing, followed by water running in the tiny pedestal sink next to the toilet.

"Well, I shoulda thought," Omega noted, as the running water sounds ceased. Echo gingerly nudged open the door with his regenerated left hand, laying the hand towel across the rack by the sink with his right. "I thought I'd go ahead and fix us some breakfast and have it ready when your mom gets here to help," she explained, "but you were still sound asleep, so when I got up and headed for the kitchen, I pulled the door mostly closed so I wouldn't disturb you. I guess it drifted all the way closed and latched, though, when the AC system came on—the temps outside bottomed out but good, last night, and it got chilly in here, so I bumped up the thermostat. Sorry about that."

"Eh. No big deal; you got to me in time," Echo said with a slight sigh. "I hate feeling like a complete invalid, though."

"Not for much longer, I don't think," Omega soothed, easing into the small toilet room and backing Echo's high-tech wheelchair out of the door, though maneuvering it in such a tight space took effort. "You're coming along great with your physical therapy, even after only a few days; Zebra told me last night that she expected to graduate you to the crutches in the next day or two."

"Really? That'll be better," he decided. "At least then, you don't have to be at my beck and call for the smallest little thing."

Omega paused, stopping the antigrav chair in the middle of their big master bathroom. She came around to the front and knelt on the floor before him, gazing up into his face, earnest.

"You know I don't mind, don't you?" she said, concerned. "You've taken care of me when I was in worse shape, in a lotta ways, you know. I'm just glad to have you home, beside me, and getting well, Alex."

* * *

"I know, Megan, honey," he murmured, meeting her eyes, grateful...yet still perturbed. "But I also see everything you're doing, and I feel like a jerk for being unable to help."

"Huh?"

"You're taking care of me like I was a child," a pained Echo explained, "because that's about all I can do for myself, right now. You take me to the bathroom, you help me bathe, you help me get dressed...hell, sometimes you even have to help me eat, when the hand's too tired from all the therapy to work right! You're doing all the cooking, doing most of the cleaning that the automated systems don't get, shuttling me back and forth to all my different medical appointments, keeping UP with those appointments, popping into the Alpha Line room to help Romeo keep the department running...and you've had to merge YOUR counseling sessions into mine, because there's no more time left in the day for 'em. A blasted forty-eight-hour day, and you've run outta time!" He broke off, then slammed his right hand—which was, fortunately, his good hand—onto the chair arm in frustration and anger. "And THEN you even have to come running in the middle of cooking when I have to take a damn piss, because I can't get there by myself!" Despairing and disgusted with himself, he put his face in his hands. "So much for your husband, your hero," came softly, muffled, from between his fingers.

"Hey, hey, honey, ease up," Omega murmured, leaning forward until she could slip her arms around him and hug him tight. Feeling her love and affection wash through him through the mind link, he responded in kind, as she continued. "You're still my hero! And you always will be! I love you with everything I've got, sweetheart. This situation is only temporary. It's gonna be okay soon."

"Is it? How do you know?" he demanded, not bothering to hide his anger and despair from her, since she could sense it through their telepathic bonding anyway; Omega had been kidnapped as a child by an intergalactic criminal and modified to have certain...unexpected...abilities, as part of a failed revenge plot against Echo. One of these turned out to be low-level, but powerful, psionic capabilities. When they had married scant weeks earlier, the telepathic Deltiri ambassador had helped them create a permanent mental link that he called an nd't'lq. And it was this link that had enabled Echo's rescue when enemy slavers had kidnapped him from their honeymoon scant weeks earlier, torturing him for information, intending to auction him off to his other enemies to be killed, once they were finished with him. "Are you sure the medlab isn't just telling us what we want to hear, until we're used to this new way of day to day...shit?"

Omega leaned back, and he could see the shock on her face.

"Um, yeah, honey, I AM sure," she told him.

"HOW?!"

"The therapists have been showing me your medical records since just before you started therapy," Omega explained. "I mean, I'm not a physician, but I AM a scientist, and with a little help here and there on exactly what I'm looking at, I can read 'em."

"Are you sure they're telling you straight, baby?"

"Why wouldn't they?"

"I dunno," Echo sighed, settling back in the antigrav chair and slumping. "I'm just..."

"You're frustrated and worried and feel useless," Omega

murmured, hugging him again. "It's okay, though. Not only do I know how it feels, I know it's gonna be temporary. You're working hard, and coming along great. And you're not useless. Just because you're not in the office doesn't mean that I'm not making good use of your brain on all the departmental stuff."

"So that's why you come home and ask me all those questions..."

"Yup. I'm picking your brain for the best way to handle things! AND passing on a lot of it to Romeo."

"Huh. Well, there's that, I guess."

"Yes, there is. Be patient, honey. It's gonna work out okay. TRUST me."

Echo drew a deep breath, trying to calm himself, then looked deep into the sapphire eyes, seeing calmness, confidence, and encouragement there.

"Trust me," she said again.

"I...okay," he agreed. "Yeah, I do."

"Okay, good." She stood, moved to the back of the chair and pushed him into the bedroom again, then released the chair handles as he took over the controls; he usually treated the thing as a mobility scooter, but they had discovered early on that maneuvering the antigrav chair through the bathroom needed the piloting of someone not seated in the chair, else it tended to bang on doorframes or cabinets, or get wedged in the water closet, thanks to the fact that the antigrav field was slightly bigger than the chair itself and nudged it this way or that if it got too close to another object. "What do you want to do now? Go back to bed? Get dressed?"

"Do you need to run back and see to breakfast? Is it gonna burn?"

"Nah," Omega replied. "I'd already finished it when I heard you call. It's waiting in the kitchen stasis field. I was in the dining room, debating what plates to use for Thanksgiving dinner. And even that is all decided by now."

"Good," Echo said, offering her a smirk. "Close the bedroom door an' c'mon back to bed with me, then."

"What, and take a nap?"

That...wasn't what I had in mind, he told her through the nd't'lq, showing her a mental image of the two of them curled together in the big bed, 'getting busy,' as she sometimes euphemistically put it.

And your mom is gonna be coming through the warp tunnels over there, she pointed at the twin closets on the far wall, *any minute now.*

No, she won't, Echo noted. *Now that we're married and moved into our joint quarters, the warp tunnels in the bedroom here are only for escape in the event of an emergency. Oh, if something bad was going down and she needed to move fast, she might come in through here, but not otherwise; she doesn't want to walk in on our intimate time by accident, so she asked me to make sure they added additional warp tunnels—which, given the size of the apartment, made sense anyhow. Anyway, she's planning to use the one in the back of the coat closet in the foyer. And we can be done before she gets here, anyway. I mean, we don't have to be, but if you're uncomfortable with her being in the den while we're in here doin' it, we can.*

Oh. Hm. Well...maybe, she considered. *An' yeah, I am. Uncomfortable about that, I mean. I, I get that it's soundproofed, but still. I mean, I heard you just now...*

Yeah, but I was yelling at the top of my lungs. And neither one of us does THAT in bed.

Well, no...but still. She's as smart as you are. She'd figure out what we were doing in a heartbeat, noise or no.

Okay, a quickie then. And no maybes allowed. Yes or no, baby.

Omega sighed, then grinned.

Okay.

* * *

Half an hour later, Echo's birth mother, the medtech called Dihl—recruited to the Division One Headquarters medlab by Omega and Fox the previous summer, partly as a surprise for Echo—was helping a still-nude Echo get settled on a special bench in the shower. Meanwhile Omega scurried about the bedroom, laying out his clothing for the day—black jeans and a white long-sleeved polo shirt, with quarter-crew socks and slip-on sneakers for ease and comfort. Echo was not a little embarrassed to have his mother helping him, but she handled matters with aplomb, and soon eased his feelings on the matter.

7

"After all, I've seen all of you many, many times before," she pointed out with a smile, as she helped him ease into position on the bench. "It has just been a while, is all. And I have done this for so many patients over the years, patients who meant nothing to me personally, save that I desired to help them heal; it is no trouble to help you and Omega now, son. Like I am certain she has told you herself, I am simply glad to have you back and once more in one piece."

"Thanks, Ma," he murmured, grateful. "I'm glad to be here in one piece, too. Being in several pieces wasn't any fun at all, believe me." He shrugged. "Don't take my reticence the wrong way, please. I'm just...used to...well..."

"You are a very private and reserved man, modest, and not prone to displaying your body. And you are still getting used to having me back, let alone having a wife," Dihl noted, shrewd and serene, as an Apache medicine woman should be. "So yes, I understand. But you must allow us to help you now. It will not last long."

"Not you, too," Echo breathed. But he hadn't counted on his mother's excellent hearing.

"And exactly what did THAT mean?" she demanded. Omega, whose augmented hearing was even better, stuck her head in the door.

"Oh good. Maybe you can help me set his mind at ease on some things," she said. "He's worried the medlab isn't telling us straight, and that he's really going to be permanently disabled or something."

"Meg," Echo grumbled.

"Ace," Omega echoed his tone. "Do you really think your very own MOM is going to be part of some big conspiracy to keep the truth from you?"

"You think we are all lying to you about your improvement?" Dihl said in astonishment. "Oh, no no no, my son. We none of us would ever do that to you. In fact, I saw your charts only this morning, and the plan is to have you out of that antigrav chair and onto either crutches or a walker by the end of this weekend, and if all goes well, on a cane inside a week thereafter. It is really more about a kind of 'reconnecting' of the nervous system, and strengthening the muscles involved. Our current techniques are excellent, and they are swift to take effect, especially given the specific supplements and medications you are on, which accelerates the healing and strengthening. You are working very hard at the therapy exercises, and are doing really quite nicely."

"And once you can get around on a cane pretty well," Omega interjected, "you'll get to come back to the office on a limited basis, until you can ditch the cane altogether and come back to work full-time."

"Oh," an encouraged Echo said, sitting up straight on the shower bench. "So...I might be back in the Alpha Line Room before Christmas?"

"If you continue improving at the rate you have been, yes, most definitely," Dihl vouchsafed. "Not full time, certainly, if for no other reason than you need the counseling first, but still. Now, son, do you adjust the water the way you like it. Omega, will you seat Echo on the bedside, or in the chair, to get dressed after his shower?"

"Chair," Echo decreed.

"We usually use the chair," Omega confirmed.

"All right, then if you will make up the bed and tidy the bedroom while he is in the shower, I shall go see about the kitchen and dining room."

"I have breakfast for the three of us in the stasis field in the kitchen," Omega noted, turning toward the bed, which was decidedly rumpled after certain recent activities. Dihl slipped out of the master suite, headed for the dining room. "So maybe pull up an extra chair at the breakfast nook, lay out some disposable plates an' stuff, and we'll eat once Echo gets dressed."

"All right," Dihl called back. "Are these the dishes you want on the dining table?"

"The stack on the corner, yeah," Omega called back, as Echo turned on the water and adjusted the temperature. "I meant to at least put those out at the place settings, but I've been here and there doing stuff, and forgot. Do the table runner and decorations look okay?"

"They look beautiful, my shich'ee'ké, my daughter."

"Oh good. I liked it, but sometimes I have weird taste, so I wanted your opinion."

"No, they are delightful, and very appropriate to the holiday. I will go ahead and set the table, then see about preparing other matters."

"What about the food you're bringing?" Omega wondered.

"That is already prepared and waiting in my quarters. I need only fetch it and warm some of the dishes at the last moment, and it will be ready."

"That's good."

* * *

At the end of his 24-hour Division-style shift around eight in the morning on Thanksgiving, Kergun returned to the taxi garage in Hell's Kitchen, some half a dozen blocks southwest of Columbus Circle and Central Park, to hand over. But while he was cleaning out the cab for the holiday—the taxi cab company was taking the rest of the holiday off, timing it to cease before the parade, and would not resume service until the following day—he discovered someone's case had been inadvertently shoved into the niche behind the spare tire and forgotten.

"Hmph," he grunted, hauling it out. He pulled up the tag, but it had been smeared with grease and was no longer readable. "Hey, Pete," he called the garage manager, "somebody forgot a piece o' luggage, here."

"Eh, what else is new?" Pete wondered. "Go put it in the lost an' found room an' if they comes lookin', I'll take care of it."

"All over it," Kergun agreed, hoisting the case and heading for the designated room in the back of the garage office.

* * *

With Dihl helping set Echo's mind more at ease, as well as generally helping around the apartment, within a bit more than an hour, the household was ready for their guests.

"Just in time for us to enjoy the parade," Dihl said with a smile, as the three settled down on the sofa and Echo, in the middle, turned on the big flat-screen television on the opposite wall. A large plate of shortbread sat on the coffee table within easy reach, and they each had mugs of spiced hot chocolate.

"Sorry I couldn't take you again this year, Meg," Echo

apologized. "Let alone getting Ma there for the first time."

"Pssht," Dihl responded, waving a dismissive hand. "Even on the television I can see the crowds this year, and I think I likely would not enjoy being in a throng of people like that. Especially as cold as it has turned."

"Yeah, it's pretty crowded all right, and it can be windy, out on the street," Omega agreed. "Echo did take me last year—between the Halloween scavenger hunt, and the Christmas accuse-Meg-an'-shoot-Echo missions, that is—and the streets were crowded. And COLD." She shrugged. "And you're right; it's colder this year! I'm glad I got the chance to do it, and yeah, one of these days, we'll take you to see it in person, Dihl, 'cause I think you'd still enjoy it, and WE have places we can watch that aren't so cold and crowded, if you get my drift. But I'm just as happy to cuddle up with my groom under the pretty throw," she flipped a certain plush throw blanket, sublimation-printed with the Orion Nebula, over the trio, "and watch the thing on TV this year."

"New family tradition, or old one?" Echo wondered, as she snuggled into his right side, and his mother settled down on his left.

"New-old, I guess," Omega said. "We used to watch the parade as a family when I was a kid. Well, Mom was in and out, I suppose, 'cause she was cooking the turkey an' dressing an' stuff. But I haven't had time to do this in a long time, let alone EVER had a husband to curl up with. And a mom-in-law I love to pieces, helping me out."

"And that mother-in-law deeply loves her daughter-in-law, as well," Dihl averred with a smile.

"Good," Echo decreed, putting an arm around both and squeezing gently. "My two favorite ladies get along great. That makes me really happy."

"Which is the best news I've had all day," Omega declared.

* * *

Once Alpha One's quarters were ready for company and the parade had ended, Dihl slipped back through the warp tunnels to her own quarters to fetch her share of what was to be an early-afternoon pot-luck dinner in Echo and Omega's dining room, attended by the 'family' Omega had collected about herself within the Division One's Earth-based Agency. Given the same criminal that had modified her had apparently seen to it that her genetic family died in a dreadful 'accident,' it was the closest thing she had to any sort of family any more, and they all took it very seriously, for her sake—though they all admitted to liking the familial feeling.

Half an hour later, the sturdy, oversized mesquite dining table and matching sideboard fairly groaned with food, as Echo—with the help of his mother and wife, one on each side— took his seat at the head of the table, whereupon Omega took the foot. Dihl, the Alpha Two husband/wife team of Agents Romeo and India, Deltiri Ambassador Zz'r'p ob Tii'rkin, Medical Chief of Staff Zarnix Chifejuz of Chesharilzi, as well as Director Fox and his wife, the assistant Chief of Staff code-named Zebra, sat down with them.

As Dihl had noted earlier, Omega had made sure to decorate the rustic mesquite table with a table runner in autumn colors— leaving the wood itself bare, to show off the intricate wood grain—as well as a lovely set of antique candlesticks and a small centerpiece of dwarf pumpkins, squash, and dried ears of blue, red, and yellow corn, being careful not to take up all the room needed for the food. All the women exclaimed over how lovely the table looked. The men all grinned, then talked about how delicious the food looked, and Omega laughed.

"To each his—or her—own! Y'all have a seat, and let's get this started," she decreed.

"Alla that," Echo threw his weight behind his wife and partner.

Everyone had contributed something: Zebra and Fox together had cooked the turkey with cornbread sage-and-onion dressing, in deference to their hosts' Southern origins; Dihl and India between them had made the traditional side dishes— mashed potatoes and gravy, a sweet potato casserole, a green bean casserole, and homemade cranberry sauce. Romeo made a huge harvest salad with apples, walnuts, and dried cranberries and a cranberry vinaigrette dressing, and India made a delicately-curried butternut squash soup. In addition, Dihl had brought an Apache version of corn pudding, and a cranberry-jalapeno slaw or relish. Omega had made a huge batch of shortbread and a pecan pie. Zarnix brought a pumpkin pie for his contribution, and Zz'r'p had obtained cheese and meat platters from the deli down the street, intended for noshing through the afternoon.

"This is a damn feast," Echo declared as the others took their places at the table.

"Yes, everyone contributed something," Zarnix agreed. Echo sobered.

"Well...not EVERYbody," he murmured, trying to hide how downcast he felt. "I wanted to try, but the antigrav chair doesn't maneuver around the kitchen that well, and I couldn't reach the top cabinets that way anyhow, but if I sat on a stool, I couldn't move around to get ingredients..."

"I told you, I'd have been happy to fetch things for you, Ace," Omega said.

"Yeah, but you were baking, and busy enough yourself," he sighed. "I didn't wanna get in the way."

"Just as a reminder," Omega noted, "you were the one who picked out the wines for the meal, hon. Four courses' worth, with two options for each course."

"Eh," he grunted. "Well, okay. Doesn't seem like much, but..."

Several surreptitious glances were exchanged among those at the table.

"I did not bake the pumpkin pie I brought, Echo," Zarnix noted. "I am not especially adept at Earth cuisine, and have no celebratory Chesharilzi recipes in my personal repertoire, in any case; I am good at making basic Chesharilzi fare, but that is the extent of my cooking ability. Instead, I ascertained with Zebra what was missing from the traditional menu, then asked an Earth friend for assistance. I purchased the ingredients according to her instructions, but she made it."

"And the appetizer trays we shall nibble this afternoon came from the deli," Zz'r'p pointed out. "Not everyone must cook in order to contribute, my friend. The wine in my glass smells delicious, and I am certain it will all go well with the meal, for you have excellent taste, based on my past visits to your domicile."

"They're right. Just kick back, Echo, and enjoy being

waited on for a few days," Zebra suggested. "It won't last long; you'll be back in the office as busy as ever, before you know it."

Echo shot a glance at Omega. *Is she sure about that?*

Looks like it to me, hon, Omega replied. *And Zarnix and India look to be in agreement, if expressions and body language are anything to go on.*

Okay. I guess I need to say grace, huh?

If you want to. Or we can ask Fox, as the patriarch, to do it.

No, I think I need to do it; I got more 'n aplenty to be thankful for, this year, he decided. *I'm alive, back in one piece, and married to the woman of my dreams. I think that's all good, no matter what else comes along.*

Aw.

"Okay, everybody, let's say grace," Echo said, holding out both hands. Within moments the table was ringed by a circle of joined hands. "It's been another year, God, and You really laid some challenges on us this time. But we're all here..."

* * *

The 'family' took their time eating; no one had to be on duty any time soon, so it was a relaxed, enjoyable meal. Echo's choices of wines were spot-on, and everyone proclaimed the dinner utterly delicious. Since the dishes had also been prepared with an eye toward a kosher diet, even Fox could partake of almost all of it with no problems.

In good time, they had finished dessert. Zarnix and Zebra helped Echo ease from the dining table into his antigrav chair, then, on Fox's orders—not as Director, but as family patriarch—Omega pushed Echo into the den. Zz'r'p moved the deli trays and the shortbread platter to the end tables in the den, and the others set to, putting away the food and cleaning Omega's dining room and kitchen.

"Guys, I can do that later," Omega called, as she helped Echo into his recliner.

"We got it, Meg," India called back. "There's so many of us, we'll have it done in just a couple more minutes. We want to do this for you, okay? You and Echo relax for a change, and put on the football game. We'll be in there in a few minutes, and your kitchen and dining room will be all clean, with plenty

14

of leftovers for you two to nosh through the weekend."

"Aw, c'mon, now," Echo grumbled, reaching for the remote. "There were enough leftovers to feed all of Alpha Line...or a small army, I'm not sure which."

"Alpha Line IS a small army," Fox's voice floated out, and Echo and Omega both snorted.

"Besides," Echo added, "y'all cooked it. Take SOME of it home with you for your own leftovers."

"What he said," Omega agreed.

"We are," Zebra noted. "We'd be in there already, but we're divvying stuff up. I brought several packs of disposable storage containers for this very purpose. It's all gonna go in your fridge until we leave."

"Oh, okay," Omega said, mollified.

"Yeah," Echo agreed. "Okay, the game's on. Y'all come on in here and I'll get into the wet bar and make folks some drinks. Or you can grab a brew outta the fridge in the kitchen, if you'd rather."

"Or some more of the wine," Omega added.

"Wet bar?" Romeo wondered, as he wandered into the den. "I didn't know you had a wet bar in the place, man. Where you got it hid?"

Echo grinned, leaned forward, and lifted the top of the coffee table, revealing a tiny refrigerator, a minuscule sink with faucet, racks of old-fashioned glasses, and numerous labeled niches for liquor bottles, some of which were already occupied.

"Pocket space warps are convenient," he noted.

"Dude! I want me one 'a those! Man, that is cool," Romeo averred, grinning from ear to ear.

"And handy," Echo agreed, fishing out a glass and his favorite whisky, then pouring himself a couple of fingers. "Meg? You want a whisky?"

"Yeah, that sounds good, Ace," she agreed, hovering nearby. He glanced up and was about to say something, when she responded, "No, I'm not playing helicopter over you, hon. I can't decide where to sit."

"Huh?"

"I could sit on the end of the couch next to you and be

close, or I could take my recliner over there and face you," she noted, pointing across the room. "I can't decide which."

"Mm," Fox said, emerging from the dining room in time to overhear, "that's a layout that wants work, then."

"Yeah, but it's symmetrical this way," Omega pointed out. "We've been trying to figure that one out."

"You want your usual Scotch, Fox?" Echo wondered.

"That would be nice, zun," the Director agreed. "And one for Zebra, too, if you would."

"If by some chance you have some kr'k'un, I will take a small glass," Zz'r'p requested, "else I will go back for some more of the delicious dessert wine."

"I got it," Echo noted, pulling a bottle and pouring the drink. "Zarnix, you want some carzgh?" he asked, as he handed the Deltiri his homeworld libation.

"You have some?" Zarnix said in surprise.

"We shopped for everybody, yesterday, after Echo's therapy," Omega said with a grin. "Fortunately the solid hologram disguise on the antigrav chair works well. Nobody in the regular stores had a clue it wasn't a wheelchair."

"Very thoughtful, kinder," Fox murmured, sitting on the sofa with his glass of Scotch, and holding out an arm for Zebra to sit next to him.

"Romeo, what about you two?" Echo asked.

"Nah. Me 'n India got brews outta the fridge, man," Romeo offered, plopping down on the far end of the big couch. "Damn, this thing's even bigger than ours."

"We needed to be able to seat everybody," Omega noted. "That sofa seats four or five, depending on who's sitting. Echo can lie down on it with room to spare. Then, with two recliners, a rocking chair, and a cushy wing chair for reading, we can comfortably seat the whole Earth-based 'family,' without having to drag in chairs from the dining room."

Five minutes later, everyone was comfortably seated around the coffee table with their preferred after-dinner libations, noshing and chatting. The football game only provided background accompaniment...though occasionally one of the human men would make an exclamation when a touchdown occurred.

* * *

"All right, everyone, I think it's time," Fox decreed, glancing at his wrist chronometer when the conversation lagged momentarily. "Romeo, would you be so kind as to help me fetch things?"

"I'd love to, Fox," Romeo said with a grin.

"I will assist," Zarnix added.

Echo and Omega exchanged puzzled glances, as their guests broke into smiles. Zarnix, Romeo, and Fox rose from their seats and headed down the hallway.

"Baby, what on earth are they talking about?" Echo wondered in surprise.

"No idea, Ace," a bemused Omega admitted.

"What we're talking about," Fox said, coming back into the den, arms full of wrapped gifts, "is a little housewarming party slash bridal shower of sorts. There wasn't time to do anything when Zebra and I merged our quarters, given everything that was going on in Dallas..."

"An' me an' India didn't make no big deal outta it," Romeo added, right behind Fox, his arms also holding presents. Zarnix, behind Romeo, carried one very large package wrapped in brown shipping paper.

"...Yet the two of you managed to provide both couples with housewarming gifts," Fox continued, stacking his armload of gifts in front of Alpha One. "Given we have a perfect holiday gathering opportunity, the 'family' put our heads together and decided this should be a joint Thanksgiving celebration and housewarming party. And, I suppose, bridal shower of a sort, as well, as I mentioned." As Romeo added his armload to the stack, and Zarnix set down his package, Fox gestured at the presents. "And there are also gifts from the offworld 'family' members, as well as a friend or two," he noted. "Most notably, 'Uncle' Pul, 'Uncle' Suud and his family, Dr. Eretigen, Doron, Dr. Taylor, and Chief Wux."

"Oh damn," Echo said blankly. "I wasn't expecting that."

"Me too, neither," Omega agreed, eyes wide. "Y'all didn't have to do this."

"We know," Zebra said, with a dimpling grin. "We wanted to. Just like you wanted to give us housewarming gifts when we merged quarters."

"C'mon over here, Meg, and gimme a hand with these," Echo said, urging his bride to sit at his feet. "I'd get down there with you, but with one leg and one hand out of commission per doctors' orders—and three of those doctors here—I'd never get back up, off the floor. Even with help."

"Not a problem, hon," Omega said, easing herself to the floor beside him. "Okay, what shall we open first?"

* * *

"Mine should probably be opened relatively soon," Zarnix noted.

"So should mine," Dihl averred.

"Okay, we put those two front and center," Omega decided.

"Open Pulgey's last," Fox decreed. Omega and Echo blinked, then glanced at each other again.

"Ho-kay," Echo agreed. "Here, baby, that silver one with the blue bow on top looks to be Zarnix's, judging by the name tag; set to on it, while I find Ma's."

"All right," Omega agreed, and commenced ripping paper. After a few seconds she exposed a box, lightly fastened and marked, THIS SIDE UP. She pulled out her trusty Swiss army knife and slit the packing tape, then opened the box lid, peering inside. "Ooo," she murmured, reaching in. "Echo, have a look at this."

Echo turned his attention to the item Omega extracted. It was a miniature tree, quite alive, with brown bark containing purple undertones, and bright blue leaves.

"Oh COOL," he exclaimed. "Is that a bonsai?"

"It is, or what you would call a bonsai," Zarnix confirmed. "It is actually a similar gardening form developed on Chesharil, and I thought you might enjoy having one. Unlike many bonsai on Earth, these are fairly simple to care for, and I obtained one in a pot that has an automated watering system. They enjoy the same frequencies of light put out by Earth's artificial lighting, so all you need do is add the enclosed plant food tablets to the water chamber twice a year, refill the chamber about once per month, and it will be good. The leaves turn gold in winter except for the edges, which remain blue, but the leaves do not fall; in the spring, they resume this blue shade. We call it a rasblun, which in English is rendered everblue."

"It's gorgeous," Omega declared.

"Yeah, that's going someplace where we can look at it, and watch the leaves change," Echo decided. "And I see why you wanted it unwrapped quickly; I bet you wrapped it just before coming over?"

"I did," Zarnix said with a nod. "We hid all the gifts in the warp passage behind the coat closet!"

Everyone laughed.

* * *

"Here's Ma's," Echo said, coming up with a large green-wrapped package with a yellow bow. He started to hand it to Omega, but Dihl cried out.

"Don't turn it over!" the older woman exclaimed, throwing out a warning hand. "Just unwrap it, son."

Omega got to her knees to watch as Echo parked the package in his lap, then pulled his multitool from his own pocket and slit the tape on the wrapping. Moments later, he was pulling out a compact, oblong, divided planter in which several aromatic plants were growing.

"A little kitchen herb garden!" Echo exclaimed. "That's great! Lessee...I see sage, cilantro, Mexican oregano, mint... what's that one?"

"I think it's rosemary," Omega said. "Several of Mom's recipes used it."

"That's right," Dihl said with a smile. "I thought you might enjoy having some fresh herbs to use in your cooking, the both of you."

"And that explains the sun lamp under the kitchen cabinets in the corner," Echo realized. "You and Fox must have worked that little detail out."

"We did," Fox acknowledged. "Some of these gifts have been in the planning stages for a few weeks, now."

"It'll go perfectly right there," Omega said, excited and happy. "It's close enough to the sinks that we can water it easy."

"And the planter has a built-in tray to catch the drainage," Echo noted. "It's perfect, Ma. Thanks!"

"Us next!" India said, grinning.

"And then ours," Zebra added.

"Okay," Omega said, scooting a large box and a small box in front of her. "Here, Ace," she said, handing up the small red-and-blue box. "I'm not even gonna try to lift this big thing into your lap."

"Okeydoke," Echo agreed, and ripped off the paper on the small, slightly oblong box.

Inside, carefully packed in foam, were two white mugs. One side had the Division One logo, the other, the Alpha Line logo. In between, and written vertically, one said ACE, the other, BABY, in the classic NASA worm font. Both members of Alpha Line burst out laughing.

"You ain't done yet," Romeo said, as he and India grinned from ear to ear. "Look inside 'em."

Both had skeletal chemical formulae inscribed on the bottom of the mugs, but each mug had a different one. Echo drew his eyebrows together, pursing his lips in thought.

"It's not...?" he began.

"It IS!" Omega shrieked in delight. "Yours is monomethyl hydrazine, and mine is nitrogen tetroxide!"

"Rocket fuel and oxidizer," Fox realized with a smirk. "Talk about personalized, his-and-her mugs!"

The room broke up laughing.

* * *

The gift from Fox and Zebra came next; it was a very large cube wrapped in silver and gold paper, with a matching gold bow. When Omega got it unwrapped, it became immediately obvious that they now had an espresso machine to go with the pod and drip brewers, as well as a small selection of coffees to be brewed in it.

"THERE we go!" Echo exclaimed, jubilant. "Mainline caffeine!"

"That'll be REAL nice, some 'a these mornings that come too early," Omega said, grinning.

"Let alone some of these cold, late nights," Echo added.

"We'll help you carry it to the kitchen and get it set up, kinder," Fox noted. "It isn't light."

"There is mine," Zz'r'p said, unassuming, as he pointed at a long, relatively narrow package wrapped in a soft turquoise foil. "Do not drop it."

Echo tore off the foil, cut open the box, and extracted a wad of packing. This, in turn, exposed a goodly-sized glass bottle full of some golden fluid. He slid it out of the packing, and stared at the label.

"Oh damn," he breathed. "Now THAT is some good stuff."

"What is it, Ace?" Omega wondered.

"It is a liquor that is made on Deltir, nn'chn," Zz'r'p explained. "It is called d'kk'l. The flavor is rather similar to one of your old Earth brandies, though it is made differently."

"Zz'r'p, am I reading the age on this correctly?" an astonished Echo wondered, studying the label. "Is this really...?"

"You are," Zz'r'p smiled, his eyes tilting up at the corners. "It is over one hundred of your years old. It is very old, and very good. I sent back to Deltir and had it taken from my personal stock."

The "Oooo!" went around the room.

* * *

"I think Suud's gift should go next, then," Fox decided, helping Omega move the big, heavy package in front of her—it was the one that Zarnix had carried. "I think, if I remember right, you'll need a bit of help with this one, too. And a place to store things. It should go in the warp pantry nicely, though."

Echo and Omega shot Fox sidelong glances, then she tore off the shipping paper, revealing a dark-green decorative wrap underneath. This too tore away, and she found a wooden case with a hinged, latched top. Unfastening the latch, she opened the lid.

"Holy shit," she exclaimed blankly.

"It's a whole case of...wine?" Echo wondered, leaning over to look inside.

"Emdalian ssrrg wine, Slisssher label," Fox noted. "Their best vintage. It's about ten or twelve years old, and should be perfect for enjoying for the next couple of years...which this should manage to cover, even if you serve it at family gatherings—though I do recommend sharing a bottle with dinner, just the two of you, on a nice, quiet evening, every now and then. The whole Guurn family, including Duuniiss, pitched in to acquire that."

* * *

Dr. Travis S. Taylor, late of Kirakalla, aka Tau Ceti f, had not forgotten them, either. He sent two tickets to see Ercwlff in concert on her homeworld of Kallos—which happened to be in Division One, so it was relatively close—with a note that told them to make it a "date night," as he put it.

Dr. Werfer Eretigen, galactic president Pulgey Entiyti's personal physician, sent them a lovely digital music album. "It contains many of my favorites," he wrote in the enclosed note, "and I have hopes you will enjoy it, too."

"And Werf has good taste in music," Fox averred. "That's a nice album."

Pan-Galactic Law Enforcement and Immigration Administration's chief, Administrator Gwag Wuxullian and his executive assistant Nargiss Nesh, gave them a tabletop waterfall set in semi-precious stones from planets all over the galaxy. The stones were lovely, and as soon as Omega initiated the ON switch, the pre-filled reservoir released its water, and the tinkling, musical sound as it flowed over the stones was delightful. A small light came on beneath the waterfall, illuminating it softly with ever-changing colors.

"Oh, there's my stress medicine," Omega sighed with a smile.

"Yeah, that's gonna be nice to sit and watch and listen to it," Echo agreed. "I always did like going down to the creek and just...sitting."

"He did," Dihl confirmed. "If his father and I could not find him anywhere else, chances were, he was down at the creek."

"I used to love to go down to the spring on the back of our property, for the same reason," Omega said. "I never got a chance to really show y'all around this past summer. Maybe we can try again when we don't have a perp on our asses."

"That's a plan," Echo agreed. "India? Romeo? Hell, all of you, if you want..."

"I'd love to see where Meg grew up," Zebra said. "Of all of you, I think Zar, Zz'r'p, and I—the Three Z's, as Echo's been calling us—are the only ones that haven't seen the place."

"I have not, as yet, either," Dihl reminded.

"We'll do that at some point, then," Omega offered. "Maybe this spring, once the weather opens up, but before it gets too hot. I think it would be nice to show my new family where my old family used to live."

"We got a couple more gifts, here, baby," Echo noted, waving a finger. "And Fox says we gotta wait until last to open Pul's. So there's Doron's. Have at it."

"Okeydoke," she said, reaching for the present.

* * *

But when she got off all the wrapping, the gift was...

...A waffle iron.

"Well, that's traditional," she said with a lopsided grin.

"And we don't have one," Echo agreed. "And I like waffles."

"It says," Omega said, turning it over to read the label, "Made in Kras...Krasno...where the hell is that?!"

"Krasnovia?" Echo wondered. "Oh, that's in the Ardrub system, baby."

"Waitaminit," Romeo exclaimed. "You mean it's a real place? I thought it was just a made-up place that the military used for war gaming!"

"No, it's a real planet," Fox confirmed. "One of the top brass in DC, the guy who came up with it for war games, isn't from around here."

"Oooh-kay," Omega said with a shrug. "Doron sent a note. It says, 'I understand from my studies that this device is essential for the preparation of one of your world's most highly respected culinary delicacies. I hope you enjoy using it.' Aw, that's sweet."

"Well, it will be, with a little maple syrup," Echo said with a grin.

* * *

"All right," Fox said. "This next one is going to be a bit tricky. Pul said it isn't just a wedding present or a housewarming gift, it's also a thank-you and a...well, you'll see in a minute. But we need Echo and Omega both standing, so I'm not sure..."

"He can lean on me," Omega offered. "Let's get you on your feet, honey."

Zarnix came to their aid, assisting the recovering Agent to his feet, and stood opposite Omega beside Echo, helping to steady him.

"There," Zarnix said. "Will that do, Fox?"

"It will," Fox said, then addressed Zebra. "Now, meyn gelibte, if you would...?"

Zebra grabbed the remote, hit several switches, then switched channels on the wide-screen television on the far wall.

Immediately a silver-white reptilian face with black horns and flame-colored eyes appeared on the screen. Behind him were several dark-green reptilians sans horns, and a red-skinned, horned reptilian.

"AH!" the white reptilian exclaimed. "THERE we are!"

"PUL!" Echo exclaimed. "Look, Meg, it's Pulgey, Suud, Duuniiss, and...that's Dr. Eretigen, isn't it?"

"Yes!" Omega said, clapping her hands. "Hi, y'all!"

"Greetings, greetings, my offworld family!" Entiyti boomed. The Draconan's wings flexed, and the artificial wing Omega had designed earlier in the year, to replace the one he had lost in a terrorist attack, flashed in the light. "And there are the newlyweds—all six of them!"

The occupants of both rooms, on Earth and Emdali, laughed.

"Now, I know that this is a special holiday for all of you there," Entiyti noted, "as well as a bit of a celebration of Alpha One's moving into their new joint quarters. So I will keep this short, though it is a celebration of Alpha One in many respects."

The others looked around, expectant and mildly confused.

"Fox, you have them?" Entiyti pressed.

"I do," Fox said, producing two small, flat boxes from a warp pocket.

"Very good," Entiyti said. "Agent Echo, Agent Omega, it is my very great privilege to present you both with the Rryssheett urr Byirr Entiyti—the Honor of the House Entiyti," he proclaimed, as Fox opened the boxes, producing two medal-like objects on ribbons. Each medal was about an inch wide, cut from a huge, single, flawless diamond, in the shape of an eight-pointed star. Fox placed each, first around Echo's neck, then Omega's. "As approved by the Emdalian Council of Lords, at my instigation," Entiyti continued, "this comes with an honorary military rank of Joint Commodores of the Grand

Fleet of Emdali. This means that either or both of you may command the Emdalian planetary fleet, should it ever become necessary. More, the two of you are equal in authority, so that you may tag-team decisions, or split the fleet into two forces."

Omega and Echo gaped at the screen in shock.

"I believe they are a bit surprised, Pul," Suud Guurn, a Reptoid and one of Entiyti's adoptive brothers, said dryly, leaning over Entiyti's shoulder, as his eldest son Duuniiss and Dr. Eretigen grinned widely. "You might wish to explain further."

"Point," Entiyti agreed. "It is very simple, children. You have both performed, as the Earth saying is, 'above and beyond the call,' in protecting each other, in protecting the galactic president—namely, me—and in protecting the entire galaxy from a tyrant's coup, for months now—again and again. The Pan-Galactic Coalition has never had call to present such matters before; as galactic civilizations go, it is still relatively young, though it would not seem so to you. But there ARE such institutions on Emdali, as we come from what was once a semi-feudalistic society. And so, with the approval of the Emdalian House of Lords, the Ennead, and Administrator Wuxullian, it was decided to give you, not only these awards, but the ability to command an additional fleet, should it ever become necessary. Echo, in the eventuality that you become Director, with command of the Division One fleet, Omega may, if she so chooses and necessity deems, call out the Emdalian Grand Fleet in your support. It is not as big as a division fleet, but as you might say, 'it is no slouch,' either. You will henceforth be formally addressed on both Emdali and Aleancë as the Lord Commodore Echo, and the Lady Commodore Omega."

"We...we..." Omega tried, as everyone in both rooms gazed at the couple in pride.

"We don't deserve this, Pul," Echo murmured, finishing his partner's statement. "We only did the right thing."

"Not enough people do that, kinder," Fox observed. "And certainly not to the degree that the two of you have been willing to do it. Repeatedly."

"THAT," Entiyti declared, firm. "Do not deter me from doing this, my adoptive niece and nephew. It needed doing.

And," he said, "I note that Echo is doing quite well after his recent ordeal."

* * *

"Huh?" Echo wondered...then realized that Zarnix had eased away, and Omega had stepped forward in shock, leaving him...

...Standing alone.

On his own two feet.

"WA-HAA!" he exclaimed in jubilation, punching both fists into the air, as the room around him erupted in surprise and excitement.

* * *

The group on Earth congratulated their honorees, Omega helped Echo sit back down before he tired out the weak leg, and Romeo and India tidied away the torn wrapping paper, as the 'family' on Earth conversed cheerfully with the 'family' on Emdali. When Entiyti finally declared that they had work to do, reluctant goodbyes were said, and the video communication ended.

"This...has been a day of surprises," Echo declared. "GOOD surprises, all around, but still."

"Amen to that," Omega offered, and the others murmured agreement.

"Gimme a piece of shortbread, baby," Echo said, "and let's get this celebration back on track."

"It never left the track, zun," Fox decreed, and everyone laughed.

* * *

"Okay, hon," Omega said from her seat on the sofa, a couple of hours later. "Time for your exercises. Yeah, you done great on that leg a while ago, but we got a ways to go yet before you're up to using it. So get with it."

Echo sighed, but immediately began performing leg extensions with his right leg, flexing and rotating his ankle as he did so.

"Guys, guys, it's THANKSGIVING!" a startled Zebra said, making a time-out symbol with her hands, as Zarnix, India, and Dihl all stared in surprise. "Echo gets a day off!"

"No," Echo demurred, "Meg and I talked about this last

night. So okay, so I DID stand on my own today, for the first time since the Cortians whacked my leg off. But I can't stand UP by myself yet, like, get out of the chair on my own. Let alone walk. I'm still recovering, with a long way to go like Meg said, and I want the best possible outcome. Just because I don't have a therapy session today doesn't give me the green light to ignore my exercises. I know what to do, and damned if I'm not gonna do 'em."

"That is a very positive, very determined outlook, Echo," Zarnix decided, "and I am glad to hear it. But it would not hurt, just for the one day. Muscles need rest and recovery time, the same as anything else."

"The therapists have already started alternating days between his hand and his leg, so one rests while the other's being worked. Besides, the last couple days, he's been doing nightly soaks in the hot tub, followed by me giving him a massage, before he crashes for the night," Omega noted. "He's resting really good, I'm feeding him as well as I know how, and we think we're seeing a difference in flexibility and strength as a result. It's subtle, but it's there. I'm hoping that, with increased massage and stimulation, the depressed scar tissue might start filling out a little more. It hasn't done so to his satisfaction, at least not yet."

"Give it time, guys," India said, crossing her eyes and grinning. "It's only been a few days, less than a week, since he was decanted from the regeneration bath."

"Impatience, thy name is Alpha One," Fox chuckled; the others laughed, and Omega and Echo flushed, then grinned sheepishly. "Still, I agree with Zar; I think it is an excellent attitude to take, kinder. And from what Zebra has been telling me, Echo is coming along extremely well."

"He really is," Zebra agreed, "and trust me, I've been keeping up with the therapists' reports from the get-go. They're just amazed at how well he's doing. Then again, as they point out, he was in great shape to begin with, so there's a firm foundation to work from."

"See?" Omega murmured, and Echo nodded, easing back in his chair in some small relief.

"Huh? What's up there?" India wondered.

Don't tell 'em I've been doubting 'em, Echo shot the message to Omega through the nd't'lq. *I know it isn't entirely logical, and I don't wanna hurt anybody's feelings. I don't mind Ma knowing, but I don't want to upset the others.*

Right, Omega responded in kind.

"Nothing much, really," she added aloud. "He's just been worried it wouldn't turn out as well as everybody's hoping. You know how that goes, I'm sure. And it ain't like he didn't go through a crap-ton of shit on the Cortian ship—I mean, they tortured him, after all—so...he's only a little anxious, I think. And he's got good reason, all things considered."

"Yeah. That's the truth. No joke," the general murmur went around the room.

"Yes, I suppose he is entitled to some angst," Zarnix agreed.

"But we are working on that, too," Zz'r'p added. "It will all come together in time."

Omega leaned over and rubbed Echo's shoulder; he shot her a half-smile, and kept doing his therapy exercises, as the relaxed, affectionate chit-chat continued.

* * *

In the end, the day ran long, though nobody minded; the others stayed for dinner, slapping together hot turkey sandwiches from leftovers, and enjoying the company. Another joint clean-up session ensued, then Fox, Zarnix, and Romeo helped the couple position the espresso machine and little herb garden on the kitchen counters, and store the crate of wine in the warp pantry. Finally they all left by ones and twos, headed for their own quarters to rest before resuming work the next day.

"Because interstellar crime doesn't take a day off," Fox pointed out.

And they were gone.

* * *

Omega helped Echo move onto the couch beside her, then they relaxed together. He slipped his arm around her and pulled her into his side, and she snuggled there, content.

"It was a good day," she decided. "A really good day."

"Yeah, it was," he agreed. "Way the hell better than I'd have thought, given what I've just been through."

"No shit," she avouched. "And you stood on your own! I'm so thrilled about that! But remember what Zz'r'p has told you—for now, don't dwell on what happened to you, and don't rehearse might-have-beens. Concentrate on what you have, right here, right now."

"I am," he said, tightening his arm around her. "One of 'em is right here beside me."

"Aw! So do you feel better about things?" Omega asked.

"Huh?"

"You had everybody here except the physical therapists," Omega pointed out. "You could observe their body language, their interactions with each other, and with you. Did you pick up anything?"

"No," Echo admitted. "Everybody was completely relaxed and okay with the idea that I'm getting back to normal, in as far as I could tell. Look, baby. I...I know I'm not being entirely rational about it. At times, I'm not at ALL rational about it! It isn't logical that they'd do that, and it doesn't fit with the people I've known for years. And I know that; I just can't help it, sometimes. I know you think I'm fearless, but I'm not. I've already told you I don't wanna lose you or Ma, and...well, now I think I'm starting to realize that I'm afraid of becoming what I almost wound up being..."

"I'm glad to hear the past tense on that," Omega noted.

"For now," he admitted. "I've...been struggling with it from the time I realized I was back in Division One hands, though."

"Huh?"

"Translate it as, 'likely to survive,'" he added by way of elaboration. "And started having to think about repercussions to what was done to me."

"Ooh," she murmured. "Which has been a few weeks. So it truly is a recurring fear, now. That means it's become part of your PTSD."

"I think so, yeah." He sighed. "So it'll come back. And probably will continue to do so, until I get myself back into shape, back to working with Alpha Line...back into the field and doing good. And maybe even then, if we get into a tight sitch. So...bear with me on that."

"Okay. Well, we'll just have to push for that as fast as we

can, then," Omega decided.

"That works for me," Echo agreed. "I'm willing to push it as hard as I can."

Chapter 2

Echo did push, and the end result was that two days later, he was placed on crutches, with a reminder to let his weight hang from his shoulders, not bracing with his hands, given the still-weak left hand.

"All your hands are there for is to stabilize the crutches' position," Zebra noted. "Not to brace yourself in place."

"Right," Echo agreed.

But it meant he could now get around their apartment on his own, including trips to the bathroom, and even get into the kitchen for the odd cooking session. All of that pleased him, though it could be tiring, hobbling about on the crutches...not to mention slow.

"Still," he told Omega, "it gives me a bit of freedom back, and it means you don't have to come running when I call, so much."

Alpha One kept the antigrav chair for the time being, since long-distance excursions could be exhausting on crutches, but unless they were going out of the apartment, Echo didn't use it.

* * *

Late that evening in the taxi company office, only two days after Thanksgiving and on the same day Echo was placed on crutches, a crackling sound came from inside the abandoned case, stowed on top of a stack of similar luggage, in a corner of the darkened lost-and-found room adjacent to the decrepit bathroom.

The fact that even the swing-shift manager was out on a run—it was, after all, the biggest shopping weekend on the planet—meant that no one heard the crackling...or the subsequent thudding that emerged from inside the room.

The next morning, Pete the garage manager found the doors to both the bathroom and lost-and-found room ajar. Just inside the lost-and-found room, the case lay on the floor, overturned. It had a large hole in it, about four or five inches in diameter, almost like something had chewed through it from inside.

There was nothing visible within except a few small shreds of what looked like thin, torn tissue paper.

Pete grunted, and threw the remains of the case in the nearby garbage can.

* * *

"All right, Echo," one of the physical therapists, Gangway by code name, told the Agent that afternoon when he came in for his session, having already worked the leg that morning, "we want to strengthen that hand, so you can use it more, and more effectively, now that we have you on crutches."

"Sounds like a plan to me," Echo agreed. "The better I can get around, and the more I can do, the better I'll like it. What do you want me to do?"

"You've been doing your grip-strength and leg exercises religiously, according to all the feedback I've gotten—and after Thanksgiving, I got plenty!—so you should be strong enough to do what I've got in mind now. So we're going to start doing some special wrist curls, but we're going to use 'cheating' form, for now," Gangway noted. "In other words, we're going to do it so that you're not putting full stress on the left hand quite yet. I have a system of pulleys you're going to use to raise a weight. I want you to do a standard curling motion, but we'll use two different hand positions for it—one, palm up, and the other, palm in. We'll start light and easy to begin with, just in case."

"Let's do it," Echo decreed, determined.

"There we go!" Gangway agreed. "Let's go."

* * *

It was difficult, especially to exert force by flexing the wrist—the 'cleavage plane,' as Omega was wont to call it, still tended toward being stiff and inflexible—but it didn't cause acute pain, so Echo pushed through it as long as he could.

But when the hand and forearm started trembling from the exertion, the therapist called a halt.

"Don't stop! I can do more," Echo protested.

"No, Echo, you did great, but now you NEED to stop," Gangway said in a gentle tone, taking the pulley grip out of Echo's shaky hand. "I know that, given everything they did to you, you're fighting to overcome some anxieties over how far back you're going to be able to come. But I want you to know that you're not only achieving every goal your team of therapists is setting for you, most days you're surpassing them—which, we think, argues you're going to make it all the way back. You just did almost twice as many reps as I expected you to be able to do. And you're going to feel that tomorrow. You said you've been taking hot soaks in the evenings, and then your life partner—er, your wife and partner—has been massaging you when you finished that, right?"

"Yeah..." Echo mopped his sweating face with the hand towel the therapist tossed him; though the muscles were small, the exercises had taken considerable effort and concentration.

"Good, that's great. Ice it over dinner, once or twice. But when you get in the hot tub, make sure you keep this hand under the hot water as much as possible, in a jet if you can, then have Omega focus on the hand and arm tonight during your massage, okay?"

"Okay."

"And it might be good if she makes you a meal where you don't need your left hand to wield utensils," Gangway added. "You worked that hand and wrist to exhaustion. That's why it's shaking now, and it'll probably be worse, later. And the reason I stopped you was because, if you'd gone any longer, you could end up pulling something when the wrist finally failed, and we don't need that now. This isn't like your usual gym workouts, where you push through until your attempt at a rep fails. We want to stop before we get quite that far."

"Oh. Well, I guess," Echo relented. "Yeah, good points, all."

"Great. Head on home, get something to eat, and rest. You done really good, pal."

The therapist helped Echo climb into the antigrav chair, and Echo headed for the agents' housing, head held high.

* * *

Omega made tomato soup—served in mugs, so they could drink it—and paninis for dinner, cutting the sandwiches into small enough wedges that Echo could easily hold one in his right hand and eat, much to his gratitude and appreciation. She also insisted that he ice the wrist off and on during dinner. To her pleasure, a ravenous Echo tucked away two mugs of soup and five panini wedges before calling it quits; Omega had one mug of soup and three wedges, then decided she was full.

Once they had finished eating, she went into the bathroom and ran water into the hot tub, adding her preferred lavender-scented bath salts—having switched when Echo protested taking a bubble bath with her, though he accepted the lavender scent after she pointed out that it was used in several popular designer men's colognes, and would blend well with his preferred fragrance—then helped him strip and ease into the tub when he entered the bathroom on his crutches, five minutes later.

"Ahhh," he sighed in relief, as he sank almost chin-deep into the hot water.

"Get that wrist over by the jet," she told him, pointing, and he obeyed without question. "There we go. Better?"

"Much. In about five minutes, I'mma feel like an overcooked spaghetti noodle."

"Good. Just relax. Do you want company?"

"If it's you? Sure. Don't expect anything but snuggles right now, though. I really am pretty worn out—they did TWO therapy sessions on me today, hand AND leg, both pretty intense."

"Yeah, 'cause they thought you were strong enough to handle it now, as well as working on you getting around an' whatnot," Omega pointed out, as she began disrobing. "Sure, I'd expect you to be worn out. But that's gonna change, as you continue to gain your stamina and strength back."

"I'm...well, I'm finally starting to believe it, now," he decided, as she slid into the tub beside him. "C'mere an' let's snuggle."

Omega eased into his side and rested her head against his shoulder.

Moments later, she heard a soft, almost-snoring sigh. She tilted her head and glanced up at his face.

Echo was sound asleep.

Omega smiled and relaxed into his body.

* * *

She had to wake him up to get him out of the tub. A groggy

Echo gingerly eased out and onto the waiting, towel-draped stool, then sat, half-slumped and barely awake, while Omega dried his body, having already towel-dried herself. Then she transferred him into the antigrav chair—since he was too out of it to use his crutches—and trundled him into the bedroom.

There, Omega took one look at the massage table in the corner, and simply moved him to the bed, managing to get him transferred once more.

"Umph," Echo grunted then. "Mm. Bed."

"Uh-huh," Omega said with a grin. "Bed."

"Mm...but my ther'pis' said we's s'posta work m' hand..."

"I know. I will. I just don't think you'll be awake enough when I'm done to get you from the table to the bed, so I went ahead and put you in the bed."

"But..."

"Trust me. I know what I'm doin' by now."

"Ah do..."

Omega fetched a couple of old, clean gym towels and slipped them under Echo's right leg and left hand, then swiped the muscle rub oil from the side holder of the massage table, and commenced working her husband's regenerated and thoroughly-worked limbs.

By the time she was finished, he was deeply asleep.

"And won't wake up until morning," she decided, using the towels to gently wipe away the excess oils on his skin, before tossing them into the laundry chute. "So...I think I'll join him."

Omega slid her own tired body into bed beside Echo's, pulled the covers over them both, and was asleep within minutes.

* * *

The Central Park Conservancy's maintenance personnel became very concerned, as the holiday season progressed, at what appeared to be an off-season infestation of clearwing borers in the park, moving gradually north from an area near the southwestern corner of the park. Evergreens were being damaged, evergreen and deciduous trees stripped of bark over wide bands, branches all but stripped of needles. A couple of trees died mysteriously. One even toppled to the ground early one morning, nearly taking out a jogger.

And all of the damage occurred overnight.

And was ongoing.

The maintenance people broke out the insecticides, then went out and sprayed the effective area, only to find that, the next morning, the affected area had shifted farther north.

* * *

Inside a Division week, and with galactic medical techniques brought to bear, Echo had progressed from crutches through a walker to a cane. Alpha One brought the antigrav chair back to the medlab and checked it back into the system; Echo bit off a jubilant exclamation as they did so.

"See, honey?" Omega told him. "No more chair!"

"Yup, an' it feels damn good," Echo admitted.

"Yeah, it should, big guy; you're coming along fast, now," Zebra, who was his personal physician, noted. "All we're really doing at this point is getting the nervous system fine-tuned and the muscles strengthened. So once the neural connections are made—and they are, or you wouldn't be able to do what you're already doing—the rest of that's gonna go fast, because you're USED to doing it."

"And it's good, because now I can start to help Meg out," Echo agreed. "She no longer has to see to me all the time, I can do a few minor housekeeping tasks to ease her load there, and hopefully y'all are gonna let me back into the office for a few hours each day, sometime soon."

"And I'm glad to have you up and about, hon," Omega declared, "because I know how you hated not being able to be independent. But I'm good, either way. I didn't mind doing it."

"I know, but...Meg, it was a heavy load for you, baby," Echo protested. "I'm getting outta your hair, I'm becoming less of a big baby for you to have to tend, and soon I'll even be able to spell you and Romeo in the Alpha Line Room."

"Yeah, I think that's a plan," Zebra decided. "Let's give it a couple of days—maybe as long as four or five; we'll wait and see how you do—on the cane for you to get a good feel for it, and ease back into your old routines, then you can go back into the office. But listen to me, both of you—I do NOT want EITHER of you in that office for an entire Division day. I don't even want you in that office for a full Earth-day shift.

36

I don't care how you work it, but to start, Echo, no more than about four hours, MAX. If some really big shit hits the fan, you can up that to about six hours. Yes, you're stronger, and yes, you were in great shape before, but you suffered some very serious trauma, both physical and mental—and that takes a toll. AND you were in the regen pod, relatively speaking, a good long while, neutrally buoyant at that, and got used to it. So you'll be surprised how fast you wear out, at least at first. You still have a lot of physical therapy to go. Now, a lot of that is going to end up being in the gym on your own recognizance and just checking in with us from time to time, but for now, we still want you working with the therapists. Never mind both of you seeing Zz'r'p. NEITHER of you is approved for field work unless it's at LEAST a Level 3 Facility Alert, and Zar and I are debating about making that a Level 2 Planetary Alert."

"In other words, a big-ass emergency," Omega noted.

"Exactly." She shrugged. "A Level 1 Division Alert and above are kinda 'all hands on deck, the shit's hittin' the fan,' and we get that, but we also checked with Fox, who double-checked GALINT, and everything looks clear at those levels."

"Okay, we can handle that," Echo concluded. "So...three days from now, I go in to the office for around four hours."

An obviously irked Zebra raised an eyebrow.

"What?" Echo wondered, startled at her reaction.

"What did I JUST tell you?" Zebra said, flinging up a hand in annoyance.

"Oh. Um. I go in to the office for NO MORE than four hours." Echo looked sheepish.

"There we go. Yes," Zebra confirmed. "But take it EASY."

"Got it."

* * *

"NYPD Dispatch. What is your emergency?"

"Moy car's been stolen!"

"Were you carjacked?"

"No. Oy came outta th' office, an' moy car wadn't theah no moah!"

"Are you certain you went to the right parking space, sir?"

"Poysitive! We got assoyned spaces in th' garage! I've had it foah yeahs!"

37

"All right. Please give me your location, and the make and model of your automobile, please."

"It's a Chevy Bolt, 'bout two yeahs old, an' it 'uz pahked on th' foath floah of th' garage off Columbus an' West 69th!"

"I have Chevy Bolt, two years old; parking garage at Columbus and West 69th, fourth floor. Please confirm?"

"'At's royht!"

"We'll send a unit right over, sir."

"Thoynks!"

"Dispatch out."

* * *

Katy turned and looked at her fellows, then grumbled, "JUST what we don't need. Looks like we got another car theft and chop shop ring setting up in Hell's Kitchen."

There was a general groan, then the dispatchers went back to answering calls and coordinating units.

* * *

Once Echo was on a cane, he was indeed able to help Omega 'around the house' a little more.

"Which means," she told him with a huge, bright smile, "that we can start decorating for Christmas now!"

"Oh," Echo said blankly. "That's right; you do Christmas big."

"Um," she replied, face falling, "well, we...we don't have to, if you don't want to."

"No," Echo decided, watching her out of the corner of his eye, his heart aching as he saw—and felt—the disappointment she was trying hard to hide, yet unable to quite block him from sensing it through the nd't'lq. "No, I think...I think this year, of all years, it's gonna be like Thanksgiving. I have a lot to celebrate, sweetheart," he told her, and saw her face light up, even as he sensed her mood lift. "Let's pull out all the stops!"

So they did.

* * *

The next car stolen was a late-model Tesla Model S, parked along Central Park West in front of an apartment building, right across West 65th Street from Holy Trinity Church; the parking valet had just brought it around, then stepped inside to notify the owner it was there, so she could go to work.

When they came out, it was gone.

* * *

"Where do you wanna put the tree, Ace?" Omega wondered, sipping coffee from her BABY mug.

"I dunno, Meg, where do you think?" Echo replied, looking around the den in consideration as he leaned on his cane. "You're the expert on Christmas decorating..."

"Well, there's a few possibilities," she decided. "It depends on if you want it private or public. I mean, we won't be here for Christmas itself..." She broke off.

"What's wrong?"

"I dunno," she said with a wry grin, then immediately sobering. "Our first Christmas as husband and wife, our first Christmas in our joint quarters, an' we won't BE here, I guess."

"Aw. Well, we don't HAVE to go to the Ranch, if you don't want to."

"No, Ace, I DO want to!" Omega told him, eyes wide. "It's only..." She sighed. "You ever wish you could be in two places at once?"

"Quite a few times, especially since I met you," Echo confessed. "Seriously, though, if you want to stay here for our first Christmas, Ma will definitely understand."

"No, we've already gone way too far down that road with our plans," Omega pointed out. "Let's follow through on it. We already did our first big holiday here. It'll be fine. I'm good. I'm actually kind of excited about it. We'll be in a FAMILY HOME for Christmas. And I haven't done that since..." She bit her lip, dropping her gaze to the floor—but not before Echo saw the blue eyes glimmer wetly.

"Since your parents and gramma died, the night before Christmas Eve?" he finished her statement, careful to keep his voice soft. "So that's important to you, too."

"...Yeah," she choked out.

"C'mere, baby," he offered, holding out his free arm. "C'mere an' lemme hold ya for a few minutes. This time of year is rough on you, I know; you wanna love it, and yet there's bad memories there."

Omega went into his embrace, burying her face in his shirt front and holding tight to his waist, as his free arm wrapped around her, cradling her close.

"There we go," he murmured. "Hang on and let it out, sweetheart. I'm here, and I won't let go until you tell me to."

"You...you wanna siddown?" she sniffled. "Don' wanna wear you out, standin' here..."

"I'm fine. Relax and let it out."

* * *

After about fifteen minutes of venting pent-up emotions, Omega raised her head, sniffled a bit, dragged the backs of her hands across her eyes, and rubbed away tearstains on her cheeks.

"Thanks, Ace," she said huskily. "I didn't know that was comin', or I'd 'a warned ya."

"I caught on to that. It's okay, baby," he told her, bending his head and depositing a gentle kiss, first on her forehead, then the tip of her nose, and finally her lips. "That's what bein' married is all about, I think. You've been there for me during my recovery, an' I'm gonna be there for you through Christmas. Try to relax about it, and realize a few things."

"What?"

"One: you're not alone any more. You have a whole new family now, in a couple senses of the word, and more, you have me, your husband. And I'm not gonna leave your side through the holidays unless you specifically tell me to." Echo met her eyes. "Okay?"

"Okay. That...sounds good. And 'one' assumes 'two'..."

"Right. Two: not only did we catch the bad guy responsible for killing your folks, that bad guy is flat-out dead. And you and I, together, did that. And all of his machinations have fallen through, and we seem to have finally reached the end of that pile of shit."

"Good point."

"Three: you have, and are, fulfilling your childhood dream, in a way you never thought possible, before."

"Uh-huh." Omega gave him a smile. It was still a bit watery, but he saw and felt an uplifted mood in it, and was satisfied.

"Four: you're a hero, on several levels, an' quite a few planets. Heroine, I guess I should say. And a heroine to me, in more ways than I got words to say it."

"Aw."

"Five an' final: you're LOVED, baby. By me, by your mom-in-law, by your adoptive family across five or six species and damn near as many planets. You. Are. LOVED. And," Echo shrugged, "don't think your mom an' dad an' gramma aren't aware of all that where they are, aren't watching an' lookin' down over you, pleased to see what you've accomplished, who you have around you. I just hope they approve of the guy you married."

"I can't see how they could possibly disapprove," Omega said, hugging him hard.

They stood like that for several more minutes, before Echo, in a light-hearted tone, said, "So okay, what are the options you had in mind for putting up the tree?"

Omega giggled, and Echo grinned.

* * *

"All right," she said, working hard to get herself back into a practical mindset, "I think we have about three options."

"Let's hear 'em."

"Option A: we put the tree up back there," Omega pointed to the rear of the den, "against the wall, between the bedroom door and the dining room door."

"Mm," Echo said, doubtful, "I dunno about that one. If either of us comes outta the bedroom in the middle of the night, it's gonna be 'cause we're headed to the kitchen for a snack. Even with a nightlight, I'm not gonna react fast enough to realize it's there an' dodge it."

"Which means one or the other of us would run square into the tree, probably knock it over, an' fall on top of it," Omega noted. "Smashing decorations, damaging the tree, and maybe getting hurt ourselves. Yeah. Good point."

"On to option B," Echo said.

"Hokay." She turned and pointed in the opposite direction. "Option B is, we shift the reading nook toward the couch a bit for the duration, and put the tree up in the corner to the left of the TV."

"That could work," Echo thought, turning to survey the corner in question. "It means we can't reach that particular bookcase so well, but it's only temporary, anyhow."

"Exactly. And if there's books in there you know you'd want, go ahead an' pull 'em before we get the tree up, an' put 'em on another shelf," Omega told him. "We don't have all the bookcases filled yet anyway."

"That'd do. Next option?"

"Next and last," Omega said. "Option C is, we put the tree in the BEDROOM, over in the corner between your nightstand an' my closet, an' we use it instead of a nightlight. The closet doors slide from the center out, so it wouldn't be in the way..."

"That could work, too," Echo agreed. "I assume that, since we're traveling for the actual holiday, we're gonna use your artificial tree this year?"

"I suppose so," she confirmed. "There's no sense in even trying to talk Fox into a real tree, with nobody here to water it or anything."

"Okay. That narrows things to two options. In the den by the TV, or in the bedroom?"

"I...dunno," Omega said, giving him a whimsical grin. "I can't decide!"

"I got an idea," Echo said with a mischievous smile. "You have more tree decorations than will go on one tree, right? Your collection, your mom's collection, your gramma's heirlooms..."

"Yeah..." Omega's eyes got big. "You aren't suggesting..."

"Yup. Let's go get another tree and we'll put up one in here, an' one in the bedroom!"

Omega squee'ed.

* * *

Three days after the Tesla was stolen, it was found in an out-of-the-way corner of Central Park. It was flipped on its roof, and the big, heavy battery pack in the floor pan had been ripped off.

What was left of the pack was found thirty feet away, with each cell systematically cracked open. In each cell, both the cathode and anode were missing, and most of the electrolyte gel was gone.

Half an hour later, the remains of the battery pack of the Chevy Bolt were found fifty feet away, in similar shape.

The Bolt itself was nowhere to be found.

* * *

Within days, Alpha One's big apartment had a festive air,

with a tree in both the den and bedroom, fat red candles with faux greenery on the end tables and coffee table; garlands over the doors; fragrance diffusers scattered about emitting a blend of evergreen, spice, and citrus; a Christmas runner and Advent wreath centerpiece on the dining table; a miniature tree in the corner of the sideboard...

...And Echo himself hung the wreath on their front door.

"Because I wasn't really up to it last year," he admitted, as a pleased Omega watched.

"And now our apartment is ready for the holidays," Omega declared.

"Time to go Christmas-present shopping," Echo agreed. "Together, this year."

Omega beamed.

* * *

An early-model Hyundai Ioniq disappeared next, stolen from the Tavern on the Green parking lot overnight; it belonged to a member of the overnight maintenance and cleaning crew.

As soon as it was reported, the unit assigned to investigate went back to the same out-of-the-way location in Central Park, hoping to catch the chop shoppers at work.

They found the Ioniq...in the same shape as the previous cars. The battery pack had been stripped from the floor pan like the others; however, this one could not be found. But there was a small lake nearby, and the police determined to drag it to see if they could find the missing battery pack.

"After all," one of them noted in dry irony, "it can't be good for the fish."

* * *

The very next morning after the Ioniq was reported stolen, Central Park Zoo officials found several animals dead in their enclosures, including two sheep and a goat in the children's petting zoo, and much to their surprise, a dead snow leopard in the main enclosures.

The zoo veterinarians were unable to determine the causes of death.

All the animals showed signs of extensive scavenging after death.

* * *

"I wanna know what the hell happened to my snow leopard!" Joshua Kanapkey, the zoo keeper in charge of the snow leopard enclosure, demanded, when he arrived for work and was informed of what had happened. Kanapkey was a strapping brunet in early middle age with eyeglasses and a heavy beard that gleamed red-gold in the sun, and a heart for the animals under his care; to say he was upset at what had happened was a considerable understatement. "How the hell did something get to Ilsa fast enough to prevent her fighting back? And why didn't any of the other leopards react?"

"We don't know yet, Josh," Curtis Ackerman, a big, burly blond with a long scar on his left forearm, caused by one of those same leopards during a rescue—he had been active in animal rescue prior to starting at the Zoo—answered, just as upset, as he was head of the animal keepers, and roughly of an age with Kanapkey. "We've got the whole staff on top of this, and the other animals are being examined; there were a couple of animals taken out the same way, over at the petting zoo, too."

"You're kidding! What, and how many?"

"A goat, and two sheep."

"Aww. I liked all the sheep. Which goat?"

"Nag."

"NO! Not Nag!" Kanapkey cried. "She was my favorite!" He shook his head in dismay. "WHAT the hell is goin' ON here?"

"I'll let you know as soon as we figure something out," Ackerman sighed. "Meantime, if you could go have a look around the enclosure and see if you see anything out of the norm, it would help. And if you figure out how who- or whatever it was got INTO the enclosure, it'd help a LOT."

"All over it," Kanapkey declared.

He turned and headed straight for the snow leopard enclosure.

* * *

"...And now that we've gone through all the more urgent items on this morning's agenda, I've got a surprise for y'all," Omega declared a couple of days later, at the morning departmental meeting in the Alpha Line Room. "C'mon in,

44

hon!" she called.

A smiling Echo, leaning on his cane and still limping just a little bit, walked through the door, dressed in his Suit.

The room, and all of the monitors from the other Offices, erupted in cheering, whooping and yelling. It went on for fully five minutes.

"Hi, y'all," he said, when the noise had died down a bit; Fox, overhearing the ruckus from his office across the Core, came to the door of the Alpha Line Room to see what was happening, then stayed to watch. "I'm back, part-time at least. I'm only allowed a few hours each day, or Medical will be down on my ass, but I'm here, in one piece, and damn glad to be back."

Another round of cheers went up. Echo raised his hand, and the Agents quieted.

"I wanted to thank everybody for...well, for ridin' to the rescue," Echo added, "and that includes, from what I understand, just about all of Alpha Line, a substantial chunk of Medical, Field, and Security, as well as the Deltiri embassy and our good Director. Plus the crew of his flagship, the *Genesis*." He nodded at Fox, who nodded back.

"Hey man," Monkey volunteered, "in the end, we didn't do that much. We just weren't sure if we'd have to fight our way through to you or not. So we went prepared."

"I know," Echo said, very solemn. "And I know what it would mean, to have to do that. To realize that my life means that much to so many people, it...I..." He choked, and broke off, dropping his gaze to the floor.

Omega, seeing what had happened, stepped to his side, laying her hand lightly on the small of his back.

"What Echo wants to say and can't quite get out," she said in a soft voice, "is that he had no idea he meant that much to y'all, and he's more grateful than he has words to say. I think he'd also like y'all to know that y'all mean just as much to him, which is one of the main reasons why he's been fighting through tons of therapy to get himself back into the department chief role, in an ACTIVE fashion, so he can go into the field beside y'all. He and I both, we care about every last damn one of y'all, and we wanna make sure that the department's run right. Which also means knowing what you have to go through to get your missions completed, and backing you up our own selves, when necessary."

Echo nodded, then jerked a thumb at his partner, mouthing, "That."

The room was dead silent for several long moments.

"We know, guys," Tare noted then, quiet. "That's why everybody in the department loves you two so much. You're right in there with us, bustin' ass to see to it that the mission gets done without any of us gettin' hurt."

"Yeah," Yankee agreed. "You two even brought us hard-heads around. Damn, girl, when you didn't have one of your own, you created a FAMILY. Way I figure it, that includes all of us, in some measure." He waved a hand around the room, including the video screens. "Even if some of us are nothin' but annoying cousins! Besides, in the end, you're the one who did the big work, going in all by yourself and hauling an unconscious Echo outta what musta amounted to the bowels of hell."

"It did, and it was," was all Echo said. Omega felt herself flush.

"I wasn't really by myself; y'all know that," she said then. "The whole Deltiri team was giving me directions, playin' mind games with the Cortians...hell, they were helping me out all kindsa ways. Look. I...we're married now, Echo an' me. I love him, or I wouldn't have married him. Yeah, this department, it's kind of our extended family. I...I mean, if any of you...we'd..."

"We'd help," Echo finished for her. "We'd do, every bit, the same for any of y'all as you did for us. And bust as much Cortian ass as it took, in the process."

Still standing in the doorway, Fox began to clap. Within moments, the rest of the department—in the room, and on the vid screens—had joined him.

"And that," the Director declared, once the room had quieted, "is why the two of you are the department leads, over and above your abilities, both individually and as a partnership. You are Alpha One, and I think it is safe to say that, when the two of you move from field duty, there will be no other.

We will retire that team code, and the two of you will always remain Alpha One, for posterity."

"Hear, hear! Amen! I second that motion!" came the cries from around the room and beyond.

"Vote?" Fox queried.

All hands went up, in the room and on the screens. Echo and Omega gaped.

"Done," Fox decreed. "I'll see the paperwork is completed this afternoon, and notify Chief Wux and the Ennead of the decision. Carry on with your meeting, tekhter and zun."

"How the hell do you carry on after something like that?" Echo wanted to know.

The room laughed.

"Well, I guess we'll start by parking our butts, and letting Romeo and Golf fill us all in on a couple of things they've been chasing," Omega said, as a smiling Fox slipped back out of the room, and they all resumed business as usual.

* * *

After the Alpha Line departmental meeting, Alpha One, Alpha Two, and Alpha Four, the lead teams in the department, met briefly to work out scheduling for managing the department.

"Because I'm only allowed a maximum of four hours a day by Medical," Echo explained, "and Meg isn't allowed a whole lot more."

"About six hours, max," Omega interjected. "But what we thought we'd try to do is to stagger ourselves a little bit. Echo can come in for his four—it won't be exactly four unless we need it to be, but he and I think he can do, say, three and a half, three hours and forty-five minutes, something like that—and then, after he's been on duty for an hour or two, I'll come in. Then he'll go home, and I'll stay for the rest of my partial shift, and hand over to one of y'all."

"That sounds like it'd work," Romeo agreed. "I been comin' in f'r you t' hand over to, Meg, an' Golf an' Easy work together, an' we split the rest of the hours between me an' them. It ain't a full shift, but you comin' in has really helped ease the command load on us."

"And the fact that she's been picking Echo's brain for us has helped, too," Golf agreed.

47

"Good, then," Echo decided. "I'm glad I've been able to provide some feedback and assistance, even though I couldn't be here."

"Dude, we just glad to see you up an' about," Romeo averred.

"Amen to that," Easy agreed.

"Be aware that I have instructions to report back to the medlab if either of you gets 'rambunctious,' as Zee put it," India said. "I know you're pushing that four-hour limit, but I'm not gonna say anything, because I think Echo's gonna have sense enough to go home if he gets tired."

"Well, sure," Echo confirmed. "I'm not stupid. I want this to work, not set me back, or worse, screw up things so I can't come back. But these guys need help," he waved at Romeo and Alpha Four. "And I want to help. I CAN help."

"Exactly," India agreed. "And I think it'll be good for you, knowing that you ARE helping, that you can still run the department, even if you have to take a reduced load until you've got your stamina back."

"So," Omega said. "We need to work out a schedule, guys, because Alpha Two and Alpha Four still have to do patrols, as well as the office work."

"Right," Echo noted. "So why don't we do it like this: I would normally start my duty shift at 8:00 am. So if I go ahead and come in then, that'd put me getting off shift about noon-ish..."

"Then I can come in about ten in the morning," Omega tag-teamed, "and we'll overlap from ten to twelve, then you go home and I stay until about four."

"I c'n come in around two or three," Romeo said, "earlier if we got somethin' goin' down like application evals, so's Meg an' me c'n work on 'em together, an' India an' I c'n do 'bout twenty, maybe twenty-one more hours in th' office after Meg leaves, hand over t' Alpha Four, do another three 'r four hours on patrol, an' we're done with our shift. Oughta only add up to th' usual twenty-four, but if it runs a couple hours over now an' then, it ain't no thang. We done more'n that on missions."

"Which means Easy and I would come in about ten or eleven in the morning the next Earth day," Golf tagged, "hand over with Romeo, do another twenty or twenty-one hours after Romeo leaves, then hand back over to Echo at eight o' clock local, and go do our own patrol. And like Romeo says," he added, "if it runs over a couple hours from time to time, it's no big deal, 'cause with Echo back, now we know it's gonna be temporary."

"This looks like it'll work," Echo decided. "It gets the office covered even better than it usually is when Meg and I are on full duty, yet still enables Two and Four to do some basic patrols, which eases the load on the other Headquarters teams."

"I think we got it, guys," Omega said. "We're good until a couple days before Christmas."

"Which we got worked out already, among ourselves," Easy said. "India's been keeping us apprised of what the medlab wants you two to do, and listen, we're in agreement: you guys need a serious break, for a change, and time away from work. Hell, even when you went on vacay last summer, things went wonky, and you ended up back on the job! So go off for the holidays and kick back and relax, okay? If something comes up, call US this time. We have your backs, I swear we do."

"Thanks, guys," Echo said, deeply grateful. "Now, you two need to go off shift already and go crash. Romeo, you and India head back home, too, and at least grab some breakfast. Meg and I got this, for a few hours, anyhow."

"All over it, boss-man," Romeo agreed, as Alpha Two and -Four headed out.

* * *

Echo did indeed start out slowly, tiring quickly after only a couple of hours. He pushed it and made it for another forty-five minutes after Omega came back to the office, then threw in the towel and went home. By the time she got off that afternoon and arrived home, she found him in his lounging clothes napping on the couch, wrapped in the nebula throw, the lights dimmed.

The second day went somewhat better; he knew more of what to expect from his body, and made sure he ate a larger breakfast, to help fuel himself. Within a couple more days, he was working the entire four hours, without skimping. And while India said she'd informed Zebra of the full duration, she'd also told Zebra that he was doing well, and had sense enough to go home when he got tired, whether he lasted as long as he wanted or not. Zebra was content with that, and approved it...provided Echo did not go longer than four hours, for the time being.

More, he was keeping up his therapy, doing the exercises even on days without therapy appointments, and was getting stronger fast.

* * *

In Central Park, early one morning as the sun was rising, a jogger on one of the paths near Umpire Rock was pleased at how well his new, custom running sneakers were doing. The bright red athletic shoes were cushioning his pounding feet excellently well.

I think this is gonna really help me improve the pace, he decided. *I might even be able to enter the next marathon and have a better showing than last time. And the shrink says it's been good for me, having a goal like that. Never mind the exercise and stress relief. Now, if Sheila just doesn't call and interrupt my pace, things'll go great.* He threw a stray thought to the cell phone strapped to his wrist, but it remained dark.

Just then, he heard an odd, scuttling sound behind him. He thought little of it until it grew louder and seemed to come closer, whereupon he glanced over his shoulder to see what was coming up behind him. His eyes abruptly grew wide; he blanched, and broke into a sprint.

* * *

Two NYPD beat cops, responsible for patrolling the Park, were chatting with the owner of one of the vendor carts along West Drive, when a bloodcurdling scream cut through the morning mist.

"That came from over around Umpire Rock!" one exclaimed.

"Let's go!" the other said, and they broke into a run.

* * *

But when they got to Umpire Rock, the area was empty.

"You go right, I'll go left, an' I'll meetcha on the far side o' the rock," the first said.

"Done," his partner agreed.

They pulled their weapons, held them in ready position pointed at the ground, and flanked the large stone outcrop.

* * *

"You see anythin', Pete?" the first said, when they met back up on the far side of the rock outcrop.

"Nothin', Bob. What 'bout 'chu?"

"Didn't see nobody," Officer Bob noted. Then he held up an object. "But I found this."

It was a brand-new, bright red, custom-made running shoe.

But part of the sole had melted.

* * *

"So how was the honeymoon, Meg?" India asked, as several of the female Alpha Line Agents sat around the table in the break room, snacking and chatting after the morning departmental staff meeting, about a week and a half after both members of Alpha One had returned to the office. Then she saw Omega's face fall, and quickly appended, "I mean, you know, all that stuff BEFORE Echo got kidnapped by the Cortians an' shit."

"Oh," Omega said, brightening. "It was really nice. Echo an' I just played tourists and newlyweds, you know, not worrying about stuff, exploring, shopping, sleeping in, kicking back and having a good time. I don't think I've ever had so much fun on a vacay."

"And the nights probably weren't half bad either, huh?" Love, of Alpha Five, teased. "I mean, Echo's built, so..."

Omega flushed, then grinned sheepishly.

"Um, yeah," she agreed. "I, um, it was...it was good. I'm...I'm happy. Really happy."

"You sound hesitant," Torino noted. "You aren't regretting it, are you? After all, you've been taking care of him since you got back from rescuing him from the Cortians. Hell of a way to start off a marriage."

"NO! No, I haven't minded that at all. Actually, I kinda like taking care of him. I like being...needed...by him. No, it's just I, um, I mean..." Omega broke off, embarrassed and unsure how to answer. *How do I tell 'em I didn't even really know what to expect on my wedding night? That I was scared?* she wondered. *Oh, I knew the mechanics...but not how I'd react emotionally. But if I try to explain, I'll just sound stupid...not to mention, forty-seven and a half kinds of naïve.*

* * *

"Guys?" India interrupted, having watched Omega's facial expressions carefully. "Remember everything Slug did to Omega, when she was a girl? Given the little 'family group' we sorta fell into, Meg and I have discussed a few things, like, well, like sisters. YOU know what I mean. Anyway, I found out it created some psychological...issues...with that sort of thing, in her subconscious. Like, letting someone get close, and being intimate, and all that. You guys understand what I'm talking about—trust issues. She trusts Echo completely, or it never would have come to them getting married, I think. I don't know for sure, 'cause I deliberately didn't ask Meg, but I do know she's admitted to me that she never really had many close romantic relationships before Echo, and I think she was kinda nervous about the whole thing, because of all that back history...and probably doesn't exactly know how to discuss it with 'us girls'..."

A flushing Omega nodded, staring at her hands in her lap, and a general soft and very sympathetic chorus of, "Oooh," went around the room. India continued.

"...So the fact that she says it was good, and she's happy being married to Echo, well, that says a lot about it, I expect." Just then, India offered Omega a smirk; Omega flushed deeper, but grinned back. "And I really think that's all we need to know about THAT."

"Yeah, uh-huh, what she said," the others agreed.

* * *

"Speaking of...that sorta thing...I did see something funny, though, while we were there, on Tiniken," Omega admitted. "It was in a bunch of the gift shops. It seems that the American Southwest is kinda popular offworld—you know, cowboys an' Indians an' horses and cattle an' all that shit...and REALLY stereotyped, but reasonably accurate, for all that—an' somebody had developed a men's fragrance they called 'Naked Cowboy'! The marketing was just over the top! It was hilarious. I swear, the label looked like one of those bodice-ripper romance novels! I dunno if Echo saw it or not;

if he did, he didn't say anything, but I picked up a bottle in the store and looked for the fragrance notes, just out of curiosity's sake, and..." she shrugged. "Assuming they got 'em right, and they're the same as they would be on Earth, I think they mighta nailed it. It was, like, musk and leather and tobacco and wood smoke..." she ticked off fingers, "and a couple other things, I think."

"Ooo, that actually sounds good," Torino decided. "Is it available on Earth?"

"I haven't seen it," Omega observed. "I dunno if it was put out by an Earth-based perfumerie or an offworld one. You might have to try to grab some on the next offworld mission y'all get."

"All over it," Torino smirked. "Did you get Echo any?"

"Nah," Omega said with a fond grin. "I got my own cowboy, and he does just fine as is. Besides, I already like the fragrance he uses. It blends really nice with his own scent, you know?"

"Yeah, I get it," Torino agreed. "What does Echo use, do you know?"

"I haven't really picked up the bottle and looked, but by the shape and color of the label, I think it's one of the Burberry men's line," Omega noted.

"Oh, that's good stuff," India averred. "I used to use one of their women's line."

"You arrived back with a great tan, Omega," Love told her, just as Echo came through the break room door en route to the snack machines; though he still used a cane for support while he continued strengthening the regrown leg, his limp now was barely noticeable to the others. But Omega, knowing him at least as well as she knew herself, saw it, though she decided it was looking good, and showed no evidence of pain or difficulty. "And from what you've said in the past, that's hard for you, with your pale skin. You didn't burn, did you?"

"No, I didn't," Omega said with a smile, offering it to Echo as he turned with a pre-packaged pastry in hand. He smiled back, then finished her statement.

"No, she didn't, because I kept on her ass about her sunscreen," he said. "Even slapped it on her a few times, my own self. She has trouble getting the middle of her back, even in a bikini, so I usually helped her, regardless." He gave his partner-wife a smirk. "And it wasn't like I didn't enjoy it. Besides, what with a blue-white star, even the sunscreen Meg got from Medical wasn't quite enough, so at a certain point each day, I shooed her back inside, so she DIDN'T burn."

"Good for you, Echo," India approved. "I know she was in some pain when she got burned at the Beach last summer—after you, uh, had to leave—and I wound up giving her some analgesics, as well as topical painkillers, and a few good swipes of Rejuvic, on top of."

"Ow." Echo winced. "Baby, you gotta be careful. I mean, I know the medlab's got the whole skin cancer thing bypassed by now, but still."

"Well, that was after y'all's whole plan to convince me... an' through me, Wright...that you were dead," Omega said in a low tone. "An' it worked—I truly thought you were dead, Ace. So I sorta wasn't really thinking about much of anything else."

The room fell silent for a moment.

"Are you two still on extended leave?" Torino wondered, by way of a gentle, semi-un-jarring diversion of topic. "I mean, you've both been in the Alpha Line Room and all, since about a week or so ago, and you got outta the medlab a couple weeks before that, Echo. In a medical antigrav chair, but still."

"Sort of," Echo explained, around a mouthful of cinnamon roll. "Right now, we're limited to just, you know, desk duty. And that, part time, as yet. We..." He broke off, eyes going distant. Finally he sighed, and continued, "The last couple months have been...hard...on both of us. I'm just glad to be back on my feet...hell, what am I saying? I'm glad to HAVE both feet. And hands, and eyes. Anyhow, Fox, Zz'r'p, Zarnix, Zebra, India, Whiskey, Rglfrz—all those guys seem to think we need some light duty, or even no duty, for a change, and plenty of time away from Headquarters, too—they want Meg an' me to head off for Christmas, maybe take an extended stay at our beach house for New Years..."

"Which we might do," Omega admitted. "New Years, I mean; we already know we're headed out for Christmas. It's not far, after all. If there was an emergency, we could come straight back."

"Yeah. Never mind some counseling for me, and MORE counseling for Meg. I don't know if we're gonna be allowed back on full Alpha Line duty before the first of the year, if that—it's already way late in the year." He shrugged. "And..."

"And they're right," Omega acknowledged with a sigh.

"I know," Echo agreed, not even trying to hide a certain moroseness. "I hate like hell to admit it, but...yeah. We been through hell and back, baby. We need the down time, you an' me."

"Yeah," Omega confirmed. "I'm just...well, it's a helluva way to do it, but...I'm glad that we're married now, so we can lean on each other so much. It...helps."

"Yeah, it does. Both ways."

"But you came out the other side, both of you, together," India pointed out. "You just need that down time, is all. Time to let your psyches unwind and chill for a bit, and Echo, time to let all of the physical therapy 'take'—you know what I mean. Nobody can maintain all this...crap...we do in Alpha Line indefinitely, without that kind of down time, and the occasional counseling session to make sure your head's on straight...and I periodically evaluate each member of the department for that very thing, and report it to the medlab so we can see to it that everybody gets what they need to keep on keeping on. And Zebra evaluates ME." She shrugged. "And I got a little counseling, too, in the aftermath of having to work on one of my best friends after the Cortians hacked him up."

"You doing better on that, India, hon?" Omega wondered, even as Echo flushed and dropped his gaze to the floor. "Did it help?"

"Yeah, it did," India confirmed, then she ticked off fingers. "I got everything down to, 'I hated to have to hurt Echo more than he was already hurt,' and 'It had to be done, so he could heal,' and 'Echo ain't Romeo, an' I ain't Meg.' And I could deal, after I fully, consciously realized those three things."

"Well, that's good, I think," Love murmured, considering the matter. "Alla that. Evaluations, and counseling, and down time, and...all of it. It keeps us as healthy as possible, in every sense of the word."

"Yeah, it is, an' it does," Omega agreed. India nodded, and

continued.

"...And the two of you, I swear, have been Ground Zero for all of the worst attacks, simply BECAUSE you're at the top of the department," India continued. "So you've caught hell more than the rest of us, even." The others voiced strong agreement. "Never mind the leftover plans of old enemies."

"No argument there, I guess," Echo averred, then glanced at his wrist chronometer. "And to that end, it's about time for me to go off-duty, or the whole medlab will have my hide. An' I've had enough of that shit already. Meg? You good for a few more hours, baby? We've been trying to stagger ourselves a little, guys, so it extends our overall time in the office a little more..."

"And Romeo appreciates it," India informed them. "For that matter, so do Golf and Easy, I think."

"Good," Echo responded. "Meg?"

"Yeah, I'm good, Ace," Omega declared. "I still gotta put together the department report for Fox, and do a couple other minor book-keeping thingies, but then I'll be on home. Are you gonna start rearranging the décor in our apartment this afternoon, like we talked about last night?"

"I thought I might start on it, yeah. The Facilities guys did a damn good job, but not everything ended up where I think we want it to be. I'm still trying to figure out how to arrange the sofa and the recliners in a better config." He shrugged. "It's mostly books and stuff, though. So that's not THAT hard. I just want to shift some categories around. And maybe adjusting some furniture positions," he held up thumb and index finger, "juuust a little. The bed needs scooting to one side, f'r instance. Right now, it's too close to the closet doors, especially with the Christmas tree in the corner. Never mind putting the dining room back in day-to-day configuration after Thanksgiving."

"Agreed. To alla that. Okay, when I get home I'll change into jeans and a t-shirt and help. Meantime, please don't be shoving the bigger furniture around until I get home, okay? That's a good way to develop an instant hernia, especially that humongously solid big bed Fox had Facilities give us! Guys, I thought it was a California king when we first moved in...but it's even bigger! Echo says it's something called an Alberta king—it's like eight feet by eight feet! I mean, it's great, and it's comfy, and it even fits Echo's height with room to spare—"

"Which ain't an easy thing to find," Echo pointed out. "I'm not short."

"No, it isn't, and no, you aren't," Omega agreed. "I remember you fussin' 'cause you'd bang your hand against the headboard of your old bed, an' stuff like that."

"Hell yeah," Echo agreed. "Helluva way to wake up in the night!"

"Oh, that," India said. "Yeah, me an' Zee an' Zar an' Fox discussed it while you two were on honeymoon. No, nothing to do with your regen, Echo, I swear," she added hastily, as Echo's brows drew together. "The whole thing took place way before that. Fox was making the arrangements with Facilities, and wanted to make sure you had a bed big enough to fit, Echo, and wanted a medical recommendation, given your height and usual levels of activity. Zar pulled up a study about mattress size relative to patient height for optimizing support and comfort, and we pretty much decided to get you the biggest bed we could wangle in the time we had. And that was the Alberta king. There's bigger beds, but they're custom and take a while to get..."

"Damn," Echo muttered, surprised. "Bigger?"

"Yup. But this one should do you two nicely," India said with a grin.

"Well, it does," Omega agreed. "That's probably the comfiest bed I've ever been in. And the rest of the bedroom furniture matches the bed! I'm not complaining, and I'm happy to have it; I'm just sayin'. So I'm thinking we might call some 'a these guys in, this weekend, to help us adjust the bedroom suite, if nobody minds."

"That'll work," Echo went along with the idea. "Even the stuff that isn't too heavy, like the dining room table, is just too BIG...you know, bulky...for one guy to move around very easily, even if he's in great shape and not recovering from an injury. And right now, I'm not that. I mean, I can, but it's damned awkward. Even with Meg working with me, it's gonna be hard for just the two of us. And frankly, being mesquite, the dining room furniture ain't too light, anyhow."

"Exactly." Omega nodded vigorously, glad to see her mate was being sensible about it; she had been slightly worried he might insist on trying to do it all himself, when the bedroom furniture, for certain, was going to be a many-multi-human job. And given he was still not that long out of the medlab after losing several limbs to the Cortians' attempts to break him, and having those limbs regrown, it probably would not be good for him to stress those limbs too much, too soon. *Never mind the fact that that leg will never be quite the same again, according to Zebra,* she thought, disheartened despite herself. *Oh, nobody except his 'family' notices the limp much, but he'll have it the rest of his life. Dammit. My poor sweetheart is the most badassest guy in the galaxy, and they went and did that to him! Part of me wishes I really HAD brain-zapped the lot, the damn bastards. At least they got theirs; PGLEIA Chief Wuxullian saw to it that they were all tried for war crimes... and they were all convicted. I think the ship's janitors are the only ones that didn't get mandatory execution. And even they ain't never gettin' outta jail.*

"We really need to adjust the dining table, and soon, though," she observed then, shaking herself out of her morbid thoughts. "It worked great for Thanksgiving, but right now, we need to put it back to the smaller size, to shift it away from the kitchen door; it's making things a little crowded, especially when we try to eat meals in the breakfast nook. I nearly took off a hipbone this morning, bringing out our plates."

"Ow. Yeah, but like I said, that's at least a two-person job. When I go home, I'll start on the books, and the pictures, an' end tables, maybe the recliners," Echo decided, thoroughly derailing the last of her morose train of thought, "'cause those actually scoot pretty easy on the carpet and only really need angling a little, so I can nudge 'em around with my hips—at least until we work out what the final furniture arrangement needs to be in there. But I'll leave the medium stuff—the couch, the dining table, all that shit—'til you get home to help, and the really big stuff 'til we got some other folks to help." He eyed her. "I know you've been worried I was gonna try to macho through it or something, not that you actually said anything, at least until just now. I recognized that look in your eye, though, and knew you were concerned. But don't worry, baby; I remember the gunshot in my gut last Christmas. And I'm still not at a hundred percent physically after the regen pod...and I know it. I still have a ways to go, though I'm working hard in the gym now, in addition to the therapy. There's being independent, and then there's just being stupid. And I have only rarely been accused of the latter."

She offered him a sheepish smile, and he grinned back at her.

"Okay," she agreed.

"Smart man. Romeo and I'll be glad to come over and help, Echo," India noted. "Just say the word."

"Adam and me, too," Torino added.

"Count Uniform and me in," Love said. "Hell, make an announcement in tomorrow's department meeting, an' you'll probably have all the volunteers you could want."

"Great!" Echo said with another smile. "That oughta get it, quick and easy, then. Thanks, y'all!"

And he was off. Omega glanced at her own wrist chronometer.

"Drat," she said with a whimsical grin. "Coffee break's over. Time to get back to work, y'all. Let's go."

Chapter 3

By the time Omega got back to her desk, the reports were coming in, not only from the Headquarters teams, but from the newly-established Alpha Line branches in several other Offices around the planet. Fox, Echo, and Omega had established those several weeks before—after the entire sequence of events surrounding 'Adita's Coup'—and decided that, for now, there needed to be at least one Alpha Line branch on each continent, and the Eurasian continent needed several. None of the branches had to be big to start, but the department needed to have a worldwide presence. And if that went as well as they expected—and as well as it had gone, so far—soon Alpha Line would begin accepting applications from the other planets in the Division.

* * *

So there were now small department branches in the Sydney, Tokyo, Moscow, London, Gaborone, and Rio de Janeiro Offices; most of them comprised no more than two or three partnership teams initially, but had grown in the interim, and the Sydney and Gaborone Office branches had already proven useful, when it was discovered that an offworld murderer and an alien terrorist, respectively, were using the cities as hideouts from their home Divisions. As yet, the less-hospitable-to-humans Offices, such as those at Atlantis and McMurdo, did not have department branches, but it was under consideration, with discussions ongoing of how best to handle the matter.

"It means the Headquarters contingent drops a bit, though," Echo had observed at the time with mild regret.

"Yeah, but we don't have to have Facilities put in that space warp to make the Alpha Line Room bigger," Omega pointed out.

"Yet," Fox had added. "I still expect that to happen in time. And glad of it; this department is proving to be an excellent concept, and quite useful, kinder. AND, by having departmental branches at the other Offices, it means you don't have to travel over the whole farkakte planet, or send your people out on wild snipe hunts."

"True," Echo had decided. "I guess it woulda helped if we'd already had this going, back when the department had to head up clearing out the fake Adita's henchmen, too."

"No argument," Fox had agreed. "It's possible, had we had it in place already, that the meshuginah momzer macher wouldn't have managed to get as entrenched as he did, to begin with."

"True dat," Omega had averred.

"Well, hindsight is always 20/20," Echo pointed out, and Fox and Omega agreed.

* * *

But this new, expanded structure meant that some of the reports were now coming in to Omega as Office reports—the teams assigned to that Office having already worked together to compile a joint report—which made it moderately easier in putting together a global report for the whole department.

"I think I'll start by collating the Headquarters report, then I can splice the various Office reports into it, and it'll be uniform in format," she concluded, after a quick glance over all the reports. "And at some point, Echo an' I'll have to work up a specific format and send it out, which'll speed things up a lot. And probably improve readability into the bargain."

So within a couple of hours, she had a full, world-wide, departmental report assembled. Omega popped it to Fox through electronic channels, then logged out, shut everything down, waved to Romeo—who was reviewing new applicants to the department for Alpha One in the far corner of the Alpha Line Room—and headed for the new, merged quarters she shared with Echo, mentally planning where she wanted to move their furniture.

* * *

But when she entered their quarters, it appeared empty. Quite a few items, including several shelves of books and the big photographic images of the Orion Nebula, had been shifted to the slightly-altered positions the pair had discussed the night before, but Echo was nowhere to be seen.

"Ace?" she called, as she moved deeper into the apartment,

61

divesting herself of Suit jacket and tie before laying them over the back of 'her' recliner. "You here?"

"Yeah, Meg," came Echo's voice from somewhere in the depths of the large apartment. "You're alone, right?"

"Well, yeah..."

"You didn't invite anybody to show up and help rearrange furniture?"

"Not until the weekend, no."

"Good. Come on back to the bedroom, then."

A smirk spread across her face, and she headed for the bedroom door, at the back of the apartment.

But when she entered the bedroom, she stopped dead in surprise: she had expected Echo to be waiting for her in bed, but instead, he stood leaning against the doorframe between their closets, one fist on his hip, weight on his good leg, heel of the other foot against the wall, toes on the floor, knee bent. He wore the cowboy boots she had given him for his last birthday, and the cowboy hat Fox and Zebra had given him at the same time...

...But in between was nothing but bare skin over taut, hard, lean muscle.

Omega's smirk turned into a smile of appreciation.

"Hubba-hubba. Or maybe that's 'hubby-hubby.' So somebody overheard a conversation in the break room this morning, huh?" she wondered.

"Yup," came the laconic reply, as he nudged the hat back on his head a bit. "I thought you might enjoy your own naked cowboy."

"Oh, I have no objections whatsoever," she decided, eyeing him from head to toe with gratified pleasure. "And the view is amazing."

"Scars an' all? I mean, things are...not everything's healed back as smooth as I'd hoped...maybe it's still too soon, but..."

"Until you said something, hon, I didn't even notice," Omega averred. "I know YOU do, though. So let me put it like this...it makes me sad to know that your gorgeous, strong, amazing body has been damaged, and I will not accept that it is permanent—for your sake, I plan on working my ass off to try to find a way to heal it all up to YOUR satisfaction. But given the choice between a few scars on your body, or not having you at all? I'll take a few scars, honey. Any day. Besides, I think I like naked cowboy a lot."

"Do I need to change my cologne, then?"

"No, no! I don't want you to change a thing, mi hombre hermoso," Omega said with a grin, closing the bedroom door behind herself.

* * *

After he got off duty that evening, zoo keeper Joshua Kanapkey decided to nose around the area and see if he could spot any clues as to who had killed the zoo's animals.

He was slipping through the shrubbery around the Children's Zoo sheep enclosure when he heard a rustling from the left; it sounded like someone pushing through the bushes. Kanapkey crouched behind a bush and waited to see who it was, sure he was about to spot the animal killer.

As he eased his head up to peep over the foliage, something hit him full in the face.

He was dead almost before the pain had a chance to register.

* * *

A couple of hours after Omega had arrived home, the pair snuggled, content, in the middle of the big bed.

"Yup, I definitely love having my very own naked cowboy," Omega said with a smirk.

"Yeah, well, naked cowgirl works pretty damn well for me, too," Echo shot back with a straight face, then grinned as she blushed. "As long as it's you, I guess."

"Aw," Omega began. "I—"

Just then, her belly let out a sound that was so loud, it was less a growl and more a roar.

"Whoa," Echo said, eyebrows shooting up. He poked her belly with a gentle index finger. "Somebody's souped-up metabolism is fussin', I'd say. Did you grab second lunch? Hell, did you eat first lunch? We were going in different directions today, chasing paperwork an' shit...I never got a chance to even find out if you ate, let alone ensured you did...wait, it's only just now getting time for second lunch, isn't it?"

"Yeah. I got a little something for first lunch, but I was planning on grabbing something more substantial for second lunch when I got home...only SOMEbody diverted me pretty thoroughly," Omega said, giggling as he tickled her belly with that same finger. "Hey now! Do you really wanna go there with me? I know how to retaliate, ya know!"

Echo froze, staring at her. *She wouldn't,* he thought. Then he remembered a certain double-ducking in the stream on the Ranch the previous summer. *Oh damn, she would...and she has. And...* he paused, considering, *it was actually kinda...fun. Okay, then. Continue, Echo, son.*

And suddenly they were in a tickle fight, laughing and flinging covers about, and whacking each other with pillows.

* * *

It only ended when Omega fell out of bed. She hit the floor on her posterior with a loud grunt, slumped onto the floor, and lay still.

"Oh damn!" Echo cried, and scrambled out of bed, kneeling beside his partner and spouse. "Meg?! Meg, baby? Are you okay?"

A loud gasp left her throat, and she began to giggle again.

"Y-yeah, Ace, I'm all right," she finally got out. "I was laughin' so hard I could barely breathe anyway, an' then when I hit the floor it sorta took the rest of the wind outta me! I'mma have a bruise on my butt, for sure, but that's about it." Abruptly her belly let out another protest, this one even louder, and she giggled again. "I guess I need to get up and go get something to eat, before my stomach decides to come out lookin' for food..."

"Urgh." Echo made a face, crossing his eyes. "Baby, that was a singularly unpleasant image. Slug didn't, I dunno, actually DO...?"

"Not that I know about," Omega declared with a snort. "If any of my internal organs have ever 'gone walkabout' as Yoke says, I never knew it. I'm not sure how survivable that would be, anyway, and near as I could tell, Slug was all about my surviving to get his revenge on you...which ain't happening. Nope, I think we've finally reached the limit of that damn gastropoid's tinkering."

"Well, that's something," Echo said, standing but remaining bent at the waist. "Lemme help you crawl back in bed, then." He held out a hand.

"Nah, Ace," Omega said, accepting his proffered hand to clamber to her feet. "I need to get into the kitchen and slap together a sandwich or something, first."

"Well, that's my point," Echo noted. "When I planned this little interlude, I figured that, at some time this afternoon, you'd need to eat, so I already got a tray ready to go in the kitchen. Soup an' paninis, staying hot in that little kitchen stasis field Fox said he added to our kitchen design...which is coming in handy, like he figured. Get back in bed while I fetch it, and we'll eat together."

"You need your cane to go that far. How are you gonna carry the tray?"

"I went by Facilities and got a little roller-cart on my way home. It folds up and goes in the warp pantry when it's not needed. Don't worry, I got this planned." He grabbed the cane, which was leaning on the armchair nearby.

"Have I mentioned lately what an incredibly considerate, thoughtful partner an' husband I have?" Omega murmured, voice gone husky.

"Once or twice," he said with a slight smile, then he sobered. "But don't think I haven't noticed all the shit you've been willing to go through over the years, just to keep me alive and free and beside you, honey. Never mind in the last few weeks. We take care of each other. That's the way it's supposed to work, whether we're business partners, best buds, or husband and wife. And we're all of the above."

He waved a hand at the bed; then, as Omega eased back between the sheets, Echo disappeared through the bedroom door, en route to the kitchen and the tray he had prepared.

* * *

But as Echo came back into the bedroom with the tray of food, Omega noticed he was limping rather more, and more severely, then had become usual for him in the last week or so. As he set the tray on the bed, she asked, "What's wrong?"

"Huh? What do you mean?"

"You're limping."

"I always limp now, baby," he said, stifling a sigh.

"No, I mean you're LIMPING," Omega declared. "Like, your normal limp is barely noticeable now; even I don't notice it any more unless I'm paying close attention. But just now, you were giving to it, like it hurt. What's wrong?"

Echo gave her a mildly chagrined glance, then admitted, "Um. Well, I think I mighta wrenched it just now, when I bailed outta bed and ran around to see about you..."

"Ooo," Omega murmured in sympathy. "Where abouts?"

"Eh," Echo grumbled, reaching for a sandwich, "just below the knee. Right where the Cortian whacked it off. I figure the tendons are fussing or something, because they're still fairly new after the regeneration process."

"Hm. Could be. Maybe a touch of mild tendonitis, even?"

"Maybe," Echo said doubtfully. "I haven't really had any kind of problem before just now. Like I said, I think I wrenched it when I launched outta bed. When you hit the floor and then slumped down and laid there, I thought something bad had happened, baby."

"Aw. It scared you?"

* * *

"Well...maybe a little." Echo met her eyes, seeing whimsical skepticism there, and 'fessed up. "Okay...yeah, it scared me. Remember, the only things that really scare me have to do with losing you or Ma."

"Aw."

"Yeah, yeah, don't make a big deal out of it," he murmured, before taking a large bite of his panini, even as Omega laid into her soup with enthusiasm. "I don't want anybody but you knowing THAT. It makes you and Ma out as targets too much. And I've already had enough of that with you as it is."

"That's true," she said, in between all but slurping the soup. "Isn't this your homemade potato-cheese soup?"

"Yup. It doesn't take that long to make, an' I thought it'd go good with the paninis," Echo noted, munching his own panini, then dipping one end in the soup and swiftly shoving it into his mouth before it could drip. "Mm. An' I was right. Wow, that's good."

"Good idea," Omega decided, following suit. "An' now I see why you brought a whole wad o' napkins!"

"Yup."

"Does your...I guess your knee area...still hurt?"

"A little." Echo winced, then scowled. "It'll be all right."

"Okay, then when we're done eating, I'mma call Zebra and see what she says. We might need to adjust the therapy schedule to accommodate it. Or maybe adjust the TYPE of therapy to help work out whatever you did to it. But we need to know beforehand. We need the physical therapy to go really well, in order to get you certified to go back into the field with me, after all."

Echo sighed, realizing she was right.

"I guess," he said, raking a hand across his face. "Or maybe I just oughta accept the fact that I'm not GONNA be suited to going back into the field, and take Fox up on that whole 'Assistant Director' position he told me about. I mean, I'm already the Assistant Director, just...more so."

Omega stopped and stared at him.

"Is that what you want?" she asked.

"*I* dunno," Echo fussed, mildly out of sorts with the whole situation. "I'm not sure it matters what I want, anyway. There's what you want, and there's what IS. Besides," he noted, "we can always look at starting a family or something, I suppose."

"Except the medlab still hasn't figured out how to fix my eggs so we'll be assured of having normal human kids, not Echo-assassins," Omega pointed out.

"Oh. Shit. I keep forgetting about that."

"Yeah. So, like you say, there's what we might want, and there's what is. And if they can't fix 'em, we ain't ever havin' kids, because I'm not gonna take the risk that one or more of our kids wouldn't try to kill you, on account of the whole 'programmed genetics' thing."

"Aw."

"'Aw' because we might not be able to have kids, or 'aw' because I care that much?"

"Both, I guess," Echo decided, polishing off the panini and picking up what was left of the mug of soup to drink. "But if the shoe was on the other foot—if our positions were reversed—I'd feel the same as you do. So I understand where you're comin' from."

"I know...now. And I appreciate it," Omega said, picking up her mug and sipping; there was nothing left of her panini but crumbs. "Wow, that was good."

"And you needed it," Echo averred. "Now your stomach isn't gonna come out looking."

* * *

"Nope," Omega said with a grin, then reached for her cell phone on the bedside table. "Go throw on some lounge clothes or something; I expect Zebra is gonna either want to come up here, or us go down to the medlab, so she can check out that knee."

"Damn, Meg, can't we just let it go? It'll probably be better by tomorrow, anyway."

"We don't know that, and I, for one, don't wanna risk messing it up," Omega pointed out. "What's wrong, Ace? You usually don't mind getting a boo-boo checked out if it's warranted. And this is warranted."

"Because I—" Echo broke off and turned his face away, rubbing the back of his neck with the hand that he had lost to the Cortian's torture and which, like the 'tweaked' leg and the gouged-out eye, had been regrown in the regeneration pod. He was silent for long moments, and Omega watched in concern. Finally she leaned over and laid a light hand on his near forearm.

"Honey? It's me. It's Meg. Your partner, your best friend, your wife. You can tell me ANYthing and I will never think badly of you for it. You KNOW that. If you can't force out the words, use the nd't'lq bond. Telepathy works way better for stuff like this, anyway."

All right, he told her, using the telepathic bond the Deltiri ambassador—and Alpha One's telepathic counselor, in the wake of multiple atrocities perpetrated on the paired team— had created for them during their wedding ceremony. *It's the same thing it was back at Thanksgiving. I'm waiting for the other shoe to drop.*

What do you mean?

I mean, I lived through having half of my leg chopped off, having my hand chopped off, having my eye gouged out. While completely conscious and aware, and undrugged. I felt all of it. If the Cortians could have figured out how to rape me to 'harvest my genetics,' they'd have done it; I'm just fortunate

68

that they were out of the tech needed to do it, with nobody 'compatible' aboard their ship. Damn, baby, I understand all too well now what you've been going through with all of Slug's shit. I just... he paused, then tried, *I don't expect to get back to what I was before, is what I'm trying to say. And...and I don't want you to get your hopes up, either. I've been working hard, really hard, but...I just...*

Hush, honey; hush. It's okay. That's not your call, or my call. That's the medics' call, and I think they've got a lot better notion of what you're capable of than you or I do, at this point. We can ask Zebra, when she examines this leg, but personally, I'd lay odds that this is your PTSD talking again, in the aftermath of being tortured. Do you want me to ping Zz'r'p, and do a quick discussion with him about it, either now, or after we talk to Zebra?

Maybe after, he decided. *You could be right, I guess. Probably are.*

Yeah. Been there, done that, after all. But you know what?

What?

I'm really glad that you're accepting the medics' professional opinions again. Omega offered him a smile.

Yeah, I guess so. Thanksgiving, I watched everything, everybody's interactions and all of it, and I realized you were right...they wouldn't do that to either of us. They ARE family, they care, and they're doing their best by us.

Exactly. But you're struggling because you really did go through a kind of hell, Ace. I understand...and you KNOW I understand.

Yeah, I know, baby. Frankly, I thought I was a dead man. Even if, somehow, they hadn't managed to auction me off to my enemies to be killed, I could tell something was wrong with what was left of that leg. Was it getting infected?

India told me it was, yeah, but only just starting. So you nailed that one. But she cleaned all that out really good once we got you back on the Genesis, *and then she and Zebra bumped you up to a stronger antipathogen in your IV, and that wiped it out. And that, well before we ever got you in a regen pod. It's fine, and it's gonna BE fine. But yeah, if that had been let go for too long, it might have taken you out, all right. I'm glad I found you and carried you out when I did.*

Me too. Echo took a deep breath, squared his shoulders, then waved at the cell phone in her hand. *Go ahead and call Zebra, and let's find out, then.*

Okay, honey.

Omega hit a speed-dial on her phone, then held it to her ear.

* * *

"Wait, wait, wait," a concerned Zebra said, as she listened to Omega's explanation. "Are YOU okay?"

"I'm fine," Omega averred. "We were playin' around, you know, pillow fights an' stuff, and I was giggling my head off, and I got too close to the edge of the bed and fell off. I was outta breath from giggling already, and hitting the floor knocked what was left outta me, is all. But it caught Echo off guard, and kinda worried him, so he jumped outta bed and ran around to see about me. And evidently wrenched the regen'ed leg in the process. I'm thinking the knee, but then that sorta torqued the tendons in what we've been calling 'the cleavage plane.' So I think we need to have you look at it. What do you think?"

"I agree," Zebra responded immediately. "We don't need any sprains or the like hosing up the PT at this point."

"Well, that's what I told him," Omega vouched. "Do you want us to come on down, or schedule an appointment, or...?"

"No, no, if he's sprained something, I want him to stay off it until I can assess it, and you turned in the antigrav chair already," Zebra ordered. "You two stay there, and I'll pop by Zar's office, tell him I'm on a semi-emergency house call to your quarters, and why, and be right up with my gear. You landed on your rump?"

"Yeah, kinda my left hip," Omega noted.

"Is it bruising?"

"Um...yeah," she said, sounding sheepish. "Already. I can see it in the mirror. I kinda landed hard, and I missed the area rug, to boot. I like the new hardwood floor in the bedroom, but owie."

"Okay. I'll bring a fresh bottle of Rejuvic, and you can drop your pants and I'll swab that down while I'm at it."

"That'll work."

"All right. I'll be up in about ten minutes."

"See you then."

* * *

"He did what? Oh damnation," Dr. Zarnix Chifejuz, chief of staff of the Medical department at Headquarters, exclaimed when Zebra, his second in command of the department, stuck her head into his office to inform him of events, and tell him she was stepping out to respond to the call. "Yes, by all means, go see about him. I can understand, from what you say, why he did what he did, but we do NOT need Echo creating more injuries in that leg."

"No shit," Zebra agreed. "Should we consider putting him in a knee brace until we get it strengthened a bit more?"

"That might be an idea," Zarnix considered. "In some respects, I hate to do it; the act of walking is the best way to strengthen and stabilize the leg FOR walking. But in a semi-somewhat-emergency situation, it would provide stability against injury, too." He bit his lip, thinking. "Let me ponder on it a while."

"Okay. And it also sounds like Meg bruised her hip but good when she fell outta the damn bed. I can bet what they were doing before they got into the pillow fight—if it WAS really a pillow fight, which I doubt—but I'm not gonna give 'em grief for having some high-spirited hijinks in their off hours, either, not after all those two have been through of late."

"And they are newlyweds, after all," Zarnix pointed out. "After nigh unto two years partnered together, it took them long enough to get on the same page about how they felt. But once they did, they pushed through with it."

"Yeah, and I think it's good for the pair of 'em," Zebra agreed. "I see a happiness in both of 'em that's really given them each an improved outlook. I think they're opening up to the rest of us a little more, too. Anyhow, I'm off. I can't say how long it'll take, but I don't have any appointments on my book, either. If something more important goes down, call me."

"Will do. Go," Zarnix said, waving her on.

She went.

* * *

When Zebra arrived, both members of Alpha One were

clad in lounge pants, t-shirts, and house shoes; Omega had thrown on a leisure bra as well, to provide a bit more coverage topside. Echo was sitting in the den in his recliner, the footrest up, an ice pack on the affected shin. Omega sat on the end of the couch nearby; two Diet Coke cans sat on coasters on the end table between them, condensation forming on them.

Mm. She must be looking after him and making sure he keeps his ass parked in the chair, with the leg up, Zebra decided. *And he's letting her. Good.*

"All right," she said, easing her kit off her shoulder and onto the substantial coffee table. "We had a little wupsie, I gather."

"Yeah," Echo said, looking and sounding a bit sheepish. "Meg and I were horsing around, you know, tickling each other, whacking each other with pillows, an' shit. And I guess she got too close to the edge of the bed just as I clobbered her with a pillow, and she lunged backward..."

"And over I went," Omega said, giggling despite herself. "Right onto my ass."

"But you said it knocked the wind out of you," Zebra said, puzzled.

"Yeah, but as hard as she was laughing, that wouldn't have been too hard," Echo said, the ghost of a grin appearing on his face. "But it caught me off guard, especially when she kinda just laid there and didn't move..."

"So you went into action," Zebra anticipated.

"Yeah. I didn't feel anything at the time," Echo began.

"Which is a good sign it wasn't too bad," Zebra decided.

"Um, okay, that's good," he interjected. "But, so she sat up and was okay, and I was twelve kinds of relieved...but then Meg's belly let out a howl, and I found out she hadn't eaten second lunch an' it was getting late, so I went into the kitchen to grab a tray I'd prepared earlier."

"'Cause he knows me, and how busy I get, and I forget to eat," Omega tag-teamed, "so he was ready with food when I came home."

"And I used my cane, and a little trundle-cart I picked up from Facilities this morning, for this kinda thing," Echo elaborated, "so I was doin' things right..."

"Yup," Omega averred, "he did. He's being careful."

"Well, that's all very good to hear," Zebra said, nodding in approval. "Not that you forgot to eat 'cause you were busy, Meg—though Fox, Zar, and I, all three, understand how THAT goes—but that Echo is looking out for you, and you're looking out for him...or I wouldn't be here."

"Right," Omega declared, reaching over and removing the ice pack from Echo's leg. "So anyway, when he came back in with the tray, he was limping kinda pronounced, and said it was twinging him, you know, in a little bit of pain. So we discussed it while we ate, and decided you ought to know, in case it needed looking at."

"Which it does," Zebra said, opening her medikit and extracting the medscanner. "And the elevation and the ice pack were good ideas, too. So stay put, and let's see here."

* * *

She slowly ran the scanner over Echo's right leg, from mid-thigh down to his toes, watching the readout intently, then repeated the motion even more slowly, before replicating it on his undamaged left leg. She drew her brows together and chewed on her lower lip for a long moment, occasionally toggling something on the scanner, and Echo and Omega watched her, then exchanged worried glances.

That doesn't look good, he told her through the nd't'lq.

Well, maybe it's okay, hon, Omega replied. *It could only be that she's trying to figure out if you really did do something, or not. Try to relax as much as you can, and wait until she says.*

* * *

Just then, Zebra looked up and saw their faces.

"No, no, no, you two calm down," she soothed. "It's not bad. In fact, I'm trying to decide if it's worth adjusting anything. Yes, Echo, there IS a small sprain in here, but it isn't serious. It does look like you twisted it, probably turning around the corner of the bed at speed or something. But the fact that it's no worse than it is...well, that's actually great news. It means your regrown tissues are strengthening right along, and handled the stress of the motion really well."

"Yay!" Omega exclaimed, punching a fist in the air. "I told ya, Ace!"

"Yeah, you did," Echo acknowledged. "It's only..." He broke off again and drew a deep breath, then confessed to Zebra, "see, I told Meg earlier, after everything that the Cortians did to me, I keep expecting the other shoe to drop."

"He thinks he won't get up to snuff, and won't be able to go back out in the field," Omega murmured. "Or, at least, part of his head thinks that. I'm not sure his WHOLE head thinks that, 'cause then he prob'ly wouldn't work QUITE as hard in the therapy. But he's bustin' ass in therapy, an' then some."

"Yup," Zebra agreed. "Echo, in case it makes you feel any better, I swear to you on all I hold holy, and that includes Fox and our relationship and marriage, that the medlab staff is NOT pulling punches with you. If we thought you couldn't do this, couldn't get back to where you were before, we'd tell you so, point-blank, and recommend to Fox that you be given a desk job. But we're all delighted with the progress you've made. You're going faster than we would have thought possible; neither Zar nor I thought you'd be getting around pretty much with only a cane BEFORE CHRISTMAS! Now, you're not quite ready physically to hit the streets with Meg yet, but damn, big guy, you're doing great! I expect—and I'd lay money that Meg has already told you this, given her own experience—that that 'other shoe dropping' feeling is your PTSD talking."

Omega nodded knowingly, and Echo's eyebrows shot up, as he threw his mate a startled glance.

"Aha," Zebra said with a grin. "Nailed that one, did I?"

"Yup," Omega confirmed. "We did discuss it, and I did tell him that very thing, and we're going to call Zz'r'p when you're finished with Echo, and see about discussing it with him. If not now, then at the next counseling session."

"I think that's an excellent plan," Zebra decreed. "As for my decision on this, what I'm going to do is to tell the therapist what happened, letting him know that it isn't a bad sprain at all, and in fact it's very encouraging that I actually had trouble finding it for a couple seconds, there."

"Wait. You did?" Echo said, straightening in his seat.

"I did," Zebra said, "scout's honor. Then I remembered, when she called, Meg had said it was near the 'cleavage plane'—not that it was exactly planar, but anyway—so I focused on that, and finally found it. It looks like you tweaked your tibialis anterior along with the proximal attachment, and I can tell for certain if you'll try one thing for me."

"What?"

"Pull your toe toward you. Flex it upward."

Echo did so, then grunted softly.

"Hurts?"

"Sort of, but not exactly HURTS," Echo decided. "Like, maybe you were pressing your thumb down on my shin, about..." he leaned forward and suited action to description, "about here." He applied light pressure on the bony part of his shin just below the scar. "Oh. Hey, that actually feels kinda good, doing that..." He started to rub the area lightly.

"Bingo," Zebra said. "And you say it feels good to apply light pressure?"

"Yeah, it does. It's subtle, but it's like the shin relaxes. And it...itches, sorta? Like, down in the tissue, not on the skin."

"Gotcha. That itching sensation is probably from lactic acid in the tissues, I'd think. Okay, then here's what we're going to do tonight," Zebra said. "Ice it, per the usual protocol..."

"Fifteen on, roughly every hour," Omega murmured.

"Right; talk to Zz'r'p about the PTSD and the other shoe dropping, too. He may not do the counseling tonight, but like you said, he needs to know to work that in there."

"Check," Omega said, and Echo nodded agreement.

"And Meg, you got the massage therapy certification, right? At some point I think I remember, you said you'd been working with Echo in the evenings, before bed?"

"Yes, ma'am," she averred, cheerful. "To alla that."

"Good. Then I want you to give Echo a massage tonight. You can make it as general as you want, but I want you to spend a good twenty to thirty minutes working ONLY on this leg, from the knee down, but principally all around the knee," Zebra ordered. "See if he's got any 'knotted' muscles in there, and loosen them. And particularly work around this area where he's got his thumb right now, and see if you can't make it feel better, especially with regard to this little sprain we have. Good blood and lymph flow is only gonna help the situation heal."

"Consider it done," Omega agreed.

"That does sound like it'd feel good," Echo decided.

"Good. I can swab it with some Rejuvic before I go, which should help, too, 'cause it soaks in a good bit," Zebra ticked off fingers, "at the same time I hit Meg's backside with it, to minimize bruising where she fell outta bed. And then I'll go back and tell your therapist Gangway all about it, and we'll discuss what we wanna change in PT when Echo comes in... when?" She glanced at Echo, querying.

"Hey, don't look at me," he said with a rueful grin. "Meg's the keeper of the calendar on all THAT."

"Tomorrow afternoon," Omega decreed, looking at her cell phone. "Right before second lunch."

"Okay, tomorrow afternoon," Zebra confirmed. "But to be honest, based on what I'm seeing? I'm going to recommend NOT that we adjust the PT to coddle that sprain, but to strengthen the leg even further, especially across the knee joint. It wants a bit more work in the rotational stabilization, I expect. I think this says you're ready for it. I'll be surprised if you're feeling this much at all tomorrow, by the time Meg and I are done with you."

"You think?" Echo wondered.

"I DO think, yes," Zebra contended. "Now, one thing we do need to know: it's getting close to Christmas. Are you two staying here, or are you going to the Ranch, like you'd talked about? 'Cause we'll need to work any treatment around that. Right now, I'm thinking you'll be done with daily therapy by then, and only have to come in once or twice a week, while doing the exercises on your own. And if you're at the Ranch, we can send down the protocols, and Dihl can handle any last things."

"That's good," Omega averred.

"Yeah, it is. We're planning on going to the Ranch," Echo said. "Ma—uh, Dihl—is already there now, and Joe and the hands are twelve kinds of enthused about us coming down for a family holiday. By now, they've all figured out who Ma and I are, relative to each other AND the Ranch, but they're keepin' it on the down-low, so nobody BUT them know. I gather that a few mods have been made to the bedroom wing in the main house—the jack and jill bedroom/bath suite, on the opposite side of the hall from the room I had as a kid, has been converted to a really nice single bedroom/sitting room/bath suite, and Ma plans to move into that...if she hasn't already."

"Really? But I thought she was staying in the master suite," Zebra wondered.

"She was," Echo said, "but I think the memories maybe became a bit too much for her. She was missing Dad, and it was affecting her more than she wanted. So she's reserving the master suite for Alpha One—me an' Meg—'cause she says we're the rightful master and mistress of the place, now."

"So we'll be in the master suite when we go down," Omega added. "I'm not sure how Echo feels about that, given he always stayed in 'his' room when he was there. But I think it..." She drew a deep breath. "I'm not sayin' this outta my own self, not my own ego, understand...but I think that it's RIGHT for him to have that, now. And I'd say that even if he was married to somebody else than me, though it would hurt. Do y'all understand?"

Zebra and Echo both nodded.

"But what are you gonna do about your annual Christmas party, Meg?" Zebra wondered then. "You usually hold that... what...the evening before Christmas Eve? It was a huge bash last year; I was sorry to have to miss it."

"Yeah," Omega admitted, "but things are different this year. I'm married to my terrific partner, and I have a new family, even if none of y'all are genetically related to me. I've...I've given it a lotta thought, and I've discussed it with Zz'r'p, and when I was ready, I brought the idea up to Echo, and he liked it. Um..." She shot a glance at Echo, who nodded and waved her on.

"Go ahead and tell her, baby," he said. "Lay out our holiday plans, 'cause the others need to know, to make it work. But be aware they may have other plans already."

"I know, and if they do, that's okay; I think I can deal, now," Omega told him. "Okay, Zebra, here's what we want to do. I've already cleared it with Dihl and with Joe at the Ranch, and they're good, too. Echo an' I are gonna go down the weekend before Christmas, but we want the family on Earth— you, Fox, Alpha Two, 'Uncle' Zarnix, and 'Uncle' Zz'r'p, though we're gonna try to get Pulgey and Suud here, too, if they can—to come down the day before Christmas Eve, and we'll have a family 'party' that night. A big Christmas dinner, gift exchange, the works. Joe will put up anybody who needs to stay over in the guest house—I'm hoping you all can, and we can do something together on Christmas Eve, too. Then you can all go wherever you want to go for Christmas and, um, and Hanukkah, without any interference. Me an' Echo an' Dihl will give our gifts to each other on Christmas morning. After Christmas, we'll come back home to Headquarters for a few days, then go to the beach house in Ipswich for New Year's Eve. We debated about staying in New York for the ball drop, but..."

"I think we all had enough of the ball drop last year," Echo said, voice as dry as the Sahara.

"That," Omega said with a wry laugh. "Especially you with a bullet hole in your gut. Damn, honey, you scared me witless on that one."

"Yeah. Sorry."

"No prob." She leaned over and kissed his cheek, and he flushed a bit. "So, but anyway, depending on the weather, we're going to the beach house, and stock up on some bottle rockets an' firecrackers an' Roman candles an' shit, fireworks, you know. Then on New Year's Eve, we'd have our own countdown, lower the force field over the beach, and shoot off fireworks."

"And since we got the modifications in to the house up there, so that we have spare bedrooms now, we wanted to invite you and Fox, and Romeo and India, and Dihl of course, to come up and join us," Echo added. "Just you five; that's really all we have room for, up there, even with the new addition. We're planning a bonfire on the beach, too, with a cookout. Nothing fancy, just burgers and kosher hot dogs. That's all provided we don't get a nor'easter instead, in which case, we might stay in New York after all. If all it does is regular thunderstorms, we can NOT do the fireworks, and keep the field up, lock it out, and still do the bonfire."

"OR, there's a big fireplace in the den, AND a fire pit directly under the house, which is on stilts over an antigrav platform buried in the bluff, so it's sheltered," Omega added. "If nothing else, marshmallow roasts are fun either place, and I speak from experience on both."

"Hmm," Zebra said, intrigued. "That sounds like it could be a lotta fun. I'll let Fox know, and we'll try to plan to be there—both 'theres,'" she amended.

"That sounds great!" Omega said, beaming.

"We'll let the others know, but if you could tell Fox and Zarnix...?" Echo wondered.

"Consider it done," Zebra said. "Now, let's see about hitting your leg, Echo, and Meg's tuchus, with some Rejuvic, then I'll clear out and let you two relax. But be sure to do the ice and the massage," she reminded.

"No problem," Omega said.

"Okay, Meg honey, help Echo hike up his pants leg, so I can get to that shin," Zebra said, fishing out a small bottle of purple liquid and a packet of large sterile swabs, "then get ready to drop your drawers."

"Okeydoke," a cheerful Omega noted, suiting action to order.

* * *

Moments later, Echo was settled, and Omega was easing the waistband of her flannel lounge pants back into place, as Zebra replaced the bottle of Rejuvic in her kit.

"Better?" she asked.

"Already, yeah," Echo asserted. "I think, by the time Meg gets done workin' it later tonight, it's gonna be good to go."

"I think that too, which is why I'm not too worried," Zebra confirmed. "That said, try not to make any sudden motions on that leg for a few more days, until we can get it good and well, and the therapist can ease you into the work to be ABLE to make those kinds of moves. In fact, Zar and I are discussing whether or not to provide you with a brace, for the times when you think you might NEED to make those kinds of moves, until you're able to stabilize the joint on your own. And I think we'll all be happily surprised and pleased at the progress you're going to make, from here on out. So I'm outta here, for now. Call me if you need me."

"Thanks hon," Omega said, standing and hugging the

other woman. Zebra leaned down to offer Echo a slight hug; he returned it in kind, and she was off.

* * *

"That," Echo decided after Zebra was gone, "was not bad at all."

"No, it wasn't," Omega said. "In fact, I'd say it sounded awfully good."

"I...think I'd agree," Echo concluded. "Which means I really need to get my head on straight about all this."

"Well, it's not surprising, hon."

"No. But still."

"Okay. Feel like a brief convo with Zz'r'p about that?" Omega wondered. "We don't have to make it a counseling session if you don't feel up to it right now. It might not be a good time for him, anyway. But he needs to know about this, for when we DO have another session."

"Well...let's call him and see, I guess," he considered.

"All over it," Omega said, pulling out her cell phone once more.

* * *

A Ford Fusion Energi disappeared next.

But this time, it disappeared from the late-night streets, complete with its driver, who was coming home from her night shift at the Lenox Hill Hospital, along the 79th Street Traverse through Central Park.

Its remains were found the next afternoon, in the same sheltered area of Central Park where the other wrecked cars had been found. Once more, the battery pack had been ripped from the car and torn open, the electrodes stolen, the electrolyte drained.

There was no sign of the driver.

* * *

Thirty minutes after Omega called him, the Deltiri Ambassador from Arcturus VII sat with Alpha One in their den, having made a 'house call' so that Echo could keep his leg elevated. The fact that Omega had informed him she had fresh-baked shortbread from earlier that morning might have influenced the Deltiri's decision, too; at the Thanksgiving 'family' dinner, he had discovered he loved the stuff, so she had a platter ready on the coffee table upon his arrival.

"...No, I can understand why you would feel like that, Echo," Zz'r'p noted after the pair had explained, leaning forward and taking a piece of shortbread from the platter on the coffee table; Omega was already eating one, but Echo uncharacteristically declined, apparently too intent on the coming discussion to be hungry, even for Omega's shortbread, which he loved as much as Zz'r'p did. "You thought you were going to die, that your life, at the very least as you had known it, was over, one way or another. Let alone the agony of being essentially butchered."

"That," Echo agreed in a low tone. Omega quickly brushed crumbs from her fingers, then took his hand and held it, squeezing gently. He turned his hand over and grasped hers tightly. "Lotta that."

"Can you accept the idea that you actually might be able to get back to your life as you have known and loved it?" Zz'r'p asked. "The full life with Omega which you have dreamed of?"

"I...I want to," Echo admitted. "It's just..." He broke off and bowed his head, staring at his lap.

"Just what?" Zz'r'p pressed. "If you need me to facilitate a mental conversation to tell me, I shall."

* * *

Echo was silent, still squeezing Omega's hand tightly in his, but he shook his head. She reached over and wrapped her other hand around the back of his, holding his hand firmly in both of hers.

"Go on, honey," she murmured. "It's okay. It's just me an' our 'Uncle' Zz'r'p. You know we both love ya to pieces. Neither of us is ever gonna think bad of you about ANYthing."

"Omega is quite correct," Zz'r'p agreed.

Echo nodded, swallowed once, then tried again.

"It's a couple of things, really," he acknowledged finally. "Some of which are just stupid, others maybe not so much, I guess."

"Let us hear them all, then," Zz'r'p offered, "and Omega and I shall endeavor to help you sort through it as best we are able."

"Well," Echo began with a sigh, "I know the medics are all telling me it's going to go well. And Zebra just swore to me they weren't pulling my good leg, not an hour ago. But..." He broke off and sighed again.

"You're afraid to believe her, after all," Omega realized.

* * *

"Part of me is, yeah," he conceded. "Despite my best efforts. Like I told you earlier, baby, it's that 'other shoe dropping' thing. Like, 'Are they just telling me this to keep me going, or do they truly mean it?'"

"And the other reasons?" Zz'r'p asked.

"Just one other one, actually," Echo revealed. "And it's the stupid one. Stupid-ER, I guess. One's stupid, the other's stupider." He shook his head. "And I know it. I can't quite control 'em, but I know it."

"Out with it, hon," Omega murmured, pressing his hand between both of hers. "Neither Zz'r'p or I care if it seems silly to you or not, if it's bothering you."

"Well said, Omega," Zz'r'p agreed.

"It's...to do with Meg," Echo confessed. "I keep wondering... okay," he broke off, then tried again. "Meg and I are married now, and I'm over the moon happy about that. It's like I've found a part of me that I didn't even know was missing, being with her like this, being her husband. But there's this crazy place in my brain that tells me that I can't have everything, and if I have her, I'll have to give up something else. Like the job that I love doing."

"So you believe you have to choose?" Zz'r'p continued his query.

"Not...really," Echo decided, biting his lip in consideration, "but evidently there's a part of my brain that does. Or, well, that's afraid I'll have to, maybe."

"And which would you choose, if you had to?" Zz'r'p asked.

"Meg, of course," Echo declared without hesitation. "I guess I'd just really like to be able to have my cake and eat it, too, as the saying goes."

* * *

"Aw!" Omega murmured, touched, then paused as a thought struck. "I wonder..."

"Wonder what, baby?"

"Well, you DID have to re-incorporate your nd't'lq download, like, RIGHT before we got married," she pointed out. "And the two versions of you sorta fought it out, there, for a while..."

"You think the 'partial me' that was left after being 'mostly dead' is the source of all this self-doubt?" Echo asked.

"I dunno," she said, shrugging. "I'm not the expert in this. But it was an idea I just had."

* * *

"Yes, and well thought, nn'chn. I currently deem it unlikely, but it is an idea that may be worth following up in a later session," Zz'r'p agreed. "But not just now, though I think it should be pursued; I should be able to tell fairly readily in a brief telepathic examination...only later, when he is less... agitated, and I will obtain a swifter and surer result. For now, let us stay on the track of Echo's uncertainties, the statements of his inner dialogue, before we go off looking for the source of that dialogue. So. Is there anything in your personal belief system, in your religion, your faith, to make you think this, Echo?" Zz'r'p wondered. "To make you think that you canNOT have both Omega as wife, and Alpha Line as occupation?"

"...No," Echo said, after thinking hard for long moments, to be sure. "I suppose I'd have to go do some specific Bible searches, or maybe go talk to Father Papa, but I think it's kind of the opposite, really."

"Yup," Omega averred. "It pretty much is, from what I know. I mean, it's not like you can wave your hand or just pray hard and suddenly be rich or nothin', but..."

"Your holy writings indicate that those who obey the Maker will be blessed with abundance, do they not?" Zz'r'p suggested.

"That's it," Omega confirmed. She patted Echo's hand. "Right, Ace?"

"Yeah, baby," he agreed. "And I'm trying to remember alla that. Only it's...hard, sometimes."

"So tell me—is there anything about your position in Alpha Line that you find to be in violation of the Maker's commands, as you understand them?"

"...No," Echo said again, after another pause to think. "In

fact, I've always kinda thought that maybe this job was a way of carrying out those commands, of helping to keep the peace, not just on Earth, but in the galaxy as a whole."

"I've looked at it the same way," Omega offered.

"Good. All right. Let us come back to this one in a bit," Zz'r'p suggested, "while I formulate a means to exercise your faith on the matter."

"Okay."

* * *

"So...tell me, Echo," Zz'r'p queried, "why would Zebra—or any of the medics, for that matter—lie to you about your prognosis? Benevolent though the intent of those lies might be?"

"Damn, Zz'r'p! Hold onto your hat on this one; it's gonna take a while. All right. A—I've already got enough head screw-ups for any twelve people over all this," Echo ticked off a finger, "and they don't wanna get me wrapped even further around the axle about it. B—they think that, if I don't have the goal of getting back into Alpha Line field work, I won't work as hard at the physical therapy. C—they think that somehow, they're sparing my feelings. D—they want to wait until I'm stronger to tell me the bad news." He paused. "I think that covers the main points. There's some kinda secondary stuff that spins off o' those, but that's the gist."

"Very well, let us take these one at a time. Let us look at your proposed rationale A: If you are already in counseling—which you are—and making progress—which you are," Zz'r'p pointed out, "then that is the BEST POSSIBLE time to give you bad news, so that I may help you deal with it as part of your treatment." He paused, allowing Echo to take in that information and process it; when the Agent finally nodded, he continued. "As for rationale B: I think we all know you better than to think you need specific motivation in order to achieve a goal, or even simply to stay in the best possible shape, so that would be somewhat pointless. Would it not?"

Zz'r'p paused again, while Echo considered the statement.

"Mm, well, yeah, I guess so," he finally agreed. "I might not work QUITE as hard, but I'm still gonna bust my ass to get in the best shape I can be, like you said, and that wouldn't be very far off the ass-busting I'm doin' now to get back in the field, 'cause I'm pretty demanding of myself. And yeah, I've known Zebra an' Zarnix for years, now. And while I gathered that Whiskey—who I haven't known as long—handled the initial procedures once y'all got me home, so they could afford to be 'family' during the worst of it, now they're the ones spearheading it at this point, so...all right. I'll buy that one."

"Very good. On to rationale C, then. How is it sparing your feelings to refuse to tell you something you already suspect, or are afraid of?" Zz'r'p pointed out. "It only adds to your suspense, tension, and general anxiety. And all of that will only tend to slow your recovery. Plus, they are surely smart enough to know that, if they do not tell you the truth of the matter now, and it turns out as you fear, you will never trust them again with anything important. Why would they risk losing your trust over something they know to be the case? Something they know you already suspicion, and which deeply concerns you?"

"Mmph," Echo grunted then. "Hadn't thought about it quite like that."

"Then start, honey," Omega murmured. "They're not gonna lie to you. We're FAMILY. They just won't."

"Yeah. Yeah, you're right."

"All right. On to rationale D," Zz'r'p said. "Please explain something to me."

"Um, if I can, okay."

"How are you weak right now?"

"Huh?"

"Why do you currently consider yourself weak? Why would anyone consider you weak right now?"

"I got a regrown hand, leg, and eye, I'm on a cane, I got a damn limp, I'm in physical therapy an' mental counseling," Echo elaborated with some significant amount of self-disgust in both his tone and his expression. "How is any of that strong?"

"You're ALIVE!" Omega burst out. "You're alive, and you're coping, and you're using every tool available to you TO cope, and you're fighting to get yourself back to normal. That's not weak, honey! Nothing about that is weak. That's STRONG. You survived a truly horrible experience, an experience intended to strip away your personal autonomy, force your knowledge out of you, and then kill you, and you're RECOVERING FROM IT! They may have damaged your body, but they didn't break your spirit, and you're pulling things back together amazingly. That is so strong I'm downright awed by you at times, sweetheart. And so proud of you, I could bust."

"Listen to your wife, Echo," Zz'r'p noted, as Echo stared at her in shocked surprise. "She is right in every particular on this. And she should know; I have said much the same to her, and she is slowly incorporating that self-knowledge into her own being, as well. In fact, it pleases me that she has learned it so well that she can now pass it on to you." He nodded. "You are both survivors, both strong of will, strong of intellect, strong of body and mind. Determined. Fierce when needed, gentle when it is called for. None of these things are weak. You are NOT weak, Echo, and in all the ways that truly count, you are as strong as ever. Therefore, holding back bad news is not necessary."

* * *

Echo was silent for long minutes, considering the points that the Deltiri counselor had presented, and mulling matters.

"That...all makes a lot of sense," he finally decided. "Okay, I...I'll try to remember all of that."

"And you have a beloved being beside you who can help remind you, when you need it, and if you will admit it to her," Zz'r'p pointed out.

"Yeah, I do," Echo said, casting a warm glance at Omega, "and yeah, I'll try. I gotta admit, the nd't'lq really helps with stuff like that. 'Cause, bein' a typical guy, I can't always force it outta my mouth, no matter how much I may WANT to."

"It does," Zz'r'p acknowledged, "and is only one of many reasons I agreed to help you both establish it. Now, as to the 'trade-off' worry, I believe you would put it...the notion that you must choose between the mate you love and the job you love..."

"Yeah?"

"Omega, would it be too much upon you to sit down and determine as many of those sacred-writings passages as possible? The ones that talk about blessings and the like?" Zz'r'p asked. "I can always approach Father Papa on your behalf; I know that you have a great deal on your shoulders at the moment, taking care of your quarters, cooking and cleaning, helping Echo care for himself, ensuring he gets to all his appointments, seeing to the department, managing your own emotional issues..."

"I could do it," Omega noted, after a moment to think it over, "and I wouldn't mind, but I honestly think Father Papa could do it way quicker and easier. I mean," she explained, "I could tell you the wavelength peak range of a given spectral class of star, almost right off the top of my head; that's just my specialty, you know? It's what I was trained in. But Papa, he can cite chapter and verse off the top of HIS head, because that's sorta HIS specialty."

"Ah. I see. Consider it done, then," Zz'r'p agreed. "I think it would be good for you both, you see; you both have a strong belief system in common, and I want to work within it to remind you of what you believe, and why, in order to help counter the negative inner dialogue."

"Okay, I get it," Echo said. "So when Father Papa gins it all up and sends it to us—what? We need to sit down each day and read through 'em?"

"That would be my preference," Zz'r'p said, "but let us see how long a list of sacred writings Papa comes up with, first. It may be that it is something you can take step-wise; say, one verse or one passage per day, and the two of you focus on it for ten or fifteen minutes or so, discussing it, breaking it down, ascertaining the full meaning of it. Were you on full, active duty, I would not suggest so comprehensive a program, but since you are not, a daily activity should fit within your schedule."

"I see," Omega said, nodding. "Like a devotional, or a short Bible study."

"Exactly," Zz'r'p confirmed. "Can you both do this?"

"Yup, I think that sounds good," Echo agreed. "And I could use the positive outlook about now, and I'm sure Meg could, too."

"Alla that," Omega vouched.

"Good. Then I think I have given you more than enough to think about for the time," Zz'r'p said, standing. "I will see you at the usual time tomorrow afternoon, after first lunch?"

"You betcha," Echo said, reaching for his cane with one hand, and the footrest lever with the other, intending to stand, in order to see the ambassador to the door.

"Park your adorable butt back in that chair, mister," Omega declared. "You just sprained that knee, remember?"

"Oh...yeah," Echo recalled, easing himself back into the seat. "Sorry, Zz'r'p."

"Not to worry, my friend," the Deltiri said with a smile. "Omega will see me out, but I do not need to be seen out. I am, after all, 'family,' as you both like to say...and as I like to be considered."

"Still," Omega said, "thank you."

"That," Echo agreed.

"You are both very welcome, children. Thank YOU for the shortbread; it was as delicious as always."

* * *

After no one had seen him in fully twenty-four hours, a missing-persons report was filed on one John Paul Davies; he had been seen the night before, entering his apartment in Midtown Manhattan near Columbus Circle, but had not reported to work in his accountant employer's office the next morning. Upon obtaining a warrant, police investigators found nothing untoward in his apartment, though a suit was laid out, ready to don, and at least one pair of shoes was missing.

It was known that he liked to jog in Central Park before going to work, and he was therefore presumed to have been accosted by a mugger while in the park.

An all-points bulletin was issued for his whereabouts.

Chapter 4

That night, Omega made certain that Echo had a nice long, hot soak in their hot tub, ensuring the jets massaged the area of his right knee. The fact that she joined him, with glasses of Emdalian wine for both, helped assure he stayed put.

The massage table stayed half-set-up in the bedroom opposite the Christmas tree, and it had been the matter of moments for Omega to finish the setup before slipping into the hot tub. So she left the hot tub first, drying herself and throwing on a robe, then helping Echo ease out without slipping, towel himself dry, and head into the bedroom. He promptly climbed onto the massage table; Omega draped him with a sheet and started work.

"Mmh," he sighed after only a couple of minutes. "You are so damn good at this, baby."

"Thanks, honey," she murmured as she worked. "You know I like that you like it, right? See, I figured it was high time somebody paid you back for caring for the people around you."

"Aw."

"Tell me, for real, how many times has anybody ever done this for you?"

"Um. Well, there's a massage therapist on staff with the medlab, an' another in the fitness center..."

"So professionally, but not just because?"

"C'mon, baby. Stop an' think. Who would I have got to do it? Me, X-ray, an' Romeo are all straight, an' straight guys, you know, hell, we barely hug each other..."

"Ohhhh," Omega said in sudden understanding as she worked. "'Cause it might get misunderstood?"

"Um, yeah," Echo admitted. "And I already had issues with that once, to deal with. I mean...you've met Agent Queen, right? He's over in the Los Angeles Office now..."

"Yeah?"

"He had a thing for me, for a while, there. I told him I didn't go that way, but he didn't believe me at first. X-ray actually offered, once when I managed to sprain my shoulder—not that he was that highly trained, but he had good instincts, my arm was in a sling, and it was hurtin', and he wanted to help—"

"Oh, I get it," Omega interrupted. "I bet he offered in front of some people, and you had to turn it down, 'cause of how it woulda looked to Queen?"

"Yeah," Echo said, and Omega could hear the sheepish grin in his voice. "An' call X-ray 'Pop' while I was about it. I thought X-ray would take my head off for that! But Queen happened to be RIGHT THERE, watching. So I got X-ray aside and explained, and he caught on. After that, he kinda helped me out with that sitch."

"Oh, that's good."

"Yeah. Queen was kinda blatant with his initial come-ons, too. Not real bad, not like the come-ons I got at the theatre, back in the fall! Let alone the idiot that tried to pat my ass!" He laughed at the recollection. "But for around here? Yeah, kinda blatant. Once I finally got him convinced that I really was straight—an' I never did figure out where he got the idea I wasn't, unless somebody told him so, for a practical joke—he accepted that I wasn't interested, and he an' I got to be good friends. We've helped each other out in tight situations more 'n once."

"But after that, I bet you were more careful, 'cause you DIDN'T know why he thought that," Omega noted.

"Right. It wasn't that I was offended; I was kinda flattered. I just don't go that way, and he flatly didn't believe me at first."

"How old were you when that happened?"

"Huh. 'Bout ten years back, I think; mid-twenties? Maybe early twenties. Still a bit wet behind the ears in some ways, I suppose..."

"So you were careful on account of you had guy partners, an' none of your girlfriends ever offered?"

"Oh, I got shoulder rubs occasionally from Ree," Echo noted, "but that was usually with my shirt on. Actually, it was usually when she wanted to subtly mark her territory in front of another female she thought might be interested in me," he chuckled. "So it was less about comfort and more about a display."

"Oh."

"You're the first person who's ever worked on me like this who's actually had a real interest in ME, personally...you know, in making me comfortable as well as healing my 'boo-boos,' as you call 'em." He paused, then added, "And I appreciate it. And you."

"Aw. Well, look, I need to shut up asking you questions, and you need to just lie here an' relax," Omega told him then. "I DO want you to feel better, and to be comfortable and relaxed, 'cause when I work the knee, it might twinge a bit, an' it'll prob'ly hurt some, even if it doesn't twinge; I expect it's tender after gettin' sprained. But it'll do it less if you're relaxed."

"I know, an' you're right; I'm talkin' too much. You accidentally got me started reminiscing," he chuckled. "I'll be hushed now."

"Good. Just unwind and enjoy it."

"Oh, I am."

* * *

He did; by the time Omega coaxed him to roll onto his back, he was half-asleep.

"Mmph," he grunted, as he settled back into a nigh-gelatinous state while she draped him. "Knee now?"

"Mm-hm. Just relax, sweetheart. I hope this won't hurt at all, but let me know if it does, and I'll ease up." She slid her freshly-oiled hands over the scar below his right knee and began to massage gently.

"Ohhh," he sighed.

"Doesn't hurt?"

"Nah. Feels...good. Itches, kinda. Bu' in...a good way..." He paused, then added, "An' you're scratchin' it, like 'at..."

"You almost asleep?"

"Uh-huh. 'S good. Real good."

"Go on to sleep then, sweetheart. I'll wake you when I'm done, and help you get into bed."

"Okay."

Omega kept massaging his knee area, gradually moving outward until his entire leg had been worked, and the skin around the knee was slightly flushed. Then she slid her hands up the length of the leg, covered it with the sheet, and moved to the other leg.

By that time, Echo was sound asleep.

He stayed that way until she was finished. She covered him lightly, then turned down the bedclothes. Returning to the massage table, she used the massage drape to lightly blot off any excess oil, gently woke him, then supported him while he sat up, slid off the table, and meandered over to the bed.

"Here we go," she told him. "Go ahead and sit down, then lean back and I'll tuck you in."

"Mm-kay."

Echo sat, turned and eased his legs under the sheet she held for him, then all but toppled back into the pillow, sound asleep again almost immediately. She grinned, stifling an affectionate giggle with an effort, then spread the covers over him.

Returning to the table, she stripped it and put the linens down the laundry chute, then pulled fresh sheets from the nearby dresser drawer, put them on the table, and folded it partway, shoving it into the corner.

Then she doffed her bathrobe, hanging it on the back of the bathroom door, and climbed into bed herself.

* * *

Two days after John Paul Davies went missing, a partial body was found in heavy foliage near The Pond, in the south corner of the Park. It had been incompletely consumed by scavengers, but one leg and foot remained.

The foot was clad in a bright-red, custom-made running shoe.

Partly melted.

* * *

The next day, Echo had his regular physical therapy session in the morning.

"Oh hey, have you talked to Zebra yet?" Echo asked, as Gangway set up for the first exercise.

"Yeah, I have," Gangway responded. "Thanks for reminding me. How is the sprained knee today? Still bothering you?"

"Nah," Echo said, shaking his head. "It's good. Zebra hit it with some Rejuvic, and Meg iced it once an hour for the rest of the day yesterday, only stopping about dinnertime. Then, before bed, we got in the hot tub for a nice long soak, and I managed to get a jet on it...sorta-kinda, 'cause the problem is on the front of the leg, so there wasn't a really good angle..."

"Yeah, I understand ya."

"So I had a nice good soak, then Meg gave me my usual massage, and worked the whole knee, concentrating on the specific place where I could feel that little pain from the sprain."

"Ah, good. How did that feel?"

"It felt really good. It sorta felt like scratching an itch," Echo tried to explain, "except the itch wasn't on the skin, it was down deep in the tissue."

"Oh, okay. Yeah, I know what you're talking about. That's a little unusual tactile response, but I've had a couple other patients describe it that way. I expect it's a lactic acid reaction."

"That's what Zebra said, too. So anyway, by the time Meg finished, even that had gone away, and it felt really good and warm. I went to bed, zonked pretty much immediately, and it feels fine today."

"That...is excellent," Gangway decided. "Really, really good."

"So what's the plan with it, going forward?" Echo wondered. "Zebra said something about a knee brace..."

"Yeah, she and Zarnix mentioned it to me this morning, when we had our daily status and planning meeting for you," Gangway said, "but I talked 'em out of it. I think I can build up the strength in the tissues pretty fast, especially given how diligent you are with your exercises and supplements. And I'd rather do that than risk your knee becoming dependent on an external support. At this stage, I'm afraid if we do that, you might never recover the full strength again."

"Then no, we don't do that," Echo decreed, firm.

"Good man. All right, let's get started."

"Wait," Echo said. "Y'all have a staff meeting...to discuss your patients?"

"Not usually, but we do for you."

"Just for me?!"

"Aw hell, Echo, stop and think," Gangway said, mildly exasperated. "You're the head of Alpha Line, you're the Assistant Director, you're the Director Successor. And you had some really bad shit done to ya, pal. If it were Fox in your shoes, you wouldn't think twice about us holding daily status update and planning meetings on him, would ya?"

"Well, no..."

"Then why should it surprise you that we put the same importance on your healing? Never mind that the chief of staff and the assistant chief of staff consider you a really close buddy, like family. We're doing everything we can to give you the best treatment possible, to ensure the outcome we ALL want for ya. And," Gangway added, "we're getting it, too. Dude, you are doing fan-freakin'-tastic."

"I...whoa," Echo murmured, surprised. "That's...I never thought about it like that."

"Well, start," Gangway said with a grin. Then he pointed at the weight machine. "Now, let's get with it, here."

* * *

After first lunch, Echo and Omega headed to Zz'r'p's office in the Deltiri embassy. It was his regularly-scheduled session, but it would be twice as long as usual, to allow for some additional matters to be discussed. This had been arranged the previous night, in order to follow up on Echo's unusually strong emotional response to the slight sprain.

"There you are," Zz'r'p said with the Deltiri equivalent of a smile. "Come, both of you, and sit down." He led them to the little conversation corner, saw them seated, then doubled back to his desk, fetching a small booklet. "Here. This is the result of my discussing the situation, and Echo's mindset and concerns, with Father Papa last night, after I left your quarters. He delivered it personally this morning." He handed them the booklet.

"Oh," Omega said, thumbing through the booklet, as Echo looked over her shoulder. "These are the scripture passages we talked about?"

"All he could find," Zz'r'p confirmed. "Then he saw to it that they were printed and placed in covers, so that it could handle much use. He told me there is enough there for you to read and meditate on for some time—roughly a year, he estimates—without ever needing to read the same passage twice."

94

"This'll be good," Echo decided. "Meg, I'm thinkin' do it over breakfast each morning?"

"Works for me, Ace," Omega agreed. "We can take turns reading 'em out loud, then discussing 'em."

"Sounds like a plan. We might have to modify it a little bit over the holidays, but I like the idea a lot, an' we'll figure it out. Thanks, Zz'r'p, and, um, please pass on our thanks to Father Papa, if you would?"

"Very good, and I will be happy to do so. Now to begin today's session, I want to check Omega's idea regarding the different versions of you that developed in the aftermath of the space plane incident," the Deltiri ambassador noted.

"Kinda figured that was gonna happen at some point," Echo said with a nod. "I'm game. But if that IS what's going on, what the hell do we do about it?"

"Leave that to me," Zz'r'p told him. "Omega, take his hand; due to the nd't'lq bond, you will be a part of this, too, so we might as well take advantage of your perceptions in addition to mine. If you notice anything unusual for Echo, let me know."

"Okay," Omega said, reaching out and taking Echo's hand. He smiled at his mate, and laced his fingers with hers.

"Very good. Now, both of you, lean your heads back, get comfortable, and relax, while I check your hypothesis, Omega."

The trio were silent for long moments, mentally and audibly, as the alien telepath searched Echo's mind, looking for the source of his anxiety. Omega mentally 'watched,' and Echo simply remained passive, letting his trusted counselor work.

Nearly fifteen minutes later, Zz'r'p came up for air. He pondered in silence for several moments, while Omega and Echo watched him. Finally he spoke.

"Anything?" he asked Omega.

"Nothing in particular," she admitted. "Nothing unusual, at least. What about you?"

"Well, it seems that Omega was most likely right," he declared, then raised a quelling hand, as a perturbed Echo started to speak. "However, I think there is little to worry about. The 'fragment' is incorporating into your psyche nicely, and in as far as it could communicate with me, said that your tactic of watching your 'family' at Thanksgiving put it much more at ease, as well. It has learned a good bit from your memories, and is now—and finally—content to fully disappear back into your mind. Do not be surprised, however, if the anxiety persists for a while yet. It is instinctive for the 'fragment,' though it indicated it is trying hard."

"Well, that's all good, I guess," Omega decided. "At least we have some idea of where that's all coming from, now. But it doesn't sound like it's going to cause Echo any more trouble than that."

"No, no, I think there is nothing at all to worry about," Zz'r'p soothed, when Echo said nothing, merely looked thoughtful. "More than likely, what we need to do is to get Echo's mind occupied with something that will make him feel useful and keep him properly busy, something that is not what he calls 'make-work,' and then his emotions will settle a bit."

"That...sounds like a plan," Echo admitted. "So far, all I'm really bein' allowed to do is the interminable paperwork that comes with running a department."

"Hmm," Omega murmured. "I'll put my head together with Romeo an' India later, and see what we can do about that. Maybe we can come up with a case that needs working, but doesn't need a lotta field work, just looking at the clues somebody else already obtained, or something like that. A cold case or something."

"This will work," Zz'r'p noted.

"Yeah," Echo agreed. "I like the sound of that."

* * *

"Yeah. I dunno offhand, Meg, but I'm bettin' we c'n prob'ly dig up somethin' that'll work pretty good," Romeo said, when Omega approached him about something substantive to keep Echo's mind occupied. "There's a few cases runnin' around, sure, but I dunno if they're anything that'll interest Echo." He shrugged. "If not, we can dig inta th' cold case files, like ya said."

"Have you got a list of the cases?" Omega asked. "You and I can go down 'em and evaluate 'em to see if it's too physical for him to do yet, or if it's more of an intellectual puzzle, or something like that."

"That'll work," Romeo agreed. "Let's go get on 'is desk

computer an' I'll pull up what we got."

"Sounds like a plan," Omega decided.

* * *

In the end, they chose a missing-persons report. It seemed that a vacationing Yelfflani named Julian W. Thompson had been exploring Central Park a few days earlier, and had left the path to sit along the Loch—not a lake, but a stream that ran through the northwest quadrant of the Park—to sit on one of the rocks and watch the water flow past...and had never returned.

"Well, this is gonna be an interesting one," Echo decided, studying the case history while looking over what few clues had been found. "One Yelfflan version of a cell phone, torn to pieces, but apparently with no missing parts; one faux animal-skin shoe that looks like it got too close to a fire; a platinum neck chain..."

"And that's significant, 'cause if it was an Earth mugger, that woulda been stolen," Omega noted.

"Point. So would the cell phone. But have you seen the photos of the site where the items were found?" Echo wondered.

"No; why?"

"Look at this mess."

Echo tossed down several still color photographs. They showed several rocks along the stream, stained and blotched with fluids, though not with anything that immediately resembled blood—human OR Yelfflan. The various items belonging to the missing being lay scattered around the stained stones, with the remains of the cell phone lying two or three stones away.

"That's...odd," Omega said, staring intently at the images, trying to understand, based on the clues, what might have happened there.

"Yeah, it is," Echo agreed. "Do you suppose the medlab would let us go look at the site and check it out? I'd like to see it in person, maybe take some samples for Forensics to analyze, something like that."

"I dunno, but we can ask," Omega said.

* * *

"Absolutely not," Zebra decreed, and Zarnix nodded his firm concurrence. "That is way too rugged an area for you to try to access while still on a cane, Echo. Yes, I know you think you're navigating well. And if that were on the path, I'd say sure, but take Meg, just in case."

"But it is not on the path," Zarnix continued. "And therefore you do not need to be going out there and navigating uneven terrain until we are convinced that leg will handle it. You just sprained a tendon across the knee joint, and that with doing nothing but rushing around the bed. Do you seriously think you can navigate rocks, tree roots, and hillocks?"

"Oh," Echo said, face falling. "I...I guess maybe workin' this case wasn't such a great idea, after all, then..."

"No, it's obviously something you're itching to sink your teeth into, Echo," Zebra said, softening her manner. "And there's nothing that says you can't. I just don't think you can get to the site yourself. Now, you could send someone out there from Forensics, to take your samples and whatnot, and that might tell you what you need to know..."

"I have an idea, Ace," Omega said. "I could go out there WITH the Forensics agent, and you can look at the site through me, using the nd't'lq. You can tell me what you want checked out specifically, and I can do it for you. Would that work?" she asked the medics.

"Yes, I think that would be acceptable," Zarnix agreed. "After all, you are getting counseling, but you are not recovering from physical injury. Zee?"

"That's actually a good idea," Zebra decided. "Does it work for YOU, Echo?"

"Yeah, that might do it," Echo considered. "I wish I could go, too, but you both have a good point. I'm probably just not quite ready for that, yet. And I don't need to be getting myself hurt even more, at this stage of things. With the relatively new tissues, I expect I could cause permanent damage, if things went south. Especially to the bones."

"Bingo," Zebra said. "I mean, we could dunk you again, but then we have to drop back and punt with all the therapy."

"Yeah, no," Echo said, pulling a face.

"Let's go talk to Forensics, then," Omega suggested.

* * *

"There's not really a lot left here," Vav, the agent from

Forensics, said, as he and Omega looked over the site. "Just the stained rocks. We figure the missing being had something in the way of a drink, and when whatever happened, happened, it got spilled."

"Yeah, and that makes a certain amount of sense," Omega agreed, "but did you get a sample of it?"

"No, the information came to the Agency through the local police department," Vav explained, "and I know we should have had someone out here sooner, but we've been a bit swamped in recent weeks. That saucer chop shop, you know."

"Ah, right," Omega said, as he took samples of the dried goo on the rocks. "Well, better now than not at all, I guess. It hasn't rained since the guy disappeared, right?"

"No, it hasn't, so we're good, there," Vav agreed. "Why did Agent Echo request you come along, though, if you don't mind my asking?"

"Oh, well, you know how he's recovering from what the Cortians did to him," Omega tried.

"HELL yes!" Vav exclaimed, vehement. "The bastards! Oh wait, I get it now. He wanted to see it himself, but since he's not up to hiking cross-country yet, he sent his partner to look, then come back and describe it to him."

"Right," Omega said. *And what he doesn't know is that you're seeing it now; I don't need to describe it,* she told Echo.

Exactly, came his reply. *But I'm not seeing anything different from what we saw in the photos. Are you?*

It's a little thicker than it came across in the pictures, I think, Omega decided. *The goo, I mean. And the rocks are more discolored. Of course, the discoloration could just be because it's been a couple of days since the photos, and the stuff has aged or something. But they look...pitted, at least in a few places. And I wasn't expecting that. And it didn't show up on the photos.* She looked around. *And none of the surrounding rocks have that pitted look.*

Hm. True. Well, maybe we'll know more when Forensics gives us an analysis of those samples.

Hopefully. Anything else you need me to do while I'm here?

I don't think so, baby. I only wanted to see it with my own eyes, and yours do just as well, all things considered. Come on

back when Vav does.
   Copy that.

* * *

At Echo's urgent request, Forensics expedited testing on the samples from the Loch. Consequently, the results came back the next morning.

"Whoa," Echo decided, looking at the printout he'd sent to the printer from the email. "Meg, come look at this."

"Whatcha got, Ace?" she wondered, rising from her desk chair and walking across the Alpha Line Room to his desk. He tipped the printout toward her, then pointed. "Oh shit. That's... what? Bodily fluids, mixed with...something else?"

"That's the way I read it, baby, yeah."

"It doesn't bode well for our missing Yelfflani, though."

"No, I'm thinking not."

"You gonna keep investigating?"

"As best I can, around recuperating," Echo noted. "I'd like to find a body, at least, before we go contacting his family on Yelfflan, though."

"Good point. I'll issue an alert to the department to keep an eye out, and copy Crutch on it, so she can tell her field agents."

"That's a plan."

* * *

Two days later, Echo obtained permission to ease into a few 'regular' exercises in the gym, with Omega spotting him, so they headed to the gym during what would have been a therapy session. The physical therapists—the lead therapist, Gangway, in particular—were pleased with his progress, and had started easing back on their sessions, concentrating more on giving Echo such 'homework' exercises instead. Echo was, as his 'family' had already noted, diligent in performing them, often with Omega's assistance, and so the plan was to continue this trend with the aid of the fitness center's equipment.

"So you can do some wrist curls and leg work, Ace," Omega told him, as she helped him ease into the leg extension machine, "only it still needs to be kinda light, relative to what we've been used to. But it'll build back up fast, and I have the therapists' permission to increase weights, repetition numbers, and sets, as I see fit, given I'm Alpha Line's training guru. And

100

we can work your core pretty hard, provided we don't stress your hands or lower legs."

"So I just need to be patient and work with you?"

"Bingo, honey."

"Okay, baby. I trust you. Let's do this." Echo gripped the handles of the machine, to stabilize his upper body. "One leg, or both legs?"

"Let's start with both legs, then we'll drop the weight on the right leg and do single-leg extensions."

"Ready when you are, then."

"Okay, start. One...two...three..."

* * *

A little under a week before Christmas, hidden deep in the heavily wooded Ramble in Central Park, though not that far from the public restrooms, the sun rose on a tree that was almost entirely shrouded in what looked like a cross between a lightweight gauze cloth and spider webbing.

But it was well off the walking trails, and no one noticed it.

Inside, just visible as a silhouette as the sun fell upon it, was an elongated elliptical shape, suspended in the tree by the webbing.

* * *

Alpha One took the Corvette and headed down to the Ranch on December 19th. Dihl was already there, and met them at the parking lot near the main house, along with Joe Beck, the Haepergen manager of the facility...which facility also happened to be Echo's family home, kept in trust by the Agency for him, while it provided down time for the agents, and earned cash for him as a civilian guest ranch...though, at Echo's insistence, that cash was now split 50:50 with Dihl. Dihl was surprised and delighted to discover how well the Ranch was prospering, as much as to be able to stay there part-time and work.

"There you are! Merry Christmas!" a happy Dihl exclaimed, hugging them both with enthusiasm as they exited their vehicle. "Oh, I am so excited to be having the family Christmas here once more!"

"Me too, Ma, me too," Echo said, grinning, as he hugged his mother. "Meg and I are both happy about it."

"Really, Omega? Are you sure?" Dihl said, suddenly uncertain, taking Omega's hands in hers. "I wasn't sure...your first Christmas married to Alex..."

"Yes, I am," Omega declared. "Okay, I admit there was part of me that wanted to spend Christmas in our new quarters...but it's more important to be HERE, I think. This is already a real home, and this is where we need to be. In future years, we might swap up, maybe; you know, alternate years. If anybody was actually living in my family home, I'd say we could all go there, like, every third year or something. But they aren't..."

"Yet," Echo interjected, hitting the remote for the trunk lid.

"Yet," she acknowledged, "and this is just great!"

Just then, a contingent of ranch hands arrived, led by Joe.

"Hey there! Welcome y'all are, every one," Joe said, flipping a couple of fingers at several waiting ranch hands to take all the luggage out of the 'Vette and into the house. "Just in private-like, y'all oughta know: We's mighty glad t' be havin' th' family back here. F'r what it's worth, alla th' hands done figured this 'uz y'all's ranch, guys. But it's awright, 'cause they's all good Agency employees. They ain't gonna say nothin', ever, an' they's all happy an' content t' stay here t' work—it's in their blood; YOU lot know what I mean—so ain't nobody gonna go someplace else an' say nothin', neither. An' when we found out what y'all wanted t' do—th' party an' celebratin' here, an all—well, I made sure we didn't have no other guests, no civilians or non-Agency personnel f'r the whole timespan ya said ya'd be here, so's y'all can have yer party, Omega, and ever'body can relax an' have a good time 'thout any risk o' bein' found out." He grinned. "Now, just so's ya DO know, we got a whole group o' civvies comin' in f'r New Years, but since ya said y'all'd be gone by then, I figgered that'd work out fine."

"Yup," Echo confirmed.

"That sounds great, Joe!" Omega said, her grin wide.

"Now, we done got most o' the decorations up around the place, 'ceptin' th' tree in th' main house," Joe went on, "It's a live tree in a pot, 'counta Dihl an' me figgered where ta plant it later on; so it's up, but it ain't dec'rated. We figgered y'all'd wanna do that."

"You figured right," Echo confirmed. "Meg even brought a few of her family's ornaments to put on the tree along with my family's ornaments. Hell, she's even got ME decorating!"

"Oh perfect," Dihl whispered, clasping her hands together. "All of it, perfect. And Cook is excited about discussing a menu with us, not only for the party, but for brunches, and Christmas and Christmas Eve dinners, let alone Christmas breakfast. She expected we would want to be involved in the preparations, given the family consideration, but she will see to it that her staff obtains all the necessary items."

"Ooo, I didn't think about havin' so much help!" Omega said, eyes widening, then she grinned broadly. "This is gonna be FUN!"

"Let's get on in the house, then, and unpack," Echo said with an affectionate smile.

* * *

By the time the trio crashed for the evening, a menu had been set for the party and the 'extended family' brunch the next morning, the tree was beautifully decorated to within an inch of its deliciously aromatic, red-juniper life, and the gifts had been placed beneath it.

They sat in the den around the tree for a long time, the only lights in the room the fireplace and the tree lights, chatting sporadically and enjoying the holiday ambiance. Dihl watched in delight as her son and his bride cuddled on the sofa. Finally she sighed.

"Time for bed, you two," Dihl decreed. "I know you are both used to Division days, but you know the Ranch doesn't keep those, because of the horses and cattle."

"True," Omega agreed. "And it's been a long day, anyhow. I think I'm for crashing soon, yeah."

"Don't forget, you are in the master suite now," Dihl reminded.

"Oooh," Omega grunted, casting a wry glance at Echo. "Does that make me the, um, like, the mistress of the ranch? 'Cause that's kinda intimidating..."

"It does, but I'm sure Ma will be glad to help out however you need to, baby," Echo noted. "You did fine with Cook this afternoon. She loved you, by the time y'all were done."

103

"She did, and you will, and I would be honored," Dihl averred. "Do NOT worry, Omega; this should be a wonderful, relaxing holiday vacation for you, and you do not need to become 'wrapped around the axle,' as you are wont to put it, over your new status here. Everything will be fine. You are, in many respects, coming home, even if you have never called this house home before. And do not feel like you are putting me out; I think this is right and good, and I stood aside voluntarily. Besides, to be honest..." She broke off and sighed. "I found, as I slept in that bed and remembered so many previous nights when I was not alone in it, I missed James more and more. I was becoming...depressed, lonely. It will be better this way. And I am quite happy with the way my suite renovation turned out, across the hall from Alex's childhood bedroom. I'll show you both tomorrow."

"Are you listening, baby?" Echo asked, nudging her in the side. "I told you, the first half of the way down. And Ma's telling you the same thing."

"Yeah, I hear both of ya," Omega confirmed with a nod. "I'll do my best. I might need a little help from time to time, to keep me from getting bent outta shape, but I'll try hard to let all that go for the holidays, and not worry."

"Good. We will see what needs doing in that regard...in the morning," Dihl decided.

"It's a plan," Omega agreed. "All right, Ace, let's go hit the hay."

"And do not worry about locking the door, either," Dihl added. "I worked out an arrangement with Joe: when the family is in residence, housekeeping does not service our rooms. In fact, all things considered, we are discussing designating the bedroom wing as private, not available for guests...which means that we can REQUEST maid service if needed, but otherwise they will not 'invade our domain,' as Joe expressed it. And no one else will enter when that door is closed. We're even considering putting a door in this end of the hallway, which can be closed off to guests, even locked."

"That's good to know, and a damn good idea, all of it," Echo said, giving his bride a mischievous glance. Omega stuck her tongue out at him. They all laughed, and headed down the hall to the bedrooms.

* * *

"I have to admit, baby, you're not the only one who thinks this feels weird," Echo confessed, as he and Omega prepared for bed in the master suite. "I always knew this as Ma an' Dad's bedroom, so bein' in here with you is a little odd."

"Is it squicky?" Omega wondered. "You know, how you don't really think about your own parents 'doin' it' or whatever...and now here we are, in their old bedroom..."

"Nah," Echo decided. "I knew from the time I was little that Dad and Ma were crazy about each other, and they had their private times, when it needed to be something really, really important for me to interrupt...and I had to knock, even then. Once I was old enough to get the 'birds and the bees' talk, I figured out pretty fast what was going on in there during those times. I never had a problem with it. I was glad they loved each other so much." He broke off, then added, "And Ma was devastated when Dad got killed. She told me once, it felt like part of her just...went away." He paused, then added, "And according to her, Gramma an' Grampa Bryant were pretty much the same, and they stayed in this room until Ma and Dad got it. An' my great-grandparents, before that. We're just the latest generation in a long line of Bryants, you an' me, taking up residence in this master suite, passing on the heritage. That's all."

"That's a very mature outlook you have, there."

"I'd like to think so." He shrugged. "Besides, now I understand exactly what Ma meant. In so many ways, about so many things, I can't begin to count 'em."

"So you won't object if I jump you as soon as we climb in bed?"

"Object? You're kidding, right?"

They laughed.

* * *

The next morning, right after breakfast, Dihl showed Alpha One her newly-renovated suite of rooms. She had taken the two bedrooms with jack-and-jill bathroom and converted them to a bedroom/bathroom with a sitting room that opened into the bedroom. The bedroom's door into the hallway was removed and sheet-rocked over, and a small TV, sofa, armchair, and desk had been added to the sitting room, along with a work table and shelf space for her herbals in one corner. Echo and Omega were delighted with how it had turned out.

"And now you have your own private space here," Echo noted, "to relax in peace and quiet, and study, or craft your herbals, or sit and read, or just watch TV, without anybody bothering you."

"Yes. Complete with new memories to be made in this space, with my son and his wife," Dihl affirmed.

"Which is a good thing," Omega agreed.

* * *

Over the ensuing days, the rest of the meal menus were determined, ingredients were acquired, and serious cooking began in earnest in the big ranch kitchen—and the cook staff for the guest ranch, Omega, Dihl, and Echo all participated.

In short order, everything was ready for the holidays.

* * *

The object enshrouded in clothlike webbing in Central Park remained thus cloaked.

But it began to change shape more drastically, becoming shorter and wider.

And it began to get bigger.

The Manhattan police were thankful that the rash of disappearances had stopped. But they continued to try to locate the missing persons, hesitant to set them aside as cold cases so soon after the disappearances.

* * *

On the evening of the 22nd, well after dark, the first guests arrived at the Ranch.

Pulgey Entiyti brought his flagship, the *Hsshthh*, to the Sol system, leaving it at the Lunar Farside Drydocks and riding a cloaked shuttle to Earth, landing it in a certain crater in a corner of the ranch, whose buried meteoric body provided a natural cloaking field to the area. He had notified Fox well in advance of his arrival time, along with a list of everyone who would be attending with him, and Joe ensured that appropriate transportation was waiting to whisk them away to the guest house.

Shortly thereafter, the Pan-Galactic Coalition President, his paramour Chassav Ssiimiilav—who also happened to be captain of his flagship and piloted the shuttle—as well as Admiral Suud Guurn and his wife Eetii, and Guurn's son Duuniiss—recently promoted to Entiyti's Chief Bodyguard— were settling into their spacious rooms in the guest house of the Ranch, after a long interstellar voyage.

* * *

The next morning, well after breakfast—the Emdali contingent, being tired, requested a sleep-in and late room service, which the Ranch staff courteously provided for their illustrious guest and his contingent—the guests from Headquarters began to arrive, all in passively-cloaked vehicles. Fox flew his souped-up BMW; Zebra was in the passenger seat, and Zarnix in the back seat. Caravanning with them, Romeo flew Alpha Two's Lexus, with India in the passenger seat, and Zz'r'p in the back seat. They landed in the parking lot beside the main house, and Joe and his hands were once more on site to whisk them and their luggage into their rooms in the guest house.

Echo and Omega had let everyone know that the 'family party' was to be informal, and to bring off-duty casual party wear; a recent and somewhat unusual-for-the-area cold snap had had Echo pinging everyone to bring WARM off-duty wear two days earlier, as the temperatures were well below freezing, and would remain so through Christmas Day.

So luncheon for everyone that day consisted of a hearty, hot and rich beefalo stew loaded with vegetables, alongside four-cheese grilled cheese sandwiches on thick slabs of homemade sourdough, and egg salad sandwiches with Dijon mustard and chopped chives, the latter provided to keep Fox kosher, since observant Jews did not consume dairy with meat. The meal was a casual affair, in deference to the heavy hors d'oeuvres that would keep the kitchen busy prior to and during that night's party.

"We're REALLY casual right now," Zebra noted, as the entire group met for the relaxed lunch in the main house, some standing, some sitting. "I mean, even Fox is wearing jeans and a long-sleeved tee. And for him to wear that outside of our

107

quarters is rare, which should say a lot to you guys about how comfortable he feels with you! You really are family, guys. But I promise we'll all get a little more gussied up for the party."

"Unlax," Omega said with a smile. "It's all cool. Yeah, so we got the galactic prez, not to mention his chief bodyguard and two previous bodyguards who are also fleet admirals, both of those admirals' wives, a flagship captain, an ambassador, an interstellar medical hospital's chief of staff and assistant chief of staff, one of the best medtechs on this or any other planet, and the four hottest Agents in the Division—"

"Not to mention the two Commodores of the Grand Fleet of Emdali," Entiyti interjected, flame-colored eyes twinkling.

"...But this is FAMILY, guys!" Omega went on as if Entiyti hadn't said anything, though she did roll her eyes and grin; Echo quickly stifled a snort of amusement. "I don't want ANY political ceremony goin' on, here. Is everybody okay with that?"

A general chorus of "Wonderful! Yes, yes! I love it! Abso-damn-lutely!" came back to her.

She and Echo beamed.

* * *

After lunch, everyone repaired to their rooms to prepare for the party, which would start about sundown.

Numerous gaily wrapped packages began appearing under the tree in the main house, most arriving in armloads delivered by ranch hands; one giant lot even came in on a cart.

Meanwhile, the big mesquite dining room table was gradually becoming loaded down with trays, platters, and casserole dishes, prepared by Echo, Omega, Dihl, and the kitchen staff over the previous days. The hot foods were kept on special galactic-tech warmers, complete with stasis fields, and the cold foods likewise on coolers. The sideboard held dark red and green linen napkins, plates, flatware, wineglasses, and several bottles of wine, as well as a large crock pot containing hot mulled syrah, and the mugs in which to serve it. All of the glassware and plates were Christmas-themed.

"And we can leave out the bottles of soda this year," Omega noted, causing Echo to deliver a monumentally-amused snort. "No Lambda Andromedans to get drunk on the carbonation."

108

"No joke," Echo agreed. "No Grendels to eat the decorations, either."

"Especially the mistletoe," Omega smirked. Then she sobered. "Um, that is, if you want, uh..."

"Of course I do. Why wouldn't I?" Echo wondered. Omega sighed.

"You couldn't see your face last year," she murmured, dropping her gaze to the floor. "I could. It really wasn't much more than a joke, because I caught most of the others in our 'family' that night, too. But..." she sighed again. "As if I hadn't needed convincing before, your expression totally satisfied me that you were NOT remotely interested in a relationship more involved than what we already had."

"Oh," Echo said, biting his lip. "I...I'm sorry, baby. I didn't mean...well, hell. Now I understand a few things about why we kept talking past each other for so long. I was still trying to deal with losing Chase at that point. No. No, if I'm honest with both of us, I was dealing with my wounded PRIDE at losing Chase, I think. And the disappointment of being alone again."

"Nuh-uh, Ace. I saw your face, saw your eyes. And I know you. Even then I knew you enough to read that. That was heartbreak, and not wanting to go there again."

Echo thought for a moment.

"Okay, fair enough," he admitted. "Yeah, I had started daydreaming about settling down with the right woman, working in the Agency, and generally doing all the stuff you and I are doing now. I just hadn't realized yet that I picked the wrong woman, the first time. She evidently had sense enough to realize we weren't right for each other, and to move on. I almost didn't."

"And you hadn't really figured that out, last Christmas?"

"Nope, not yet, at least. Oh, I'd started realizing I'd fallen for you, but..." Echo turned away slightly. "Look, Meg. You were my fourth girlfriend, at least as an adult. I had a girlfriend in high school, but I honestly can't say now how serious it really was, or whether it would have held up through my going to college, so arguably fifth. But Linda was ripped from me when I was sucked into the Agency, so I never got a chance to find out. Kar'nun and I...it was a mutual decision to break up, but she instigated the conversation when she realized how young I really was, for an agent. Ree-ree dumped me, again because I was too young for what she wanted. And Chase dumped me for another guy. So, while I know you think I'm a hunk—and I appreciate that more than you know, though I don't really think about it, most of the time, or think of myself in those terms— let's face it: my track record in relationships has been kinda one-sided. I flatly wasn't ready to risk getting dumped again, especially not by somebody I liked and respected as much as you. Never mind by my partner and best friend."

"Holy shit," Omega said in surprise. "Alex, I never even considered it like that. Wow. That all makes sense of what was going on, as well as what I saw on your face, in your eyes...and that makes it a LOT less painful a memory...for ME."

"You understand why I reacted like that?"

"Yeah. Not only do I understand, I can 'feel' it through the nd't'lq. I'm so sorry, honey," she murmured, coming to his side and easing an arm around his waist. "I didn't mean to hurt you."

"I didn't mean to hurt you, either, Meg."

"I know that now," she admitted. "It's okay. But yeah, that's the main reason why I stopped looking for anything from you. Which means, yes, it's why we talked past each other so long."

"In that case," Echo said, grabbing her by the arm and towing her into the den, "where'd Ma hang that mistletoe? We need to make up for lost time."

Omega giggled, and followed him to the sprig of greenery hanging from the ceiling.

* * *

Their guests arrived for the party just as Echo planted a deep, passionate kiss on Omega. They stopped and clustered just inside the back door, which opened into a rear foyer and thence the den, and watched the couple, who were not yet aware they had company. Smiles spread across all the faces.

"Now that's more like it," Romeo declared in a soft voice. "'Bout damn time, too. Took 'em a whole year t' get around to it."

"No Grendels to eat the mistletoe," Fox observed, and the group laughed.

That brought Alpha One up for air, and they both flushed as they became aware of their audience.

"The party has begun," Dihl declared with a wide smile, standing in the doorway from the bedroom wing.

* * *

In short order, everyone had loaded plates of food, along with glasses of wine, and chatted quietly as soft Christmas music played in the background on the house's sound system. They sat or stood, and the various couples took turns under the mistletoe...though Fox had to explain it to the Emdalian couples. He took distinct advantage of it with Zebra, however, much to the delight of Alpha One and Two.

"Is everybody comfortable in their rooms?" Omega wondered, once they had all taken seats on the various items of overstuffed furniture in the den. "I hope you all have plenty of room."

"They're really nice, Meg," India said. "Do they, like, have some small space warps in there, like at Headquarters? Because Romeo and I are convinced that the insides of all of our rooms, combined, are bigger than the whole building, and there's other rooms..."

"They do," Echo confirmed. "But they tried to keep it subtle, so the civvie guests wouldn't pick up on it."

"And they should have put you all into the suites, rather than the standard rooms," Dihl noted. "So you would have plenty of space to be comfortable, and to feel at home. That was our desire, at any rate." She gestured to herself and Alpha One.

"They did, Dihl," Zarnix said. "It is amazingly comfortable, bordering on luxurious. Not what I would expect of a working ranch. Not that I am complaining!"

"Sometimes we get planetary potentates and the like, coming through," Echo explained. "The suites were put in for them."

"And now we have the Director, an ambassador, an admiral, and the Coalition President, staying there, among others," Dihl pointed out.

"We have FAMILY staying there," Omega said firmly.

* * *

"I suppose we ought to help you guys clean up the place a bit," India said quite a few hours later—it was well after midnight—looking around at the party detritus with a grin, "and then get back to our rooms, huh? It's been a long, if really fun, day."

"It has been wonderful," Entiyti agreed. "I think I rather like this holiday, Franz. I know Hanukkah much better, of course, because of you; but I would like to know more of Christmas."

"No, no, we're not quite done yet, y'all," Omega decreed, "and this last little tradition, Echo and I decided to share with all of you, and we hope you won't mind. And...I think it'll help answer some of Uncle Pul's questions about the holiday. Echo?"

Echo picked up a certain old book, wrapped in worn black leather and lying on the nearest end table, and opened it to the bookmark he had placed there earlier.

"And it came to pass in those days, that there went out a decree from Caesar Augustus, that all the world should be taxed..." he began to read.

* * *

"...Well, I can definitely see where your Jesus would have had problems with the Jewish religious authorities, let alone the Roman," Suud said thoughtfully, some time later. "After so long working with Franz, I think Pul and I know the Jewish religion almost as well as he does."

"Not quite, I expect," Entiyti noted, "but 'pretty damn well,' as Echo is wont to say. But yes, I can see that. I can also see how it could be, without violating Jewish law, however."

"It is an interesting conundrum, isn't it?" Fox wondered. "We have a few Jewish Christian agents in our organization, and I have had some intriguing discussions from time to time. They argue, quite persuasively, that Yeshua—as he would have been known in Hebrew—was the fulfilment of the prophets. At times like this, I ponder it and I wonder."

"This reading from your scriptures," Zz'r'p interjected, "it is a holiday tradition for you, Omega? Or is it something you and Echo decided to add, as a result of everything that has happened in recent weeks?"

"Oh, it's a family tradition for Meg, of long standing," Echo said. "Like, all the way back to her earliest childhood. She and I talked about it last year. You'll note I read it, not her?"

"Yes?"

"Her father used to do it, when she was growing up. She says she finds the timbre of the male voice makes it feel 'right' to her, in a way that reading it out loud herself...doesn't."

"Ah," Fox murmured. "That is good to know, tekhter. We'll all remember that for the future, just in case we're needed to 'spell' Echo, because he has a cold or the like."

"Okay," Omega said, offering them a wobbly, but pleased, smile. "That sounds good, Abba Fox. And thank you. I know that it isn't your belief system..."

"But it is yours," Fox said, quiet. "And it is important to you both. And you are both important to me. So I will deal."

"Would anyone like a bit more wine, or perhaps some coffee?" Dihl asked, voice gentle as she eased the topic of conversation in a different direction. "While it has been brought up already, please know that we are in no hurry to rush anyone off. The three of us had discussed it, and rather hoped the gathering would last late into the night, with talk and laughter, good food and drink, and love and contentment."

"Nicely said," Zarnix noted. "Is there any coffee already prepared? If there is not, I shall simply fetch a glass of soda with ice."

"There is coffee," Omega said. "I saw Cook slip into the dining room with a couple of fresh pots, not two minutes ago. Let me go get a tray with the coffee, some mugs, cream and sugar, and I'll set it on the coffee table and serve everybody that wants some. Echo, can you handle those that want wine, whether regular or mulled? I had Facilities send ahead with another of those trundle carts like you have at home, so you can load stuff on it."

"That'll work, baby," Echo said, grabbing his cane, using it to lever himself upright, and following her into the dining room, swinging it at his side.

* * *

Five minutes later, everyone was partaking of their preferred beverage, Cook having assured Omega that one pot contained 'high test,' the other 'unleaded,' so that those who were sensitive to the caffeine could choose not to be kept awake. As Omega detoured back to the dining room to fetch more mugs, she glanced out the window, then stopped dead.

"Oh...my gosh," Omega murmured blankly, as she gazed out the window on the moonlit landscape. "Ace! Honey! Come look!"

Echo came to her side and looked out, then grinned widely.

"Snow! It's SNOWING!" he declared, pleased. "Hard! We've already got nearly half a foot, and it's really coming down!"

"Just in time for Christmas!" Omega cried, clapping her hands together in delight.

"And with this cold snap, it'll stick around a while," Echo added. "The Ranch is gonna have a white Christmas!"

At that moment, Echo's cell phone rang. He answered it in speaker mode, in case Fox needed to hear something.

"Hey, Echo, it's Joe," the Haepergen ranch overseer said. "I won't keep ya. I only wanted ya t' know that it's snowin' right along out there..."

"Yeah, we just now spotted it through the windows, Joe," Echo answered, still grinning like a schoolboy.

"Well, I thought I'd tell ya—since you, Meg, an' yer mom are th' rightful owners o' th' place—we done got th' horses up in th' stable with blankets on 'em an' a hot-mash feed f'r supper, an' the boys an' girls are runnin' th' all-terrain vehicles an' tractor right now, t' put out a couple extra hay rolls an' feed f'r th' cattle. We done had heaters in th' water troughs already, on 'counta th' cold snap; it's right cold out there tonight. So anyhow, I think we managed t' get all th' animals proper taken care of. Oh, and since we ain't got no civvie guests, we ran up a couple a' those Ererot pop-up outbuildings, so yer guests' vehicles are all under cover now, an' they can get from th' main house to th' guest house under cover iffen they wanna. The vehicles'll stay warm an' ice-free, so ev'rybody can head out tomorrow on time without no trouble, scrapin' windshields an' whatnot."

"That sounds great, Joe, and thank you, though I expect some of us might go out and build a snowman, here, before too long! Thank the 'boys an' girls,' too, if you would."

"Sure thing, pal. Y'all havin' a good time in there?"

"We sure are, Joe!" Omega declared. "Echo's gotcha on speaker, 'cause we were afraid something had gone wrong someplace, so I heard. Thanks ever so much!"

"And I 'third' that," Dihl said with a mischievous grin.

"Awright. Y'all have fun, an' we'll see ya in th' mornin'."

"Good deal. Echo—and family; the WHOLE family— out."

"Joe out."

"Looks like it's going to be a lovely holiday for you guys," Zebra said, coming over to look out. "Oh wow! Fox, come look, honey! This is gorgeous, especially with the moon shining through the breaks..."

Fox and the rest of the 'family' gathered by the windows, excited and exclaiming in cheer over the event, so rare in that part of Texas.

Then they clustered by the roaring fire with glasses of wine to toast the season.

* * *

About an hour later, a contingent —the entire party, in fact—went out to build a snowman in the back yard of the main house. Mischievous, they wound up building two, one male, one female, though Zz'r'p and the Emdalian contingent had to be showed how.

As Pulgey Entiyti placed a dead pecan branch in the middle ball of the male snowman to serve as an arm, he felt a cold, wet blob smack him in the back of the head, and spun, just in time to catch a second snowball in the face.

"Argh!" he cried, shaking his head to clear his eyes and breathing slits of the snow. "What...?"

Zebra was doubled over laughing, and Fox grinned from ear to ear, as he formed a third snowball.

"FOX! This means WAR!" Entiyti bellowed.

"SNOWBALL FIGHT!" Romeo cried, as everyone scrambled to take sides.

* * *

Division One teamed up against The Rest of the Galaxy, as Pulgey put it. Alpha One, Alpha Two, Fox, and Zebra took on Entiyti, Captain Ssiimiilav, Suud Guurn, Duuniiss Guurn,

115

Zz'r'p, and Zarnix.

A shy, somewhat flabbergasted Eetii Guurn ducked and dodged until she was well out of the line of fire. Moments later, Dihl joined her, then the pair watched in amusement as the snow missiles flew. Occasionally they had to step out of the way of an errant projectile, but they both stayed on the sidelines, watching, laughing, and commenting to one another. Within a couple of minutes, they were joined by Joe and several ranch hands, drawn by the whooping and hollering. They all stood around watching with big grins.

Division One had better accuracy, being more familiar with the projectiles and their composition and aiming, but strength was on the side of The Rest of the Galaxy, and the humans found it needful to dodge when a snowball came their way. One snowball, aimed and thrown by Zarnix, clobbered Zebra hard enough to knock her on her backside into a snowdrift; Duuniiss managed to take one of Echo's legs out from under him—it was his good leg, when the other foot was in the air to maximize momentum during a throw—causing a similar effect. But Fox, coupled with the Alpha Line leads—Echo, Omega, and Romeo—had amazing strategic planning, and used their coded signals to coordinate bombardment attacks on the offworlders to good effect.

"HALT! All halt!" Pulgey finally cried, holding up both hands. "All halt, please!"

It took a few moments, but eventually everyone stopped.

"I do not know about the rest of you, but I am soaked to the scales, with snow down the tops of my boots," Entiyti declared. "And I do not see either side gaining a great advantage over the other, save that we are all becoming wetter and colder."

"Truce?" Fox offered with a grin.

"Truce," Pulgey agreed, matching the grin of his brother in all but blood.

Everyone nodded concurrence, still smiling.

"Then let's go back inside by the fire where it's warm," Echo suggested. "Joe, that includes you and the guys, there. C'mon! We have coffee and the spiced wine, and I can add shots of something stronger to drinks, if anybody wants it."

"I think some of us will," Fox declared, still grinning.

* * *

Once everyone grew warm and clothing more or less dried, Joe and the ranch hands slipped out, headed back to the bunkhouse, and the rest finally called it a night.

"That was the best damn Christmas party I've ever even BEEN to, let alone thrown!" a happy Omega said, as she, Echo, and Dihl hugged their guests, escorting them out the back door and through the inflated passage to the guest house before coming back to the main house.

"I'd have to agree, tekhter," a smiling Fox averred.

"I have never been to a Christmas party before," Duuniiss said, "but if that is what they are like, I should not mind in the least coming again, 'cousins.'"

"I think it's a plan," Echo declared, grinning.

"Then we shall all be here," Entiyti determined.

* * *

Everyone slept in a bit the next morning, then the Ranch cook served them all an enormous western-style breakfast, clustered around the huge family table. Since Entiyti brought along his 'girlfriend,' Captain Chassav Ssiimiilav, and Suud Guurn brought along his wife Eetii as well as son Duuniiss, all the leaves had to be put in the table, and another table brought in to be placed end-to-end with the big table; there were a grand total of fourteen members of this delightfully unique 'family' partaking.

"This is wonderful," Dihl murmured, happy and content. "I cannot recall the last time a big family meal was held at this table."

"Nor yet such a varied one," Fox chuckled, tossing Entiyti and Guurn a mischievous grin. "We have Earth humans pretty well covered for their diverse nationalities, plus Draconans, Reptoids, Chesharilzi, and Deltiri! All in one big, happy family!"

"We do!" Omega averred. "And glad of it!"

"Amen," Echo agreed. "Merry Christmas, everyone."

* * *

Breakfast—or perhaps brunch described it better—was a casual affair, the dishes handed around Southern-family style, simple and filling, with care taken to the various dietary restrictions, whether innate or religious in nature. The end result was that everyone was thoroughly sated and happy when all was said and done.

Then they all repaired to the den, there to open presents around the Christmas tree.

* * *

In New York, deep in Central Park, everything remained as quiet as the countryside in a western Texas snowstorm.

A certain tree, hidden deep in the Ramble, remained shrouded in a strange webbing.

The object buried deep in the web-like material hung, still and quiet, as the Moon, scudding between clouds, briefly illumined it in a silvery sheen.

* * *

With so many people exchanging gifts, the Ranch's den was soon awash in torn and discarded wrapping paper. Soon they were all donning new clothing, or trying out new tools, or exploring the use of new gadgets, while looking over each others' gifts.

"This will be vunderlekh for working on my vehicles," Fox decided, investigating the new acoustic turnscrew Echo and Omega had gotten him. "It has all the latest bells and whistles!"

"And I'm loving the Yiddish cookbook!" Zebra said, as she flipped through its pages. "I'm thinking Fox is gonna adore my experiments with this."

"You know it, bubeleh!"

"...But what did you and Omega get each other, Echo?" Entiyti wondered, sporting the special cloak Alpha One had had made, and which had slits to accommodate his wings—the natural and the artificial. His paramour, Captain Ssiimiilav, had a crisp new cap to match her uniform, complete with lots of 'scrambled eggs,' as the gilded decoration was called in the American military services...and carefully tailored to allow for her own horns.

"Oh, we haven't exchanged our presents yet, Uncle Pul," Omega explained. "Normally families exchange presents on Christmas morning, which is tomorrow. And that's when Dihl and Echo and I will exchange gifts. But we wanted to be able to exchange gifts with the rest of you, too, without interfering too much with those of you who need to leave later today, either to return to work, or to celebrate your own holiday."

"So, since we planned it to allow y'all to stay over until Christmas Eve, Meg and I figured this counted, since some families do gift exchanges then," Echo finished the explanation. "That way, we treat this like a really true family, lacking only the genetics."

* * *

"And that is appreciated more than you know, zun," Fox said, voice grown very quiet. There was a brief lull in the rustle of wrapping paper, as the 'family patriarch' spoke. "Granted, I had brothers in all but blood, and they are here now, and have been greatly appreciated, over the years...but I have not had a full FAMILY in pushing a century, now—more than seventy years—and..." He broke off, dropping his gaze to his lap.

The room fell completely silent. Zebra leaned over to him and eased an arm around his shoulders.

"Finish it, honey," she breathed in his ear. He nodded.

"I...had not realized...how much I... missed it," he finally got out, his voice cracking once.

Omega, who sat on the other side of Fox, reached out and took his hand.

"Thank you," she murmured, "for consenting to be ABBA Fox for us."

Then she leaned over and kissed his cheek.

"She's right, ya know," Romeo agreed.

"Every bit," Echo averred.

"You bet," India added.

Nods went around the room.

"Even those of us older than you find your little clan to be delightful, Fox," Zz'r'p noted. "Zarnix and I were discussing that very thing before we all sat down to brunch this morning."

"Yes, indeed," Zarnix confirmed. "We are pleased to be considered uncles in this family."

"And you know your brothers and their families are pleased for you, Franz," Suud pointed out. "Never mind pleased that your clan accepts us as members, as well."

"Uncle Franz," Duuniiss said, putting an arm around his mother, who was shyly nodding her agreement, "you may find

119

this...strange. But after recent months, and interacting so much with you all, I find myself feeling every bit as much a part of this clan as I do the Guurn clan on Emdali. And just as proud to be so."

"I am the elder statesman here," Entiyti noted, "but I find I cannot speak more eloquently to the matter than these, your beloved family members, have already done, Franz."

Fox paused, looking around the room, at the sincere faces that looked back at him with love and friendship.

"And that," he said, voice still very quiet, "may well be the best gift I have gotten, the entire season."

"Hear, hear," Zarnix decreed.

"Absolutely," Dihl agreed.

"Happy Hanukkah, Merry Christmas, and Tthuusst Llaagaarssht," Fox said then, adding the Emdalian solstice holiday to the list with a slightly wobbly smile on his face, as he reached for his wineglass and raised it. The others followed suit, and soon a chorus of holiday greetings—Earth-based, and not—ran around the room in soft, happy murmurings.

* * *

The first to leave were Fox and Zebra, with Zarnix and Zz'r'p accompanying, a few hours later.

"I hate to have to break up the holiday celebrations, kinder, but I have a Directors' meeting the day AFTER Christmas," Fox explained, "and the Boys need some holiday downtime, too."

"And we need to get back as well," Zarnix added, gesturing to himself and Zz'r'p, "because not every offworlder celebrates Christmas, and so we have appointments and other things to deal with. No, no, India, Romeo, we have already discussed it, Fox and Zz'r'p and I; there is plenty of room in Fox's car. We will both ride back with him, and you can stay a bit longer, if you like."

"It's been great to have y'all," Echo said, instinctively standing without need of a cane, and taking several steps on his own to provide hugs all around, as Omega shadowed him, and for the same reason. "Thanks for coming, ALL of ya."

"Thank you for having us, zun, tekhter," Fox replied, giving the younger man an unusually fierce hug.

120

"Alla that," Zebra said, hugging Omega just as hard. "Relax, unwind, make some new holiday traditions, and make some new versions of old holiday traditions."

"I think we made a great start on that already," Omega said with a soft smile. "And they're all good."

"Indeed," Dihl agreed. "And I am delighted to have, not only my son given back to me by his very caring colleagues, but a daughter as well."

"It's a really good Christmas," Echo decided.

"And it's not even over yet," Omega pointed out.

* * *

Alpha Two departed around forty-five minutes later, followed within the hour by Entiyti, Ssiimiilav, and the Guurn family, who had all traveled together on Entiyti's flagship; the shuttle that would take them back to orbit was sitting in a certain crater not so far away from the ranch house.

"I'll git 'em over there," Joe, the ranch manager, offered. "Then I'll come back t' the bunk house an' see th' boys an' girls have a good holiday, too."

"Tell Cook to take the rest of today and all day tomorrow off, Joe," Echo said. "Ma an' Meg an' me can handle the cooking for the rest of it."

"Oh, now, she done got tomorrow's dinner all planned for y'all," Joe noted. "I expect you can prob'ly just heat it all up right fine on your own, but I'll check."

And they were gone.

Dihl, Echo, and Omega sat around the fire the rest of the afternoon, talking quietly, playing Christmas music, and watching holiday movies on the television.

* * *

That night, Echo and Omega cuddled in the big master bed together in the dark. Moonlight, reflecting off the snowfall, trickled in through the curtains at the window, allowing for slight illumination of the room here and there.

"Merry Christmas, baby," Echo said, smiling at her; his teeth flashed white in the faint light.

"Merry Christmas, Ace," Omega replied, returning his smile. "I take it, you're happy?"

"More than I can say," Echo admitted. "This is a dream

come true for me, having you here, celebrating Christmas with you, having you with me in the master suite of the house I grew up in...as master and mistress of that house. Complete with Ma, even. I can't begin to express..." He paused, then sent her a wave of love, happiness, and contentment through the mental bond. *There. Did that help express it?*

Yeah, it did, honey, Omega answered. *I'm thrilled to be here, too. I love you so much, and to have the privilege of sharing this special holiday here at your family home, with you, as your wife...I'm so happy.*

Good. Then can I make a suggestion?

Of course. What?

I think we need to start another holiday tradition.

What's that? she asked.

Well, it starts like this...

And he pulled her close, as he trailed kisses across her face.

Oh, I like that idea, she told him, sliding her hands around him.

* * *

The next morning, Alpha One inaugurated another new holiday tradition, virtually identical to the one the previous night, then rose and threw on lounge clothing—to approximate the pajamas they never bothered wearing any more—tied robes over that clothing, and meandered down the hall toward the den.

Dihl awaited them there in the big overstuffed armchair, with a coffee service on the coffee table, two mugs waiting, her own in hand as she sipped from it. The lights on the tree had already been turned on, and the same selection of Christmas music they had used at the party now played softly once more on the sound system.

Omega and Echo seated themselves on the couch, then made cups of coffee for each other, leaning back and sipping in contentment. Echo put his arm around Omega's shoulders, and she snuggled into his side.

"Mm," she sighed. "Merry Christmas, y'all. I don't think life gets any better, does it?"

"Merry Christmas, shich'ee'ké-é. Merry Christmas, shiyee'-é, my dear daughter and son," Dihl replied with a smile.

"Merry Christmas, Ma, Meg," Echo murmured, hugging his partner. "And no, Meg, I don't think it does." He paused long enough to sip his coffee, then wondered, "Breakfast first, or presents?"

"Presents!" both women exclaimed, and Echo laughed.

* * *

First, they refilled coffee mugs.

Then they took turns opening gifts, so that the others could watch reactions, but even so, a little over an hour later, they began to tidy away wrapping paper while admiring their new presents.

Her son and daughter-in-law had put their heads together and given Dihl a delightful, tiny squash blossom necklace, little more than a silver and turquoise choker, with matching earrings; it was exquisitely made, without being flashy or obvious, and given her duty time in west Texas on a guest ranch, Fox had approved its wear with her black scrubs.

Some girl talk over Thanksgiving had revealed that Dihl's preferred fragrance was a high-end brand that, heretofore, she could rarely afford and even more rarely find. So Omega had gone down to the big mall near Alpha One's favorite pub, locating a gift set of the scent—perfume, cologne, body lotion, and dusting powder—and acquiring it for her.

Echo had obtained some leather and sinew, as well as a few small beads, and handcrafted a pair of moccasins for his mother, that she could use as slippers if she wished. He then proceeded to hand-decorate the toe with the beads, creating a classic Native American sun symbol—similar to what was found on the New Mexican state flag, but in the colors of the four directions. The fact that it enabled him to exercise the dexterity and strength of the regenerated hand only pleased his physical therapists, who were almost as excited over the finished product as Dihl was.

In turn, Dihl had commissioned matching silver engraved belt buckles for both members of Alpha One; when they looked closer, they realized the Alpha Line logo had been cleverly worked into the engraving. She also got them matching tooled leather belts. Both buckle and belt were subtle, and while they would not work with their Suits, the items would fit in quite nicely at the Ranch and other southwestern environs in their off hours, with jeans.

For each other, Echo and Omega sported plush new, floor-length, hooded, terrycloth spa robes, with sheepskin fleece bootie slippers, for their private 'spa days.' Echo also got Omega a couple of lacy, delicate négligées, one in a delicate pink, the other in the perfect shade of blue to match her eyes... and her own cowboy hat. In turn, Omega managed to find a suitable pair of men's knit-silk lounging pajamas that would fit Echo's tall frame and that he could wear to wander around their quarters in their off hours...then got two of them, with a matching robe.

While she was shopping for Dihl's fragrance, Omega also picked up a bottle of Echo's favorite cologne; it was in the Burberry line, and she adored how it melded perfectly with his own natural scent.

"Ha!" Echo said, after he'd opened the package to find the cologne. He handed her a medium-sized package. "Open that next, and tell me we don't think alike, baby."

Omega ripped off the gift wrap, slit the tape on the box, and opened it. There were fully half a dozen bottles of her signature 'Heavenly Bodies' custom perfume inside.

"Oh good heavens," Dihl said in dumbfoundment. "You DO think alike!"

"Yeah, I managed to do a bit of sleuthing and find out who made the stuff for you, then I asked them about it, saying I'd recently married 'Dr. McAllister's friend' who'd had 'em continue the scent. So they said they needed to mix up a small batch of it, because you'd bought the last of what they had a few months back." He shrugged. "So they did, and I bought the whole batch. I don't want anybody but you wearing it, baby. I may not have mentioned it, but it's drool-worthy on you."

"Good, 'cause I think the same about yours!" Omega shot back with a grin.

Echo also got his bride a small star-shaped pendant, made of the same offworld precious-metal alloy as their wedding rings.

"Because you have a star-shaped solitaire ring, and Romeo gave you those star-shaped earrings last Christmas," Echo pointed out. "I thought you should have a set. And this way, you do."

"I love it, honey!" Omega said, leaning up and kissing him just before donning the necklace. He fingered it, where it lay in the hollow of her throat.

"It...looks good there," he decided, voice gruff.

"It does," Dihl agreed quietly.

"Here's your last one from me," Omega said, handing Echo a largish and rather heavy package.

"Ooo," Echo said, accepting it and beginning to slit adhesive tape with his knife.

It was a leather-bound set of books, a compendium of many of Echo's favorite short stories in an elegant boxed set.

"Oh damn, baby," he murmured, awed and delighted. "This is gorgeous. Tooled, gilded leather, in a different color for each volume? And the whole thing in a tooled leather box? That's gonna take pride of place on our bookshelves."

"It better get read OFF our bookshelves," Omega noted, raising her eyebrow in mock-irritation.

"Oh, it's gonna, baby! It's gonna!" Echo decreed, pulling one of the volumes and leafing through it.

"We are now out of coffee," Dihl noted, as she attempted to freshen her mug. "And I am beginning to feel a bit peckish, as James would have said. Might the two of you be ready for brunch?"

Echo looked up from the book, and he and Omega glanced at each other.

"I think we could be talked into it," Echo averred.

* * *

Brunch was quick to fix; Cook had left a huge casserole, very similar to Echo's classic breakfast casserole, in the refrigerator, along with a baking pan of orange-spice rolls. They only wanted heating in the oven to be ready. There was also a big platter of already-made gingerbread doughnuts.

"Oh man, I'mma get spoiled by this," Omega decided, as she slid the casserole into the bottom rack of the oven, and the spice rolls on the top.

"Tell me about it," Echo said. "I don't remember either the doughnuts or the spice rolls from family recipes..."

125

"They aren't," Dihl noted, busy brewing another pot of coffee as Echo transferred the platter of doughnuts to the dining table, then doubled back for the pitcher of orange juice and jug of milk. "Cook told me the other day, that was something she learned in...is it chef school? Whatever culinary school she attended. I have yet to try either, but they sounded utterly delicious, to judge by her description."

Within a few minutes, the trio was seated around the gaily-decorated breakfast table, laughing and talking and eating a delicious and very special Christmas breakfast.

* * *

The trio then bundled up and spent the rest of the morning riding three wooly equines through a gorgeous snowy landscape. They returned just in time to get cleaned up and dressed to welcome the ranch hands to a holiday buffet, which, Omega had been informed, was a tradition the Bryants had long held, and which the management of the Ranch had seen fit to keep up—along with a small holiday bonus for each hand.

Cook popped back in with her staff, bringing tray upon tray of food and setting it out on the big dining table...then joining the crowd of Ranch staff noshing and greeting the true owners of Meteor Mountain Ranch.

After about an hour or so, most of the staff departed, and Joe and his principal overseers stayed, seating themselves with Echo, Omega, and Dihl in the den with mugs of spiked hot cocoa. Echo rose to stoke the fireplace, but Joe waved him back.

"Not quite yet, there, pal," he said. "You look to be doin' purty good with that regrown hand, not t' mention th' rest of it, an' we're all pleased as punch about that, but let's not risk it just yet, okay?"

So Joe stoked the fire for Echo, then they all sat around and talked about galactic politics, ranch work, Alpha One's adventures, and anything and everything that the group enjoyed.

The ranch management left well before sunset, and the little Bryant family found one last gift from the Ranch staff: a baked ham dinner with all the sides, one of the classic Southern Christmas dinners.

"We are gonna have so many leftovers," Echo observed, as they sat down to eat.

"But it's been a wonderful Christmas," Omega declared. "I hate to see the sun set on it."

"We still have the rest of the evening together, baby," Echo pointed out. "We'll throw in some Christmas movies and keep the theme going."

"With several days more to come, plus there is New Years in a week's time," Dihl added.

"Fair enough. I can live with that," Omega decided.

Chapter 5

Three days after Christmas, Alpha One headed back to Headquarters; Dihl rode with them.

"We need to swap out a few clothes, pick up some clean laundry, and put away gifts," Echo noted as he drove the airborne Corvette. "We can spend a couple days in our new quarters, then head up to the beach house the day before New Years Eve, put everything to rights for company there, run out and do some shopping, and have everything ready for our guests on New Years Eve itself."

"Sounds good, Ace," Omega agreed. "Part of me hates to leave the Ranch, though. That was an utterly delightful Christmas."

"Yes, it was," Dihl said from the back seat. "I cannot tell you how happy it made me to have my son back, complete with his bride. To see the two of you staying in the master suite was the culmination of a lifetime of dreams. Dreams that, until this past summer, I had thought dead with my son." She paused, shaking her head. "I am almost rapturously happy."

"Aw," Omega murmured, as Echo flushed slightly.

"I'm pretty damn happy about it too, Ma," he said quietly. "All of it. It felt...right."

They were quiet the rest of the trip...but it was the quiet of contentment.

* * *

The shrouded tree in Central Park remained as it was, though the object encased within it had changed shape slightly. From time to time it shifted position a bit, but in general the tree...and the structure within it...remained quiet.

The mysterious disappearances within the Park ceased... for the time.

* * *

On December 30, Alpha One headed north, aiming for Ipswich, Massachusetts and their beach house on Plum Island. Dihl chose to stay behind and ride up the next day with Zebra and Fox.

"Because there are a couple of new procedures Zebra intends to show me," she explained to her son and daughter-in-law. "I'll spend the day doing that, then go back to my quarters and pack, and be ready to go with them the next morning."

So Echo and Omega flew the 'Vette up to Ipswich and across the sound to the southern end of the island, landing on the lone road and decloaking only after verifying there was no one upon it, or within sight.

Five minutes later, the security system had allowed them access, and they entered the beach house that Echo had bought several years earlier.

* * *

"Are you good with this, baby?" Echo wondered, as they walked into the den. "I mean, the last time we were here, we were kinda...on the run..." He shrugged. "I don't want you to be uncomfortable with being here."

"No, I think I'm good," Omega decided after a moment to consider. "And we had those mods made, so it's gonna be a little bit different, anyway. If for no other reason than it has another floor, two new hallways, and about ten new rooms."

"Heh! True," Echo agreed. "Structural space warps do wonders for floor layouts."

"Ain't it the truth."

"I expect we need to go through and throw out some things from the last time we were here," Echo noted. "We left in kind of a hurry, there, and I didn't bother to take time to chuck the contents of the fridge into the disposal. Never mind not finding time to get back up here to remedy that."

"Ugh," Omega grunted, wrinkling her nose. "That's gonna stiiiiiiink..."

"Yeah, there's gonna be science experiments growin' in there, for sure."

"Well, good thing we came up early, then. Let's set to it."

* * *

With both of them hard at work, it didn't take too long to clean things out and put everything to rights.

"And now we need to go get supplies for the trip," Omega decreed, once the house sparkled. "Food for the gathering, extra linens for the four new bedroom/bathroom suites we got, paper products, fireworks..."

"Yeah, the weather forecast shows we're gonna have good weather, so that oughta work," Echo confirmed. "Tell ya what. Let's drive into town and run by the mall for bath towels an' bed sheets an' shit, then I'll drop you off at the supermarket I used to use, while I go buy the fireworks."

"That works," Omega decided. "Let's go."

* * *

Their enthusiastic guests showed up by about nine in the morning on New Year's Eve. Dihl rode with Fox and Zebra, and once more, Alpha Two caravanned behind. But since the celebration was planned for evening, they brought a potluck luncheon for seven, a multicultural buffet: beef and chicken fajitas, a big potato kugel, Korean purple rice, a creamy fruit salad, and an enormous Native-American style corn pudding for dessert...the majority of which was in the Lexus' warp trunk. Most of the dishes were in portable stasis fields, set to either heat or cool, as needed—a technology that, Fox decreed, was one of the handiest trade negotiations he and Sugar had made in recent years.

In short order, the two cars were unloaded, tucked safely into the garage against the elements alongside the Corvette, and Echo showed their guests to their rooms, while Omega set out the food—next to the chips, dips, and salsa, and the cheese tray, that Alpha One had provided as their contribution to the meal.

Soon everyone was settled in—Dihl was in the new bedroom across the hall from the master suite, the others were in rooms in the 'new downstairs'—and had gathered around the fireplace; the cold storm system that had given snow to the Ranch in Texas had reached New England, leaving a dusting of snow over the ground, and the fire felt good, so early in the morning. There was normally more snow by that time of year, but it had been largely dry in Massachusetts since the storms had come through in early autumn, the last time Alpha One had been at the beach house.

"And it's not supposed to stick around long," Omega noted. "It'll be cool, but by day after tomorrow, it's supposed to warm up a little bit."

"Just enough nip in the air to make this fun, though," India said with a grin.

"Meg and I went for a walk on the beach late yesterday afternoon, about sunset, and collected a crap-ton of driftwood," Echo noted, "so we have plenty for the fireplace AND a bonfire. And we can cook on any of the fires—fireplace, fire pit under the house, or bonfire. So. Time for a vote: all in favor of the fireplace?"

"Only if the weather turns bad," Fox said. "And by bad, I mean storms with wind and rain."

"What he said," Romeo agreed. "REALLY bad."

"Yup," Zebra confirmed.

"I agree," Dihl noted.

"Okay, fireplace is a last resort, weather fallback," Echo confirmed. "Fire pit under the house?"

"Perfect if it rains or snows," Fox stated. "And I don't think the forecast calls for that. Therefore, I'm holding out for a bonfire on the beach."

"Hear, hear! Yeah! Alla that!" came the responses.

"It's unanimous, Ace," Omega said with a grin.

"Bonfire on the beach, it is," Echo said, returning her grin. "Fox, if you and Romeo would be so kind as to help me dig a pit...?"

"Oh no, you don't," Zebra piped up, jabbing a finger at Echo. "That's mandated on your 'do not do until your medics say so' list. And we ain't said so!"

"Aw, c'mon, Zebra," Echo said, slumping in disgust and dismay. "Don't do this to me. Not now. I don't even use the cane any more; I only keep it around because y'all insist. You KNOW I'm doing okay now."

"And we wanna KEEP it that way," Zebra averred, unswerving. "You will not be doing any digging. Period. End of discussion."

An upset Echo raked a hand across his face and up into his hair, as Omega came to his side, putting her hand on the small of his back and rubbing gently, attempting to soothe.

"It's okay, honey," she murmured. "I can use a shovel just as well as you can. I grew up on a farm, after all."

"I know, Meg, but you were gonna get the food ready," Echo said with a sigh.

"Actually, Echo, if you'll supervise and let us know where you want it, and how wide and how deep it needs to be, I expect Romeo and I can get it knocked out pretty quickly," Fox pointed out. "It's only sand."

"Yeah, man," Romeo agreed. "Me an'...lessee, Meg calls ya 'Abba Fox'...me an' Abba Fox c'n get this part, bro. We don't mind."

"You're sure? I mean, guests an' all..."

"No. FAMILY," Fox said, voice firm. "We may be visiting, and we may not have been here before, but we are family, and we will make ourselves at home and HELP. Like Romeo says, let your abba and your brother help out, this time. You wanted our help anyway; the only difference from what you asked and what you're getting is that you're not going to be wielding a shovel personally. We still need to be told where to put it, how deep it needs to be, how wide..."

"They have a point, Ace," Omega said.

"Okay," Echo capitulated. "That'll do...THIS time."

"Next time you throw one of these beach house gatherings, you'll be back up to speed," Zebra noted. "Now, we all picked up folding chairs and tossed 'em in with everything else, so India, what say you and I fetch those and carry 'em all down to the beach, while the guys build the fire, and Meg and Dihl get the food ready to go?"

"And by the time we have that all done, it will be lunchtime," Dihl observed. "And after that, we can SET the fire and wait for it to reach the proper temperatures."

"Plan," Echo said, and they all headed off to their respective tasks.

* * *

After lunch, unpacking, beach walks, Echo's therapy exercises, and getting the chairs set up in the sand around the newly-dug fire pit, Echo lit the fire. Then they all sat around, chatting and watching the surf as the sun grew lower and the fire crackled, wrapped in the inexpensive spare blankets Omega had gotten expressly for the purpose of being dragged through the sand.

A bit over an hour later, Omega returned to the house and brought down a large folding table, erecting it nearby, then— during the course of several trips to the house and back— putting hamburger and hot dog buns, condiments, lettuce, sliced tomato, sliced and diced onions, kosher pickle chips, pickle relish, sauerkraut, and a couple of varieties of sliced cheeses on it. Several different kinds of chips, dips, and Echo's homemade salsa added to the menu, along with several huge bags of marshmallows. She and Echo had collected around a dozen slim branches from the front yard the night before, sharpening the tips, and now they lay on the sand beside the table, as she fetched the hamburger patties and hot dogs, and Echo set up a grill over the coals on one side of the fire.

"Fox, just so you know, those hot dogs are kosher," Omega noted, as Echo began putting the meat on the grill. "I can't say about the ground beef..."

"It should be," Echo contended, "That store's butcher supplies the meat for pretty much the entire Jewish community in the Ipswich area."

"That sounds vunderlekh, kinder," Fox said with a smile. "Provided I keep the cheese from the vicinity, I think I will be good."

"I've kept everything separate," Omega informed Fox. "I mean, we don't keep a kosher kitchen, but we've tried hard to accommodate."

"I noticed the kraut and the pickles were kosher style too," Zebra observed. "Meg, I think you and Echo did great. And I can't wait to roast marshmallows! I haven't done that since... since I was a kid, I guess!"

"We've got chocolate bars and graham crackers if folks want s'mores for dessert," Omega informed them. "I just haven't brought 'em down yet 'cause the table doesn't have room."

"And there's more general party food for later tonight, once we go in to watch the ball drop on TV," Echo said, flipping the burgers. "Deli trays, cheese trays, relish trays, a tin of Meg's homemade shortbread, some sorta little finger cake things..."

"Petit fours," Omega filled in. "We done good by y'all. You won't leave tomorrow saying you were hungry."

"It sounds like it!" India laughed.

"Watch the ball drop on TV? I thought we were going to shoot off fireworks," Dihl wondered.

"We are...from the deck," Echo said. "We can get the first fireworks ready and still watch the ball drop on the TV. Hell, with those big picture windows, we can watch the ball drop FROM the deck, if folks want to."

"But it'll be cold," Omega reminded them. "Echo and I kinda thought a chance to warm up inside would be good. Then we can come back outside for the fireworks."

"Meg made more of that mulled wine like we had at Christmas, just in case," Echo said. "It's on a corner of the counter in the kitchen, in a crock pot, staying hot."

"Ooo," Zebra murmured. "That stuff was good."

"Indeed," Fox agreed.

"But we got beers and chocolate stout to go with the burgers and dogs, as well as soda, if somebody wants it," Omega added. "I was wondering if one of y'all would mind coming back up with me and helping me carry down the cooler; I wagged it to the back door by myself, but no way could I carry that thing down the stairs without taking a bad tumble. I swear, it's half as big as I am."

"Hey, pretty lady, no sweat, we c'n get this; you stay here an' help Echo," Romeo said, standing. "Fox, you feel like some more manual labor t' help out?"

"Sure," Fox said, getting up. "Let's go, zun."

"It's not fancy, guys, but it'll be good," Echo said. "We coulda done a big fancy shindig in our quarters at Headquarters, but we thought this might be a nice change of pace."

"I think it's great," India declared. "You already did the fancy shindig for Christmas, anyway. Besides, you two need the down time, and for that matter, I think we all could use it."

"That was the idea," Omega said. "Ace, honey, do you have everything?"

"Ease that clean platter over here within reach, baby, and put the used platters on the sand under the table," Echo said, pointing. "These burgers are almost ready to take off the fire, and the dogs are close, too."

Omega moved clean platters within Echo's easy arm reach,

as Fox and Romeo toted the cooler down the steps from the deck. Then she threw her blanket across her shoulders and sat down in her chair by the fire, as the other men eased the cooler down beside the table.

Moments later, Echo was setting a big platter of hamburgers and hot dogs on the table, declaring, "Soup's on!" and they all moved to the table.

* * *

After dinner, they sat around the fire roasting marshmallows until well after full night had fallen, talking, telling stories on each other, listening to the sounds of the waves crashing on the beach, stargazing from their chairs with Omega's guidance, watching the multicolored flames from the salt-impregnated driftwood, and occasionally watching the sparks fly as Echo added a few more sticks of driftwood. Suddenly Omega's cell phone bleated, and everyone jumped.

"Oh shit," India grumbled. "Now what?"

"No, no sweat, y'all," Omega said, pulling the device. "That's just the alarm to tell me it's ten o' clock! We need to bank the fire—that way, we can come back down later, if y'all want to—and move up to the house. Echo will get the fireworks ready, an' I'll get out the party food an' turn on the TV to one of the Times Square broadcasts. The champagne has been chilling since this afternoon!"

Dihl helped Echo bank the fire—it was well away from any foliage or anything combustible, and the sea breeze was blowing out to sea, as it was solid dark—then the lot trooped up to the beach house to ramp up the celebration.

* * *

In the end, Echo rowed the fireworks—mostly rockets and small mortars—along the edge of the deck, facing seaward, while Omega adjusted the security force field, opening it toward the ocean, then got out the party food. Dihl offered to handle the champagne, and Romeo switched on the flat-screen TV and found the Times Square broadcast that featured the younger brother of 'The World's Oldest Teenager,' believed deceased, but in reality, 'not from around here' and thus possessed of a longer lifespan than the human norm. Then Romeo added a few pieces of driftwood to the fireplace, while India and Zebra lit the candles that Echo and Omega had scattered about the den, keeping the lighting low.

Dihl opened the back door, propping it open, so that Echo could watch AND hear as the ball drop neared, while still prepping their fireworks. Then she ensured everyone, including her son, had a flute of champagne. As the ball touched down, Echo set off the first mortar amid cheers from the others, then hit a switch on a little control panel; he had brought equipment from Headquarters and automated the fireworks display, so that he could pay attention to his bride and their guests.

"To a new year!" he cried, raising his glass in a toast as the others joined him on the deck. "May it be better for us than this last year, weddings notwithstanding."

"Hear, hear!" came the response, as they all clinked glasses and sipped.

Then Echo set aside his glass on the railing as the others joined him on the deck to watch the fireworks. He took Omega's glass and set it beside his; then, during a pre-programmed lull in the fireworks, he pulled her into his arms.

"Happy New Year, baby," he told her.

"Back atcha, Ace," she said with a grin. Then he kissed her thoroughly.

"Good idea," Fox muttered, and took Zebra in his arms.

"What 'e said," Romeo affirmed, joining suit.

Dihl stood, beaming in happiness, watching the happy couples as she sipped her champagne.

They only came up for air when the fireworks resumed.

* * *

Once the fireworks ended, they all trooped back down to the beach and Echo stoked the bonfire again.

They sat and talked, joked, and laughed until well into the wee small hours. Eventually, they decided in mutual accord that it was high time to go to bed.

So Romeo grabbed a bucket, sitting nearby for the purpose, wandered down to the water's edge, filled it, and brought it back, dumping it on the fire.

Then they trooped back to the house.

* * *

"Nothing fancy, but damn, that was fun," Echo decided,

when he lay in bed beside Omega.

"No shit," she agreed. "We might wanna try to make this a semi-sorta annual thing."

"Not a bad idea," Echo considered. "Or at least, every other year or so, provided we're not on a mission. I'll talk to Fox about whether that's a reasonable consideration, given the high ranks of the personnel involved. Oh, by the way, Zebra said they're looking at making Ma one of the medtech chiefs. She's more than got the experience in nursing, and she's nailed everything they've taught her to do."

"That's great!" a pleased Omega exclaimed. "I think that's a fine idea."

"Good. I got another fine idea."

"What?"

"Guess."

And he pulled her close.

* * *

New Years morning at the beach house was late, relaxed, and mildly lethargic; everyone, especially Fox, was decidedly more laid-back than usual. They turned on the flat-screen TV over the fireplace and watched the Rose Parade while everyone participated in cooking a big communal brunch. In short order, they were chowing down from huge platters of scrambled eggs, smoked salmon, turkey sausage, and smoked bacon, with grits, toast, and bagels with cream cheese. Even Fox had plenty to eat while still keeping kosher.

"This has been an outstanding New Years," he noted, as he tucked away the last bite of bagel with cream cheese and smoked salmon, a dollop of scrambled egg garnishing the top. "And my compliments on the cooking and preparation! You had something for everyone, both at Christmas and New Years!"

"We tried really hard, Fox," Echo said with a smile. "We want our whole family to enjoy our company, and that means ensuring everybody's happy an' well fed, without any dietary problems to upset matters."

"Among other things," Omega agreed.

"Well, you did an excellent job, children. I know I am certainly nicely full," Dihl observed, content. "And my room

137

was delightful, my bed soft and warm, and I feel as good as I felt after waking from my regeneration last summer!"

"That's what we like to hear!" Omega declared. "Now, the parade's over with, and the football games haven't started yet. How about we all bundle up against the winter sea breeze and go for a walk along the beach? We can work off some of that food we just ate."

"Hear, hear! Amen! Wonderful idea!" came the exclamations.

* * *

"Meg, you and Echo have a dream vacation spot up here," India told her 'adoptive sibling' as the group of seven strolled down the beach. "Thank you so much for inviting us all to enjoy it!"

"Never mind adding rooms for all of us," Zebra added. "That lower floor with all the bedroom suites is delightful. And the beach-facing windows were wonderful!"

"She means it," Fox asserted. "She stayed up rather late last night, sitting at the window and watching the surf by moonlight, even after we all supposedly went to bed."

"And you sat right beside me," Zebra retorted.

"I did," Fox admitted with a chuckle.

"We did, too," India confessed. "So...yeah. Thanks!"

"Well," Echo said, "back in the summer, when Meg and I were here to get away from Wright, we talked about having a 'family gathering' up here. We both loved the idea, and even before she and I started seeing each other romantically, we'd started talking about how to modify the house so everybody could visit and not have to worry about heading home right off. Maybe in the summer, we can do a clambake or lobster boil, or something."

"I like th' way you two think!" Romeo declared with a grin. "That sounds good!"

"Well, I'd have to bow out of that part," Fox noted. "Neither clams nor lobster are kosher. But I expect, knowing you two, you have work-arounds in mind, even for that."

"A few," Omega said with a grin. "We'll have to verify a few things with you first, to make sure we do it right, though."

"And you know I'm always open to that, kinder," Fox

agreed immediately. He paused, chewing his lower lip for a moment, then said, "Bear with me a moment, everyone; what I want to say may be a bit difficult to get out."

The group paused, focusing on the 'family patriarch,' as he pondered wording.

"All right," he sighed. "Everyone here knows where I spent a good portion of my adolescence. And where I saw the last living member of my genetic family."

They all nodded their understanding; thanks to galactic medical techniques, Fox was considerably older than the early fifty-something he appeared to be; the events he referenced occurred in the Nazis' Majdanek concentration camp, where he lost every member of his genetically-related family during World War II.

"It's been over seventy years," he continued, "since I've had a family of ANY sort, other than, I suppose, Pul and Suud, who are legal, if not genetic, brothers. Somewhere along the way, I stopped worrying about it, stopped missing it...at least, I thought I had. But when Omega put together this meshugge kleyn mishpakah, this crazy little family of ours...at first I worried about her ability to handle the kind of work we do. I thought she might be too soft for the hardness of the work. She proved me wrong, of course...essentially right off the bat. Then, somewhere along the way, I realized..." Fox broke off and shook his head. "It's my family, too, I guess is what I'm trying to say. And I LIKE having that family."

Zebra elbowed him then, and he glanced at her.

"What?"

"Say it right, honey," she told him. He sighed again.

"All right," he confessed. "I LOVE this family. Every last crazy one of you."

"And we love you, too, Abba Fox," Omega murmured, pulling him into a gentle embrace. "Even the guys, though they have a harder time sayin' it."

"Yeah," Echo agreed, gruff.

"Group hug," Romeo declared, as they all joined in.

* * *

When they returned from their walk, the rest of the afternoon was spent before the fireplace toasting more marshmallows, with football games on the television, in camaraderie and contentment.

"Just like any family should," Omega proclaimed.

"Amein, tekhter," Fox agreed.

"Marshmallows!" Zebra sang, and they all laughed.

* * *

As the first day of the new year waned at last, and the sun drew on toward the western horizon, Alpha One's guests got ready to leave.

"It's been wonderful, kinder, more than I can say. The whole holiday season," Fox declared, as he hugged both Echo and Omega, dropping a light kiss on Omega's cheek. "Getting away from Headquarters twice in a week was good, too!"

"Tell me about it!" Zebra agreed, giving Omega and Echo hugs and kisses. "It was a blast! Any time you want to invite us up here, we'll do our damnedest to make it!"

"Alla that!" Romeo agreed, gingerly hugging Omega and offering Echo what the younger man termed a 'bro-hug.'

"What they said!" India averred, joining the impromptu departure line. "You two have a damn fine weekend getaway, right here!"

"And you're welcome to come up and join us, guys," Omega invited, as Dihl gave her and Echo a motherly hug each.

"Well, perhaps after the newlyweds have settled into their married status a bit more," Dihl pointed out. "The two of you need your private times, especially right now."

"They do, and we will," Fox concurred. "But I must agree, this is an excellent hideaway, and while none of us would be so rude as to intrude on your private time, whenever you may want company here, you have only to say the word. You are both excellent hosts, and this is a fine location for a small gathering."

"I expect Meg an' me are gonna be doing this sorta thing fairly often," Echo noted with a grin. "We've been talking about exactly what Romeo said—using this place as a getaway on our days off."

"Yeah," Omega chimed in. "It's close enough that an emergency call will bring us into Headquarters inside a couple hours, but far enough out to be quiet and relaxing."

"That will work," Fox decided. "And now, we need to be off, kinder, because we DO have a couple of hours in the air ahead of us."

"'Bye! Goodbye! Happy New Year!" came the calls, as the group departed.

Moments later, two 'special' vehicles were cloaked, morphed, and airborne, headed south, back toward the Big Apple.

"Well, we've got the place all to ourselves," Omega murmured, as she and Echo stood on the small front porch, waving. "It's gonna seem empty now."

"Nah," Echo said with a devilish grin, as he slipped his arm around her waist. "I got plenty in mind to keep you busy."

She laughed.

* * *

The next day, Alpha One slept in, relaxing and reveling in their privacy and their relationship. Eventually they rose, showered together, then threw on clothes suited to the season— jeans and sweatshirt, in Omega's case, and sweatshirt and workout pants, in Echo's, though both still wore house shoes— and made breakfast. Over that meal, they decided what to do for the day.

"The weather looks like it's gonna be good," Echo concluded, studying the Agency's meteorological app on his cell phone. "Cool, of course, because hell, it's January Second in Massachusetts. But warming up over what it's been, so we can probably go for a beachcombing walk without freezing our asses off, if you wanted to."

"And you can work out and maybe even go for a jog on the beach," Omega pointed out. "The cooler weather will be good for working out. And Zebra said that'd be really good for your legs and feet, 'cause the sand will work you in ways that regular walking or jogging won't do."

"Yeah, I thought that sounded like a plan, too."

"I'm glad we thought to put in a workout room downstairs, when we made the additions, though," Omega noted. "We can work out and stay in physical shape while we mentally unwind. Regardless of the weather."

"And I can do all my therapy exercises," Echo added. "I

pretty much gotta start using significant weights on all those, now. The weight of my own limbs just isn't close to enough any more."

"I've been noticing that," Omega observed with a pleased smile. "I think you're comin' along great, Ace."

"As between us, India pulled me aside last night and said that she—and all the rest of the medical staff who've been workin' on me—agreed with you," Echo told her then. "I'm approved to go without the cane now, not that I wasn't already doin' that anyway, at least when I thought I could get away with it." He gave her a mischievous smirk, and she smiled.

"That's great!"

"Yeah. So I think...lessee. Zebra said running barefooted in the packed sand by the surf was what would be good for the foot muscles, right?"

"Yeah. Just be careful not to step on any shipwreck driftwood or something."

"I think I know where I can do that and be safe from puttin' a nail or a stob through my foot," Echo considered, mulling over the matter in his mind. "I'm gonna let breakfast digest, then head down."

"I'm glad it has warmed up a little, or your poor feet would freeze. Want a companion jogger?"

"If you wanna join me, I'd love it, baby. But yeah, we're gonna keep to a jog today, not a flat-out run. I don't think I'm ready to do wind sprints in the sand an' surf, not quite yet. Let alone continuous running at speed."

"Okay. Let's do it, then."

* * *

Later that morning, the pair headed down to the beach, wearing their surf shoes, and Echo took Omega to the section of beach he expected to be safe. They used special apps on their Agency-issue, galactic-tech phones to verify there was nothing dangerous in the sand near enough to the surface to hurt them along their entire planned route, then they left their surf shoes on a big rock outcrop, stretched, and began to jog slowly down the beach, gradually picking up the pace until they were moving briskly, but not at an unduly rapid pace, lest it stress Echo's regenerated foot and lower leg.

"Oh, this feels amazingly good," Echo declared after only a few minutes of the activity. "The way my feet feel, flexing in the sand...that's awful damn nice."

"I bet," Omega said with a grin. "Been there, done that. And we've got enough room to make several up-and-back laps without getting bored."

"Yup. This was a plan."

"Good. We can do it every day, and you can go a little farther and a little faster, each day."

"DEFINITE plan!"

They laughed.

* * *

By the time they came in from their run, then hit the workout room to finish Omega's training and Echo's therapy, it was lunchtime; since the beach house had no outside artificial lighting to speak of—nor did they particularly want it—whenever they were there, they kept normal Earth hours. Party leftovers made up the principal components of their luncheon, mostly cobbled together into sandwiches.

"Though I'm thinking some of that leftover cheese might make for a nice fondue tonight," Omega decided, looking at the various platters she'd extracted from the refrigerator, sitting before them on the kitchen table.

"I like that idea," Echo agreed. "Between the veggie tray, the fruit tray, an' the bread, plus about a pound each of four different cheeses, we could probably make a really nice fondue meal, and STILL have lotsa stuff left over for salads and sandwiches. Let's do it."

"Okay."

"Beachcombing this afternoon?"

"Followed by a soak in the hot tub, then lounging in the hammock?"

"With glasses of something, yup."

"I can definitely get into this, for a change," Omega decided. "You know, I enjoyed it when you brought me here the first time...or I would have, if I hadn't been running from Mark Wright. I still loved it, I just wasn't quite allowed to enjoy it, you know?"

"Yeah, I get it. And now?"

"This is absolutely great, Alex," Omega told him, sincere and grateful. "Nice and quiet and safe, and nobody bothering us, nobody breathin' down our necks. Nothing to do but what WE WANT to do, for a change. An' I dunno about you, but..." She looked up at him and met the dark eyes. "I've NEEDED this."

* * *

Echo looked deep into the sapphire gaze, seeing and sensing the beginnings of a profound, contented peace forming there—perhaps since the first time he had met her—and something in him responded in kind.

"Yeah," he agreed, letting out a relaxed sigh. "Yeah, me too."

* * *

Within a matter of days, Echo was not merely jogging, but running, and shortly thereafter, he started wind sprints up and down the deck stairs to the beach.

"Damn, Ace," Omega said, watching from the hammock. "You're doin' great!"

"It feels...really good," he panted, as he thundered up the stairs for the final time, then paused before her to catch his breath. "Nothin' hurts, everything feels strong and pumped and...like it's supposed to be, I guess. At this point, I honestly can't tell this," he patted his right knee, "isn't the entire leg I was born with." He shrugged, then paced back and forth on the deck, cooling down. "Oh, I guess if I stop and pay attention, I can feel the slight limp. But unless I AM payin' attention, I don't."

"And that's fantastic," Omega said with a grin. "I'm so proud of you I could bust!"

* * *

"Aw," he said, offering her a slightly sheepish smile. "Well, I'm glad, sweetheart. It...means a lot to me, that you're proud of me. I hope you'll always be proud of me."

"I can't imagine ever NOT bein' proud of you, honey," she replied. "C'mere an' stretch out here with me an' cool off. I got a bottle of water with your name on it."

"That sounds good," he agreed, easing into the hammock beside her and accepting the chilled bottle she pulled from the small cooler on the shelf under the blankets, opening and sipping it. "How are you doing?"

"Me? I'm doin'...okay," she said, but he caught the slight hesitation.

"Just okay? I thought you were startin' to relax," he tried, not wanting to press her, but concerned.

"Eh. I had a nightmare last night," she admitted then. "Those are happening less and less, but I still get 'em, now and then. And yes, I already talked to Zz'r'p about it," she added. "That's why I sat up here and watched while you ran; I was so occupied with a little long-distance session with him that, if I'd tried to run with you, I'd probably have fallen over my own feet, right into the surf."

"I wondered about that," he said, taking another deep swig of the water. "I mean, this is the only day you haven't gone running WITH me, an' I was a little worried what was up, from the get-go. I picked up you were preoccupied, through the nd't'lq; I just couldn't quite make out why. Did the counseling session help?"

"I think so, yeah," she mused, thoughtful. "I mean, it's like he and I discussed—I'm probably always gonna have the odd nightmare about...about the kidnapping and 'augmentations,' about Wright tryin' to rape me under the influence of his programming, about you getting tortured..." She shrugged. "That's just the way it is for me. But you didn't know about last night's dream, did you?"

"No, I didn't. At all. And frankly, I'd have expected you to wake up screaming or something," Echo confessed. "I heard about the flashback dream you had when I was in the regeneration pod."

"Mm. I was sorta hoping nobody would tell you," she said, scrunching her face.

"Well, I think Zarnix wanted me to be prepared, in case you did it after we were married," Echo explained. "I mean, if you screamed like I was told you did, right next to me in the middle of the night with us both sound asleep, it's gonna give me a coronary anyway, but at least I'd know what was happening."

"Oh. That makes sense, I guess. An' I'm glad I HAVEN'T done that to you! I think that was actually 'bout the only time

I've screamed during a nightmare...an' I think that was 'cause it was a flashback inside a nightmare. But no, this wasn't anywhere close to that," Omega told him. "Yeah, it was a nightmare, but it wasn't a FLASHBACK, as such. An' this time, I KNEW it was a dream, and was able to partly take control over it."

"You took it lucid. Nice. Did Zz'r'p teach you how?"

"Yeah, he did. And yes, it helped. Because this time, when Slug tried to catch me in his tractor beam, I pulled out a tachyon-splitter rifle from somewhere an' blew a hole in him," Omega declared with a grin. "Twelve-year-old me, an' all."

"GOOD for you!" Echo exclaimed, putting an arm around his wife and partner, and hugging her in exultation. "That's GREAT, baby!"

"Yeah, I was pleased," Omega averred with a lopsided smile. "But...well, it's still gonna be disturbing, at least a little, you know? I mean, just the subject matter is gonna tend to upset me a little bit."

"Yeah, I understand, honey," he said. "But it sounds like you're making good progress, too."

"Zz'r'p agreed."

"Good. Whatcha wanna do now?"

"I dunno. Do you need to go shower?"

"Probably. You wanna join?"

"I was thinkin' more along the lines of, I wait here for you, an' we just lie around here an' watch the clouds, listen to the surf, an' generally chill. At least until it's time to eat."

"I can get into that, too," he said, draining the water bottle and standing. "I'll toss this, then hit the shower, and be back in fifteen."

"I'll be here."

* * *

That set the pattern for Alpha One's days.

They grew relaxed and stronger, mentally and physically. They slept well, ate well and healthily, spent plenty of time on the beach and in the water, as well as in the fitness room. They took turns giving each other massages, then soaked in the hot tub or cuddled in the hammock, and watched the world go by, peaceful and content.

* * *

Roughly two and a half weeks after New Year's Day, the webbing that encased the tree in the Ramble began to move, then to writhe. Within moments, the entire tree started to shake. Minutes later the webbing ripped open from within, and a creature emerged like nothing ever before seen on Earth... though certain filmmakers had tried to imagine it.

Its body was about four to five feet long and at least a foot wide, covered in spiky gray 'fur,' and its tandem, triangular, ribbed wings, decorated with a mottled gray/tan pattern, were wrinkled from where it had emerged from its cocoon. Its face somewhat resembled a bat's, though it was also possessed of huge, black, composite eyes and feather-like antennae that, at the moment, lay back along the top of its muscular body. The overlapping tandem wings, while spanning fully four times as wide as its entire body length, were stubby, only about two feet long from their leading to trailing edges, and at rest, they swept back like a delta-wing, enabling it to fit into a space of no more than a third to half as wide as its body length.

The gigantic moth-like creature moved into an opening, a kind of small glade between trees, and spread its wings to their full twenty-foot span, then flexed them, basking in the sun for a bit and drying its wings as it pumped them full of blood and shook out the wrinkles.

After about an hour of this leisurely business, it apparently decided to become more active. It began to beat its wings, faster and faster and faster, until they appeared as blurred as the wings of a hummingbird in flight.

This fanned the air around it at an ever more rapid rate, until it blew the forest-floor debris about. Several dead limbs broke off nearby trees, but instead of crashing to the ground they were blown away; a dead, half-rotted tree snapped some five feet off the ground and toppled to the forest floor several feet from the base of its trunk.

With a slight push of its furry, clawed legs, the giant creature took off, rose above the trees and surveyed the area with those big black, compound eyes, then headed for the nearby high-rise district.

* * *

The force of the creature's rapidly beating wings was akin to a powerful helicopter rotor, and as the creature flew and banked through the buildings, moving close for camouflage, windows were blown out or shattered, injuring people inside the buildings and on the street below.

One woman happened to be walking past a window in her company's office when it abruptly shattered, pelting her with glass shards. She cried out, flinging up her arms to shield her face from the broken glass...

...Just as the creature's wake washed through the room, sending papers, desk implements, chairs, and wastebaskets flying about, knocking over cubicle partitions, and wreaking havoc on the office.

"Brenda! LOOK OUT!" someone cried.

* * *

The powerful wind caught up the woman, and whipped her right through the opening where the window had been, before she knew what was happening.

Suddenly Brenda found herself in open air, her clothing flapping wildly around her, and feeling an odd, weightless sensation, even as someone in the distance shouted her name over the roar of the wind. She looked down...and suddenly realized she was falling.

I'm going to die, Brenda thought in horrified realization, seeing the sidewalk far below. *I'm going to die.*

She began to scream.

All the way down.

* * *

Officer Stacy Armand, the 9-1-1 dispatcher, took the first call.

"9-1-1, please state the nature of your emergency."

"There's a—a THING—flying around the buildin's, blowin' out windows, an' killin' people! Brenda just got blown out th' window an' fell to the sidewalk! An' we're on the TWENTY-SIXTH FLOOR!"

"Wait, calm down, please, and repeat. You say someone jumped from the twenty-sixth floor?"

"NO!" the caller yelled. "She got BLOWN OUT THE WINDOW, after it BROKE! There's a THING flyin' around down here, blowin' out windows on th' buildings! There's people on the sidewalks hit by big chunks of glass! One guy's bleedin' all over, an' I can see it from way up here!"

Armand stared blankly at her console for a moment, then continued.

"All right, you have an airborne object breaking windows among the buildings? And the debris injuring people on the sidewalks below?"

"YES! And then the wind from it sucked Brenda right out the busted window, an' she fell!"

"Is it an aircraft?"

"I dunno! I don't...don't THINK so...it looks like..." the caller broke off abruptly.

"What does it look like?"

"You'll think I'm nuts."

"No, I won't, I swear. What does it look like?"

"Like some giant butterfly! Like, right outta th' old 1950s movies!"

"A...butterfly?"

"YEAH! Or...or maybe a giant, I dunno, hummingbird? Its wings go so fast they're blurred!"

"All right. We have an emergency situation involving an unidentified flying object, falling debris, shattered windows, at least one person who has fallen from a broken window. Does that cover it? Do you have a fire?"

"No!" Just then, in the background, Armand heard an alarm sound. "Check that," the caller said, "I guess we do, now! Wonder if today can get any worse?"

"What is your location?"

"Northwest corner o' Columbus an' West 66th Street."

"Copy that. Columbus and West 66th, northwest corner. Dispatching police, fire, and paramedics momentarily. Are you on a cell phone, or a land line?"

"Cell."

"Good. Please follow evacuation orders, but stay on the line."

"Thanks!"

Armand switched communications loops.

"This is 9-1-1 dispatcher. We need 20th Precinct NYPD

response to the northwest corner of Columbus and West 66th Street. Recommend at least three units. We have reports of a drone in the area, damaging high-rise windows and injuring people on the streets below. We may also have had a jumper. Send fire and paramedics to the location, and be prepared for a high-rise fire."

"Dispatch, 20th copies. Units Adam-12, Adam-38, Adam-42, please respond to emergency."

"Adam-12, en route."

"Adam-42, on our way."

"Adam-38, rolling."

"Roger, Dispatch. FDNY Engine 44, Division 3, Ladder 25, Rescue 1, please respond."

"Engine 44, rolling."

"FDNY Division 3, rolling with all units."

"9-1-1 Dispatch, this is EMS; do you require ambulance service?"

"Affirmative, EMS. Unfortunately, at this time, I don't have a feel for how many injured there are. It sounds like there may be at least two dead..."

"Copy that, Dispatch. We'll get at least three units rolling."

"That's g—"

The phone rang. Armand switched comm loops.

"9-1-1 Dispatch. What is your emergency?"

"DEAH GOD! Wot IS this thing?!" the nigh-hysterical caller screamed. "We need help! Somethin' is floyin' around down heah next t' Central Park, shootin' at th' sides o' buildin's, bustin' out windahs, an' killin' people!"

"What is your location?" Armand asked...just as the phone rang again.

"Ssh, Stace, keep going, I've got it," the dispatcher at the next console said.

"Jus' down fr'm West 69th an' Central Pahk West; ya cahn't miss it," the caller said...as the switchboard lit up with emergency calls.

"...Got it," the dispatcher to Armand's right said. "243 West 70th. Sending paramedics and an ambulance."

"325 Amsterdam?" the dispatcher to her left commented. "Sending paramedics and an ambulance."

As the telephones continued to ring, the dispatchers rapidly became overloaded with requests for paramedics, ambulances, fire rescue, and police. The cause was reported to be anything from 'a drone shooting out windows' to 'one of those giant kaiju things like you see in the Japanese movies.'

"I think we might have us a terrorist attack under way," Armand's colleague to the right decided—just before taking yet another call.

Huh. Maybe. But it sure doesn't sound like it to me. I think maybe I better put in a call for some special backup, Armand concluded.

And dialed a very specific, and restricted, number.

* * *

"There's a WHAT?" Fox exclaimed, his Agency cell phone held to his ear.

"You heard me, sir," Armand's low voice said. "We've got a very serious situation, and it doesn't sound like it's from 'around here.' Either we've got a very unusual terror attack under way and ongoing, or this is in your jurisdiction. Regardless of which it is, we're probably going to need backup. Dispatch is already having to call in units from outside the Upper West Side to respond."

"Right," Fox said then. "Let me get my people on it, and we'll see what we can find out. If nothing else, maybe we can give you some subtle assistance."

"Believe me, that would be much appreciated right now, either way," Armand replied. "Like I said, we've already mobilized most of the PD and FD in the Upper West Side, and are starting to call in units from all around Manhattan. We've got serious casualties. Hell, we've got probable fatalities."

"All right, I'll get on it immediately. Fox out."

"Dispatch out."

Fox laid his phone on his desk and stared at it for a long moment, thinking. Then he thumbed a switch on his desktop.

"Lima here, Boss. Whatcha need?"

"Lima, get Crutch up here, please. As quickly as possible. And see if you can't get some video eyes on whatever the hell is buzzing Midtown Manhattan up through the Upper West Side, and parts of Central Park."

151

"On it, Boss."

* * *

As the hours passed all too swiftly, more and more odd, even mysterious, reports came in to New York's 9-1-1 Dispatch. It seemed that, in addition to a terror attack by a drone, there was a crime spree underway—car thieves were striking the Upper West Side, immediately west of Central Park.

"Well, it's really been going on for a few weeks now," Stacy noted. "It's just...there was a lull there, for a couple weeks over the holidays, and now it's ramped way up or something. I expect the chop shop is using the terror attack as a distraction to hit as many cars as they can."

"Like we weren't busy enough," a dispatcher coming in for the next shift complained.

"No shit," Armand agreed. "This has been the shift from hell. Fires, deaths, attacks on buildings, car thefts, you name it. And it doesn't look like slowing down, so get ready."

"The odd thing is," Armand's neighbor dispatcher, Betsy, noted, "they only want either electric or hybrid electric cars."

"Yeah," Joanne agreed. "That's...different. And they're only going after the batteries, according to all the feedback on the street that I've seen."

"Stop and think about it, though," Stacy said. "Other thieves go after copper an' aluminum an' stuff. Why not go after the...what is it...lithium?"

"Yeah, it's lithium," Joanne confirmed. "My boyfriend works on 'em sometimes. Have they found the latest one yet?"

"Not ye—" Betsy began, as a radio call came in to her station. "Stand by, guys," she tossed off, as she answered. "NYPD Dispatcher. Yes, go ahead, unit 12. You did? Let's see; that was..." she grabbed a clipboard and leafed through it, "that was the stolen Beemer I-3, right? It—wait. What? You're kidding. Oh, da— uh, that's not good. No. The owner's NOT gonna like THAT. Yeah, I'll pass it up the chain. Dispatch out."

"What's up?" Stacy asked, as Joanne leaned forward to listen.

"Adam-12 just found that stolen BMW electric," Betsy told them. "They're not sure what's going on, but it was torn to pieces."

"Well, chop shops tend not to care what shape the car's in afterward," Joanne observed with a shrug.

"No, Joanne, you don't get it," Betsy countered. "I don't mean chopped up. I mean TORN up. Like, shredded. Adam-12 said the METAL looked like the jaws of life had been used on it, all over the car," she added. "The only thing missing was the battery pack."

The three dispatchers stared at each other.

* * *

Within the next ten minutes, five more reports came in to Dispatch, all of electric or hybrid cars found ripped apart, with batteries missing...along with two more fires, six more buildings under attack, and three more known casualties.

"And only in the area where the drone is operating," Joanne noticed.

"Yeah, there's gotta be a connection," Betsy agreed. "You suppose they're using the batteries to power their drone or something?"

"Could be," Joanne decided. "What I'd like to know is, why rip the car up if all they want is the battery?"

"Hey, they're terrorists. They destroy stuff. It's what they do," Betsy observed.

"Okay. But HOW are they rippin' 'em up that bad?"

No one could answer that.

Chapter 6

"Yeah, Fox," Lima said, as he sat in the Director's office with Agent Crutch, the head of the Field Agents department. "There's a situation, all right. We've got at least two dead that I've been able to find out about so far—one woman got sucked out of a broken window and fell over twenty stories to her death, another guy basically got transfixed by a big shard of broken glass, and bled out on the sidewalk. There's a couple more that are pretty iffy; one had an entire pane of that 'shatterproof' glass land on top of 'im from over ten stories up, and another had a brick fall on his head."

"Damn," Crutch said, perturbed, as she and Fox both winced. "What's doing it, do we know yet?"

"Best I can tell, it's this thing," Lima said, tossing down the printout of an image.

"What the hell is that?" Crutch wanted to know. "It looks like a giant flying...wooly bear or something. A caterpillar with a built-in antigrav unit?"

"Close, Crutch," Fox said, studying it. "It looks like a giant moth, only the wings are moving so fast they're blurred. Look here." He pointed to the slight smudges on either side of the body of the creature. "Lima, have you or Bravo been able to identify this thing?"

"No, Fox, we haven't," Lima said. "It's evidently either rare, not from an Earth-like planet, or both. Nobody at Headquarters recognizes it. We've put out a call through the Offices and offworlders for anyone who can identify the thing to contact us at once."

"Good man."

"Huh," Crutch said, studying the photo. "So its wings are moving so fast you can barely see 'em..."

"Yeah, but they're there," Lima said. "Here. We actually managed to snag a video with a drone...before it attacked the drone." He handed the two his personal tablet, triggering the video to loop.

"Attacked it?!" Fox repeated, glancing at Lima, before looking over Crutch's shoulder at the slowed, enhanced image of the giant moth flying.

"Yeah," Lima confirmed. "Fortunately it was fairly basic Earth tech, or we'd have had to initiate the destruct mechanism. Our remote-sensing people found it—well, what was left of it—in the street, pretty much torn to pieces. Even the rechargeable battery had been cracked open; half the lithium electrolyte sludge stuff was gone, and the lithium cathode was completely gone. We dunno what happened to that."

"Odd," Crutch noted, puzzled.

"No shit, as Echo might say," Fox decided. "So...Crutch. Is this something you think your people can get eyes on, maybe take out?"

"I dunno, Fox," Crutch said, considering, while she studied the video snippet as it looped through the footage. "This thing is damn fast, and it seems pretty...strong. If it can tear apart a drone and crack open the battery case—which is my take on what happened, though I have no idea WHY—well, it's no slouch. I mean, we can try, but it's gonna be hard. And I'm not sure Alpha Line is gonna have any advantage over my people, advanced training or no; this thing ain't like anything I've ever seen before, an' I've got about as much experience as Echo on that shit."

"Do you think it's worth even trying?"

"Hey, we can try, sure," Crutch said with a shrug. "But I'd feel better if those personal force fields had ever gotten into production, so I can ensure all my people come home safe."

"I hear that one," Fox said with a sigh. "From what I've understood, it's just too much of a power drain to make 'em properly useful in the field. Never mind things like full-spectrum protection and the like. We need a breakthrough in the power pack technology to make it really useful."

"Yes, Omega's little incident with the Cortians demonstrated all that, eh?"

"It did, in spades. But Echo had already been testing some hand-helds. Unfortunately, the force shield itself nearly got him killed in a firefight."

"Oh yeah, I remember his after-action report on THAT

one," Crutch said with a wry chuckle. "That boy doesn't pull any punches, does he?"

"Not over something like that, no."

"Lima," Crutch said, turning to the younger man, "can you pop this video, and some of the photographic images, to my personal tablet?"

"Yes ma'am," Lima averred. "I can have it waiting for you by the time you get back to your office."

"Good. Do that. I'm going to head back and call an emergency department meeting, see if I can get a bunch of volunteers out in the field," she said. "If we can keep people out of harm's way, get some more intel on it, maybe even take it out, and do it FAST, we might be able to contain this mess."

"Exactly," Fox agreed. "Go, alter khaverte, and keep me posted."

"Gone," Crutch said, rising and heading out.

* * *

"Do we have any more information about what's going on in Manhattan?" Fox asked Lima then.

"Not a lot," Lima said. "There's a few other things going on that are interesting, though, and I can't think they're coincidences."

"Oh? Like what?"

"Like people gone missing," Lima ticked off fingers, "several fires in high-rises and a couple back alleys, and...you're gonna think I'm crazy...several of the newer style electric cars have been stolen and seriously vandalized—transported to another location, ripped apart, and the batteries gone missing."

"Huh? What does that have to do with anything?" Fox wondered, confused by the addendum.

"We're not sure," Lima said, "but given what the...well, Bravo and I've taken to calling it the 'mega moth'...what the mega moth apparently did to the drone, it made us wonder."

"Mm," Fox murmured, considering. Finally he came up for air. "Well, I don't have enough knowledge of the thing to figure out THAT conundrum, zun. Did you call Stacy Armand back, and find out if anything else was developing?"

"What, you mean the 9-1-1 dispatcher that immigrated to Earth from Kref?"

"The same. She's the one who notified me of this little situation. I gather the dispatch office is going nuts with all the calls."

"Yes sir, I called her back. She barely had time to talk, they had so many reports coming in. But I've already told you everything she was able to tell me, in what time she managed to talk."

"What's the general consensus of the NYPD on what's happening?"

"Terrorist attack of some sort."

"Right. That should work," Fox decided. "But it's definitely in our wheelhouse."

"Without doubt, sir."

"All right. I need you two working on finding out what the hell it is, and what its weaknesses are. Ping the Sciences department and get them working with you on that."

"Right, Boss."

"Good. Now go."

Lima went.

* * *

An hour later, yet another report of a stolen electric car came in. This one was high-end, a latest-model Porsche Taycan. It was found in a distant part of Central Park, in at least five main pieces and many smaller ones. The battery pack was found fully fifty feet away, cracked open, with the cathode and the electrolyte solution completely missing.

Unsurprisingly, the owner was not happy with the report.

* * *

"Bravo!" Fox called, as the younger agent scurried through the Core, nearly two hours after Lima had left the Director's office.

"Here, boss!"

Bravo looked up and immediately detoured up the ramp to Fox's office. As soon as he entered, Fox gestured to him to close the door, then take one of the visitor chairs.

"So. What does the Sciences department have for us on this 'mega moth,' as you two call it?"

"Nothing, Fox," Bravo said, shaking his head ruefully. "Chief Item says it's obviously an offworld creature, and some sort of exo-lep-something-or-other—giant offworld butterfly, I gathered it meant—but she says our butterfly insectoid expert, Agent Vinegar, is in the field on Flibitz, and out of reach of even our comm systems."

"And nobody else in the entire department has a clue?"

"No sir. And Item pinged the sciences departments of every Office and Station on the planet. AND called in the extraterrestrial experts. We got nothing."

"Mmph," Fox grumbled, stifling the multilingual curse he had been about to deliver.

"But," Bravo continued, "I might have something for you anyway."

"What?"

"We might have a handle on how this thing got here. In which case, we might be able to trace it back, figure out what it is, and how to kill it."

"Let's hear it," Fox demanded.

"You'll need to meet some people, first," Bravo said. "And that might take a little bit."

* * *

Two hours later, a small offworld family sat in Fox's office. It comprised a mother, father, a daughter of somewhat indeterminate age, and a toddler son. All four resembled nothing so much as giant koalas of various ages.

"Yes, Director Fox, I am afraid so," the male Kydeen sighed in response to his questions, then scowled at his elder child. "My daughter claims this is her...'pet.' I have no idea where she obtained it."

The Meechuub family hailed from Kydeen's capital city of Neeso, and had arrived on Earth just before Thanksgiving, coming in through Grand Central Station, downstairs. Sedeb Meechuub was the father, Zuugli Meechuub the mother. Andep was the younger of two children, a male, still being carried by his mother, and Deeruna was the elder child, a female.

"Would you like to explain to the Director, aclin?" Zuugli addressed her daughter.

"No," came the sullen response.

"WHAT did you say?!" Sedeb nearly erupted.

"Um...no, SIR?" Deeruna tried.

"Aclin cha, you will TELL Director Fox how you came by this...thing, or I swear upon the spear point of your great-great-great-great grandsire, you will be grounded for the rest of your natural life, and then some!" a fiercely angry Sedeb Meechuub ordered, and his daughter cringed, then sighed.

"It was supposed to be a science project for school," Deeruna admitted then. "There is a...I think you Earthers call it a 'science fair,' sir? So I contacted some researchers and asked for the egg. I had it incubating; I was going to hatch it and raise it through the larval stage to adult, then show it for the school science competition. But," she added, pouting and verging on what looked like tears to Fox, "somehow, the incubating case was lost after we arrived on Earth. I have been looking everywhere for it!"

"Youngling," Fox said, "do you have any idea how big it is, or how strong?"

"Oh, it is not that big," Deeruna declared, confident. "Maybe two or three pawspans across." She held up her paws to demonstrate.

"Two or three...? Child, its body is longer than you are tall!" Fox exclaimed, and the child gaped in shock. "Its wingspan is wider than thrice MY height! Its wings beat so fast they're barely visible, and it has blown out many windows in our buildings in Manhattan! At least one person was blown out one of those broken windows to her death, and several other people have died after being hit by the debris falling to the streets!"

"Oh, great Maker," Zuugli Meechuub breathed, shocked. "There are humans dead?"

"I now have a tally of four so far, with several times that number in hospital, and at least twice, maybe three times, that number missing," Fox said, reining in his anger. "This is a VERY serious situation. And so far, this...this...we are calling it a 'mega moth,' because we have not yet identified what it IS...my agents have NOT been able to catch it, because it is so fast."

A horrified Deeruna sat down hard on the floor of Fox's office.

"That...that big?" she whispered. "It...it has killed humans?"

"It has," Fox averred, gentling his voice, as he began

understanding that this was, indeed, a child, probably not even an adolescent of her species, and very immature despite her obvious intelligence. "We have an extremely serious problem here, youngling. Your little 'pet'...isn't. Not at all."

"I...I did not think it would...it cannot be!" she cried, upset. "The egg was only this big!" She measured out a large pawful of air. "How did it become that big? Are you SURE it is Dukeer, my science project?"

"What's a 'Dukeer'?" Fox wondered.

"That is evidently what she has named it," Sedeb explained. "It means 'little flying one' in our language. It does not sound to be very little."

"No, it's not," Fox agreed. "Here. Let me play some video of it in flight for you."

He had the adults sit in visitor chairs, facing the wall screens; Deeruna remained where she was on the floor, and the baby stayed in its mother's arms.

* * *

"Oh no," Deeruna whispered, when the drone footage ended. "No, no, no. It wasn't supposed to be like THAT."

"What did you think it would be, young one?" her father demanded. "Is that what I think it is?"

"I...I..." Deeruna stammered, eyes wide with fear and distress. "Y-yes."

"Dear Maker, aclin cha!" Zuugli addressed her daughter. "You have put us all at risk! Do you realize what might have happened to US? And now it is loose among the humans, and it is KILLING!"

Deeruna let out a wail, and began to weep.

* * *

"I gather you recognize this creature?" Fox asked the father.

"After a fashion, yes," Sedeb Meechuub admitted. "I am not a specialist, but I have seen a couple of documentaries and nature shows which mention it, in recent lunations. I cannot think of the name of the thing, but I know who to contact on Kydeen..."

"You can help us deal with it, then?"

"No, no, I have no expertise on this," Sedeb told Fox, while his wife attempted to calm their nigh-hysterical daughter. "I think, unless you intend to charge us, that perhaps we should return home and attempt to contact the appropriate people there to provide you the help you need. That is all I can think of to do; we can be of no help to you here."

"Your daughter has made a serious error," Fox pointed out. "She may not be of the age of majority yet—"

"Oh, she is what you would term 'elementary school' age, Lord Levy. She has more than two of our decades before she reaches her majority."

"I see," Fox said, considering, "but she is still responsible for several deaths—perhaps more, by the time we can end this."

"I know," Sedeb sighed, bleak. "She is a good girl, and very smart, much smarter than her age would indicate, but she is too impulsive; she simply does not think things through before she acts. We have tried and tried to teach her the necessity, but it is like water off a gluub's back. And now it has gone as badly as it is possible to go, I think. I fear this will not end well for us, no matter what we do...especially for her. I will provide you our contact information, and we will make ourselves available for... whatever you decide is right and just." He paused. "Unless you prefer we stay here, in your custody. School resumes soon, and Deeruna should be going back, but under the circumstances, we will do as you say, sir."

"No; the rest of you had nothing to do with this," Fox said. "And you have another child to care for. Go home, but leave your contact information with me, check through the appropriate channels between here and your home, THEN check in with the PGLEIA Office nearest your home, and I will get in touch once we have matters under control. And if you CAN send us some expert assistance from your homeworld, that would be greatly appreciated."

"I do not know that I can, but I will try," Sedeb said. "This is a creature I have heard of, but about which our people know little."

"That...does not sound good," Fox decided.

"No, I do not think it is."

"Stay in touch."

"Yes sir, Lord Levy."

* * *

161

After the family left, Fox called 'the Boys.'

"You got us," Lima said over the closed intercom system. "Whatcha need, Fox?"

"I need for you two to track down the agent who handled customs for the Meechuub family, right before Thanksgiving," Fox ordered.

"All over it, Boss," Bravo said. "I expect we can have that information to you inside half an hour, unless there's something weird in the shift records."

"Good. Thank you, kinder."

"Does..." Bravo began, then silenced as Lima shushed him.

"Does what, zun?"

"Noth-nothing, Fox."

"Come now, Bravo, you know me better than that," Fox said in a soft voice. "When have I ever chastised you for curiosity, or wanting to know something?"

"This...was gonna be a little more than that, Fox," Lima said. "He's twelve kinds of red right now, because what he was thinking popped out, only it isn't our place..."

"Ask me anyway."

"You called us 'kinder,'" Bravo pointed out in a small voice. "I was wondering if..." He broke off, and Fox heard the swallow, even over the intercom system. "...If that meant we were part of that whole family thing you and Alpha One and Alpha Two an' all have..."

"Ah," Fox said with a smile. "Well, as far as I am concerned, you would be. But as I am old enough to be your grandfather... hell, I'm old enough to be Alpha One's GREAT-grandfather! I shudder to think what that would make me to you two!" They all laughed. "Anyway, I may be the patriarch, but it was Omega who actually put it together, though I don't think she quite meant to. And given the ages, I'm not sure where you'd fit. Maybe exceptionally young sons, maybe GRANDsons, in which case, you'd need to get either Alpha One or Two to 'adopt' you..." He shrugged. "You're all but brothers, anyhow."

"We are, that," Lima agreed, the smile audible in his voice. "Would...do you think Echo and Omega would object to, um, to our approaching 'em...?"

"Provided they aren't busy, I don't think they'd mind," Fox

decided, "although I'm not sure how they'd react! Neither of 'em is really quite old enough to be the parent of a teenager, let alone a twentysomething. Eh," Fox added, "given the crazy ages in this meshuginah family we have, I'm not sure it would matter! In any case, if you do, tell them I suggested it."

"Thanks, Fox," Bravo said, sounding shy. "Just knowing that YOU think of us as family...means worlds."

"Good," Fox said, growing gruff. "Now, off with you, and see if you can't dig up the customs agent for me. I want to know how such a thing as this...mega moth...got through our system to begin with."

"Ooo. Good point," Lima said. "We'll try to set a speed record, Fox. The Boys out."

"Fox out."

* * *

Half an hour later, Agent Actor sat in Fox's office.

"No sir, I honestly don't recall," Actor noted, biting her lip. "That was a month and a half ago. And we get a LOT of people coming through Customs."

"Fair enough," Fox decided. "Is there anything about that situation, as I've described it, that would send up a red flag for you?"

"Not particularly, no sir," Actor said. "Pets are allowed, and it's not uncommon for students to come through with projects in work. I'm sure that there would have been the appropriate paperwork..."

"Yes, my administrative assistants have already uncovered that," Fox admitted. "Nothing was flagged on it, either." He ticked off fingers. "The 'pet' and 'school project' boxes were both checked, as well as the 'safe' block."

"Right. Now, obviously, if it was a dangerous animal, like a gurfdin or the like, that would be different," Actor noted. "But if I can't find anything like it on the 'proscribed dangerous animal' lists, then I let it go through."

"Mm. Well, given we don't even seem to know what the thing IS, I suppose that means it wouldn't be on the lists," Fox pondered. "Which might say something about the procedures we're using, but there it is. I think we'll be looking into changing things in future, though."

"Wait. You're saying that this...thing...that's attacking the Upper West Side...that's killed people...THAT was this kid's science project? Her pet?" Actor asked, as the puzzle pieces suddenly fell into place for her. "And it came through on my watch?"

"That, unfortunately, is exactly what I'm saying, tekhter," Fox sighed. "How it grew from an egg that fit easily in a standard luggage-sized case, to THAT thing, I don't know. But evidently it did, because the child identified it. SHE didn't know it would get that big, either, and her father is the only being I've yet found that seems to vaguely recognize it, and even he couldn't put a name to the thing. None of my contacts on Kydeen recognize it, either."

"Ohhh, that's bad." Actor bit her lips, forehead puckering in distress.

"It isn't good."

"I am SO sorry," Actor murmured, shocked and horrified. "I...if I'd known..."

"No, I understand that now," Fox said, holding up a staying hand and keeping his voice low and calm. "You are not in any trouble. But I may want your help to work with your department chief to change protocols, so we can prevent this happening again."

"You have it, sir! Just yell, and I'll be there."

"Thank you, Actor. Dismissed," Fox said, nodding and waving toward the door.

"Thank you, sir. I'll get with my supervisor and let her know what happened."

"That's appreciated; I need to figure out how to round up this meshuge riz zhuk."

And she was gone.

Fox sighed.

* * *

Two days after the creature's first appearance, something strange happened.

A sudden, unearthly shriek, sounding of pain and frustration, echoed through the high rises of the Upper West Side of Manhattan.

Then a loud whirring sounded in the streets, and the mega

moth flew wildly among the buildings, running into several structures, and diving at vehicles on the streets below. At least half a dozen people were seriously injured from falling debris as windows shattered, and more than fifty sustained minor injuries. Four vehicular accidents resulted from the 'dive-bombing drone,' as drivers instinctively swerved to avoid it. Pedestrians fled for the nearest door or subway entrance.

When this circumstance continued into the next day with only a slight decrease in the 'terrorist' activity overnight, local officials called for a temporary evacuation of the Upper West Side from West 54th up to 96th Street, and from Central Park and 7th Avenue to West End.

And very few of the denizens complained.

* * *

"That tears it," Fox declared, on the intercom to Lima. "I need Zarnix, Uncle, Crutch, Alpha Two, and Alpha Four in my office right away."

"On it, boss-daddy," Lima responded.

Fox snorted despite himself.

* * *

Five minutes later, the requested agents sat or stood in Fox's office.

"...So we have a situation," Fox said. "We were given a heads-up when this moth-creature first appeared, several days ago, by one of 'our' people in the city 9-1-1 Dispatch office, and when the city officials put out the call to evacuate the area, Peter Johannsen, who knows about us, and is responsible for contacting us when City jurisdiction overlaps ours, placed a coded phrase into the announcement: 'We are calling for help from elsewhere.'" That means the city leaders are asking for Agency help on this thing, because they've realized it's in our jurisdiction, and they know they don't have the ability to handle it; they're hoping we do."

"Have we identified it yet?" Crutch wondered.

"Yes and no," Fox replied. "We don't know exactly what it is, but we now know that it comes from the Kydeen system, and it's evidently a rare creature on their world, because I haven't been able to dig up any real information on it, even going through my PGLEIA contacts on Kydeen."

165

"What are its weaknesses?" Golf asked.

"We don't know," Fox said.

"What are its stats?" India asked.

"Body, approximately one and a half meters long and half a meter in diameter at the broadest point," Fox enumerated, "wingspan somewhere between four and a half, and six, meters. Weight, unknown. Wingbeat frequency when in motion is roughly sixty beats per second, or around about hummingbird speeds...but much bigger. And that makes it dangerous, in itself—the winds and turbulence in its wake are substantial, enough to blow out windows and the like. The thing has to have some serious nourishment to sustain that, according to our Sciences people, but as yet, we don't know what it eats."

"Shit," Romeo grumbled. "Ain't none 'o this good."

"No, it is not," Fox agreed with a sigh. "But we have to do something to help. And it IS in our jurisdiction. At least we have the means to handle it; the city, not so much. There have been casualties, people."

Everyone winced.

"So," Fox continued, "I am calling a Maximum General Emergency. Do I hear any counter arguments to that call?"

The office was silent.

"Good. Well, NOT good, but you know what I mean. Now, since it flies, I think we are going to use morphed cars in flight mode, but make sure to use full cloaking, kinder," Fox determined. "Just because a given area is evacuated doesn't mean it is 100% free of people. And there will still be people in the buildings on the periphery of the evacuated area."

"Not to mention, if they're evacuating, a lot of the island will be closed off," India reminded. "Flight is probably gonna be the only way to get on or off Manhattan Island."

"Point, and yes," Fox confirmed.

"How fast do we need t' be on this?" Romeo wondered.

"How fast can we get set up to roll?" Fox asked. "We need to be out there, locating and containing this thing, as fast as we can."

"Well," Romeo said, thinking fast, "if y'r assistants c'n do some o' th' logistical coordination, I expect we can be set up and sendin' out search teams in about two hours, maybe three."

"Good. I was planning on pulling them in anyway, for that very purpose."

"But what about the locals?" Uncle, head of the Security department, wondered.

"Once I got that coded message from Johannsen, I pinged him," Fox explained. "It's being cleared; he knows what we need, and he told his colleagues he's arranged to bring in a special classified military unit of considerable strength. Which... is true, after a fashion, I suppose. We're more a paramilitary unit, I think, depending on your definition, but still. We'll have all the space we need, without anyone getting in the way, or asking questions we don't want."

"Let's go, then," Crutch decreed.

* * *

Roughly two and a half hours later, Fox, Lima, and Bravo were coordinating efforts at Columbus Circle, while Romeo commanded Alpha Line—all Alpha Line Agents not already assigned to missions were being called into the effort, usually heading up teams of field agents, commanded by Crutch, in a search of the area. Uncle's Security people were sent out to locate the incident sites, along with a number of Sciences department personnel, in an effort to glean information on what, exactly, was happening, and why.

But fifteen minutes after they sent out the first search team, Fox and Lima took an emergency call.

"BREAK BREAK! THIS IS ALPHA TWO ROMEO! WE HAVE AGENTS DOWN! REPEAT, AGENTS DOWN! I'M CALLING AN ALPHA-TWO-ORANGE! WE NEED MEDICS AT THE CORNER OF 80TH AND AMSTERDAM! REPEAT, 80TH AND AMSTERDAM!"

"Romeo, this is Fox," the Director said into his cell phone; he had placed it into what the agents referred to as 'walkie-talkie' mode. "What happened, zun?"

"Th' damn moth thingie came through at speed, Fox," Romeo replied. "Hard by Berta an' Carmen's car. The wake sent 'em spinnin', and they went down!"

"Damnation!" Fox exclaimed. "How bad?"

"I dunno yet, Fox," Romeo answered. "That's why I called th' medics in. Couple cars in my team have set down beside

167

'em, an' are goin' t' see about 'em while the rest of us set up a defensive perimeter in the air, t' watch f'r the thing comin' back."

"Copy that," Fox said. "Be careful, zun. All of you."

"We are," Romeo said. "Hell, I had a damn hard time o' handlin' th' Lexus my own self. Th' way those wings move, it leaves a helluva wake."

"Mm. Perhaps I need to look at a heavier vehicle, then," Fox considered.

"That might be a good idea, Fox," India said then. "I was glad to be strapped in, because we bucked all over the sky, even though Romeo had it controlled."

"Ugh. All right; I'll get on that right away. Any more word on the downed team?"

"They's gettin' outta their car, Fox," Romeo said. "They look t' be mostly okay, though they's bein' helped by th' others. Kinda wobbly...not that I can blame 'em."

"Are the medics there yet?"

"Th' medical airskimmer just put down, boss-man. Zebra's on th' ball; she's loadin' 'em into th' airskimmer. But we's gonna need a wrecker or somethin' t' get their car back t' Headquarters."

"Very good. All teams, this is Director Fox. Bring it back to the staging center; we need heavier vehicles than morphed automobiles."

"Roger that," came the responses from many voices.

* * *

"...Yes, Chocolate, I think we're going to need airskimmers to attempt to wrangle it," Fox decided, as he called the vehicle hangar master on his cell. "That way, we can use the solid hologram capabilities and disguise them as...helicopters or something. Play around with it and see what works best, then use it. We're already working on setting up a staging area at Columbus Circle and expanding into the corner of Central Park, so we can use the major streets as 'runways' of sorts. You'll just have to be careful to avoid the high rises along the periphery."

"All right, Fox, I can do that," Chocolate responded. The sound of key clacks was audible in the background. "The

Vehicle Maintenance sub-department saw the Maximum General Emergency and called in the troops, just in case, so we can cover this. I'll start ferrying airskimmers to you in about five minutes. And...there. Orders issued; the first flight of airskimmers will lift off in five, and arrive at the staging area a couple of minutes later. And I have a retrieval vehicle en route to fetch the damaged car, as well."

"Copy that, Chocolate; thank you," Fox said.

"No problem, Fox. The dispatcher that gave you the heads-up about this thing is a close friend of mine. I'd sorta been expecting something like this, so I gave my line management the down-low about it. We're ready."

"Vunderlekh! Very, very good! I'll keep you posted as we need repair and maintenance. Fox out."

"Chocolate out."

* * *

The sun was setting as the agents brought back their specialized automobiles, landing in the area to the northwest of Columbus Circle; meanwhile, the vehicle hangar personnel brought in airskimmers south of Central Park. As the field agents landed, they left their cars running, and ran to Bravo or Lima, who assigned airskimmers to them if they were standard field agents; Alpha Line Agents already had designated skimmers, and they ingressed as their skimmers arrived.

Meanwhile, additional personnel debarked the arriving skimmers and began setting up lights along the streets being used as runways; as twilight transitioned to night, it would enable the agents in the air to see the staging area better, and align their craft for proper landings as needed. Then they reported to 'the Boys' to provide traffic assistance and direction.

Bravo and Lima smoothly coordinated the entire operation, as field agents transferred to airskimmers, and the hangar personnel bringing in skimmers left in the discarded autos, returning them to their proper locations in the vehicle hangar.

Within minutes, agents were back on the search in airskimmers, as the autos were cleared from the staging area.

* * *

But it didn't make a lot of difference. While the airskimmers weren't as vulnerable as the cars had been, the mega moth's wake still caused the heavier vehicles to drift. And they simply were not fast enough to keep up with the giant creature's erratic movements. They could outstrip it on a straight stretch, but the mega moth was far more maneuverable. And much more difficult to spot in the lower light levels.

"This ain't workin,' Fox," Romeo told the Director when Alpha Two and their search team came back so the agents could take a brief break. "We find it, it zooms up, dodges all of us, and heads off. Then we just gotta find it all over again."

"He's right, Boss," Golf agreed. "My team has located it three times already. We just can't figure out how to catch or kill it. And believe me, we've tried."

"We've spotted it four times," India averred. "Same thing."

"And we've had to rescue no less than five Sciences personnel, that I'm aware of," Crutch grumbled. "They get out there, investigating things, and lose track of what's around 'em. One poor devil actually fell off a roof when the mega moth came by."

"It blew him off?" Fox wondered.

"Oh HELL no," Crutch fussed. "He was tryin' to get a better look at it, and the damn fool leaned too far."

"Farkakte," Fox murmured, raking his hand down his face. "LIMA!"

Lima's head, tilted sideways, popped around an airskimmer. "Yeah, boss?"

"New orders: ALL Sciences personnel are to report back to Headquarters immediately. I DO NOT want them stirring their too-curious noses outside the damn building, on pain of confinement to quarters."

"Uh...okay," Lima said, puzzled. "What am I gonna give Chief Item as a rationale?"

"Failure to maintain situational awareness, leading to my field agents having to rescue them instead of taking down the mega moth," Fox retorted.

"Got it," Lima said, pulling his cell phone. "I'll have 'em off the streets in about fifteen, and load 'em into a skimmer for a quick shuttle back to HQ."

"Good man."

"So what are we gonna do, Fox?" India asked. "We need

more info on this thing. We're essentially operating in the dark, because we don't know what it is, and we don't know what its weaknesses are."

"Well, I know a bit more than that, now," Fox said. "I've has a communiqué from my counterpart on Kydeen. It's some sort of creature from Kydeen's moon Zheen, which has an environment somewhat akin to Venus, and therefore is relatively unexplored. But that's about ALL I know. All ANYone seems to know."

"But that'll mean it's tough as shoe leather," Easy commented.

"Yeah. And now we don't have any science people out there to learn anything more," India noted.

"Honey, they weren't really learning much," Crutch told the younger woman. "Curious cats, sure. But whenever I'd ask one what they'd figured out about it, every last one said they'd have to go back to Headquarters and study the data, and maybe they could tell me in a few days."

"The city will be toast in a few days," Easy observed. Just then, they were interrupted by a call that annunciated on all their phones at once.

"BREAK BREAK! CODE RED! WE HAVE A FIRE ON THE TWELFTH FLOOR OF 364 AMSTERDAM AVENUE! REPEAT, WE HAVE A FIRE ON THE TWELFTH FLOOR OF 364 AMSTERDAM AVENUE! ALL FIELD TEAMS, PLEASE PREP FOR FIRE SUPPRESSION!"

"BRAVO!" Fox bellowed.

"Already on it, Fox!" Bravo called back. "Breaking out those new fire suppression grenades that we got in the trade agreement, and loading them on the skimmers!"

"Toast is right," Romeo grumbled.

"We need Meg," India decided. "And Echo, too. Meg's got the scientific expertise; she might be able to shed some light on this beastie for us. And Echo's got the gray matter, too; he can help her logic through it. Never mind his experience. I've seen those two brainstorming together before. It's definitely synergistic."

"I hate to, though," Fox said. "I'm not sure they're ready yet."

"They don't have to go up doing rescues and entrapment attempts and stuff," India pointed out. "But I'm betting that brain of Meg's will make something of this, especially in concert with Echo. And both of them already know how to remain situationally aware, and conduct themselves in the field."

"She got a point, Fox," Romeo agreed.

Fox sighed deeply. Then he gestured to Alpha Two.

"Come with me," he said. "The rest of you, get back in the air and scout this mess out. See if you can figure out what's started that fire, because it isn't the first, based on what Stacy Armand told me at the beginning of this meshuge mess."

* * *

Fox turned and walked away from the group, Alpha Two following. Once they were out of earshot of the others, he turned.

"India, pull your cell phone and see if you can get Zebra and Zarnix on a joint call," he ordered, "then put it in speaker mode. I want to see if we have a united front in Medical about whether or not to call in Alpha One."

India immediately extracted her cell from her Suit jacket pocket.

* * *

"No, if you need their noggins, I can sure see it, honey," Zebra confirmed. "I just don't wanna see 'em joining in with the rest of their department on this thing. Echo's not ready physically, and I dunno if either of 'em are ready mentally."

"I must concur," Zarnix added. "Though I think Echo is doing rather nicely physically, based on what I saw at Christmas. Half the time he did not even think to use his cane."

"True," India agreed. "I think he's a lot closer than we might be aware. He might be back up to speed already."

"But now is NOT the time to find out," Zebra argued.

"Well, I have to agree with that," Fox concluded. "But you don't mind if I bring them in and have them look things over, see if they can help us figure out a weakness we can exploit?"

"Given what I am seeing of the injuries already coming into the medlab, Fox, I think the faster we can deal with this creature, the better," Zarnix said. "So yes—I recommend calling them in."

"I concur," Zebra added.

Fox nodded, then turned to Romeo.

"Send an Alpha Line Alert to Alpha One," he decreed.

* * *

Echo and Omega had just gotten ready for bed, and were sitting in front of the windows overlooking the ocean, eating a bedtime snack, when their cell phones, already on the charger stands in the bedroom, let out high-volume tocsins. The pair stared at each other.

"Uh-oh," Omega murmured.

"Yeah," Echo said.

They both leaped up and ran for the bedroom.

* * *

"I'm glad you had Wardrobe load a couple spare Suits for each of us into the closets at the beach house, Ace," Omega said, as Echo flew the Corvette back toward New York. "At least this time, we had a chance to deal with the extra food."

"Yeah, that new stasis freezer will handle it until we can get back," Echo agreed. "And the stuff that was too far gone will feed the landscaping nicely."

"I don't think I've ever packed that much, that fast," Omega considered. "Do we know what's going down?"

"Not any more than what the alert said, baby. Something is attacking New York, it's not from around here, nobody knows WHAT it is, and they need your scientific expertise."

"But they got a whole SCIENCE department!" Omega expostulated. "Why do they need us, in particular? I don't mind, I just don't get it."

"If something's actively attacking, the Sciences guys don't have the field training needed to stay safe, if they go out investigating," Echo said. "I'm betting somebody got into hot water, and hadda have their asses saved by a field team that could have been better served going after the attacker."

"Mm. Good point," Omega pondered. "Well, I guess we'll know once we get back to Headquarters."

"Yeah, but it's gonna take us a little longer than normal, even flooring it. I have express instructions to veer way out to sea, and approach Brooklyn over Jamaica Bay."

"Whoa."

"Yeah."

* * *

Upon arriving at Headquarters, Alpha One headed straight for the Core and the Alpha Line Room. None of Alpha Line awaited them, but Item, head of the Sciences department, waited there.

"No, they're all out in the field, with Fox, the Field department, and as much of Security as could be spared," she explained. "And I have to head back to my office to keep on top of Fox's inquiries, but we were hoping the pair of you, being more well-traveled than most of my department, might recognize some of this."

She handed Echo a large manila envelope. "If either of you come up with anything important, Fox left instructions for you to ping him and me both, and we'll try to figure out how to make it work strategically."

"Right," Omega said, as Echo opened the folder and Item headed for the door.

"Whoa," Echo said, as an electronic tablet, and nearly a dozen 8"x10" still photos, dumped onto his desk. "Where should we start?"

"I'm betting something important is on the tablet," Omega said, "video of the whatsit or something. And then the photos are enlarged stills to show detail. So check the tablet first."

"Okay."

* * *

"Ohhh, shit," Echo murmured, as soon as he got a look at the imagery and video of the mega moth.

"That's...wild," Omega agreed.

"It is, that. And I think it's gonna be bad news, if it isn't already."

"Yeah. But I just don't get it," Omega said, looking at the information displayed on the tablet, in a small legend pop-up in the corner of the screen; it depicted known data about the creature, largely length, width, wingbeat frequency, and speed.

"Huh? What don't you get, baby?" Echo wondered.

"It looks almost exactly like a giant lepidopteran—a kind of mega-moth, or something, like Lima and Bravo keep calling it," she said. "But how the hell is it even alive, let alone flying?"

"I...still don't understand where you're going with that."

"The reason why most insects don't get really huge, even in the fossil record," Omega explained, "is because they don't have internal skeletons like we do, they have exoskeletons—armor plate, effectively. That's pretty much what supports their bodies, too, just like our internal skeletons do for us. Past a certain size, though, that armor plate gets so big and heavy that the insect risks being crushed by the weight of its own exoskeleton! Never mind the weight it would have to lift in order to fly!"

"Oh," Echo said, as the light dawned. "I see. Well, if this were really an Earth-based organism, you'd be right, Meg. But it's not. I'm pretty sure it's a Zheen exoheteroc—Zheen is one of the moons of Kydeen; think, um, think a kind of cross between Venus and Titan."

"Oh, so large-ish, hot, dense toxic atmosphere, an' very definitely not Earth-like?"

"Exactly. And yes, the 'mega moth' has a partial exoskeleton of sorts, but that's for protection, not support. The thing has an internal skeleton, more or less like Earth mammals, sorta, but different in design. Think...think kind of like birds, with lightweight, almost hollow bones, then muscle, then lightweight plate armor over various body parts, like the legs, that would tend to be more vulnerable otherwise."

"And the 'fur' over their bodies?" Omega queried, fascinated. "On Earth species, that's a kind of chitinous scale, like on the wings, but shaped differently..."

"It's similar," Echo recalled, "but I don't know that it's the same as what we know as chitin. It's all a really lightweight polymer, like chitin is, but even lighter, and without the need for the outer 'armor plate' to be quite so thick. In fact, if I remember right..." Echo did a quick search on the tablet they had been using to look at the video and photo imagery of the creature, "Yeah, here it is—the polymer is a silicon polymer instead of a carbon polymer, and kind of similar to...maybe one of the harder micas? It's a two-dimensional polymer, in that it tends to form plates or sheets, with some interlinks between the sheets in the third dimension that strengthens the overall structure. But those interlinks are long, like small chains themselves, so the sheets are farther apart, with plenty of open space between, which helps make it lighter than even a mica." He shook his head. "I'd have to show you. I remember the picture in the course book, but it's hard to describe, and I'm not finding it in my Agency web search. And other than a dead one that got dissected—which I was present to see, and is the only reason I have a clue what the hell this thing is—and a couple of brief, *in situ* videos of one in the wild—which, given Zheen's murky atmosphere, weren't real clear—we don't really know a lot more about 'em than that. Like I said, Zheen is kind of somewhere between Titan and Venus, and there are no known sapient species that can live on it...and precious few drones or probes that can survive long, either. So it's really hard to obtain reliable information about the surface, or anything that DOES live on it. Know what I mean?"

"Yeah, I get what you're saying," Omega decided, thinking. "Hm. That says interesting things for its biochemistry, I think, maybe. I'm a little surprised that it can live in an oxygen atmosphere."

"Oh. It doesn't have lungs, as such," Echo explained, double-checking the article he had found, "'cause they dissected it, like I said, and there weren't any. It seems to rely exclusively on what it eats for all nutrients, including oxidizing agents."

"Mm. So our air isn't toxic to it, as such."

"I wouldn't think so, no. It has a mouth, and a proboscis-like tongue-thing, and a recognizable digestive tract, so it apparently eats sort of like we'd expect of lepidopterans on Earth. I got no idea about how it excretes or whatever, or even if it does; it might be able to make almost complete use of the materials it takes in. It just has a very different sort of plate armor on it."

"So...it's not as heavy as an Earth insect of that size would be?"

"Not hardly, no," Echo confirmed. "That said, you still probably don't want to be downwind of one, because the wings are big and powerful; the leading edge is reinforced with bone, the muscles are strong, and the majority of the wing is that mica-like polymer, so they're damn strong, they beat fast, and generate a lot of lift. Think...not quite hummingbird speed, but plenty fast. And a damn sight bigger." He pointed. "You need to go back and look at that video of it flying, then realize that it's been slowed down by around fifty to a hundred times."

"Whoa. It's flapping that fast?"

"Every bit. And like I said, you don't wanna be close by."

"Meaning...?"

"Meaning, unless you're hanging onto something, you'll probably get blown 'ass over teakettle,' as Sir Mike likes to say," Echo elaborated. "And anything not tied down, or otherwise firmly fixed in place, will go flying. And anything too fragile is probably gonna be smashed up."

"Oh shit," Omega breathed, eyes widening. "The skyscraper windows. The ones that broke out and fell on people."

"Exactly," Echo said, grim. "Never mind the woman that 'fell' out."

"Damn," Omega whispered.

* * *

"Did you see this, Meg?" Echo asked, flipping through the images taken from the various damage sites. "Look. Dead dog on the rooftop. And according to the annotation, the penthouse owner didn't own a dog."

"That's interesting," Omega noted, taking the photo he handed her. "I don't know of any eagles resident in the Big Apple. And while there are hawks, I don't think a hawk is big enough to carry a dog—" she broke off and stared at the photo. "That's...that's not a, a lap dog," she stammered. "That's a freakin' Labrador retriever!"

"Well, it was," Echo noted with a sigh. "I guess something ate it."

"But, but, they aren't small," Omega protested, flabbergasted. "There's not an eagle on Earth that can carry THAT!"

"No," Echo mused. "Which might mean we need to reconsider how much like an Earth moth this thing really is."

"What do you mean?" Omega wondered.

"Don't some of 'em eat the liquids that carcasses exude?"

"Ugh. But yeah, you're right. So our giant moth-thing may

177

have been feeding on what was left of it," Omega decided. "I'm still wondering how it got up there, though."

"Meg, baby, you're missing what's right under your nose," Echo pointed out.

"Huh?"

"What if the giant moth-thing ITSELF is what brought it up there?"

"Hm. Well," she considered, "it's big enough, I guess. And it has claws on its legs—insect-like, but claws for all that. If it can generate the kinds of lift from the wingbeats that you're talking about, I guess it could find a dead dog and carry it someplace where it could feed off it in peace..."

"Or it killed it and took it there to feed," Echo pointed out.

"Oh, come on, hon," Omega said, an incredulous grin forming on her face. "How the hell is a giant moth gonna kill something? What kinda weapon does it even have to DO that?"

"I dunno," Echo admitted. "But no more than we know about the things, I think it's a possibility we don't need to exclude just 'cause Earth moths can't."

Omega screwed up her face, thinking.

"Yeah, okay," she said. "Fair enough. We consider that a possibility, but unless I see some evidence to support it, it's unlikely."

"Hey," Echo said, "does that image say WHERE it was?"

Omega flipped over the photo and looked at the information written on the back of the photographic paper.

"Yeah, 63 West 67th Street," she read off. "Near the corner with Columbus."

* * *

"...No. Absolutely not," Fox's voice on Echo's cell phone decreed; the head of Alpha Line had it set in speaker mode so both he and his partner could hear and speak. "Alpha One is on MEDICAL LEAVE. I called the two of you in here to use your experience and expertise to help us devise a plan to defeat this creature, not to go out in the field."

"C'mon, Fox," Echo grumbled. "If you want us to give you our best evaluations, we gotta at least SEE the damn thing."

"I know you two better than that," came the retort. "You see it, you'll be after it in nothing flat. NO. You'll

178

work from Headquarters, in conjunction with the Sciences department. I have all of Alpha Line out here already, under Romeo's command, along with every field agent and security agent in the city, trying both to corral this thing and to run rescue operations, as well as clandestinely helping the city's emergency responders with all the rest of it."

"How's it going?" Omega wondered, keeping her voice gentle.

"Not as well as I'd like, tekhter," Fox confessed then. "We've had some fires start in some of the high-rises, though we're not quite sure why; some of them are pretty severe, and we are concerned that the buildings may collapse. We do NOT need another Twin Towers disaster in the city. So. We have offworld firefighting foam grenades, expressly intended for these sorts of situations, but we're having trouble getting them to the right places to extinguish the fires, oddly enough. And dodging the backwash from the giant insect zooming around out there isn't helping. Which is why we need YOU two to figure out how to take it down...and preferably, out."

"Are we sure it's not sentient?" Omega asked.

"According to the family that inadvertently brought it to Earth, no, it's not," Fox replied.

"Wait, wait, wait," Echo interrupted. "Brought it to Earth? We know who?"

"Yes, and yes, though it doesn't help much," Fox sighed. "A Kydeen family name of Meechuub came to Earth along about Thanksgiving, and their precocious elder child, who looks like being a scientist one of these days but is still in what we'd consider elementary school, had somehow managed to get hold of an egg. I have NO IDEA how...but I would really love to know. She wanted to study it for a school project, but I don't think she had any real understanding of how BIG the thing was gonna get. Anyway, the child brought the thing to Earth in her luggage, unbeknownst to the parents, who knew she was working on a school science project, just not WHAT. And somewhere between landing on Earth and arriving at their hotel, the damn case was lost. For rather over a month."

"And mega moth rampages are the result," Echo finished for him.

"Exactly."

"So...we need to contact Kydeen to obtain more info," Omega tried.

"No; been there, tried that," Fox admitted. "As soon as the family came in and told us what had happened—which only occurred when the child recognized 'her' creature on the evening news, and apparently went ballistic with excitement—I contacted the main Kydeen Division Office and asked for assistance. It turns out that this thing is not far off being their version of the Loch Ness Monster; they don't really know any more about it than we do, because it's such a rare creature— from their moon, which some of their commercial exploration teams are only just now beginning to develop sufficient technology to explore, and nobody ELSE even comes close. I have no idea how this child got her hands on it...though I rather suspect that whoever she obtained it from thinks she's older, more experienced, and has a few more degrees, than she has, or is, in reality."

"I've encountered some kids capable of that, so yeah, I can believe it," Echo said. "And I'm betting that's exactly what happened. 'We need somebody knowledgeable to tell us what we've got. Put out a call,' and the kid managed to gin up a reasonable facsimile of an offer...which the exploration team then took her up on."

"Okay, wait. Do we really wanna be killing it, then, if it's so rare?" Omega pressed.

"We don't know if it's rare on Zheen, baby," Echo pointed out. "Just that it's rare for anybody to SEE one, because of the environment on Zheen."

"Well, but still..."

"Look, Omega, if you can figure out a way to stop it wiping out half the city without killing it, I'll listen," Fox declared, mildly exasperated. "But if you saw what this thing is doing out here..."

"Which was kinda the point of this call," Echo noted.

There was a long sigh on the other end of the line, then silence for several moments.

"All right, under ONE CONDITION," Fox finally responded.

"And that is?"

"You OBSERVE ONLY, and DO NOT get involved in any operations."

"Done," Omega declared. "Let's go, Ace."

"Wait," Fox's voice said, just before Echo broke the comm.

"Yeah, Fox?" he said, holding it back up so they could hear.

"How had you planned to get over here?"

"Take the 'Vette up, I thought."

"No. It's too small, and too light. If that thing so much as flies by you, you're apt to auger in before you have time to blink."

"That bad?" Echo wondered.

"That bad."

"What do you suggest, then?" Omega wondered.

"Mm. Okay, take the 'Vette, but don't morph and go airborne. I want you to drive it here, ON THE STREET, in standard automobile form, to the staging center in Central Park, and I'll figure something out by the time you arrive. Well, you'll have to take it airborne over the river; they've closed all the bridges and tunnels, just like they did for 9-11. But stay low, just above the water, and make sure you've activated all the cloaking it's got when you do. Try to stay well away from anything that may be airborne in the area, or you could end up in the drink." He paused, then added, "Oh, and put your cell phones in emergency continuous mode."

"You mean what the field agents call 'walkie-talkie mode'?" Echo verified.

"The same. I need you hearing and relaying any emergency calls you may encounter while you're out there."

"Roger that. Be there shortly, Fox," Echo said, and this time he did deactivate the phone. But he also pulled up the settings and made the adjustments Fox had ordered, even as Omega did the same thing to hers. Then they slipped them back into their pockets.

"All right. Let's go," Omega said.

Chapter 7

By the time they arrived on Manhattan Island, it was morning. At the first site they had set out to explore, there was little to see. But nearby—some fifteen feet away from the place the creature had been seen—Echo spotted something odd about an entryway.

Hey baby, he thought at her, as he walked over and studied the door. *Come have a look at this.*

"What is it, Ace?" Omega wondered, wandering over.

"Look." He pointed at the wooden door frame.

"Wow," Omega murmured, puzzled, studying the door frame. "It looks like it's...melted, or something."

"Yeah. Now, I'd expect splintering, or maybe gnawing, or just possibly insect tunneling. But wood doesn't...melt."

"Not normally, no," his partner agreed. "Though it doesn't look melted so much as...maybe dissolved?"

"Yeah, maybe," Echo decided, pulling his cell, triggering the camera app, and taking several photos. "It's really strange, though."

"It is, that. Anything else?"

"Not that I can see. There's some charring next to it, though. See here?" He pointed.

"Yup, and that's weird in itself," Omega decided. "Any acid or whatnot that would dissolve the cellulose should be aqueous—containing water. Which also should mean that it would be wet, and NOT burn or char."

"Exactly." Echo narrowed his eyes, thinking. "Eh. I got nothin'."

"Well, let's keep looking. Maybe we'll eventually hit the clue that makes it all make sense."

"On to the next site, then?"

"Yeah, let's go."

* * *

"Hey, Echo," Omega said, as they headed between sites they were investigating. "Have a look at the emergency graphic display on your phone."

Their next stop was 63 West 67th Street, the site where the dead dog had been located on the rooftop, but they were traveling to Columbus from Broadway on foot to avoid the risk of encountering the exoheteroc, and had yet to quite reach 67th, being still in the previous block.

Echo toggled the screen on his phone, then whistled.

"We got...that looks like maybe a day care...?" he decided. "And a fire in the upper stories of the building. Shit. Yeah, there it is. The 'Little Sprouts Day Care Center'? I thought this was an office building..."

"It is," Omega noted, "but having a day care in the same building with your office is a convenience that some companies like to offer. It's easy to get to, so you bring your kid with you to work and drop it off on the way to your own office, then pick 'em up on the way home. No detours, no running late because the traffic around the day care was wonked. Generally easier for everybody all around."

"Then why didn't the parents grab the kids on the way out? It doesn't look like there's many people still inside the building," Echo pointed out, "and the ones that are, are all coming out over there." He pointed at the main entrance, where a steady stream of people emerged.

"We couldn't! They wouldn't let us!" one of the distraught evacuees, close enough to hear, replied. "They said that the day care workers would bring 'em out, and we weren't to go there, just evacuate ourselves. What they don't realize is that one of the day care workers is disabled; I mean, he can get around on his feet, but several flights of stairs? Maybe carrying kids? I dunno; they might not be ABLE to get them out without help! At least not all of 'em!"

"Well, shit," Echo grumbled. "Why aren't y'all evacuated already?"

"We're a financial firm," another said. "The other companies in the building ARE gone, but we've been trying frantically to lock down our records and transfer 'em to the Philly office, just in case things go really south here. We finished fifteen minutes ago, and now we're clearing the area as fast as we can, on account of the fire that started in the upper levels."

"Mm," Omega murmured, noncommittal.

"All right, you gotta do what you gotta do," Echo decided. "Is there anything else you can tell us that might let us know what to do about the day care?"

"They're on the fourth floor," the first evacuee noted. "If you take the northeast stairwell, you'll come out at the end of the hall. They've got the fourth suite on the right."

"Got it," Omega noted...just as the swift beat of wings could be heard.

"EVERYBODY GET UNDER COVER!" Echo shouted, as the mega moth came down the street.

* * *

As everyone dived for shelter, inside or beside parked cars, sheltered in doorways, or huddled under bus stop canopies—not the best cover if something heavy fell, but better than nothing—the mega moth shot down the street overhead. Several windows shattered in its wake, taken out by the atmospheric overpressure of the powerful, swift wingbeats, and the glass came clattering to the sidewalk, fortunately missing everyone.

But one poor woman, frightened into immobility, stood where she was on the sidewalk, staring at the creature in horror.

Abruptly the mega moth diverted its flight, diving right at the paralyzed woman.

"Oh no, you don't!" Echo exclaimed, darting out from the doorway overhang where he and Omega sheltered, pulling his blaster as he went. He fired—

—But missed, as the mega moth, spotting him, dodged with hummingbird-like agility. Out of the corner of his eye, the Agent thought he saw something fly into a broken window, some twenty-five feet up and perhaps fifty feet farther down the sidewalk, but he was trying to draw a bead on what amounted to that giant hummingbird in terms of flight profile, and ignored it.

"Dammit!" he exclaimed as it darted away again, before he could even line up on it.

Two blocks to the northeast, it banked around a corner and was gone.

"All right!" Omega called, as Echo quickly holstered his blaster, and the woman's friends came running to help her.

"Everybody out of here! Head home as fast as you can. If your car isn't here already, DO NOT TAKE THE STREETS. Take the subway; that, um, drone is too big to get through the doors into the tunnels. You can come back for your cars once we've made it safe for people."

At that, several of the cars revved their engines, pulled out of parking spaces with squealing tires, and headed down the street...away from the place where the mega moth was last seen.

"Are you the police? FBI?" one of the building's evacuees queried Omega, skeptical. Echo whipped out his *carte noir*, which promptly morphed.

"Plainclothes police, sir," he noted. "We're part of the special team responding to this terrorist threat. But yes, we're working with the FBI on the case."

"Is that what it is?" another whispered. "Terrorists? They're trying to take down buildings with a bombing drone?"

"Pretty much," Omega said, lying through her teeth. "As you can see, it's pretty high-tech, and we're having to use some special equipment in our efforts to take it down."

"What about our children?" the first evacuee cried, upset. "They're still in there!"

"But you're not doing them any good by staying out here and making yourselves targets," Echo pointed out. "We know they're there, and we'll see to getting them evacuated. Please follow my partner's instructions and head for the subway," he added, pointing down the street in the opposite direction from the one the mega moth had taken. "The Lincoln Center station is only right around the corner and down the street to Broadway, in front of Julliard. GO! We'll take care of this, and see that your children get home safe."

Several of the worried parents scanned the pair up and down, as the workers without children obeyed orders, most jogging down the street at speed, others outrightly sprinting. Finally, the parents joined the exodus, somewhat reluctant, but understanding that they did their children no good by getting killed when broken glass and other dangerous debris fell on them.

"Okay, that takes care of that," Omega murmured, when

the last person was out of earshot. "Now we gotta see that day care gets out safely."

"Lemme see if I can raise Fox on the horn and get somebody over here to help." Echo pulled out his cell phone.

"That works," Omega decided.

* * *

But Echo couldn't raise Fox, nor could he reach Lima or Bravo, who had been pinch-hitting whenever Fox was handling something.

"And that argues for them ALL being too damn busy to answer the call," he pointed out.

"Yeah, but we got smoke coming from an upper floor in that building, so there IS a fire," Omega noted, pointing. "But it should just be a case of helping them lead the kids out, 'cause the smoke is well above their floor level, according to my display. They'll have to come down the stairs, granted, but still."

"Well, if I try to do anything, what with my leg, Medical will pitch thirty-eight kinds of unholy fits," Echo grumbled. "So...what? We stay here and keep trying to raise Fox?"

"Nope. YOU stay here and keep trying to raise Fox," Omega said with a grin. "MY legs are fine, and I can climb stairs with the best of 'em. So I'll go in and lead 'em out. It shouldn't take long," she told him.

"I do NOT like that," Echo griped. "No backup? I should be beside you, baby..."

"Well, you can't, until the medlab releases you."

"You shouldn't, either. You're recovering from a bad case of PTSD."

"Yeah, but this isn't gonna trigger that. I'm just gonna run up the stairs and help 'em get out," Omega said. "It's gonna be dark inside with the emergency lighting, and they probably just need somebody to come show 'em the way to get down to the ground." She shrugged. "It looks like the fire is well above 'em, and not that bad. The sprinkler and fire suppression systems will probably have it out by the time I can get to 'em."

"And I probably don't need to be running multiple flights of stairs until I'm given the all-clear," Echo sighed. "Never mind that I've been working hard on the stair-climber in the gym, AND running the stairs at the beach house..."

"Patience, honey," Omega soothed. "Now, are you okay with me doing this, or not?"

"I don't guess I have a lotta choice," Echo admitted. "There's kids in there. Besides, you're probably right; they just need help finding the exit with a buncha kids in tow, and it'll take you maybe fifteen, twenty minutes to do it. So...go ahead and go."

"All right. I'm gone," she said, leaning up to kiss him, then turning and heading for the door at a steady jog.

* * *

The day care center was on the fourth floor of the high-rise, so it was only a few flights up, and Omega had no problems reaching it. She would have been less than enthusiastic about anything above the tenth floor, but would have gone, just the same; she and Echo trained for long-distance exertion that was much more demanding than a few flights of stairs. Fortunately, while the emergency lighting was on and the warning lights still flashed, the siren had gone silent. She jogged up three flights of the northeast stairs, then went through the firewall door into the fourth floor.

She headed down the hall for the fourth door to her right; it was glass, and the sign painted on it read, *Little Sprouts Day Care Center*. Several small pre-schoolers could be seen just inside. Omega opened the door and entered.

"Hello!" she called, "is anyone in charge here?" and a woman with a ginger complexion and smiling hazel eyes behind eyeglasses emerged from a small office.

"Hi! Are you here to help us evacuate?" she asked.

"Yes, I am," a cheerful Omega verified.

"Oh, good," the other woman said, her relief obvious. "DAVE! We have help now!"

A man on a mobility scooter came out of another room, a group of children following him. He had a look of alertness in the brown eyes, which lit up when he saw Omega, and a smile spread beneath his brown salt-and-pepper beard.

"THERE we go!" he declared. "And it's an Agent, no less. We're in good hands, Joanna."

"Really?" Joanna replied, glancing between Dave and

Omega. "Are you an Agent?"

"Um," Omega began, thinking fast.

"Joanna, did you introduce us?" Dave asked. "Security, you know."

"Oh!" Joanna exclaimed. "No, I didn't. I'm Joanna Weiner, and this is my husband, Dave. We, um, we're...'not from around here.' We moved here from Agra'Thoth on Tu'Ven about two years ago, and work at the day care now."

"Aha," Omega said with a broad grin. "Well, yes I am, then. So let's—"

Just then, the alarms sounded again.

"Oh dear," Joanna said, concerned.

* * *

Echo? Omega called through the nd't'lq. *The fire alarm just went off again. Can you tell what's going on?*

Yeah, baby, I think so, came his reply. *There's smoke coming out of a broken window on the third floor, as of just a couple of minutes ago. Looks like we got another fire going in there. I dunno how it started, but it's spreading fast, I think.*

Well, shit. Whereabouts? Relative to my position, I mean. I turned on the beacon app on my phone when I came in, so you should be able to find me, if there's not too much interference from the buildings.

Oh, okay, good. Hang on and I'll try to tell you. After a few moments he 'spoke' again. *Near as I can tell, it's one floor below you, and to your northeast.*

Mm. That could be bad. Stand by one.

Standing by.

* * *

Omega glanced at the Weiners, who were watching her with puzzled expressions.

"Were you communicating with someone?" Dave Weiner asked the female Agent.

"Yeah, I was talking with my partner," Omega noted. "Agent Echo."

"ECHO?! And you said you're Omega?? Oh, damn, Joanna!" he exclaimed. "Do you know who this is? This is half of the Alpha One team!"

"You're kidding!" Joanna Weiner said, shocked. "The top

team in the whole Division? The very first full-on, officially married partnership in the Agency?"

"I dunno about all that," Omega said, flushing, "but we're the Alpha One team, yeah. And um, yeah, we're married now."

"We're in good hands, then," Joanna noted, just as the blaring alarm silenced. "Oh, that's better. My head was starting to hurt!"

"And that explains something else, too," Dave said. "Substantial, credible rumor has it that the two of you have a Deltiri nd't'lq bond, now?"

"We do," Omega admitted. "And yes, that's how I was speaking to him just now. We don't talk publicly about it a lot, just so it's not widespread knowledge, but we don't keep it a secret, either. Though I'd appreciate it if y'all kept it to yourselves, just the same. So stand by a sec, here; based on something he told me, I need to check on something."

"Of course we'll keep it private," Dave determined. "It's your business, after all."

"And we're not going anywhere until you take us," Joanna agreed.

* * *

Omega opened the door to the day care and stepped into the hall.

Hm, she thought, looking around. *It's hotter out here than it was. And...* she glanced down the hall, toward the door into the stairwell she had ascended. Heat waves could be seen rising from the floor; the carpeting was beginning to discolor. *Oh, that's SO not good. We need to move fast, but not go that way. Hey, Echo?*

Yeah?

It's bad. It's right down from us, and the carpet's just before igniting in the hall. I gotta move fast, here.

Do what you need to. Yell if you need me to send help.

You got help to send, yet?

Nope. But I'll do what needs doing.

Okay.

She turned and entered the day care.

* * *

"Okay, we gotta go, and go NOW," she told the Weiners.

"Get the kids together and be prepared to follow me."

"What's wrong?" Dave wondered. "I thought the big danger was in an upper floor; we were just waiting for someone to show us how to get the kids out of here."

"It was. It's not now," Omega said. "There's another fire on the floor below us. It's down that way," she pointed, "and the carpeting in the hall on THIS floor is starting to smolder."

"Oh shit," Dave murmured under his breath, so the children would not hear. "We DO need to go."

"Kids!" Joanna called. "Come gather around me, please."

There was the sound of a small stampede, and more than a dozen preschoolers came running to cluster around her.

"There we go," she said with a smile. "We need to go with this nice lady. This is, um, Ms. Omega, and she's going to show us the way out. I need you to stay close, because there may be a fire in the building, and we want to get you all out safe and to your mommies and daddies."

There was a frightened murmur.

"Hi, y'all," Omega said then, with her brightest smile. "Everything's okay, but we need to go now, all right? All that y'all have to do is to follow me, and I'll get you out. I promise."

The murmuring changed from frightened to eager.

"Okay, kids," Dave said, "follow Ms. Omega, and we'll follow you."

Joanna held the door, and Omega, like a black-clad pied piper, led a line of small children into the hall, turning right, away from the fire.

* * *

"Okay," Omega said, pulling up an app on her cell phone. "So...to get to the other exit stairwell, we have to go through the building's atrium?"

"Around it," Joanna noted; she and Dave had gotten the children to form a double line, so she was riding herd only a couple of feet behind Omega, and Dave brought up the rear, a few feet behind that. "It's all balconies overlooking the atrium on this level."

"Mm...all right, I see," Omega said. "So tell me, Mr. Weiner—"

"Please call me Dave," he said.

"And I'm Joanna," his wife added.

"Okay." She threw a smile over her shoulder. "Tell me, Dave, can you walk without that scooter?"

"I can, but not really far, because it hurts," he explained. "I was in a spac-er, an aircraft crash a few years back, and it left me with some long-term injuries."

"Can you take a couple of flights of stairs?"

"Not...really. Not any more."

"How are we gonna get you down the stairs, then? The elevators aren't a good plan, with a fire upstairs...and we need to get out, as quick as we can, before something starts to give way..."

"Oh, the stairs are not an issue," Dave said with a grin, tapping the control bar of the scooter. "This came here with me from back home."

"Ah. It's a floater?" Omega wondered, letting the mischief show in her eyes as she glanced back.

"Bingo," Dave said. "With a bit of camo tech, if you get me."

"I do," Omega confirmed. "So you can manage the stairs?"

"Not a problem."

"Could you, say, go out the window and float to the ground? Maybe with a couple of small passengers? If we could use it as a shuttle, it would be faster," she considered.

"No, I can't do that," Dave admitted. "It isn't designed for it, and the manual that I got with it indicated that the field is structured for the weight distribution it has right now, with a passenger in the seat..." He shook his head. "I can, and have, managed to carry one child in my lap, but that's as much as it'll withstand. And it has a max height of about a foot off the floor, and that's built in. Try to exceed the limits, and it automatically shuts down. I guess they didn't want somebody flying around in the thing, when it isn't made for that and doesn't have the instrumentation to do it safely..."

"But then how does it handle stairs?" Omega wondered.

"Oh, I have to set the mode," Dave explained. "It reads the height of the next step, and adjusts the field to accommodate IT, not the previous step. So it'll handle most stairs fairly readily. But no. I can't do what you suggest. It would drop like a rock, and probably overbalance and pitch us all out, while it was at it. Assuming it didn't just shut down before dropping like a rock. And still pitch us out."

"Well, drat," Omega grumbled, careful to use an expression that would be safe around the young children. "Let me think, here."

"It won't be a problem, trust me," Dave reiterated. "We're only on the fourth floor. It'll follow you all down three flights of stairs without any issues."

"You're sure?"

"I'm positive."

But that turned out not to be the problem.

* * *

When they got to the southwest stairwell, there was considerable burning debris two landings down, sending copious smoke up the stairwell, and making it impossible to pass the second floor.

"Oh great," Joanna Wiener grumbled. "Those idiots on the twelfth floor insisted on storing spare furniture and files on the landings despite fire marshal regs, and NOW look what we've got."

"Looks like one of the upper fire doors failed," Omega observed, craning her neck to look upward, even as more burning debris fell past the door through which they watched.

"More likely, somebody left it open," Dave Weiner explained in disgust. "Like Joanna said, some of the companies that leased space in this building liked to hire idiots who defied fire codes."

"And any other rules they could find to break," Joanna added.

"Mm," Omega murmured, pulling out her cell phone once more. "If I had my regular equipment with me, I could probably handle this, but I don't; I've been on...holiday leave...and got called back in for the emergency. Oh well. Lemme see if there are any other easy routes down."

"There aren't," Joanna Weiner noted, worried. "There IS another stairwell, but it's an internal one, and only intended to connect to certain suites within the building. It doesn't have a ground-floor exit at all."

"Crud," Omega grumbled, shoving her phone back into her pocket. "This might be harder than a simple evacuation, after all."

"What do you want to do?" Dave asked. Omega shrugged.

"We go up," she declared. "We can't go down, and we can't stay here. Maybe we can find a floor in between the fires where we can break out a window, and some of my people can bring a craft by and get us out...before the building's structure heads south." She turned to Joanna. "Where's this other stairwell?"

"This way," Joanna Weiner said, waving, as she headed back the way they had come.

* * *

As they passed back through the atrium, Omega paused by the railing.

"Hang on, guys," she said, reaching over the rail and hauling up a bright red pennant, about a foot and a half wide but around eight or ten feet long. "Help me get this thing pulled back and rolled up."

"But...why?" Joanna wondered, as she moved to help.

"Attention," Omega said with a grin, as she pulled out a knife and cut the cords attaching it to the spindles of the railing. "Good. Now let's roll it up so it'll be easier to carry."

"Here," Dave said. "Put it in the basket on El Carrito."

"El what?" Omega wondered, handing the rolled red cloth to the male.

"El Carrito," he repeated, grinning widely, as he plopped the rolled cloth into the basket. "About a year after we arrived here, we took a trip to Mexico. The locals liked my little go-cart, and that's what they called it!"

"Ha!" Omega exclaimed, as a titter ran through the children. "The little cart!"

"Exactly!" Dave said, grinning even wider.

"Come on, guys, we need to go," Joanna urged.

They went.

* * *

In the third stairwell, since it was intended as a connector rather than a route out of the building, only certain floors were accessible. They climbed up to the next exit, which turned out to be the eighth floor, but as soon as Omega entered one of the offices, she shook her head.

"No, this won't do," she said. "This floor has support struts across all the windows; they block too much of the windows. We can't get out here."

"Keep going up?" Dave wondered.

"Keep going up," Omega confirmed.

They re-entered the stairwell.

* * *

"We're going da wong way," one anxious little one murmured, as they climbed. "We need to go DOWN to get out."

"We can't go down, Suzy," Joanna said. "There's fire down there."

"Dere's fire up DERE, too!" Suzy said, pointing up the stairwell. "We can't get out, can we, Mrs. Joanna?"

"It's going to be hard, sweetie."

"...Are we gonna die?"

At that query, Omega stopped, then turned and sat down on one of the steps.

"Suzy?" she called. "Come here, honey."

Suzy came to her. The little girl was about four, perhaps five, though slightly built, with long brown hair pulled back in a ponytail, and hazel eyes. Her forehead was puckered with worry, and her eyes held unshed tears. Omega put her arms around the little girl and pulled her into her own chest.

"Now listen," she said, loud enough for the other children to hear, as they clustered around the pair. "I know you're scared, but I have friends who have some really cool gadgets they can use to reach us, no matter how high up we have to go. But I have to find a place where the windows are open enough for them TO reach us. So I need you to trust me, and I need you to stay with me."

"But I'm tired," she almost whispered. "We climbed a lotta stairs, Ms. 'Mega."

"Then I'll carry you," Omega said. "Mrs. Joanna and I can't carry all of you at once, but we can let you take turns and rest a few minutes."

"I think, if I sit one of them in my lap, I can fool El Carrito into letting me carry someone for a few minutes," Dave offered.

"There we go," Omega said. "Can you handle that, Suzy?"

"Awen't you scared?" Suzy wondered.

"No, Suzy, I'm not," Omega told her, calm.

"Why not?!"

"Because my husband is outside the building, waiting for me," Omega explained, "and he'll see to it that our friends get us out, and probably help them to do it. And he never lets me down."

"Never?"

"Never ever."

"Okay, let's go, den."

Omega picked up Suzy, setting her on one hip. Joanna picked up another child, a wee two-year-old boy, and handed him to Omega, who set the child on the other hip. Another child went into Dave's lap, and Joanna took a fourth.

They resumed climbing the stairs, with eleven more children following close.

* * *

Meg? came the familiar mental voice as Omega climbed. *Where are you, baby? Did y'all come out on the other side of the building or something?*

No, Ace, Omega replied. *I'm afraid things got a lot more complicated. Evidently the fire on the higher floors got into the other stairwell, and people were keeping shit on the landings against codes...which is also probably how the fire got into the stairwell, since that was SUPPOSED to be one of the firewalled exits. Anyway, flaming debris was falling down the stairwell; a bunch had fallen on the landing two floors below us, and it was really too dangerous to try to get out that way, what with all of the stuff on fire falling around us, even if it hadn't blocked the landing. If I had my usual gear with me, I could probably have taken care of it, but...I don't.*

Oh shit. So where ARE you?

There's a third stairwell, Omega explained. *It isn't an escape route, it's a link between office suites, so it doesn't even have doors to every floor, just about every seventh one or something; it's a little weird, but who knows what the architects were thinking. I believe we're above the tenth floor now, but the eighth floor doesn't have clear windows. I need you to contact*

195

Fox as soon as you can, and get him to send something capable of hovering next to an open window that we can climb into with a bunch of kids in tow.

Damn. Okay, baby, I'll see how fast I can raise him.

Thanks, hon.

No problem, sweetheart. Be careful, baby.

You know what YOUR reply is to that, Ace.

Yup. 'Always.'

Right. Me, too.

Okay. Fair 'nuff.

* * *

In the end, they wound up on the fifteenth floor. They could not go any farther, because the original fire was only a few floors above them, with bits of debris beginning to fall down the stairwell, and smoke from the fire below was collecting in the higher floors anyway. Omega ducked into the corridor, then swiftly checked the nearest offices to verify that the windows were clear.

"Okay, this'll work," she said as she came back to the stairway door, where the others waited. "Come on, let's go in here and see about getting out."

Omega stepped onto the landing and held the door as the children, led by Joanna, entered the corridor. Dave, in El Carrito, brought up the rear, and Omega pulled the door open wider as he eased onto the landing and straightened El Carrito, then aimed for the doorway.

But just as he got across the threshold, a loud groan sounded from somewhere up the stairwell, followed by an odd, metallic *ping-pop!* sound. Omega glanced up, her eyes widening, then lunged for the door herself.

She didn't quite make it.

* * *

A sudden clatter and clang sounded from above, and an entire landing, the metal structure having failed in the heat of the fire several floors above, crashed down in pieces. Omega lunged for the doorway, but masonry came down with the rest of the debris, wedging the door open and caroming off her lower leg. Suddenly she was on the floor, sprawled across the threshold, her legs pinned down by bent metal as pieces of concrete and cinder block pelted the landing.

"Uhn," she groaned, when the racket ceased. "Ow ow ow."

"Oh wow!" Dave exclaimed, as Joanna gave a shocked cry. "Are you okay, Omega?"

"I dunno, I—oh shi-uh, shoot," Omega said then. "The landing just wobbled under me..."

"Oh no! Then we gotta get you out NOW!" Dave Weiner exclaimed. "How bad are your legs?"

"I dunno; I think they're reasonably intact," Omega decided. "I'm just pinned down by the weight."

"Is it burning you? Is it hot?"

"Not too bad, no. And my Suit protects me from most of that, if you understand me."

"Right. Joanna, we're gonna make extra use of this banner," Dave decreed, pulling it out of El Carrito's basket and unfurling it.

"How?" Joanna wondered, as Dave commenced tying one end to one of the handles of the scooter.

"Like this," he said, and ran El Carrito as close to Omega as he could get without hitting her...and without crossing the threshold onto the landing. "Oh damn; I can feel the floor sagging! Help her get it under her arms and around her back, then give me the free end. Stand back, kids; I'm gonna need some room for this."

The children immediately scurried back several tens of feet, as Suzy fussed and rode herd on them, in order to allow 'our Ms. 'Mega' to be rescued without the Weiners having to mind them.

"Right," Omega said, "I see what you're gonna do, but whatever you do, stay well inside the threshold. I don't know if the landing will support any more weight. It's starting to give rather alarmingly now."

"Never mind the flaming pieces that are starting to fall down," Joanna noted.

"Yeah. We really need to hurry," Dave decreed. "The flooring near the threshold isn't as stable as I'd like, either. When it goes, we need to not be anywhere close."

Within moments, the banner—which was a relatively heavyweight, embroidered silk, though designed to drape and flutter in the breeze—was under Omega's arms, wrapped around her back, and both ends tied off to Dave Weiner's scooter handles. He shifted El Carrito into reverse and eased up the throttle, giving it power, until Omega began to slide out from under the debris. She grunted, and he eased back, but she waved him off, rotating her hand to indicate he should go faster.

"Hurry!" she exclaimed. "It's gonna go any second."

"If I redline it, are you gonna lose a leg or something?" he asked.

"No, everything's sliding, I just still can't get out on my own," Omega replied. "I can't get enough leverage with my arms to pull myself out yet. But the landing is sagging worse by the moment."

So Weiner maxxed out the throttle, and Omega slid across the threshold and into the corridor...

...Just as the landing began to give way entirely.

"GO!" Omega cried. "Joanna, GET THE KIDS DOWN THE HALL! Dave, haul ass!"

They did. Moments later, the whole door frame had joined the cacophony falling down the stairwell, and the end of the corridor yawned into the opening.

But their entire group was halfway down the corridor, safe.

* * *

"Are you okay?" Joanna said, helping Omega get free of the banner, as Dave began rolling it up again.

"I dunno," Omega admitted, sitting up and rubbing her ankle. "This foot and leg hurt a lot."

"Can you stand?"

"Lemme see."

Omega planted her good foot firmly on the floor, pushing up on one arm, then performed a one-legged reverse squat, pressing up on the good leg, until she was upright. Joanna Weiner stood close, steadying her, and Omega gratefully put a hand on her shoulder to help steady herself as she rose, until she could put the other foot on the floor.

But as soon as she attempted to put weight on it, the ankle tried to buckle, and she stifled a cry of pain.

"Whu-oh," Dave remarked, watching. "That doesn't look

good."

"It feels worse, trust me," Omega said with a grimace, as she hung onto Joanna's shoulder for dear life, keeping the bad foot off the floor. "Suzy, honey, can you and a couple of your friends do something for me?"

"What, Ms. 'Mega?" Suzy said, scampering over to stand before the wounded Agent.

"Can you go into that room there, where I left the door open, find one of those rolling desk chairs, and push it in here? I can sit in it and roll where we need to go."

"We gots it, Ms. 'Mega!" Suzy declared, and she and two friends ran through the door, coming back moments later with the requested chair.

"Good," Omega said with a smile. "Thank you, Suzy and Friends."

"You're welcome, Ms. 'Mega," came the chorused response.

"Now, Suzy, I want you to lead the kids into that same room," Omega said, "right beside Mr. Dave. Mrs. Joanna, could you help by pushing me into the room, too? We'll need to close and brace the door behind us," Omega added.

"Sure thing, Omega," Joanna agreed, as Dave—and Suzy—led the children into the office suite.

* * *

Ace? Omega called through the nd't'lq. *Honey, can you hear me?*

I'm right here, baby, came the immediate reply. *I gather you had to carry some kids? Has something happened? I picked up that you got a hell of an adrenaline surge just a bit ago...*

Yeah, something has happened. There was a partial collapse in the stairwell we were going up, just as we were leaving it. One of the higher landings, up by the fire, collapsed onto the landing we were just getting off, and it collapsed, too—and took the doorframe, part of the wall, and the end of the corridor with it. AND it's starting to set this floor on fire, what with flaming debris falling down and drifting into the corridor through the big hole it left. We closed the door to this office suite, but there's no firewall here; it's not gonna last long. We need to get out of here, and fast.

199

Oh shit. HOW fast? Immediately? 'Cause I got nothin' here. I haven't been able to raise Fox, OR Lima or Bravo. Not yet.

No, not immediately, but inside twenty minutes maybe, half an hour max, would be really good now.

Okay, lemme see if I can't call something up more directly.

All right. We're on the fifteenth floor, and should be on your side of the building.

Got it.

* * *

"Oh shit," Echo repeated the murmur aloud, once he understood the situation. "That ain't good. At. All. And me sidelined medically." He pulled out his cell phone and keyed it in walkie-talkie mode. "Break-break. This is Agent Echo. I have an emergency situation. Repeat, Agent Echo has an emergency situation."

"What's up, Echo? You did it, didn't you?" Fox's voice responded, sounding vaguely annoyed. "You walked into a rescue."

"No, Fox, I didn't. But Meg did; we didn't have any choice. There's a day care center in one of these buildings that has a fire on the upper level, and they needed help negotiating their way out. We're talking little bitty kids, here, and I gather only two caregivers for 'em, and one of those handicapped. We didn't think it would be any big deal, just go in and show 'em the way down a few flights of stairs with no elevators, but then she found out the guy was in a mobility scooter, and THEN the new fire started on a LOWER level, and..."

"Oh damnation," Fox muttered. "I see, now. A simple lend-a-hand turned into an emergency."

"Right. Worse, I think Meg's hurt. She hasn't said anything, but I'm picking up that she's in pain. Nobody wants ME going in there, so I need an agent to come pluck 'em off the fifteenth floor, I think it is."

"Where are you, zun?"

"Mm," Echo spun, looking for street signs, "West 66th and Amsterdam."

"Fox," a female voice entered the comm, "this is Crutch. I'm about a block away from him, and I just finished tossing a couple foam bombs into a building over here. I'll go help out."

"Thank you, meyn khaverte."

Thank God, Echo thought in relief. *Crutch to the rescue, 'cause Echo ain't allowed to.*

* * *

Moments later, Crutch came in on a hoverpod and landed beside Echo, as he stood on the sidewalk on a deserted street; after broken window shards and fragments of masonry had injured dozens and killed several in only a couple of days, the streets had mostly cleared of pedestrians...and most vehicles, as well.

West Midtown and Hell's Kitchen through the Upper West Side all the way to West 97th had largely evacuated; it hadn't taken a great deal of prompting on the part of first responders, either. The building that Alpha One had been helping to clear was the last holdout, largely because upper management of the companies housed in it had been stubborn and refused to recognize the danger. *Idiots. Not unlike some of their employees, I suppose, by the sound of it,* Echo thought with disdain.

No one among the general population knew what was really going on; few had actually seen the mega moth, and those that had, mostly from a distance. Given its gray-and-tan mottled coloring made fairly effective urban camo and it moved amazingly swiftly, the combination made it hard to spot in any event...unless you knew what you were looking for. The Agency already knew what cover story it would put out in the aftermath, with little in the way of brain bleach needed; some of the original emergency calls had assumed it to be a terror attack, and Omega and Echo had played off it earlier, as they urged the building's evacuees to flee.

"Hey there, big guy," Crutch said, as she opened the gate of the hoverpod and stepped out, onto the sidewalk. "Where are they now?"

"Near as I've understood from Meg," Echo turned and pointed upward, "they're on about the fourteenth or fifteenth floor of that building there."

"How many we got, counting Omega?"

He thought for a moment, pulling up the mental imagery he'd gotten from his partner-spouse, then counting heads.

"Somewhere between fifteen and twenty, Crutch; I'm not sure of the exact number," Echo decided. "That's counting Meg; I'm pretty sure she's got a bum foot and is probably gonna need some help, her own self. And another of 'em is in a mobility scooter. But most of 'em are little kids."

"Well, damn," Crutch grumbled. "Kids or no, I'm not gettin' 'em down in this thing. I guess I can pop up there and do a quick reconnoiter, though, then call in the cavalry in airskimmers or the like. If Omega's injured, that means the emergency medical response teams, and they got airskimmers out the wazoo for this operation."

"That'll work. We just gotta move. Notice the smoke coming out of the windows a couple floors above 'em? Long story short, it's set their floor on fire, what with flaming debris falling down a stairwell..."

"Ooo shit. Yeah, lemme get moving here, big fella," Crutch said, heading back for her hoverpod. "Keep an eye out for the humongous airborne blowhard, and gimme a yell if you see it coming; this hoverpod's not worth shit in a breeze like that."

"Roger that," Echo agreed.

Crutch entered the hoverpod, activated it, turned on the force field, and headed up.

* * *

Crutch kept a careful eye out as she ascended, staying well away from the building as she neared the lower floors from which the flames licked, then easing to one side and continuing up some ten more floors. There, through a window, she spotted a room full of children, with a few adult heads in the midst— one of which had a white-blonde braid. She waved, and several children pointed.

The braided head popped up, and Omega spotted her, waving back. Then she gestured, indicating all of the children.

Crutch put the hoverpod into stationkeeping mode, then held up both hands, opening and closing them several times, asking, *How many?*

Omega nodded, then pointed to herself and held up three fingers. Then she pointed at the nearest child, and held up one finger on one hand, and five on the other. Crutch got the message.

202

Three adults, and fifteen little ones. And according to Echo, one of the adults in a scooter. Right. We should be able to get them out in at most a couple of airskimmer loads, but we need to get them to an opening first...or make one.

She pantomimed raising a club and hitting the window, and Omega nodded, then made a throwing motion, followed by both hands 'exploding' outward, and Crutch knew she understood.

Crutch nodded then, and held up her hand to the side of her head, thumb and little finger extended in the universal *I'll call* gesture, then swooped her hand in like an airplane...or an airskimmer.

Omega nodded her understanding of the message, *I'll call for a rescue craft*, and gave her a thumbs-up.

Crutch pointed at Omega, frowned, and ran a hand down her body, asking if Omega was all right. She watched as Omega drew a deep breath, then shook her head.

The younger Agent pushed against the desk that stood between her and the window, moving into the open, and Crutch realized she was sitting in a rolling desk chair. As soon as her feet were visible, she leaned down and rubbed her left ankle, then flopped her hand over on her wrist, to indicate that she had turned her ankle rather badly, and Crutch nodded her understanding.

Crutch 'walked' her index and middle fingers, then held out a hand, and Omega shook her head—*No, I can't walk.*

"Damn," Crutch expostulated with some vehemence. "First Echo, now Omega."

In response, Omega offered a wry smile and shrugged.

Crutch waved a dismissive hand, threw her an OK sign, then gave her a thumbs-up. Then she jerked her thumb over her shoulder. *Everything's gonna be okay. I'll go see to it now.*

Omega nodded, and brushed her hand in the universal *go on, git* gesture.

Crutch grinned and left.

* * *

"Hey, Joanna, Dave, come here a moment, please," Omega said, as Joanna put one of the children up on a desk; the floor was now getting unpleasantly warm, indicating that the fire was likely starting to move under the false flooring that allowed for the HVAC air ducting, and they had everyone that could manage it sitting in chairs or on desks and tabletops. However, to Omega's relief, there was no indication of the carpeting beginning to discolor, which meant the fire was not yet under them. Dave Weiner watched out the window, looking down at the street far below, and the tiny being in black who impatiently awaited there. At Omega's call, he turned his scooter.

"Sure thing, Omega," he said, trundling over to where she sat. "What's up?"

"We are where we're gonna be, now," Omega explained as Joanna walked over. "And my people know where we are, and are going for a rescue craft. So in order for us to get out TO that craft, we have to make a hole."

Joanna and Dave glanced at each other.

"The window," they said in unison.

"Exactly," Omega confirmed. "And since I'm off my feet, YOU TWO will have to be the ones to handle that."

They glanced at each other again.

"Umm..." Joanna began.

"Come on, honey, we can do this," Dave urged. "It's just a window. We broke our share of those as kids, by accident."

"Well...okay," she agreed.

"Good," Omega decreed. "Now, here's how we're gonna do it..."

* * *

Echo stood on the sidewalk on the opposite side of the street, watching the signaled communication from a distance via goggle-glasses assistance, and keeping one eye and both ears peeled for the mega moth, which was prone to basking in the sunshine on the side of a building for an hour or so, then taking off and swooping through the concrete canyons in search of no one knew what.

A mate, maybe, Echo considered. *Or food. Or both. What the hell does a giant moth-creature EAT, anyway?*

Finally Crutch started down, calling to Echo on the emergency frequency of his cell phone.

"Exactly what you said, Echo," she noted. "Omega's injured, probably gonna have a hard time walking, and she's got two more adults in there and a bunch of kids, but I think an airskimmer—"

Just then the beating whir of gigantic wings made itself known, and Echo glanced around quickly, then pointed in horror.

"CRUTCH! Get down here NOW! It's coming up the street!"

Instinctively, Crutch spun to look in the direction Echo pointed.

That was her mistake.

Because, before she could react further, the mega moth rounded the corner and flew past overhead. One of the wake vortices caught her, and the little hoverpod suddenly spun out of control...

...Right into the side of the building.

Then dropped.

Chapter 8

Fortunately, Crutch had already made it a little more than two-thirds of the way down before disaster had struck. The antigrav unit on the hoverpod, damaged by the impact with the building's concrete façade, slowed Crutch's descent, but falling was still falling, especially from a couple of stories up. Granted, it appeared to be more like falling on Mars, and she had a force field—hoverpod force fields were almost always set on 'soft'—to protect her. Still, the transfer of momentum was substantial; falling three stories on Mars was the equivalent of being hit by a truck going forty miles an hour. The force field's 'soft' setting tended to make collisions nearly perfectly elastic, which meant she bounced...but as Echo and Omega had found out back in late summer, the trampoline effect alone could be dangerous.

By the time Crutch's limp form, slumped in the hoverpod, settled to the street, Echo had chased her down and was already on the 'walkie-talkie' cell phone.

"MEDIC!" he yelled into it. "CODE BLACK! AGENT DOWN! Agent Crutch is down! The damn mega moth knocked her out of the air! I need a trauma team to the corner of West 67th and Columbus!"

"Agent Echo, this is Whiskey, monitoring," came the reply. "My team will be en route as soon as we can divert our course. But I thought I heard you telling Fox earlier that you were on West 66th?"

"I was," Echo explained, even as the hoverpod sputtered and died, releasing the injured agent from the force field. He quickly knelt and reached for a pulse in her throat. "That's how far Crutch got knocked."

"Oh damn. Is she still alive?"

The background chatter between field teams died to complete silence as Echo felt for a pulse. He got it.

"Yeah," he reported. "I got a pulse. It's weak and slow, but reasonably steady. She has blood coming from her nose and mouth, though."

"On my way, Echo. Bringing my trauma team and a couple of evac units."

"Good man. Thanks."

* * *

Three minutes later, Whiskey and his team were easing an unconscious Crutch out of the hoverpod and into a basket stretcher; the physician had already ascertained it was safe to do so by running several swift sweeps with his medscanner.

"But she's in bad shape, just the same," he told Echo. "Did she not see it coming?"

"No," Echo verified, "and I was helping her watch. The damn thing must have been right over on the next block sunning, or something. It was just suddenly THERE."

"Mmph," Whiskey grunted, shaking his head. "We have to stop this thing."

"I know. Listen, the reason Crutch was up there is that Meg is trying to get a day care group out of there, and she's injured," Echo explained, pointing to the building. "You got two airskimmers here; can you use one to take Crutch to the medlab, and the other to get them out before the fire gets to 'em?"

"Oh, we're not qualified for search and rescue, Agent Echo," one of the medtechs noted. "I mean, the field agents are, but not us."

"You don't have to be," Echo said. "I've got that much under control myself. I know pretty well where they are, and I know what to do. I just need help getting to them and bringing them down."

"If I were you, I wouldn't use this thing if my life depended on it," one of the field agents said, as they left their airskimmer sitting in the street nearby. "We got some serious steering and attitude control problems with it; add in the giant pest zooming all over the damn sky, and it was all we could do not to end up like Crutch."

"Have you installed that new software patch that came down?" Echo wondered.

"I have no idea," the other agent noted. "This isn't OUR airskimmer—it's one that came out of the vehicle hangar as a spare; ours is in the shop. I don't know what's been done to it and what hasn't, and I haven't had time to find out."

"What are you going to do?" Whiskey asked them.

"Given Crutch is our boss, we were hoping to ride back with her, kind of see to her," the first field agent said. "Once she's properly seen to, we'll go by the vehicle hangar, report in the problem and where we left the skimmer, and see about obtaining another, more reliable ride."

"That works," Whiskey decided. "Echo, I'll try to send someone back to help when I get Crutch stabilized."

"Thanks, Whiskey," Echo said, and opened his mouth to say more, but they were already loading their patient into the remaining airskimmer.

Scant seconds later, they were gone.

* * *

Shit, Echo thought. *Meg, can you hear me, baby?*

I'm here, Ace. We saw what happened. Well, the kids didn't; we kept them away from the windows. Is she gonna be okay?

I don't know. It was a pretty bad crash. How are things there?

Okay so far. But they won't be for long. The floor is feeling pretty warm, the door is turning downright hot, and smoke is starting to collect up near the ceiling.

Sprinkler system?

Seems to be out through the whole building. I'm thinking the pipes might have burned through or something. Water pressure's at zero, from what I can tell in the water fountains an' shit.

All right, baby. Lemme see what I can do.

* * *

This time, when Echo grabbed his cell phone, he hit the speed-dial straight through to the Director—which automatically caused it to exit 'walkie-talkie' mode for the duration of the call, in favor of a more secure mode.

"Fox. That you again, Echo?"

"Yeah, Fox. You got anybody freed up yet?"

"No, zun, I'm sorry. What's up? I thought Crutch was going to handle things for you."

"She tried, but things went south, hard. Meg's trapped by

208

two different fires on an upper floor of a high-rise; one's above her, and one's below her...and the floor she's on has caught now, too. Building codes or no, it's only a matter of time before this one goes, if nothing else gets done, and I don't want her and those kids to be in there when it does! I grabbed Crutch on her way back from that other firefighting excursion, and she tried to go up in a hoverpod to assess the sitch, but the damn mega moth came through again and...well, it turns out that the propulsion systems on hoverpods aren't nearly strong enough to maintain control against what amounts to jet wash."

"Oh damn. How bad?"

"I...don't know. It looked bad. She was unconscious, pale, bleeding from nose and mouth, and...well. I just sent her off with a medic team, and they were headed for the medlab at emergency speeds."

"Farkakte, verdammt, merde, glagaram, cachu, khro, abdab, argdun, and gronk!" Fox cursed with feeling.

"Alla that," Echo agreed. "Plus a few. Anyway, I got an airskimmer here, though it's damaged..."

"How bad?"

"It's flyable," Echo said. "I think it maybe just needs that new software patch installed. The agents that set it down said the attitude control was acting up, and they weren't thrilled about trying to use it with the equivalent of a damn jet engine zipping around among the skyscrapers. The Venturi effect around the buildings is apparently bad enough on it without adding that into the mix."

"Yes, and of course we'd have a storm system moving in and increasing the winds today," Fox grumbled. "I don't think it's gonna actually dump anything, but we sure as hell didn't need the wind."

"No shit, Boss." Echo paused. "So, Meg's got a handicapped offworlder, his wife, and a room full of little kids—it was a day care, I understand, so think preschool—a couple fires on their heels, and nowhere else to go; there's been some sort of collapse in the stairwell, I gathered. So they need help, as soon as we can get it to 'em, or none of 'em is gonna make it. Worse, she's injured, and barely able to walk. I think she sprained an ankle but good, though it might be broken."

There was a foreboding silence on the other end of the line. Echo held his breath.

"Zun, I literally have no one else to send," Fox said in a low voice. "I've been going in and doing rescues myself. And they aren't always exactly successful, our rescues, even with all our tech. I've got at least a dozen agents in the medlab already, maybe more, and that was before you told me about Crutch."

"But Fox...!" Echo said, as he felt uncharacteristic panic rise up inside. "It's MEG!"

"Believe me, I know. The agent nearest to being my own daughter, the one I understand best, who understands me best—because we've both been there. I know. Listen, zun," Fox interrupted. "You were doing really well over Christmas and New Years, right?"

"Well, yeah..."

"And you've kept up the exercises? You're still doing all the therapy and the workouts and whatnot?"

"Yeah..."

"Good. Then I say do what you need to do. If the medlab should pitch a fit in the aftermath—assuming we have an aftermath for them to pitch fits through, at this rate—well, then this call never happened, and you had an emergency situation on your hands with no other backup after Crutch was injured. All of which is true, except for the call. Do you understand?"

"Um, yeah, Fox, but what if—" Echo began, uncertain.

"No 'what ifs,' alter khaver," Fox admonished. "You can do this. You could always do this. You KNOW that. Based on what I saw at New Years, you're back up to speed. And as between us, in our pillow talk, Zebra agreed; the medlab is just being cautious, as is their prerogative. Now GO. Rescue your partner, and the people she was trying to rescue. But be careful."

And the communiqué disconnected.

Echo stared at his cell phone in something akin to horror.

* * *

I gotta do this, he thought, looking up at the smoke pouring from a broken window of the high-rise. *Otherwise a bunch of people are gonna die, most of whom are little kids, and one will be my baby—my wife and partner, and the woman I'm crazy in love with, the woman I want, one day, to be the mother of my own children. And that's just not acceptable at all. Fox is right. You CAN do this. Man up, Echo, and get this done.*

He ran for the airskimmer.

* * *

Echo performed a quick check-out of the airskimmer, ascertaining the nature of the attitude control problem and executing a swift software patch on it to try to minimize the difficulty. Then he sat down and strapped into the pilot's seat, scrolling rapidly through the solid hologram camouflage options, finally selecting a generic tilt-rotor vertical-takeoff-and-landing aircraft and initiating it. From the outside, the airskimmer immediately 'became' a standard tilt-rotor aircraft.

Hang on, baby, he told Omega through the nd't'lq. *I'm on my way.*

He lifted off.

* * *

Having been told the floor on which Omega and her group were stranded, Echo counted carefully as he ascended in the airskimmer, moving almost straight up as the maglev propulsion system enabled the vertical take-off, slowing as he neared the stories containing the fire. This was a newer building, having been constructed with the updated codes that were instituted in the wake of the 9-11 attack on the World Trade Center, so he deemed the likelihood of collapse low...but not nonexistent.

And it doesn't matter if it doesn't collapse, if it kills all the people in the fire, or through smoke inhalation, he thought. *Dead is dead. So I need to hurry up and cram 'em all on board. I just hope they'll all fit. If it wasn't for the fact that most of 'em are little kids, I'd be worried, 'cause I'd have to make several trips. But at one point, I'm pretty sure I 'saw' Meg carrying at least two—before she got hurt, anyway—which means they're not gonna be very big. I MIGHT have to make two trips, but I'm betting we can get 'em all in here at once, even if we have to have 'em sitting in each other's laps. Assuming the mobility scooter fits, I guess. If it doesn't, we get him on board and leave the scooter behind. Those can be replaced.*

With that thought, he adjusted the magnetic levitation field to increase its power; after Omega's little race to save his life in their own airskimmer, the *SchmaltzBlitz*—which had been the first of the airskimmer fleet—Fox had had all of the airskimmers outfitted with the ability to adjust the magnetic flux from the command console, increasing or decreasing power and speed at will—effectively a variable throttle. *Which is handy now,* he considered.

* * *

All right, baby, he told her mentally, *I'm getting close. Where are y'all?*

Hang on just a second, Ace, Omega replied. *I planned for this. Stay back from the building, and verify for me there's nobody below on the sidewalk.*

Echo banked the airskimmer to get a good look. *Nope. Sidewalk is clear, Meg. You are go for whatever you need to do.*

* * *

"Okay, he's getting close, but he's out of the way of debris, and the street's clear," Omega told Joanna and Dave, as she slipped her goggle-glasses from a pocket and donned them. "Do it like I told you."

Dave picked up the nearest visitor chair, which happened to have a steel frame, then moved to the side of the window and switched off El Carrito. It settled to the floor and he locked it into place.

"Okay, kids," Omega said, as Joanna eased away from the window and covered her face with her arms. "Come over here near me, turn your backs to Mr. Weiner, and cover your faces like I showed you."

When the children had obeyed, Omega nodded at Dave. He averted his face, covering it with his other arm, then swung the chair with all the force he possessed at the window.

The window exploded outward, as he released the chair at the peak of his swing. Glass and chair flew out of the building and fell toward the sidewalk, many stories below. Dave grabbed another chair as he reactivated El Carrito. He swiveled until he faced the broken window and wielded the chair like a lion-tamer, poking at the shards of glass still attached along the entire sill, until they had fallen out, into the air, and the perimeter of the floor-to-ceiling window was safe to pass through. Only then did he discard the second chair.

"Great," Omega decreed. "Joanna, it's your turn."

Joanna nodded, then eased over to the broken window and tossed out one end of the banner they had swiped from the ballroom, then stuffed the end she still held into the open drawer of the nearby desk, closing the drawer and bracing it with the nearest visitor's chair to ensure it stayed closed, as the banner fluttered in the wind.

"There," she said. "That should do it, Omega."

"But we need to hurry," Dave noted, pointing at the far wall, which was starting to blacken. "The increased air flow is gonna draw the fire in here fast now."

"Right," Omega agreed. "Stand by."

* * *

Okay, Ace, you should be able to see us now. If the exploding window didn't give away our location, that big red banner ought to.

Yeah, I see it, baby. I'm coming in. Y'all be ready.

I'll have 'em ready, hon. But you need to hurry. The increased oxygen from the busted window is fanning the fire. We got a nice chimney draw going through here now.

Roger that.

* * *

Echo brought in the airskimmer hard by the open window, nudging the hatch to within inches of the high-rise's wall. He set the skimmer for station-keeping hover mode, then unstrapped and, leaving his cane aboard to allow for the use of both hands, he hurried to the airlock hatch on the starboard side of the craft. He opened the inner door, then locked it into position so it would remain open, and opened the outer door, stepping through into the office.

"Okay, guys, the cavalry's arrived," he declared, as he surveyed the room. *Mm. Two adults—one handicapped on a mobility chair—and...one, two, three...fourteen kids. Where's Me-oh, there she is,* he thought, finally spotting Omega sitting in a desk chair nearby, bent over and talking to one of the children, who was crying in fear. *Make that fifteen kids, then. Let's get the handicapped guy aboard first, then the kids, then the other adult, and Meg can see to herding things.*

"Sir," he said, addressing Dave Wiener, "how skilled are

you at maneuvering your mobility chair?"

"Almost as good as you are at maneuvering your ship outside," Dave replied with a grin. "El Carrito and I have been to probably as many planets as you have."

"So you're not from around here." Echo raised an eyebrow.

"Nope," Joanna declared cheerfully. "Hurry up, there, Dave. The smoke is getting worse."

Dave Weiner turned El Carrito toward the window, gunned the throttle, and shot across the four-inch gap and into the airskimmer. Echo glanced through and saw that he was pushing the scooter as far into the port-side rear flight deck as he could manage to work the thing. *We might have to go to some effort to get it out again, but we can take our time with that,* Echo decided, *once we're on the damn ground.*

"Ma'am?" Echo addressed Joanna. "I've gathered from communications with my partner," he nodded at Omega, "that you two are the day care people for these children?"

"That's right, sir," Joanna noted. "You probably want me to ride herd. Kids? Kids, can I have your attention?"

"Yes, Mrs. Wiener?" one of the little girls asked, as the others turned to pay attention.

"I need you all to line up in front of the window, and follow Mr. Wiener into the nice man's helicopter," Joanna said. "He's got it just outside, and it's going to be very safe, and he'll take us away from the fire."

"NOOOOoooo!" one of the children screamed, then began to cry. "It's too high! I'll fawl! Faw down go boom like da other lady! Like Ms. 'Mega!"

"No, honey, no, it'll be okay," Joanna said, shushing the other children, who began to get frightened as well. "It'll be fine. We'll get on board and be safe."

But the little one was not consoled. She continued to cry harder and louder, until all the other children were whimpering in fear.

"Suzy," Omega said then, "come here, baby. Come listen to me."

A tentative Suzy, trying to hold back tears, moved toward Omega, who smiled and gestured her closer, until the female Agent could hug the sniffling child.

"Now listen, honey," Omega told Suzy then. "See that man over there?" She pointed at Echo. "The man that flew the helicopter up here?"

"Uh-huh?"

"That's my husband."

"Ooo. He's kyoot."

Echo felt himself flush.

"Yes, he is," Omega agreed with a devilish grin. "Now, did you think I took good care of all of you to get you here?"

"Yes, Ms. 'Mega. Even when you faw down go boom, you 'uz still taking care ob us."

"Do you know who taught me how to take such good care of you?"

"Noooo..."

"My husband, Mr. Echo. He's GOOD, Suzy. He knows what he's doing. He'll..."

Just then, there was a *whoosh* as part of the door crumbled away, exposing fire outside in the corridor. A wave of heat washed through the room, and flames wafted through the opening, beginning to catch the walls and ceiling near the door.

"NOO!" Suzy screamed, badly frightened. "We're gonna die, we' re gonna die, we' re gonna die..."

"HUSH," Omega ordered, growing stern. "Hush, everybody. We have time to do this. You need to trust me, and trust Mr. Echo, and do what Mrs. Joanna says. She would never tell you wrong. Can you do that for me? Can you be brave?"

"Like you, Ms. 'Mega?" Suzy wondered, trying not to whimper.

"Like Ms. Omega, yes," Echo averred. "Like Mr. and Mrs. Wiener, too."

Anxiously chewing the end of her ponytail, Suzy considered, while all the other children, pale and frightened, watched. Finally Suzy responded.

"Yes, I'll be bwave like Ms. 'Mega," she declared. "Mrs. Weiner, let's go!"

Within seconds all of the children were lined up, with Suzy in front, holding Joanna's hand until she was well inside the airskimmer's airlock. One by one, Joanna Weiner shepherded the children through the broken window, across the small gap of empty space, and into the airskimmer, following hard on the heels of the last child, herself. Echo heard her say, "All right, children, everyone have a seat on the floor next to Mr. Weiner, as close together as you can get, and let's wait for Mr. Echo to bring Ms. Omega in, then we'll be off."

"How about we all sing a song?" Dave Weiner suggested then, followed by affirming exclamations.

* * *

"Come on, Meg," Echo said, as the rest of the doorway collapsed, and the fire began to lick harder at the walls and ceiling of the room. The papers on the receptionist's desk ignited then, sending up a burst of flame. "We're outta time. We gotta go."

"I'll do the best I can, Ace," Omega said, pushing up from the desk chair and trying to step forward. But she stumbled with a cry when the bad ankle gave way, and Echo caught her before she could fall.

* * *

"Oh no," Suzy said, pointing out the windscreen of the airskimmer. "Here comes da big bug again!"

"Hang on, kids!" Dave exclaimed, locking down El Carrito. "Grab something and hang on!"

They did, just in time. The airskimmer bucked and shimmied in the wake of the mega moth, even bumping the side of the building and bouncing off it.

* * *

"Here," Echo said. "Let's do it like this." He bent and scooped Omega into his arms.

"Ace, no!" Omega cried. "You can't carry me yet!"

"Baby, if I can pick up and lunge-walk across the room with a barbell this size, I can carry you," he pointed out. "And you know I'm already doing that in the gym, and have been, for a while. Besides, right now I got some adrenaline up." He nodded upward; the fire had caught the ceiling tiles and was already nearly overhead. "So let's go." He headed for the window and the airskimmer beyond.

But when they got to the window, the airskimmer hatch was a good yard away and drifting outward.

"What happened?!" Omega wondered, dismayed.

"It was the damn exoheteroc!" Dave called across the intervening space. "The thing flew by here and we bucked all over the sky!"

"Do either of you know how to fly an airskimmer?" Echo called over the beating of the thankfully-now-distant exoheteroc. "Can one of you get into the pilot's seat and nudge this thing over closer to the window?"

Dave and Joanna Weiner both shook their heads in the negative.

"Oh shit," Omega murmured. "Echo, leave me and take them. Without my weight, you can make the jump—I've seen you jumping to the 'fireman's pole' at the beach house—and send someone back for me."

"There's nobody to send back for you, baby, and no time to even try," Echo said, eyeing the distance. "That's why I'm here, when I'm supposed to be off field duty. And I'm not leaving you behind. Put your arms around me and hold on tight."

"Oh, Echo! With MY weight—"

"Hush, and do what I tell you," he said, turning and moving deeper into the room, toward the fire, even as burning bits of the ceiling tiles began to fall. "Put your arms around me, hang on tight, and pull yourself in as close to my body as you can get. If we don't hit either of the openings straight, we're done."

Omega obeyed, as Echo turned to face the window opening once more.

"Ready?" he asked, and she nodded against his chest, tucking as close to him as she could get without interfering with his movements. "Here we go!"

And he took off in a dead sprint, accelerating toward the window as hard as he could.

* * *

Echo leaped right on the edge of the window sill, driving forward as hard as he could with both legs, his injured wife and partner held tight in his arms, lunging toward the hatch of the airskimmer, now over four feet away and drifting farther with every moment.

Omega looked down as they crossed empty space, and stifled a gasp as she realized just how high they were.

And then they were surrounded by the hatch, as Echo

rolled to keep Omega on top, the pair sliding onto the flight deck and into the nearest layer of children, who had quickly and instinctively formed a flexible wall by turning their backs and bracing against each other.

* * *

"We did it," Echo murmured, releasing Omega and sitting up, amid cheers from the children.

"YOU did it, honey," Omega replied. "My hero came through again."

"If you say so." He flushed.

"I do. Hey, listen. You don't happen to have any foam grenades loaded in the launchers of this thing, do you?"

"I got no idea," Echo said, scrambling to his feet and helping her into the co-pilot's chair. "It was having attitude orientation issues, what with the dam-er, dang mega moth, and the agents who were flying it left it on the street and went to find something they could control better. I did a software patch on it to make it flyable, and took it up. Have a look-see, while I get this hatch sealed."

Omega strapped in and commenced stabilizing the airskimmer's station-keeping, while studying the weapons instrumentation. Meanwhile, Echo grabbed the nearest rail—in case the mega moth came past again, while he was near enough to the hatch to fall out—and cycled the airlock closed.

* * *

Then he hurried to the pilot's seat, sat down, and strapped into the seat.

"What did you find, Meg?" he asked.

"We got 'em and to spare," Omega determined. "Turn this baby and gimme a good angle to see inside, and I'll fire a couple in here. While we were moving through the building, I watched the burning areas, studied 'em; I think I figured out how to aim and place the things to make this work. If you can arrange to go past a few openings on the way down, I can run a few tests; we might be able to put this building out."

"That works," Echo decided, turning the airskimmer so it faced the open window frame. "Here you go. Have at it, baby."

"And...away," Omega said, launching two small canisters deep into the opening.

Seconds later there was a low-pitched *FWUMP*, and the flames visible through the window began to die back.

"YES!" Omega cried.

"YAY!" the children shouted.

* * *

By the time they got the Weiners and their small charges to a safe haven on the ground, the Alpha One team had managed to put out no less than four more high-rise fires, all but two in different buildings. Echo eased the airskimmer to the pad near Fox's command center, then hit the automatic hatch release and extended the ramp.

"Here we go, guys," he said, turning in the pilot's chair. "I'm glad everyone enjoyed the ride in my cool helicopter. Mr. and Mrs. Weiner," he addressed the adults, "there should be someone waiting for you over on the sidewalk that you can check in with, and see about getting the kids' parents notified that they're safe."

"Thank you both, so much," Joanna Weiner murmured, taking first Echo's hand, then Omega's.

"Yes, you saved our lives," her husband Dave agreed, following her lead. "Never mind keeping all the children calm."

"Hey, it's sorta what we do," Omega responded with a soft smile. "We were glad to help. Besides, you probably saved my life with El Carrito, there, dragging me out of the rubble before the whole mess went down."

The Weiners smiled, then rounded up the children and debarked the craft.

* * *

"Whoof," Echo said then, slumping slightly in his seat.

"Lotta that," Omega agreed, then grimaced. "Unf."

"Uh-oh," Echo said, sitting back up straight. "Somebody's hurting."

"I'm afraid so," Omega admitted. "I'm starting to get worried that something's broken, or maybe torn."

Just then, Bravo appeared in the open hatch.

"Oh great! It IS you two!" he exclaimed. "Fox got your reports of putting out the high-rise fires. He wants to know how many more of the foam grenades you have in the magazines."

"Um," Omega said, pulling up the information on the

weapons console. "Looks like maybe a dozen more."

"How many does it take per building fire?" Bravo pressed. Echo and Omega glanced at each other.

"What, maybe four per floor?" Echo wondered.

"That sounds about right, yeah," Omega agreed. "If we catch it early, only one floor is usually involved. But if it's been going for a half-hour or better, there's usually three or four floors."

"So that might only do one building," Bravo considered.

"Right."

"Okay, I'm gonna have the Weapons teams load you up with foam grenades, and you can go back up and put out some more of these fires," Bravo noted. "And you can show the other teams the technique you worked out, because everybody else is having trouble with it—the foam grenades are knocking the fires back, but not extinguishing 'em. The tilt-rotor hologram disguise is a good one, too. Keep that one going, and pass it on to everybody."

"But—" Echo began.

Shush, Ace, Omega told him. *I can do this. I've gone this long, I can go a while longer if it saves some lives. Never mind prevents downtown Manhattan from burning to the ground.*

Are you sure, baby? If you tore a tendon or muscle, we need to get it looked at as soon as possible.

I'm sure. I've already notified Zz'r'p, and he said he'd tell Zebra as soon as he has time to think—he's trying to help coordinate some of the rescue efforts, telepathically—so the medics will be waiting when we're done. The faster we go now, the sooner we can get me to her. And like I said, maybe save some lives in the doing.

Right. Let's get going, then.

"Load 'em up," Echo ordered.

* * *

While the Weapons team was loading the special munitions into the airskimmer and Omega was compiling a quick message to all other airborne Agency teams about how to best tackle the fires, Echo dug through the airskimmer's stowage and extracted the medikit. Scrabbling through it, he pulled out the medscanner and examined Omega's foot and ankle.

"Mmph," he grunted in displeasure, "it looks like the theater injury times ten, baby. I see hairline fractures, sprains, and... shit. It does look like you probably have a tear in the peroneal tendon. It's not all the way through, but you don't need to be walking on it, for sure."

"Shit. The one on the outside of the foot? Runs up just behind the ankle?"

"That's it, yeah. What happened? You lose footing and turn it all the way on its side?"

"Oh hell yes. For a split-second there, I was walking ON the ankle. I was trying to get out of the way of a collapse and didn't quite make it."

"What kind of collapse?"

"Oh hell, every kind, Ace. A landing up above failed and came down on top of me, bringing part of the adjacent wall with it. And kept pelting me with pieces of brick an' shit. THEN the impact, and the weight of the upper landing, started to tear loose the landing I was pinned down on. Mr. Weiner had to use his antigrav chair to haul me out from under before IT all went down—and took the door, the wall, part of the floor, and all with IT—so I'm gonna be black and blue tomorrow into the bargain."

"Ow. Damn, baby. If this is the worst that came outta all that, you're damn lucky, I'd say."

"Yup. I coulda gone down with it. Can you strap up that ankle and maybe give me a little something for the pain, Ace?" Omega wondered, as she sent the brief report to Fox, to forward to the other teams. "That should get me through until we can see Zebra. 'Cause if we're flying the airskimmer, I'm not gonna be walking, anyway."

"Yeah, I was planning on that." He crouched down and eased off her shoe and sock as gently as he could; it still produced some grunts and hissing from his partner. "Hang in there, baby," he told her. "I can't take it off and be any easier."

"I know. It just hurts. A lot. I'm stifling most of it; given what-all Slug did to me while I was conscious, I guess I kinda have a high pain threshold now."

"Shit. Well...yeah. I hear you, and I've noticed something similar developing in me lately."

"I sorta figured. Anyway, just do what you gotta, and I'll deal, hon."

"Wilco, sweetheart. And yeah, you're already about forty-eight kinds of blue, purple, and black, here. Hang in there; I'll be as gentle and quick as I can."

"I know."

A couple of minutes later, Echo had the foot and ankle strapped from just behind the ball of the foot to halfway up her calf, to ensure maximum stability. He slipped her sock over it, then eased the shoe on her foot, but did not lace it.

"There," he said. "Do you still need something for pain?"

"I sure wouldn't argue," Omega confessed. "But if you do, make it something light, that won't dope me up. I need my wits about me to do this firefighting stuff. Not to mention help you with the airskimmer if that damn giant cootie comes through again."

Echo snorted despite himself.

"What?"

"'Giant cootie,'" Echo noted, snorting in amusement again.

"Well, it is," she grumbled. "Pain shit, please."

"On it," Echo said with a gentle grin, scrounging through the kit and finding a preloaded syringe of the same painkiller he had given her the previous September, when she had broken her foot on a hidden flyrail weight backstage, while working undercover as an actress on Broadway. "Slip off your Suit jacket, roll up your sleeve, and I'll hit you with it."

With Echo's help, Omega managed the request, just barely; she was becoming very stiff in the aftermath of the wall collapse and subsequent fall, and simply taking off the jacket was proving much harder than Echo had expected.

By the time he got the osmotic syringe pumped into her, the Weapons personnel were waving a go-ahead through the windscreen.

The pair strapped back in and lifted off, headed out to try to help control the fires raging...while the mega moth continued to run loose through the city.

* * *

Twenty hours later, Alpha One returned in the airskimmer to the staging area at Columbus Circle. They were out of foam grenades, and had personally put out fires in over a dozen skyscrapers and taught the other agents how to do so, as well as assisting in several rooftop rescues—Omega flying while Echo exited, only when necessary; for the most part, all they had to do was hover just over the rooftop and open the hatch, and the rescued people scrambled into the airskimmer.

Since the THIRD dose of painkiller had worn off by that time, Omega's foot and ankle were aching quite badly as a result, and the rest of her body wasn't doing much better. Echo had noticed she was even having trouble sitting still in the co-pilot's chair, and was squirming slightly, because of the pain. Unfortunately, that only had the effect of further annoying stiff, sore muscles and bruising, making matters that much worse.

So when the Weapons team approached with another load of foam grenades, Echo waved them off and opened the hatch, extending the ramp. Then he unstrapped and turned to his partner-mate.

"Come on, Meg," he told her, reaching for her straps. "Let's get you to Zebra and some medical care. It's way past time to have you seen to."

"Okay," she sighed, and didn't protest when he scooped her into his arms once more.

* * *

Bravo was still running the staging area, and when he saw Echo wave off the Weapons team, he contacted Fox, who hurried over. When they saw Echo carrying Omega off the airskimmer, Fox exclaimed, "Farkakt!" and headed for the ramp. "Bravo, call Zebra and tell her to get over here, preferably five minutes ago," he ordered over his shoulder.

"Roger that, Fox," Bravo noted, reaching for his phone's earpiece.

* * *

"What happened?" Fox wondered, as Echo eased Omega down on a nearby bench. "Did something go wrong with a rescue?"

"Not recently," Echo noted, as a quiet Omega leaned against the bench's back-rest. "Remember when I was trying to find someone to help me get Meg out, with that day care group?"

"Yes?"

"This was one of the reasons she couldn't get 'em out on her own," Echo explained. "A damn stair landing and part of a wall collapsed on her, based on what she told me. According to the medscanner on the airskimmer I borrowed, she's got a couple of hairline fractures, at least one full fracture, some sprains, and a torn peroneal tendon on the outside of her ankle."

"Oh damnation," Fox breathed. "How bad? Is it all the way through?"

"No, but I haven't let her walk on it since then, or it might be. I strapped it up, and gave her some pain meds—three times," Echo noted, and Fox realized Omega still hadn't said a word...and was very pale.

"Wait," Fox said, as it suddenly hit him, "you mean the two of you went back out into the field to put out fires and rescue civilians, with Omega having breaks and tears in that foot?"

"Yup," Echo confirmed. "AND bruises and contusions all over from the rubble that fell on her. Bravo said you needed us to do that, and help the others work out the best way to hit the fires with the grenades, so we did. Meg said if it saved lives and kept the city from burning down, she'd deal."

"Oh, tekhter," Fox murmured, bending and stroking Omega's white-blonde hair with one hand, as he looked into her eyes. "Oh, meyn kleyn maydele! You should have said something!"

"It needed doing, Abba Fox," Omega sighed, as Echo sat down beside her, slouched slightly, and eased her around until she could rest her head in his lap, and lie along the bench. "But oh, I'm so tired now. It hurts..."

"That's 'cause you need more pain meds, baby," Echo explained. "But I figured Zebra needed to have a look, first. We've been at this for around twenty hours or so now; I don't think we should let it go any longer."

"No, you're right," Fox agreed. He turned and called across the circle. "BRAVO!"

"Yes, boss?" The executive assistant came running.

"What's Zebra's ETA?"

Bravo glanced at his wrist chronometer.

"Mm, 'bout another minute, minute and a half, max. Any

moment, really."

Just then, a motorcycle roared up, a single rider in black leather aboard.

"Oh, there she is now," Fox said, as the rider switched off the engine and dismounted, then pulled off a black helmet.

"Isn't that your cycle, Fox?" Echo wondered, as Zebra grabbed her medikit out of the saddlebag in the back.

"It is," Fox acknowledged. "It's proven useful to help her get from place to place as she's needed. And as you know, it isn't quite...standard...especially by the time I was done with it, so it can really move. But it stays on the ground and out of the way of the worst of the damn moth's wake..."

"What's up?" Zebra called as she approached. Then she saw the two members of Alpha One sitting on the bench, and stopped dead. "Oh shit! Echo, you're supposed to be on medical leave! What did you go and do to yourself?"

"Nothing," Fox said, "but Omega apparently has broken bones and torn tendons in her foot and ankle."

"WHAT?!" Zebra sprinted the rest of the way to the trio, extracting her medscanner as she went.

* * *

"Yup, she did a number on it, all right," Zebra said ten minutes later, when Echo and Omega had finished explaining what happened to injure her, and the physician had performed a thorough examination of the ankle and foot. "This is even worse than what you did to it when you were in that Broadway show, undercover, a few months back. And the rest of you is even worse banged up, as well."

"Yeah, an' it hurts 'bout like, too," Omega agreed, and Echo winced in sympathy. "I guess that's what you get when a landing an' part of a wall falls on ya an' the people you're trying to rescue have to pull you out b'fore the whole thing collapses under ya an' carries you down with it."

"What I want to know is, with it busted up like this, how did you get OUT of that building?" Zebra wondered.

"Echo carried me," Omega said with a proud grin. "He brought the airskimmer right up to the window after we busted it out, then shepherded all the little kids on with their caretakers, THEN came back and picked me up. But by the time we got to the window, the damn moth-thing had come through again and drifted the airskimmer about three or four feet away. Meanwhile, the fire had burned through the door and caught the ceiling, so we hadda get out fast."

"Meg," Echo murmured, as he saw Zebra's eyes widen. *Baby, maybe you don't need to tell her this. Remember, I'm supposed to be on medical leave...*

"Keep going," Zebra said.

Omega stopped with her mouth open, staring at Echo. *Oh shit. I just got you in trouble, didn't I?*

I dunno. I—

"Keep GOING," Zebra insisted.

"It was an emergency, Zebra," Echo said with a sigh. "It was that, or let her die in the fire. She couldn't walk at all. And we had no backup."

"He ran and jumped the distance," Omega explained, now hesitant, "carrying me. We sailed right into the open hatch, then he rolled so he landed on the deck with me on top, rather than his weight landing on me when I was already hurt, and we slid across...an' the kids were watching, and managed to form kind of a bumper-stop for us, and we were fine. Echo got me into the co-pilot's seat, closed the hatch, then I shot a couple of the foam grenades into the fire, an' we got the hell out."

Zebra sat down heavily on the far end of the bench.

"So much for medical-mandated leave," she grumbled.

"Bubeleh, it was an EMERGENCY," Fox reminded her. "Echo called me several times, hoping I had someone to send to do the job, so he didn't have to violate his medical leave. But I DIDN'T. I've been performing rescues my own self, just trying to fill in where needed. And when Crutch came by, she tried to help, but..."

"That's what she was doing when the mega moth knocked her into the building," Echo explained. "Which is why she's in the mess that she's in now."

"How is she?" Omega wondered, as Zebra commenced work on her ankle, unstrapping it so she could see more external detail, palpating gently.

"Dunno yet," Zebra sighed, as Omega hissed in pain. "Zar was still working on her, last I heard. She was in bad shape.

She...might not make it."

"Gronk and abdab," Fox said in a low tone. "That would be a serious loss. The field agents love her as much as the Alpha Line loves these two. Never mind that she is a very old and very good friend. You know," he added, "she is not designated an Original, but that was ONLY because she was not present at the First Contact. She WAS already a member of what our historians term the 'pre-Agency.' She just wasn't in Texas with the rest of us."

"Oh wow," Zebra murmured. "So was she one of the first you met who weren't there...?"

"She was, yes. THE first I met who wasn't already there."

"I'm sorry, Fox," Echo sighed, slumping farther. "It...it all happened too fast. There was—"

"Hush, zun, hush," Fox said then. "I looked up the incident report you submitted while Zebra was examining Omega. I understand. There was nothing you could have done. The damn moth is just too fast."

The four were silent for long moments, pondering.

"Well, the good news is, if Echo really did everything Meg is saying he did," Zebra began.

"He did," Omega averred. "I made the mistake of looking down while we were airborne. Shit. And I'm not even acrophobic."

"...Then I guess the therapy worked damn well, and he's back to normal."

"Which means he can go back on duty?" Fox asked, raising a surprised eyebrow.

"Like, field duty?" Omega followed the query, pushing upward.

"You lie back down there, young lady," Zebra ordered. "You have a broken bone in here that is NOT where it needs to be, and I'm gonna have to set it, and that's not gonna feel good. AT. ALL."

"Painkiller and taking her back to Headquarters?" Fox pressed. "Surely you weren't going to perform what amounts to field-dressing it, bubeleh...?"

"Wait. She doesn't have painkiller in her already?"

"It wore off about ten or twenty minutes before we pulled

back into the staging center," Echo said. "We'd already been at it for way more than half of another shift, closing on a full shift, and damn if I was gonna go any longer without this getting seen to, city-wide emergency or no. Only," he added, "I figured it might be better if YOU—or whichever one of the medics was available—chose the proper pain med to use next. But yeah," he added, "my baby, there—she's hurtin,' all right."

"That's good, then," Zebra decided. "Not that she's hurting, but that you finally got help for her. And yes, we need to get some painkiller into her, and yes, once I have time to breathe, I'll formally clear Echo for field duty again. Omega, dear, how long have you been on your feet, so to speak? Not from the time you got here, from the time you last woke up?"

"She's been going since, um, we had just been thinking about crashing for the night when y'all recalled us," Echo recollected. "And we've worked about...what, baby, about thirty hours since then?"

"Ish," Omega decided, wobbling a hand in the air to indicate the approximation. "I think a bit less than that; maybe twenty-six, twenty-seven? Something over a normal Division shift, but not a whole lot over..."

"Right. So figure we've been up for..." Echo paused, estimating, "forty-two, forty-three hours, or thereabouts, rounded approximation?"

"Damn," Fox said, surprised, "you two have been going longer than anyone else here as yet; we at least started off with shift operations, though that's kind of gone to Gehennem in a handbasket. But one way and another, no one has relieved you two?"

"Well, first we drove in to Headquarters, but we had to detour way out to sea, so it took longer than usual. Then we spent some time in our office, going over what info we had, an' trying to gather more information. Based on that, we went out and were trying to scout out info on the mega moth, by lookin' at some of the locations it had been sighted an' stuff. Then we realized the day care group was stuck, so I went into the building, trying to help the kids get out, and that took a few hours, 'cause none of it went according to plan," Omega noted with a weary sigh. "Then I managed to figure out exactly where to hit with the foam grenades to get the fire out, so we put out a few on our way to offload the day care group. Then we started firefighting duty, and showing the others how to aim the grenades for maximum effect...we assisted in several more rescues, put out a buncha fires..." She rubbed a hand across her eyes and sighed again.

"Right," Fox said, shaking his head. "When you're supposed to be one of the main teams helping us figure out how to stop this thing. I knew you'd end up sucked into this, one way or another, even if you tried not to be. And I know," he said, holding up a forestalling hand, "that you DID try hard not to be, both of you. But neither of you is morally capable of standing by and watching an innocent die if there is anything you can do to prevent it, and I understand that, too—and approve."

"So do I," Zebra admitted.

"Good," Fox said with a smile. "I knew there was a reason I married you, bubeleh. Zebra, get 'em back to the medlab, get Omega patched up, and see they get some sleep, whether there or in their quarters, I don't care; whatever you need 'em to do. The rest of us will hold the line until we figure out how to stop this thing. Which these two are likely to be instrumental in doing."

"All over that one, hon," Zebra told her mate. "How do you want me to get 'em back there?"

"Echo, take the airskimmer, and hand it over to the hangar master," Fox ordered. "Whoever's on duty will know what to do with it. By the sound, it probably needs a little maintenance before being sent back out, in any case."

"Yeah, the attitude control is a bit wonky," Echo agreed. "I ran that software patch on it, which helped, but it still needs some work. It definitely gets tricky when the mega moth is flying in the area."

"If Echo wasn't such a damn good pilot, it woulda been one hell of a roller coaster ride," Omega observed. "It could get a little rough, even so."

"Damnation. I'll bet," Fox agreed. "You two, load Omega on it, then go back to Headquarters as fast as you can get her there. I'll see the cycle gets back to HQ for you, Zee; don't worry about it, my dear heart."

"All right, Fox, hon; thanks. And now I wanna see YOU carry her," Zebra told Echo. "I want to walk behind you and watch your gait and make sure you're not straining something."

"Okay," Echo said, "but nothing's hurting at all."

"Go," Zebra ordered, as he picked up his wife and partner. "I'll be the judge of that."

Chapter 9

By the time they reached the medlab in Headquarters—having had to dodge a few airborne obstacles in the process, including the mega moth and at least one news media helicopter—Zebra was fully satisfied with Echo's ability to move and work, including his reaction time and coordination as he maneuvered the airskimmer.

So they got Omega into the medlab and anesthetized, then Zebra set the bones in her foot, working delicately with a special Higgs-field medical device that gently nudged the bone fragments into the desired positions without the need for a more invasive surgical technique. Then, with Echo's assistance—since the medlab was as overworked as the field teams—she carefully slipped a specialized, removable cast onto Omega's foot, followed by hooking her up to an IV with regen fluid that she had formulated expressly to heal bone and tendon.

"What about the regen pills?" Omega wondered.

"Oh," Zebra said. "I'll have you run by the pharmacy and pick up some of those later, but they take a while to compound properly; I've already put in the order, but it'll take probably a couple of hours for them to do this, minimum. Meantime, I can mix the fluid here, and run an IV on you, and you can go home and get some sleep and pick up the pills later."

"Aha," Echo said. "So first things first, when we wake up, is go pick up those?"

"That'll work, yeah. All right, here's what we're gonna do for now," Zebra told Echo then. "You both need some rest, and Meg needs down time for that foot to heal. So once the IV goes in her, I'll finish it off with a dose of pain medication, then I'm sending you both home to eat and sleep. It's not great timing given what's happening on the streets, but if I know you two, you've been going hell bent for leather ever since you got back to New York, and you'll need some rest if either of you is gonna work with the rest of the Sciences department to figure out how to stop this thing. So both of you, go try to get a few hours' sleep. Echo, I'll send oral pain meds home with you for Meg, and if you need something to help you sleep—I mean, if you're, like, hyper or something—just say the word and I'll send a couple sleep tabs for YOU home with you, too." She eyed him, but he shook his head. "Okay, that's fine. But if you get restless, CALL the medlab, because YOU need to rest, too. I can't say I'll be here, 'cause I probably won't, but somebody will be."

"Okay."

* * *

Half an hour later, the regen fluid IV was complete, and the pain medication administered in its last drops. Within moments, Omega relaxed as it took full effect.

"There we go, baby," Echo noted. "I bet that feels better."

"Uh-huh," she responded, sighing. "Wow, does that help. I was starting to really hurt all over."

"Good. I want Meg to stay off that foot for a good Division day at a minimum," Zebra instructed Echo. "The same IV that will speed her foot healing will also help all the other contusions, none of which looked serious, but I can definitely see why she hurt all over! Be prepared, Echo, 'cause she's gonna be black and blue everywhere. And she needs to come back in here and let somebody examine that tendon before she gets back on her feet. We don't need it tearing the rest of the way; that'd mean surgery to repair it, or at least tack it back together before getting dunked in the regeneration pod. And that would take her out of the whole shootin' match goin' on out there," she waved a hand at the wall, denoting the battle to contain the mega moth, "because the sooner it's reattached, the better the prognosis, so we'd have to cut and then dunk, pretty much immediately. Which also takes the surgical team away from our part of the fight, and could result in us losing somebody."

"Nuh-uh," a tired, somewhat groggy Omega grunted. "Nope. No' gonna do that. Nope, nope, nope."

Echo and Zebra chuckled in gentle affection.

"Right," Echo agreed. "Not a plan."

"So when you wake up," Zebra continued, "eat well, then call Zar, pick up her 'script, check in with Fox, and report to the Sciences people for the latest data. Work with them to try to figure out a way to stop this thing, or kill it, or whatever."

"All over it, Zebra."

"Okay. Lemme log out an antigrav chair for you, and the two of you head straight on home. She's gonna be zonking out on you real soon anyway, now that I've given her the pain meds. Completely aside from how long you guys have been going, the pain has worn her out; the meds shouldn't actually knock her out, but she's so tired, they've already kicked her onto her ass."

"Mm," Echo hummed, "yeah. Been there, done that. No t-shirt, though."

"No matter what you do, nobody ever seems to actually give ya one of those things, do they?" Zebra observed, and they laughed.

Minutes later, Echo was pushing a half-asleep Omega out of the medlab, headed for the agents' housing.

* * *

Echo trundled Omega into their quarters, going straight back to the bedroom. There, he turned down the bedclothes, then knelt in front of her.

"Meg. Meg? Wake up, baby." He took hold of her shoulder, very lightly shaking it. "We're home. Can you sit up on the side of the bed while I undress you?"

"Mmph," she grunted, rousing from a medication-and-exhaustion-induced stupor. "Urgh. If you c'n get me to th' bed, Ah'll try t' sit. Can't promise Ah won't fall over..."

"Let's do that, then," Echo decided, standing, slipping his arms under her shoulders and pivoting carefully, as he transferred her from the chair to the bedside; she attempted to help him move her, but her legs were wobbly at best, and her knees refused to lock out, so other than taking some of the weight, her efforts accomplished little. "If you fall over, try to fall backward, okay? That way, you'll land on the bed. I don't need you pitching into the floor and breaking your nose or concussing yourself or something..."

"Hokay."

Echo nudged the antigrav chair out of the way, then commenced stripping clothing and weapons holsters from his

233

partner, laying it all on the foot of the bed, to put away later.

"Hey, listen," he said, as he worked, "do you want your pajama top on? Are you cold?"

Omega stared at him with big, blue, unfocused eyes. *Wow,* he thought, not sure whether to stifle a laugh or offer sympathy. *She looks pretty out of it.*

"Are you comin' t' bed, too?" she asked then.

"Huh?"

"You comin' t' bed, too?"

"No, Meg, I'm asking if you're cold, baby. Do you want your pajama top?"

Omega blinked slowly.

"Are you comin' t' bed, too?" she repeated for the second time.

"Baby, what does that have to do with—" Echo broke off, then smeared his hand across his face as understanding arrived. "Because if I come to bed, you can snuggle up to me an' get warm?"

"Uh-huh," she confirmed, nodding a slightly wobbly head. "So 'f you're comin' t' bed, no, Ah don' need it. But if you're not, Ah wan' it."

"Okay, I understand now. I won't be coming to bed immediately, 'cause I gotta do a couple things first, but really soon quick, yeah, I'll be coming to bed. 'Cause frankly, I'm pretty tired, too."

"Hokay. Then no 'jammies."

"All right." Echo paused in his work long enough to meet her eyes...whose focus had not improved through that conversation. "Are you okay there?"

"Kiiiiiiinda loopy," she admitted in a slow drawl, trying to make a circular looping motion with one hand, though it was more an oval, and precessed significantly. "Not 's bad as th' Broadway show thing was; Ah think Zee gave me sumpin' diff'runt this time. But still purty loopy. Yup."

"Okay. You gonna be all right, though?"

"Yup. Better Ah git hor'zontal purty soon now though, don't Ah'mma fall over."

"Gotcha. Remember, go backward if you fall over."

"Yup."

She paused, then pointed in several different directions, glancing at him for clarification. Echo pointed straight back, over her shoulder, and she mouthed, "Oh," jerked her thumb over her shoulder—nearly toppling backward in the process—then nodded a decidedly wobbly head.

When he had her stripped down to bare skin, he helped her turn and lift her legs—complete with cast—into the bed, then spread the covers over her as she finally 'got horizontal.'

"There," he said, as he shifted her discarded clothing to the armchair nearby; her warp pockets could be sorted once they woke. "Just lie there and relax, but try not to go to sleep yet. We both need to eat, so I'm gonna run into the kitchen real quick and see if I can't throw something together that doesn't require a lotta effort, and bring it back here on a tray. I won't be five minutes. All right?"

"Hokay," she said again.

"Are you hurting?"

"Nope. Not so loopy now Ah'm layin' down, either. Meds Zee gave me 're workin' purty good, Ah think. Ah'm not all goofy like last time, though. Least, Ah don't think..." She looked up at him with an adorably muddled expression, and he was tempted to plant a full kiss on her in that moment. "Am Ah? Or did Ah ask 'at awready?"

"I don't think you are, no," he said, deciding to ignore the repetition. "Groggy as hell, an' a little confused, but not so... out of it." Echo also made the decision to stifle the urge to kiss her; she needed food, rest, and healing, in that order, not amorous affections from her spouse. *That can come later, when we have some actual TIME,* he thought. *Never mind energy. 'Cause I'm about ready to keel over, too.*

"Mmkay, 'at's good," Omega observed with a sigh.

"Good. I'll be right back."

* * *

A scant five minutes later as promised, Echo returned with a tray full of grapes, pre-sliced cheese, a couple of the Agency's special complete-nutrition meal bars, and one piece of shortbread apiece. To complement the menu, he had bottled water and glasses of milk to drink.

Despite her best efforts to stay awake as he had asked,

Omega had been just starting to doze off when he returned. So he gently woke her and helped her sit up, propping her with pillows, before placing the tray over her lap and sitting down beside her, helping her eat, as well as sharing the food with her.

Ten minutes after that, the empty tray was on the dresser, the antigrav chair was switched off, plugged in to recharge, and locked down nearby, and Echo was stripped and in bed beside Omega, his discarded clothing on the chair arm opposite Omega's. She rolled over and snuggled into his side with a sigh, as he eased an arm around her battered, weary body.

Five minutes after THAT, they were both sound asleep.

* * *

Back in Manhattan, Fox & Co. were waging an all-out war against the fires. For some reason the agents could not fathom, as soon as they got nearly finished putting out known fires, more fires would break out.

"At least Alpha One figured out how to use the firefighting foam grenades to best effect," Lima noted.

"Yes, we only just got those in, and no one has had the training on them as yet," Fox pointed out. "I'm very glad Omega figured it out. I also think there is something odd about these fires that is making it more difficult than it should be. Never mind how all the damn farshtinkener, meshuginah things are being ignited!"

"It has to be something to do with the mega moth," Bravo decided. "We're only getting those fires in the areas it's frequenting."

"Agreed, but what is it doing?" Fox wondered. "Is it fanning the flames with its wingbeats? Is it blowing something loose, then creating sparks? Or is whatever it's blowing loose what's creating sparks? What is the connection between the moth-creature and the fires?" He paused. "And more importantly, do we have everyone evacuated out of that area of the city?"

"Yes and no, I think," Lima said, checking his tablet. "According to the local beat cops, there are a few homeless people and panhandlers that stay in the area, but the good news there is that they've all gone down, into the subways, and the mega moth is too big to get into the subway tunnels."

"Well, there is something, I suppose," a weary Fox decided.

"And nothing has pulled a Twin Towers and collapsed," Bravo added. "Which would probably invalidate the subways as safe spaces."

"Yet," Fox sighed. "Please, HaShem, may it not."

"Amen," Bravo and Lima—who were finally trying to hand over, between emergency calls—said in unison.

"BREAK-BREAK!" their cell phones barked. "We have a fire over off West 70th and West End, and it's spreading fast! Send fire suppression immediately!"

"Here we go again," Lima said, stepping onto the pad and waving another airskimmer into the air.

* * *

Six hours later, Omega woke in pain when her medications wore off. As she stirred restlessly, Echo woke, as well.

"Hey, baby, how are you?" he asked, keeping his voice soft.

"Hurtin' over here," she noted. "Kinda bad."

"Okay, I'm on that," he said, reaching for the pill bottle and carafe on his nightstand. "Here." He got out a tablet and handed it to her, pouring a glass of water as she popped the pill into her mouth. Seconds later, she had downed the medication and laid back down.

"You gonna be all right?" he asked then.

"As soon as that med kicks in, yeah, I think so," she decided. "You doin' okay? Not sore or anything, are you? I mean, from all that runnin' an' jumpin' while carrying me..."

"Nah, nothing unusual after a mission like that," Echo averred. "I've been sleeping pretty well."

"You woke up when I got restless."

* * *

"Well, yeah," Echo said with a grin. "You have no idea how...aware...I am of you being around me, do you, baby? Especially in bed?"

Omega snorted.

"No, no, I don't mean like that...although yeah, that too," he admitted. "No, I mean..." He broke off, then gnawed his lip, thinking of how to explain. "You're part of me now," he tried. "In ways I never even dreamed of, before. You're in here," he laid his hand on his chest, "and in here," he touched his temple. "And I'm just...AWARE of you. No," he said, anticipating her, "it isn't all the nd't'lq, either. Part of it, I'm sure, is just subliminal clues—your perfume, your body heat, stuff like that. But...not all. So even if I'm sound asleep, if you're beside me and you start movin' around, it registers on my subconscious and I wake up enough to make sure you're all right. And to take care of you, if you're not."

"Huh," Omega murmured, thoughtful. "That says a lot, comin' from 'Mr. Walks Into A Wall 'Cause He's Not Really Awake,' I think."

It was Echo's turn to snort.

"You're never gonna let me live that down, are ya?" he asked, grinning. "I was doped to the gills on pain meds after gettin' shot, baby. It isn't like I'm that way ALL the time."

"No, I'm not, an' you know I'm just pickin' at ya, Ace." It was Omega's turn to grin. "But you have to admit, you did sleep pretty soundly when we were at home and not on a mission, back before we got married. So I'm bettin' it's that same subconscious awareness you use when we have to rest during a mission."

"You could be right." He shrugged. "I haven't really tried to analyze it. I just go with it."

"Does that mean you don't get rested enough, though?" Omega said, and Echo saw the worry lines crease themselves on her forehead. "I mean, 'cause now I'm here in bed with you, an' you're lookin' out for me?"

"Not that I've noticed," he decided after only a moment to consider. "If anything, I think I'm sleepin' better 'cause you're next to me. I feel...more complete, if that makes sense. Happier. And that relaxes me."

"Yeah, it does make sense, at least to me," Omega confessed, "because I feel the same way."

"Good, then," Echo said. "I gather the meds have eased the pain already? You got chatty..."

"Yeah, they kick in pretty quick, which is nice," she agreed. "But I don't think the oral stuff is at the same dose as what she gave me in the IV, 'cause I don't feel so muddled now."

"Well, that's good, I guess."

"Yeah. Hey, Echo..."

"What?"

"Changing the subject," she began. "Did you...notice anything unusual about that dog's body?"

"The one on the roof? From the photo?"

"Uh-huh..."

"I'm glad you brought it up, 'cause I meant to, but then we got busy and I forgot," he said. "Because yeah, I did. At least, in afterthought."

"What did YOU notice?"

"Well, you could see where I guess some buzzards or whatever had gotten to it," Echo noted, thinking back, "maybe crows, I dunno. Scavenger birds of some sort. Rip and shred—you know what I mean. But that didn't look like the original injury..."

"No, it didn't," Omega agreed. "What did it look like to you?"

"Like...like the dog...melted, sorta."

* * *

"Exactly," Omega said, grim. "See, now I'm wondering if the giant cootie—"

Echo stifled a guffaw. A puzzled Omega stared at him, then mentally replayed her statement, and grinned at him, somewhat rueful.

"You get a kick outta that name for it, huh?"

"Yeah," Echo snorted, still trying to control an urge to laugh. "You keep using it, and I nearly lose it every time. It so perfectly summarizes our feelings about the thing." He waved a hand. "Keep going. I'm listening, even if I'm snickering."

"Okay. So I'm wondering if the thing is, maybe, like a Froon, you know, with acid spit or something," Omega speculated. "Or even—oh shit!" she exclaimed, sitting upright, as an idea struck. "Oh shit, oh shit, oh shit."

"You just glommed onto something important," Echo realized, sitting up with her.

"Yeah, I think I did," Omega confirmed. "The fires, and no water in the pipes, and the torn-up electric cars, and...oh damn. This...this is bad." She began scrabbling at the bed covers, throwing them aside and trying to ease her cast out of bed, despite the intense stiffness in her body.

"Whoa, baby," he said, reaching for her. "What the hell are

you doing? You need to stay off that foot for a couple days, minimum, or you might be in the regen pod for a couple of WEEKS. And we still need you working on this. Especially if you just figured something out, which it sure as hell sounds like you did. What's wrong?"

"Several things," Omega declared, still trying to untangle her legs from the sheets. "If I'm right, the mega moth is what's starting the fires, directly. Not intentionally, but still. And...do we know that there was only the one egg in that kid's science project?"

Echo gaped at her in something akin to horror.

"I don't," he finally said. "That doesn't mean that Fox doesn't know, or that we couldn't find out."

"We need to know," Omega decreed. "Otherwise, we could end up with a firestorm on our hands, and an awful lot of dead people."

"Oh shit. Lemme help you get dressed," Echo said, climbing out of bed and heading for the closets.

* * *

Half an hour later, they sat in the office of Item, department chief for Sciences at Headquarters, Omega in her antigrav chair, Echo in a visitor chair.

"No, not that I'm aware of," Item informed them. "In as far as I was told, the child only laid her hands on the one egg."

"That's...good," Omega decided, "but maybe we need to verify that? Is that Kydeen family still on-planet?"

"I don't know offhand," the other woman said, "but I'll find out. Because you're exactly right; we need to know if there could be more than one of these things. The sightings are sporadic enough that it COULD be more than one, based on what I remember of the map."

"Something else," Omega continued, as Echo watched and listened with folded arms and grim visage. "Have any of y'all found any unusual...liquid, or dried liquid...residue, either near one of the bodies, or near the ignition point of any of the fires?"

"Mm, no, not that anyone has reported to me," Item said, after a moment to consider.

"Is there any connection between all the deaths? Anything that the victims had in common?"

"Not that I'm really aware of," Item said. "So far, however, there are at least three people missing and unaccounted for, possibly as many as six or eight. Three bodies have been found in Central Park that weren't much more than skeletons with a few bits of desiccated tissue, even though they weren't reported missing more than a day or so prior to discovery of the bodies. Eight or ten have been killed due to falling debris or glass; thirty-seven hospitalized for same. Three were killed when they fell from, or were sucked out of, broken windows, and fell to the street below. There's around, oh, half a dozen animals that I'm aware of that have died under mysterious circumstances, too, at least two of which were found alongside the owner's bodies, likewise desiccated." She pulled up a file on her laptop. "Let me just check, and see if anything has been flagged since the last time I looked." Item scanned down through the spreadsheet, then raised an eyebrow, and opened up several additional files. "Huh. That's interesting. All three of the bodies in Central Park belonged to psychiatric patients. One was schizophrenic, the other two were bipolar..."

"What kinds of medication were they on, do you know?" Omega pressed.

"According to these forensic reports, the schizophrenic was on lithium...one of the bipolar patients was on olanzapine and lithium...and the other was on asenapine and lithium," Item reported.

"What about the missing persons?" Echo wondered.

"Let me check," Item said, then pulled up another file. After several moments, she looked up at them, her eyes troubled. "Well, I think we've found a common thread, here. All of the missing persons but one were also psychiatric patients, diagnosed with one of three things: bipolar disorder, schizophrenia, or something called 'major depressive disorder.' And all of them were on lithium salts as part of their treatment, most with something else prescribed, as well."

"Oh shit," Omega breathed. "Oh shit." She turned to Echo. "Ace, don't Yelfflani have a dietary need for lithium? I mean, that should be one of their essential minerals, right?"

"Yeah, that's what I recall," Echo confirmed. "Why?"

"Well, that means there's a higher amount of lithium in a

Yelfflani's body than in a human's..."

"Oh shit," Echo said, suddenly understanding. "My missing-persons case. Julian W. Thompson."

"Bingo."

"Damn. Well, that's a possible resolution I wasn't expecting. Item, who's the 'but one' you mentioned?" Echo asked.

"Oh. Evidently there have also been some odd deaths among the animals at the Central Park Zoo," Item noted, reading over the reports. "One of the keepers was upset, because they were animals he tended personally. On the afternoon before he went missing, he said something to a coworker about trying to investigate after he got off work. Then he never showed back up the next day."

"Ooo," Omega murmured. "When was that?"

"Mm. Mid-December, it looks like."

"Okay. Did the animal deaths match the dead bodies that have been discovered?"

"Judging by the photographs, I'd say yes," Item decided. "Which may mean that the zoo keeper ran across this thing. And since there has been a very odd, and very intense, cold-weather insect infestation reported in the foliage of the Park through most of December, I'm betting the thing might have been...larval, at that point?"

"Huh," Omega grunted, considering. "Good idea. Maybe it started out on the plants, then sniffed out the higher lithium in the patients, THEN either decided that all animal-type creatures were good to eat, or maybe it assumed they'd all have lithium...or maybe it was just hungry, or felt threatened..."

"Any or all of those would probably work," Item decided. "Especially if all the humans were carrying cell phones, with their lithium-ion batteries...which lithium, I gather, is important?"

"Mmph," Omega grunted again. "Yeah, I think so. Think...a shot of minerals with a little...fiber."

"Ah. Something like, yeah," Item agreed, then chuckled grimly. "I suppose we're lucky it didn't glom one of the offworld visitors or something. Oh wait, you said it might have..."

"Yeah, it sure looks like it. Okay, that's several points down, it sounds like. On to the next, I guess. Anything unusual about those desiccated bodies, other than the desiccation?" Echo wondered.

"Yes, a couple of my people said it looked like parts of the bones had sort of...melted," Item answered. "Not the usual cut marks of tool or teeth or claws. Nor yet scorch marks. They didn't know what to make of it." She waved her tablet. "And these images substantiate their descriptions, in my educated opinion."

Echo and Omega exchanged glances. Omega bit her lip.

"Okay, that means something to the two of you," Item observed. "What's up, and what do we need to be looking for?"

"Have you ever heard of organolithium reagents?" Omega asked.

* * *

"...I suppose that explains the focus on lithium in the diet. So the proof of your hypothesis will be if there is excess lithium near the fires?" Item verified, after Omega had explained.

"Exactly," Omega confirmed. "And that means we need to go out there and test for lithium everywhere we can."

"Well, after a couple of my people were a bit too preoccupied with their finds and nearly got themselves killed—almost blown off a rooftop, I was told, though I have my suspicions regarding that—about a day ago, I'm afraid Fox has restricted us to the facility," Item said, apologetic. "We're not field agents, after all. You know how we scientists can get, Omega. You're one of the more...alert...I've seen."

"Yeah, well," Omega murmured. "Turns out some o' that came along with the 'enhancements.'"

"Oh. I'm sorry; I didn't mean to bring up a hurtful topic."

"That's okay. You didn't know. But yeah, I do know what you're talking about. Which means," Omega added, "that Echo and I need to go do that."

"I think we probably need to check in with the medlab about that busted foot first, baby," Echo recommended.

* * *

"Absolutely not," Zarnix decreed.

"But Zarnix," Omega protested. "If we're gonna stop this thing, we need to know."

"Then someone else will be finding out," Zarnix riposted.

"YOU are on medical leave from field work. I do not mind if you do in-house scientific analysis, as long as you stay off that foot. So you are NOT on sick leave; I am simply not approving you for field work. And going out to take samples is field work! There is no way you can do what you are proposing and remain in that antigrav chair. Especially if the exoheteroc comes after you! And if you get up and start walking around on that ankle at this point—let alone running from the exoheteroc— assuming you survive, you WILL tear the tendon completely, and you WILL require surgery to repair it, and you WILL end up in a regeneration pod for several weeks while it heals. And depending on how you tear it, and how badly, it could end up being YOU who cannot go back into the field. Ever."

Both members of Alpha One paled at that.

"No, baby," Echo said then. "You stay here. I've got an idea how we can do this, you an' me, that won't put you at risk. Zarnix, did you or Zebra ever put the go-ahead for me to go back in the field into the system?"

"We did, but it was around other things, like putting Crutch into a regen pod," Zarnix noted.

"Crutch is in a regen pod? She'll be okay, then?" Omega asked, perking up.

"I...do not know yet," Zarnix admitted, face falling. "Suffice it to say, it was a last-ditch effort. We may only decant her to send her off to a well-earned retirement...if not in her original condition. And...perhaps not even that."

"You still don't know if she'll survive?" Omega whispered, horrified.

"...No. The damage to internal organs was...severe. Let alone the severity of the concussion. And you, of all people, Echo, should understand about the problems inherent in healing brain damage with a regeneration process."

"Damn," Echo muttered, running a hand through his hair.

"Lotta that," Omega agreed, guilt-ridden. "Shit. All because I got myself into a situation I couldn't get out of on my own."

"And I wasn't supposed to help get you out of it," Echo added, disheartened.

"Yeah, but I cheerfully walked right into it," Omega pointed out, discouraged and annoyed with herself. "Dumbass that I am."

"No, do not blame yourselves," Zarnix said, firm but consoling. "I have had the entire story from both Fox and Zebra, and we all understand. It was only supposed to be providing assistance, not a rescue, as such. It simply turned into one between the time Omega entered the building and the time she could attempt to lead them out."

"And we still don't know why, for sure," Echo noted. "Not yet, at least."

"Yeah," Omega agreed, downcast. "Still..."

"Hush, adoptive niece. Had it not been this, it would likely have been something else. It is NOT your fault," Zarnix decreed, checking something on his tablet. "Ah, there it is. Yes, Echo, your active status is back in the system and has gone live."

"Okay, then how about this: Meg, I'll go to one or two of the sites with whatever equipment you put together for me to take," Echo suggested, "and you can 'watch' through the nd't'lq and tell me what needs doing. Then I'll perform the field testing and you can see the results." He grinned. "I'll be your remote drone, as it were."

"Ohhh, I don't know if I like that," Omega admitted, perturbed by the notion. "All by yourself? With you just going back into the field after everything that's happened to you, and the risk?"

"She has a point, Echo," Zarnix agreed. "Is there any chance of obtaining backup to go with you?"

"I seriously doubt it," Echo pointed out. "I couldn't even get help to get Meg outta the burning building with the kids an' all. The field agents are spread thin, and Fox even said something about calling in as many field agents from other Offices as he could shake loose. The field agents are flat runnin' ragged out there."

"According to what he said when we pinged Fox earlier over a quick breakfast, before we went to see Item, they have more and more new fires starting, and haven't figured out why," Omega explained. "Which, if I get the test results I expect from this little excursion we're talking about, I CAN explain it, and maybe even figure out how to prevent it. But in the meantime, they're going nuts trying to stop 'em before something collapses."

"Mm. That is not at all good. All right. If you do this, Echo, you will need to make sure you are particularly vigilant and cautious."

"I can do that, especially with Meg's help," Echo pointed out. "After all, didn't we already determine that she's one of the most...AWARE...humans that's ever been?"

"Zee did tell me something about that, yes," Zarnix recalled. "All right. I am game for you to try it if Omega is."

"IIIII...dunno," Omega murmured, hesitant.

* * *

"Wait," Echo said, his brow furrowing in worry. "Don't tell me you have a 'bad feeling' about this..."

"No, nothing like that," Omega said, and Echo relaxed. "I'm just...I'm worried about ya, Ace. You already almost bit it a couple times an' got hell beat outta ya, all in about a month or so. I just..." Abruptly she exhaled heavily and bowed her head, partly hiding her face. "When you get right down to it, I didn't actually have a whole lot in the way of a life until you came along, honey. I had a goal, but really nothing else. And now I have the world, the universe. Because you showed it to me. I...I don't...I can't..."

"Hush, baby," Echo murmured, sensing through the nd't'lq what she could not manage to choke out. "It's okay. I understand. I've had a few too many really close shaves lately—"

"Like, micrometer close," she interjected.

"Yeah, and it has you unnerved. And I guess I can't blame you. If it helps at all, I've been there with you, too. Especially after the Cortians toasted you. So I know what you're feeling right now."

"I know," Omega sighed. "And I know you gotta do this. It's really the only way to do it properly."

"Well, we DO have actual drones and remotes, ya know," Echo pointed out. "I've trained you how to use 'em. If you really don't want me to go, I won't."

"I really don't want you to, but I don't think a drone could..." Omega broke off, rubbed her hands over her face, and thought for a long moment. "Well, I guess we could try that,

246

first, and see what happens. We might get it to work."

"That sounds good," Zarnix noted; he had remained quiet through Alpha One's discussion, allowing them to talk through the matter without his interference, but now he interjected his professional opinion. "If neither of you goes into the field, I have nothing to worry about. But if it does not work, Echo, you are back on active duty and may do as you think best."

"Thanks, Zarnix," Echo said. "C'mon, Meg. Let's go survey the fleet of drones and see what we can come up with."

"First, go pick up your Regenic prescription," Zarnix reminded Omega.

"Oh, right," she replied.

* * *

When Alpha One showed up at the medlab pharmacy, Agent Prep was working the counter. The short, red-haired agent with a subtle, fashionable stubble-beard raised both eyebrows as he saw Echo trundling Omega up to the window in an antigrav chair.

"Not again," Prep said, his unusual blue eyes sparkling gold and silver with amusement. "Girl, what did you go and do to yourself this time?"

"Got a buncha little bitty kids out of a high-rise fire," Echo said before Omega had a chance, "and had part of the building fall on her in the process."

"Oh DAMN!" Prep exclaimed, shocked. "I was joking, guys! You two need to be more careful!"

"We try," a discouraged Omega said with a sigh. "Shit seems to follow us around just to happen to us."

"Yeah," Echo agreed. "Some days, I feel like that guy from th' ol' Sunday funnies who had the little rain cloud followin' him around."

"THAT," Omega declared with feeling.

"All right," Prep said, "I assume it's Omega that needs the 'script, this time?"

"Yeah," Omega affirmed. "Should be a bottle of Regenic pills back there for me?"

"Oh, I remember that," Prep said, disappearing into the back as his voice drifted forward. "Hang on just a sec. Mmm... you also have a prescription for pain, here..."

"Okay, that's good," Echo said. "She only had enough for about one more dose, from what Zebra gave her...whenever it was."

Prep came out with two pill bottles.

"Here you go," he said. "You gonna keep up with it, or you want me to give 'em to Echo?"

"How dopey will the pain med make me?" Omega wondered.

"Shouldn't make you dopey at all," Prep said, double-checking the label. "Nah, this one's good. Zebra had in mind that you'd need to think clearly."

"Okay, I'll keep up with it, then," Omega said, and Prep gave her the bottles, which she tucked into a pocket.

"You good for now, baby?" Echo asked.

"Yeah, I think so," Omega said. "It'll be a little while before I need more."

"Hey, listen, before you go," Prep said, "is it true about that giant insect in Manhattan?"

"Is it ever," Omega said, rolling her eyes. "We got a mess out there."

"Well, I knew I was filling orders right and left, I just wasn't sure what was going on," the other agent admitted. "That's the disadvantage to bein' stuck back here alla time."

"Oh, I get it. Okay. It's called an exoheteroc, and it's supposed to be on Zheen, one of Kydeen's moons," Echo explained. "It looks like a giant moth, with a wingspan probably a good fifteen or twenty feet across, though it's kinda hard to tell, 'cause it moves more like a hummingbird."

"Worse, it's the same color as the buildings, so it blends in," Omega added. "And it might be what's causing the fires... and maybe killing people."

"Oh DAMN!" a horrified Prep exclaimed again. "Okay, y'all go get 'im. Or, well, just be careful."

"That's the idea," Echo averred, as he and Omega turned and headed for the Surveillance Equipment Section. "Time to go pick a drone, baby."

* * *

In the end, they chose a drone that had long range, a substantial frame, offworld tech, and fairly sophisticated sample collection and return capability.

"I'm not entirely thrilled about bringing a sample back to Headquarters," Omega noted, "but if it's already dried and has been lying out there a while, it should be safe."

"And this drone has an isolation compartment for the samples," Echo pointed out. "We'll have the drone master load it with a dry nitrogen atmosphere to keep everything neutral and inert. That should work pretty good, right?"

"Yeah, that should work," Omega agreed. "Provided we can actually get a sample and return it with this thing. After what happened to Crutch, who was in a much more powerful prop unit, I have my doubts."

"I understand, but we need to at least try," Echo encouraged. "If this DOES work, it saves us a lotta trouble."

"I know, and I'm cool with that," Omega averred. "Now let's get this thing outfitted and send it out."

* * *

In short order, the drone master, Kaf, had set up their drone to have a dry nitrogen atmosphere in the sample chamber, and Omega had looked over the locations she wanted to sample and gotten street addresses and specific positions.

"All right," Kaf told Alpha One. "Echo, you go ahead and take the drone up to the roof of the building and activate it. Once it lifts off, come back down here. I'll set it up so you and Omega can 'drive' it, and leave you to it. Omega, yell if you run into trouble, or need help."

"Right," the two heads of Alpha Line said in unison.

Echo took the drone and headed out, and Omega settled down at the console, watching closely as Kaf instructed her in its use to control the drone.

* * *

Echo emerged onto the rooftop of Headquarters near Omega's little observatory dome. He sat the drone on its landing gear, placing it on a small metal table Omega sometimes used for notebooks and whatnot, when she was stargazing as an automated observation ran in the dome. Then he began flipping a group of switches in a specific sequence, activating the drone.

Okay, Meg, he told her through their bond. *It's ready to go.*

And we have liftoff, came the whimsical reply, as the

maglev initiated and the propeller blades that helped steer the drone spun up. The drone eased off the tabletop, rising straight up some fifty feet, then it headed for the East River.

Echo turned for the stairs.

* * *

Moments later, Echo was taking a seat at the control console beside Omega, watching the video being transmitted by the drone as she flew it toward the site where the dog's body had been found on the rooftop.

"Here," he said, "you want me to do that? You'll need to be fresh when we reach the site, so you can run it to get the samples. I can spell you until then; it's almost time for your next med dose anyway."

"Okay, that makes a lotta sense," Omega said, scooting over to let him take the controls. "I WAS starting to hurt again."

"Yeah, you're well inside fifteen minutes or so; why don't you go ahead and take 'em?" Echo suggested, as he began commanding the drone. "Otherwise, we'll be tryin' to juggle landing the drone an' you taking your meds, 'cause that's about the ETA on the drone."

"All right; fair enough." She extracted a couple of little pill bottles from her pocket—the pain medication, and the Regenic—and a chilled water bottle from the storage in the antigrav chair. Moments later, the medications were in her belly. She waited patiently, trying to ignore the pain, for them to take effect, and watched as Echo skillfully piloted the drone toward the desired rooftop.

* * *

By the time the drone reached the rooftop some fifteen minutes later, Omega's pain medication had taken full effect; she was free of pain, but fully alert and active. Echo brought the drone down to the rooftop's level, then put it in station-keeping mode and handed over control to his partner. Omega took control and brought the drone up a bit, scanning the rooftop; the dog's body had been removed, but there were still stains and smudges showing where it had been, and a small puddle of dried fluid beside it.

"There we go," she said, setting down the drone right next to the dried material. "Lemme see what I can do with this, then."

"Wow, you're good," Echo said, as he watched his wife and partner delicately operate the controls of the remote to obtain the sample.

"Thanks," she said with a grin. "I worked one whole year with a remote lander intended for Mars, so we had to figure out how things needed to be done, as much in advance of the need as we could. I got the job of playing with an actual RCV to work out the best ways to do everything."

"Makes sense," he decided.

Inside five minutes, she had managed to use the remote's non-metallic sampler to scrape up a decent-sized sample from the dried puddle, placing it into a glass tube inside the sample compartment, and remotely sealing it.

"There," she said. "That's sample one."

"Now where to?" Echo wondered, as he resumed piloting the device.

"Over by Central Park, where they found a couple of the human bodies," Omega instructed. "Look here." She pushed a street address, scribbled on a satellite map printout, across the console top.

"Aha," he said, studying the map. "Got it."

He zoomed the drone upward and headed east with it.

* * *

Echo directed the drone over to the western edge of Central Park; there, several of the dead bodies had been found, just over a rise along Central Park West, under a copse of trees... several of which showed signs of the 'infestation' that park officials had been fighting over the holidays.

Unfortunately, the natural environment made it harder to locate the exact places where the bodies had been, and he and Omega had to scan the terrain carefully in order to find them.

At last Omega spotted the mottled, discolored, yellowed grass where the bodies had lain—apparently placed there by the mega moth as a safe place to return with its prey to feed, at least based on Omega's hypothesis—and Echo brought the drone down close, so she could look for specific signs of the substance for which she searched.

"Hmmm," she grumbled, frustrated. "This is taking too

long."

"What do you mean?" Echo wondered. "It takes as long as it takes."

"No, I mean, the longer this takes, the higher the probability becomes of our drone running into the giant cootie," she fussed, then waited for the snort she knew he would make, before continuing. "I wanted to go in here, grab the samples, and get out, before we had to try to negotiate the thing's wake. Never mind that—well, you did notice I was careful to pick out a drone with an off-world power pack, right?"

"I did, yeah."

"And you know why?"

"Yeah. Or, well, I can make a pretty good guess."

"Okay, let's—oh, there we go!" Omega exclaimed. "There's what I want. Lemme take over now."

"Have at it, baby," Echo said, rolling his desk chair a couple of feet to the side, to allow her easier access to the drone's remote controls.

With the same skill she had demonstrated previously, Omega obtained a sample of the soil and dead grass, tucking it into the sample container and stowing it, before moving the drone some ten or twelve feet to the left and repeating the process. "One more time," she decided, moving the drone five or six feet forward, and taking a third sample. "I want several, because I can't be sure these soil samples are gonna really yield us much of anything; if the liquid mostly drained away into the dirt, there won't BE anything, much. But I think that's why all the grass there is dead, now."

"Chemical burns?"

"Basically, yeah."

"Are you gonna try to get samples from another location?"

"No, I think I wanna just try to head back with the ones we already have. If we don't turn up anything on these, I might try some more, yeah. But then I might just be wrong, too."

"Somehow, I doubt that," Echo said, considering. "It makes too much sense, and fits too much of what's happening, to be wrong."

"I hope so," Omega said with a sigh. "Because it also might give us a way to defeat the thing. Anyway, let's get those back here, so we can start the analysis."

"Right. Returning to base with the samples." Echo resumed control as Omega moved aside, and brought the little drone to cruising altitude, turning it toward Brooklyn and the Headquarters location.

But before the drone had even crossed Central Park, the camera view went berserk, and the gyroscopic stabilizer went dead. Several lights on their control panel began flashing red, and an audible alert sounded. At that, Kaf came running into the control room.

"Shit!" Omega cried, as an odd, insectoid claw became visible along the side of the field of view. "Guess who?!"

"Giant cootie! Damn it!" Echo exclaimed, wrestling with the controls as he attempted to free the drone. Unfortunately, if the debris that fell within the field of view was anything to go by, a significant portion of the flight surfaces had been ripped away, along with at least two of the attitude propellers. Moments later, the view showed the ground rushing toward the camera, as the drone dropped like a rock.

"KILL IT!" Kaf cried.

"We'd like to!" Echo responded.

"NO! The DRONE! Hit the destruct button!" Kaf elaborated. "It's offworld tech! We can't afford it being found!"

Kaf flipped up a plexiglass cover over a big red button, then slammed his hand down on it. Fractions of a second later, the video image onscreen broke up, and was replaced with static.

"Damn," Echo and Omega said simultaneously.

* * *

"Well, you were right," Echo said, as they headed for the Alpha Line Room to ponder matters. "The drone was completely defenseless against that thing."

"Yeah, I was afraid of that," Omega sighed. "And since we had to destroy the drone, we lost our samples, too. I was hoping we might be able to retrieve 'em."

"Yeah, me too." Echo paused his comment as they entered the big, empty room; the rest of Alpha Line was on the streets of Manhattan, trying to help figure out how to corral the 'giant cootie' while fighting fires. He watched as Omega moved to her desk, woke the computer, and checked for messages and emails, before adding in a quiet voice, "You know what we need to do next, baby."

Omega stiffened, but did not turn around.

"And you know how I feel about it," she replied. "I vote we contact Fox or Romeo and see if we can't get a team out there, either with instructions as to how to get what we want, or with someone from the Sciences department to do it while they play bodyguard."

"If you really think there's anybody to shake loose to do that, that'll be fine," Echo agreed.

"Then let's see what we can see," Omega decreed.

* * *

"...I'm sorry, Meg," Romeo said on the cell phone, which Omega had in speaker mode. "I c'n put out an Alpha Line Alert so that, if any of our people go by one o' th' sites, they should contact you on instructions f'r gettin' a sample. But I can't say when, or even if, that'd happen, let alone when they'd be able t' get the sample back to ya."

"Where IS everybody?" Omega asked then. "I thought the area was already evacuated."

"It is...mostly," Romeo admitted. "At least, o' th' people who 're usually here. But now we got idiots comin' in, wantin' t' see th' mega moth, news media tryin' t' get shots of 'the terrorist drone fleet,' an' all kindsa shit like that. An' we're th' ones Fox tasked with not only keepin' their asses in one piece, but keepin' 'em from findin' out what's really goin' on. Never mind the reg'lar first responders tryin' ta put out fires an' junk."

"Shit," Echo murmured. "Klydonian invasion, take two."

"Pretty much, yup," Romeo agreed. "Least it's not the whole damn planet this time. Huge pain in th' ass, but it's gotta be done. So anyway, half of Alpha Line is out here, doin' all that, an' th' other half is back at Headquarters, sleepin' like th' dead after a shift o' doin' all that."

"Right; gotcha. Okay, hon, lemme let ya get back to it," Omega said, stifling a sigh. "Y'all be safe. ALL of you."

"Doin' our best, 'sis,'" Romeo said. "India sends 'er love, by th' way."

"Back atcha both," Omega said with a smile. "Omega out."

"Romeo out."

* * *

"...No, tekhter," Fox said, "I'm not in any better shape than Romeo, I'm afraid. We are still having new fires breaking out, and we cannot ascertain what is causing them. The Boys and I have decided that, since there is a complete overlap between the exoheteroc's...territory, for want of a better term...and the perimeter within which the fires are occurring, that there has to be a cause and effect, but we cannot determine what."

"Well, that's just it, Fox," Omega told him, as Echo leaned over her shoulder. "If I'm right, then I know what that cause IS. But I need these samples to test, to verify that I'm right."

"Mm. I see," Fox hummed, thoughtful. "In that case, I really want to help even more than I did at first. But what I WANT doesn't matter, kinder; I simply don't have any more resources at the moment to accommodate the request."

"Anytime soon?" Omega pressed, hopeful.

"No, meyn kind, I'm sorry," Fox said with a weary sigh. "I sent Zebra off to bed, with instructions for her to tell Zarnix to do likewise; Whiskey and Rglfrz are next up, though Whiskey hasn't had that much sleep, either. I've been calling the Atlanta and Chicago Offices for assistance, both with medical personnel and field agents. Even the Los Angeles Office is sending assistance. But it will be some few hours before any of them arrive; I instructed them NOT to fly, as that seems to be the sure way to attract this farshiltn zakh's attention. So they'll be coming in to Grand Central Station...probably early tomorrow morning."

"I need to find this out, Fox," Omega insisted. "If I can determine this, then not only can I tell you for certain how the giant cootie is—"

"The what?!"

"Giant cootie is what Meg has taken to calling the exoheteroc, Fox," Echo said with a chuckle. "I know we've got a serious situation, but damn if that epithet doesn't make me laugh every time."

There was a snort from the other end of the line.

"I can see why," Fox said, a grin audible in his voice. "Thank you, tekhter, I needed that. And yes, I think I vaguely recall hearing that term before, from Echo, now that I think about it. I gather that, if you can obtain these samples, you may be able to tell me what is going on, and potentially how to stop this thing, this 'giant cootie,' as you put it?"

"I think so, Fox," Omega said, serious. "At least, I can start to formulate some ideas that stand a decent chance of working."

"Can you and Echo not do this?"

"Zarnix refuses to clear me medically," Omega explained, "and I don't think Echo needs to be going out there against that thing without some sort of backup...which we ain't got, right now. We already tried to retrieve samples with a drone, and the giant cootie tore it to shreds."

"Damnation!"

"Exactly. I don't want Echo ending up as another unexplained casualty in all this by going out there by himself, if we can help it."

"Understood. I'll see if I can't scare up a loose agent to go with him, then. Would that do?"

"That would help," Omega decided, biting her lip. "To tell the truth, with him just coming back on active duty, I'd rather not send him out at all..."

"Baby, I'm doing fine," Echo murmured. "I can DO this."

"You probably can," she agreed. "I just...I already told you, you've had too many close shaves lately for me to..."

"Well, she has a point there, Echo," Fox noted. "And I can understand it. But daughter, you may not have much choice, if you want to get this done in anything like a timely fashion."

"I know," Omega said with a deep sigh. "And the longer we wait, the higher the probability that the damn cootie starts a mess that we can't stop. Okay, if you can get Echo some backup, that'll have to do."

"Echo, gather up whatever equipment Omega says you'll need, and come over here in the Corvette, the same way you did last time, when you two scoped things out," Fox said. "I'll see what I can work out between now and the time you get here."

"Is the 'Vette back in the vehicle hangar?" Echo asked in surprise.

"Yes; once the two of you set off in the airskimmer, I had it sent back," Fox explained. "The vehicle maintenance personnel have been shuttling vehicles back and forth for us. So by the time you get over here to my command center, I should have someone lined up to go with you."

"Consider it done, Fox," Echo said. "I should be there in... what, Meg? Half an hour?"

"Make it forty-five minutes," she corrected. "I wanna make sure we go over the sampling equipment and procedures before you go."

"Got it," Fox said. "I'll be looking for you, Echo."

"I'll be there. Alpha One out."

"Fox out."

* * *

As soon as Echo left to meet Fox, Omega headed straight for their quarters.

Once there, she did NOT turn on any lights or the television. Instead, she went all the way through to the bedroom, where she closed all the doors, locked herself into the room, and turned the lights down as low as they would go, even unplugging all but one of the night lights.

Then she dragged out a sleep mask and earplugs from the nightstand drawer, donned them, and waited in her medical antigrav chair, anxious.

Chapter 10

Not quite an hour later, Echo showed up at the staging area in the Corvette, alone, but with several small items of equipment tucked into various warp pockets. As he exited, he tossed the keys to Lima, who pointed toward Fox, and Echo turned, heading for the Director.

"Hey, Fox," he said, as Fox glanced up from the electronic tablet which he was using to coordinate fire-fighting efforts, all while trying to locate the mega moth. "I made it."

"Oh, hello, zun," Fox said, somewhat absently. "Hang on a moment; we have a situation."

"What's up?"

"Evidently our mega moth, giant cootie, or whatever the hell we're currently calling the thing, has decided to crawl into the broken window of a high-rise to feed on something, and in the process, it has set a fire that we're having a hard time reaching," Fox explained. "It's spreading into the building's core, and we're getting concerned we're going to have a collapse. It doesn't take that much heat to cause structural steel to lose structural INTEGRITY, after all."

"True," Echo noted. "It's really more about uneven heating, isn't it? I mean, if part of the girder is heated and tries to expand, while another part is in a cool section and doesn't, or maybe even wants to contract, you get some pretty severe thermal stresses within the girder, and the steel can start to distort..."

"Exactly," Fox confirmed. "And as soon as that shape begins to change, the applied forces shift their angles..."

"And a house of cards collapses," Echo said, nodding. "Yeah, I remember that firefighting course you put me through after, ah, certain historic events some years ago."

"You were young, but that's a good sign it took," Fox said, pleased. "So let me see what I can do, here, then we'll talk. Give me a minute or two..."

"Right."

Echo waited while Fox issued orders, both via text and voice command on his 'walkie-talkie' cell phone. Finally Fox looked up.

"All right," he said with a tired sigh. "Hopefully THAT sequence of attack will enable 'em to get the fire out before something bad happens. I hope that's not one of your sample sites."

"Where is it?"

Fox showed him the map display on his tablet, pointing to the location.

"Ah. No, we're good," Echo said. "I got a couple places in Central Park proper, then a rooftop a couple blocks away from there, and if I can do all those, I should be all right."

"That's good," Fox said. "Even better would be if you can just grab samples from the Central Park sites. I can get you backup to THOSE, since we have people guarding it as a crime scene, but if you go into the high-rise district, we could have a problem."

"Hm. Well, shit," Echo grumbled. "According to Meg, my priorities are exactly the opposite from that. The Central Park samples are gonna be harder to extract chemicals from, so she'd prefer I hit up the rooftop site, if it came down to it."

"Damnation," Fox cursed. "And shit, glagaram, abdab, and gronk, while I'm about it."

"You don't have any backup available for me at all, other than the guards on the crime scene?" Echo wondered.

"No, zun, I'm sorry. Between trying to put out fires, this bad new fire, trying to ensure that the subway tunnels underneath it are closed and evacuated in case it comes down, and fending off the exoheteroc, never mind working on figuring out why it's causing fires AND how to take it out..." Fox sighed and shook his head. "You're just going to grab a couple of material samples, right? Do you really think you'll need backup?"

"No; I'm not planning on attracting the thing's attention," Echo pointed out. "But Meg...after everything that's happened in recent months—especially my kidnapping and torture by the Cortians—she's...not comfortable with it..." He shrugged. "And frankly, I understand that."

"Ah. Yes, I see. Well, let's just try to get it over and done, and you back to Headquarters with the samples she needs for her analysis, as fast as we can, then," Fox decided. "The faster you go, the less are the chances of something having TIME to happen, anyway."

"True," Echo agreed. "Okay, Fox, I'm off, then. It's all within a few blocks, and I figure if I'm on foot and stick to cover, I'm unlikely to attract much attention."

"Good point. Be careful, zun."

"Always, Fox. Always."

* * *

Echo headed out, slipping from tree to bush to rock and never allowing himself out in the open for more than a couple of seconds, paralleling Central Park West until he reached the slight rise on his left, near the bus stop.

Then he walked over the rise and leaned against the stone fence, checking for anything flying at speed down the street, before he located the blotched, yellow turf that marked the site where the bodies had been found.

Just then, three agents stepped out of their coverts and threw him several hand gestures by way of acknowledgement of his presence; Echo realized they'd already heard from Fox, and would provide lookout, assistance, and backup if it became needed. He raised a hand in greeting, and they nodded, then disappeared back into their hiding places.

Okay, baby, I'm at the first site, he told Omega through their link, as he got out a pair of heavy-duty, chemical-resistant nitrile gloves. *You went over how to take the samples pretty thoroughly with me, so I think I'm good with that. Show me WHERE you want me to get the samples.*

All right, Ace, came the reply. *Look over to your right. See that deep yellow, dead patch of grass? Get one in the middle of that. As near to the deepest yellow part as you can. And be REALLY careful not to get anything on your skin or clothes.*

On it.

* * *

It took about half an hour to obtain four samples at the Central Park site, as Omega used Echo's eyes to survey the area and decide exactly where she wanted the samples extracted, then show him the precise place.

But soon he had them tucked into a special padded pouch lined with nitrile—which pouch, in its turn, went into a warp pocket. Each sample bottle had its own little padded pocket within the pouch, ensuring it would remain undamaged rather than bash against the other bottles.

There, he told her. *And I haven't seen hide nor hair of the 'giant cootie' mega moth.*

Good. Let's hope it stays that way.

Me too. Now, on to the rooftop dog site?

Yes. That's the most important one, but also probably the most dangerous. You won't have much, if any, in the way of cover there. And you'll be up at its flight level. So BE CAREFUL.

You know the answer to that, baby. Help me keep aware, all right?

Of course.

* * *

It took Echo a bit over ten minutes to reach the address where the dog's body had been found on the roof; he could have arrived sooner because it was not that far from the Central Park site, but he was keeping a close watch out for the mega moth, and exercising a great deal of stealth in the process. Since this building had not had a fire—the only possible indication that the mega moth had visited it was the dog body on the roof, and that section of roof was covered in stone pavers to accommodate the penthouse owner—he took the elevator to the currently-unoccupied penthouse, as the owner had evacuated. There, he used an electronic lockpick to enter, and headed straight for the door onto the rooftop.

Before he exited onto the roof, however, he looked outside, scanning the horizon as far as he could see throughout the field of view of the French doors, even as he put the nitrile gloves back on his hands.

Hm. I don't see anything, he decided. *Meg, baby, do YOU see anything?*

* * *

Back at Headquarters, Omega sat in the dark in their bedroom, in what she thought of as a 'meditative telepathic state,' in order to focus on Echo's environment to the best of her ability, as she perceived it through his senses. Now she

261

scanned intently, knowing that her partner/husband's life could depend upon it.

No, Ace, I'm not seeing anything, she admitted. *Of course, it could be behind the penthouse from us.*

I know. That's what worries me. Well, I guess once I get out, I'll do a three-sixty and see what we see.

And sprint for cover if we see the damn thing.

Right.

DAMN, but I wish we had a suit made of the gloves' material, or something.

No argument there. Something to gin up in the aftermath, I guess.

Yeah.

* * *

Echo opened the door and stepped out, immediately turning in circles as he scanned the area as best he could.

I'm not seeing anything, he said. *Baby?*

Me too neither. Let's go ahead and get this done as quick as we can. I want you outta there as fast as you can git.

Do you still want two samples from here?

If you can do 'em fast. Otherwise, just grab one.

Okay.

Echo turned and headed for the pale blotch on the paving stones where the dog's body had been partially dissolved, extracting the sample collection kit from a pocket as he went.

* * *

Huh, he grunted mentally, as he stood beside the blotched spot on the roof. *Look at this, baby. The paving stones are pitted.*

Yeah, you're right. Just like the rocks back at the Loch, where your Yelfflani guy went missing.

Somehow that doesn't bode well to me.

Me neither. Well, let's hurry up and grab the samples and get you outta there.

Right.

Echo immediately knelt beside the dried fluids and delicately scraped up a sample with the special non-metallic spatula Omega had given him—she hadn't wanted to chance a random spark igniting the stuff while Echo was handling it—before depositing it in another bottle and sealing it, then placing the bottle in the nitrile-lined collection pouch.

Then he scraped up another sample from a different portion of the dried patch, placing it in a fresh sample container.

* * *

Omega, having eliminated as much of her own sensory experiences as she could to maximize her concentration, was focused solely on Echo's eyes and ears. Since her mind had been finely tuned by Slug to perceive all sensory input in a more sensitive and detailed fashion than most humans, she knew it behooved her to help Echo detect the mega moth if it was in the near vicinity.

So when she 'heard' the faint, beating whir in the distance, growing louder all too swiftly, horror swept through her being.

ECHO! she shouted. *IT'S COMING! HEAD FOR THE PENTHOUSE* NOW!

* * *

"Oh shit," Echo breathed aloud, glancing up as the sound of rapid wingbeats became audible to him, as well. "It's coming up behind me!"

He had just tucked the second sample into the collection bottle; he took the time to seal it, shove it into the nitrile bag, and throw the bag into a pocket, then he leaped directly from his kneeling position into a sprint, straight for the rooftop door of the penthouse.

But when a big blob of some viscous gray fluid hit the stonework just in front of him, he eluded it—somehow managing to avoid all the splatter—and headed for the rooftop garden shed instead.

The mega moth flanked him, hovering, and he ducked, just before the exoheteroc shot another mucus-like blob of saliva out of its proboscis. It passed over Echo's head, striking an arborvitae, which immediately began to dissolve.

Well, that confirms my hypothesis, he 'heard' Omega's random thought, and agreed. *Damn.*

Echo lunged behind the shed, and watched as a fusillade of the deadly saliva globules flew past, taking out a lounge chair, a plastic end table, and part of a miniature lemon tree; they melted down into puddles of organics, though the concrete planter in which the lemon tree had stood did not, instead doing a reasonable job of containing what remained of the tree. He tried to catch his breath, taking quick inventory to ensure he hadn't been contacted by a droplet of the viscous, caustic fluid...

...When the exoheteroc came around the corner of the shed. Echo ran.

* * *

The next several minutes were a nightmare of ducking and dodging, as Echo tried to work himself closer to the penthouse door without so much as being splattered by the backsplash from the surprisingly powerfully-projected sputum. He darted from structure to structure, using the side of the penthouse, the gardening shed, a little gazebo, and the pool house— fortunately the pool had been drained for the winter, else it would have constituted an even worse danger when the lithium reagent combusted on contact with the water, generating a steam explosion.

But at no time did the mega moth let him get close to the penthouse door.

Left! LEFT! Omega's mental voice cried in his head, and he obeyed without question, leaping to the left, just as another glob of spittle flew past him to the right. He ducked around the corner of the penthouse and pressed against the wall, panting.

Is this thing intelligent? Echo wondered then. *It's like it knows I'm trying to get through that door.*

I dunno, hon, Omega replied. *You know as much as I do, on that score. But, I mean, Earth cats an' dogs have intelligence 'bout like human six-year-olds, so...* He felt the mental shrug.

Ummph. Wonderful. Dammit, I gotta get outta here somehow, he told her, *but I don't think it's gonna let me anywhere close to that door. Can you raise me some emergency help?*

I dunno, but damn if I'm not gonna try, came the answer.

* * *

Rousing from her 'telepathic meditative state,' Omega pulled her cell phone. She swiftly hit the 'walkie-talkie' mode on the device, then shouted into it.

"BREAK-BREAK! EMERGENCY! ALPHA ONE RED EMERGENCY! This is Agent Omega! I need any aerial unit near 63 West 67th Street to divert to that location at once! Echo is under attack by the mega moth! Repeat, I need an aerial unit near 63 West 67th Street to divert to that location at once! Echo is under attack by the mega moth!"

"Omega, this is Romeo," came the reply, as the rest of the comm chatter silenced. "We's only 'bout a block away, in our airskimmer, th' *Crash Cart*. Divertin' from fire response to your location at th' maximum speed we c'n manage in these high-rises."

"I'm not there, just Echo," Omega noted. "Be prepared for anything."

"Right."

* * *

Echo, Alpha Two will be there in seconds, Omega told him as he swerved and weaved, diving in and out between the penthouse structures, as the exoheteroc tried to hit him with a burst of its caustic saliva, ejected through its proboscis-tongue, and she tried to help him watch for the spit. *They're in an airskimmer.*

I'm not gonna have time for them to land and open the hatch, baby, Echo sent the brief thought at her. *Never mind the fact that, as soon as they appear on the rooftop, they'll become a target, too.*

Um. Good point. Okay, the airskimmers have handholds on the hull, right? For working on it?

Uh, yeah, WOOP! Echo mentally exclaimed, as a blob of the mega moth's spit came much closer than he liked, and he sidestepped the splatter. *Whew, missed me. Yeah, it does. Why?*

Do you think you can hit it from the rooftop, if it's just below the roof? I mean, like, land on it?

Oh, you've gotta be kidding me, baby.

Have you got a better idea?

No. I guess I stand a better chance that way, than against this thing, I suppose. Okay, just lemme know where it is, and when I need to jump.

Wilco.

* * *

"Omega to Alpha Two," Omega called on her cell phone, trying to split her awareness between assisting Echo, and contacting their colleagues. "Omega to Alpha Two. Please come in."

"Alpha Two here," India's voice said. "Almost there, Meg."

"Good. Whatever you do, stay BELOW the rooftop level, by at least one story, but no more than two, or you'll become a target," Omega informed them. "In other words, stay out of the exoheteroc's line of sight."

"But Meg," Romeo expostulated, "how we s'posed t' get Echo if..."

"Drop your force field, be prepared for an abrupt hull impact, and KEEP THE IMPACTOR ON THE HULL," Omega replied, trying not to bite her lip at what she expected would be their response. Several background gasps went up on the comm, as other teams listened to the emergency communication.

"Oh shit," India murmured, her voice registering horror. "You don't mean..."

"I do mean," Omega said, firm. "And turn on the skimmer's beacon locator, please. I—um, I mean we, Echo an' me—have to time this just right."

"Beacon on," India said, and Omega pulled up the app on her phone. "Do you read our location?"

"I gotcha," Omega said, seeing the airskimmer's position moving between the buildings. "Keep going, and hover about four or five feet out, once you're next to the building he's on."

"Wilco," Romeo averred. "ETA in ten seconds."

* * *

All right, Ace, Omega told Echo. *Get ready. They're coming up West 68th Street, and staying out of a line of sight to the mega moth. They'll pause and hover as soon as they get even with the end of the building, and they'll be about four or five feet away from the building, maybe a story, story and a half, below you. So just remember us flying through the glide park on Emdali with Uncle Pul.*

Roger that, Echo replied. With Omega's help, he had managed to evade the mega moth's view, and was currently pressed up against the wall of the penthouse suite's garden shed again, catching his breath. *I'm...lessee, I need to get across the corner of the building, then. WHERE exactly along that end of the building will they be?*

266

I don't know yet, Ace. But I have them on the beacon app, and I'm 'looking' through your eyes. I'll be able to compare and tell you exactly where to jump.

Okay, baby. I trust you.

I know. I'm workin' hard, here, to earn that trust.

You earned it a long, long time ago, honey. Even if this doesn't go well, I'll know you did your absolute dead-level best.

Don't talk like that, now.

No, seriously, though. And know I'll be waitin' for ya on the other side.

O-okay. But let's talk about THAT later. Otherwise I'm not gonna be able to concentrate on this, and it WILL go south.

Ah. Right. They're in their personal airskimmer, then? What'd she name it...Crash Cart?

Yeah, an' yeah. And—

* * *

"We're here, Meg," India called. "Romeo's fine-tuning the positioning now."

"Copy fine-tuning," Omega replied, checking the beacon app for their location relative to the side of the building, and comparing it to the view she was getting from Echo.

"Aaaand...GO!" Romeo exclaimed.

* * *

Go NOW, Ace! GO NOW! Omega cried. *HERE! Jump right there!* And she mentally showed him exactly where to jump along the parapet.

Echo took off at a dead run.

The screech and whir of wings behind him told him the exoheteroc had spotted him.

He reached the parapet and dove over it.

"Oh SHIIIIIT!" he yelled as his feet left the rooftop.

* * *

As soon as he cleared the building, Echo spread-eagled, moving into the classic skydiver position, as he watched the roof of the airskimmer rushing up at him. He scanned its roof, looking for appropriately-placed hand-and footholds, then adjusted his body position in a sophisticated skydiving maneuver, aiming for those grips on the airskimmer's hull.

Within seconds, his torso slammed into the hull, extracting

a grunt of pain from him, as the impact knocked a significant portion of the air out of his lungs. Reflexively, Echo's hands sought and wrapped around the nearest hand grips, even as the airskimmer shifted slightly beneath him, both to compensate for the impact, and to ensure he did not slide off. He sucked in air, grateful for Romeo's skill in the pilot's seat—even if it had been at his own instruction—and sought the foot grips with his toes.

Once he was secure on the roof—a matter of scant seconds—he released one grip, rapped on the roof with his fist, then grabbed hold once more...

...Even as a large shadow fell across his body.

* * *

The thud on the roof indicated Echo's arrival to Alpha Two, and Romeo quickly adjusted the airskimmer's attitude, compensating for the impact, the increased weight, and the modified weight distribution. Moments later, a lighter double-thump denoted he had been successful in stabilizing himself.

"There," he said. "We got 'im. Initiate force field."

"Done," India replied, hitting a couple of buttons. "Hopefully that'll protect all of us against that thing."

"Yeah, and ensure Echo c'n breathe once we start haulin' ass," Romeo agreed.

Just then, Omega's voice came over the comm once more.

"Okay, you have him. Bring the force field up!"

"It's already done, Meg," Romeo averred. "Hopefully that thing won't be able t' get through THAT."

"It can't spit through it, either," she said.

"Huh?"

"Never mind right now; I'll explain later. Get outta there!"

"Goin'," Romeo replied. "Gonna accelerate slow; don't wanna accidentally dislodge Echo."

Just then, a smaller thud made itself known from somewhere, and the weapons console indicated a strike on the force field.

"Aw shit," Romeo grumbled. "Surely it didn't."

* * *

"Oh shit," Echo murmured, glancing up to determine the shadow's source—not that he didn't already know—to see the exoheteroc hovering right overhead. "Oh SHIT!"

It spit.

Echo instinctively flinched in an effort to avoid the liquid projectile, but the blob of saliva impacted an invisible surface some three feet over his head, sliding off and falling away, even as the airskimmer began to move forward, slowly building up speed.

Thank God, he thought, fervent and grateful. *See if I go out on a mission without my partner backing me up physically, ever again.*

Somewhere in the distance, he 'heard' a mental giggle.

Told ya, came the response.

* * *

"Okay, Meg, we got 'im, an' the mega moth did hit us with somethin', but it impacted the force field an' didn't come through. So we's all safe an' away," Romeo reported. "Where ya want 'im delivered? Th' stagin' area?"

"No," Omega said. "He's got some samples for me, that might help me figure out how the mega moth is starting those fires, as well as how to STOP those fires, and maybe the moth, too."

"Ooo."

"Yeah. So I need you to bring Echo back to Headquarters as soon as possible. Although, well, yeah, you might wanna land at the staging area so he doesn't have to hang onto the outside of the airskimmer the whole time. That could get bad if he gets tired and his grip goes out. If he left the 'Vette there, he can come back on his own; if not, could y'all ferry him home real quick?"

"Roger that, 'an sure thing, Meg," Romeo agreed. "Especially if it means takin' down th' fires, an' takin' OUT th' mega moth! Okay, one layover at th' stagin' area t' take 'im aboard, then 'e goes straight to HQ, one way or another."

* * *

Echo held on for all he was worth as the *Crash Cart* accelerated, thankful for the force field around him, both for the protection it afforded against the mega moth—which could not keep up with the airskimmer on a straightaway, and now was falling behind rapidly—and for the fact it blocked the airflow, enabling him to breathe with no difficulty. Soon the exoheteroc veered off and headed elsewhere, disappearing among the high-rises, as the *Crash Cart* made its approach to the staging area and was waved straight in to land, being given priority over other skimmers on approach...much to Echo's gratitude.

The *Crash Cart* sat down gently on the designated landing area, and this time Echo saw the yellow flicker that marked the force field being dropped. Moments later, the hatch was open, and Romeo and India were fetching a special ladder, placing it against the side of the airskimmer's fuselage, and calling to him.

Echo slid his feet out of their restraints, released the hand-holds with some difficulty, massaged his stiff, sore hands, and sat up.

"Well, that was some ride," he told them, as he crawled across the hull roof toward the ladder. "Never mind the game of hide-and-seek that came before it."

* * *

Echo climbed down from the top of the airskimmer, and Whiskey, who was back on duty and had been called to attend by Fox—along with a brief explanation of why, provided by Omega while the *Crash Cart* was en route—gave him a quick check-out to ensure that none of the caustic chemicals in the exoheteroc's saliva had splattered on him secondary to landing elsewhere on the rooftop. Fortunately it had not, else even his Suit might have combusted on his body, and Echo knew it.

The instant Whiskey was finished and verified his health—though he did recommend Echo get a once-over upon arriving back at Headquarters, at his earliest opportunity—Echo notified a waiting Fox that the rooftop likely needed firefighting efforts, if not already, then within minutes.

"From what, zun?"

"The exoheteroc, Fox. I got some samples," he patted a pocket, "an' Meg still has to test 'em, but she thinks that its spit may be really, really bad. It might even be what's causing the fires. AND that the mysterious deaths we got—you know, where the bodies looked sorta melted?—were the damn thing's prey."

"PREY?!" Fox exclaimed in shock. "You mean it ATE them?!"

"That's our working hypothesis right now, yeah," Echo confirmed. "She's the expert, but I wanted you to know, especially since the 'giant cootie' as she calls it, was spitting all over the rooftop, trying to snag ME. An' everything remotely organic that it hit melted down, except the stone, concrete, some of the metals, an' shit like that. I watched two small trees in planters turn into puddles in those planters."

"Ugh. So we definitely need to keep our people away from it."

"That is an excellent plan going forward, yeah," Echo averred. "Force fields stop the spit, though. I think we've been lucky so far that we haven't actually lost anyone. At least... um...have we heard about Crutch...?"

"Not lately," Fox said with a sigh. "Given Zebra told me she was in a regeneration pod, I think that might be good news...but I'm not sure."

"Right. Well, I'm headed back to Headquarters to deliver these samples to Meg. If I hear anything about Crutch, you want me to let ya know?"

"Please."

"Okay. Wilco. Um, where did the 'Vette get to, do you know?"

"LIMA!" Fox bellowed. Lima appeared around a just-landed airskimmer.

"Yeah, Boss?" he called.

"Alpha One's Corvette? Where...?"

Lima waved Echo over.

"C'mon an' I'll show you where we parked it, Echo."

Echo nodded, then turned to Fox, grabbing his hand.

"Later, Fox," he murmured. "Stay safe, pal. We don't need to lose our patriarch."

"I'll do my best, zun," Fox responded, voice quiet. "But like you and your partner, I cannot stand by and see innocents die. You and Omega, hurry and tell me how to handle this damn beast. Before something really bad DOES happen."

"On it," Echo said, and headed for Lima, even as Alpha Two boarded their airskimmer once more.

* * *

Omega waited for him in the vehicle hangar, still in her

antigrav chair. She looked tired, pale, and stressed. Once he switched off the Corvette and got out, she flung out her arms.

"Oh, ECHO!" she cried, biting her lip as her bright blue eyes glimmered with unshed tears.

Echo knelt before her, gathering her into his arms, letting her physically feel him against her body. She promptly wrapped her own arms tight about him, refusing to let go, all but pulling him into the antigrav chair with her.

"Hush, baby, shush," he murmured, rubbing a gentle hand over her back in an effort to soothe. "It's all over, it's done, I'm home an' intact, and I've got what you need to run your tests. It's all done, and I'm safe. I'm right here with you."

"I know," she whispered, burying her face in his shoulder. "I know. I'm just...I..."

"You just still have PTSD, after everything you've been through, an' my little game of dodge-ball up on the roof did NOT help that," Echo noted. "Especially since, with the nd't'lq, you lived it with me, every step. But it's okay. It's okay, baby. I'm fine. I'm home and in one piece, for a change. I swear to you, we'll get through all of this...together."

He held her for several more minutes, as she hung on tightly and struggled to maintain her shaky emotional control. Finally she drew in a long, shuddering breath, let it out slowly, and raised her head.

"Okay," she said in a wavering voice, offering him a wobbly, but sincere, smile. "I'm gonna be all right now. Thanks for...for understanding, an' being willing to hang on with me..."

"Damn, Meg, after what you did to get me away from the Cortians, let alone helping me survive what we just did, this sure wasn't any big deal," he pointed out. "You just needed some tactile reassurance, that's all, baby. An' I understand that, too. Remember my nightmares after our first run-in with the Cortians? An' how you let me do the same thing you just did? It's okay."

"Eh. Well. Um. All right." She flushed. "You said you got the samples?"

"All of 'em in a warp pocket, right here," he said, patting his side. "Are you up to analyzing 'em?"

"I'm a little bit spazzed," she admitted, "but Item told me

to notify her when we had the samples, and she'd personally help with the analysis—she's a chemist, herself. So if I can't get settled, she'll keep things on track."

"That works," Echo decided.

"C'mon," she said, holding out a hand, "let's go."

He took her hand, and they went.

* * *

Item, who was indeed a skilled and experienced chemist, brought Omega into her personal lab in the Sciences department to work, as the pair studied the samples to determine what compounds were contained within them, using everything from x-ray diffraction and gas chromatography to mass spectrography, as well as some more sophisticated offworld technology, including bosonic field mappers and gluon flux counters. Soon, as Echo observed in some relief, Omega was engrossed in the attempts to identify chemicals in the residue samples.

So he slipped out and headed for Medical, extracting his cell phone as he went.

* * *

"Oh, that does not sound as good as I had hoped," Zarnix noted in his private office, once Zz'r'p had arrived and Echo had finished telling the two males about the force and intensity of Omega's reaction to his return in the vehicle hangar.

"No, but it is logical and understandable," Zz'r'p agreed. "Our human niece has been through much in recent months, Zarnix. And her attachment to and love for Echo is incredibly strong."

"But I didn't think she was THAT..." Echo began. "I mean, before we became involved, she didn't..."

Suddenly a memory struck. *Antarctica,* he thought. *Our very first mission together as Alpha One. When I gave her instructions to go off and leave me if anything happened when I confronted the assassin. And she was NOT happy about that. So unhappy that, for a moment there, I thought she was gonna disobey my orders. Mama Bear. And that was, by her own admission, before she'd fallen for me.*

"Ah, you realize," Zz'r'p said with a smile. "Yes, her affections are strong, are Omega's. And if she has become fond of you, she becomes...how did you once express it, Echo? A mama bear?"

"Yeah," Echo agreed. "And yeah, I was wrong just now. If she loves you in any way, she fights for you, with everything she's got. And she loves me. In all possible ways, now, I think."

"Deeply," Zarnix added. "More than anyone else on this, or any other planet, I believe."

"She does, more than words could express. But she could NOT fight for you," Zz'r'p pointed out. "Not in this instance. She was completely helpless to do anything except watch through your eyes, instruct you on taking the sample, and hope you would see the 'giant cootie' coming."

"Well, she did more than THAT," Echo pointed out. "A lot more. SHE heard it coming, using my ears, and then warned me! And once the thing started attacking me, she helped me analyze and locate sufficient cover, helped me watch for the damn thing—I mean, between the two of us, I think we had my entire field of vision, top to bottom, side to side, scrutinized—AND she put out the emergency call for help, THEN coordinated getting me offa that damn roof."

"Yes, but she could not ACT; she could not MOVE. She had no way to vent her own adrenaline, and so she was still quite frightened," Zarnix noted. "Badly so, if her reaction when you returned was any indication."

"Well, yeah," Echo agreed. "That's why I'm here. It... worried me. I've never seen her like that before."

"I have," Zz'r'p observed. "When we were rescuing you from the Cortians."

"Oh," Echo said, subdued. "Well, I still think maybe we need to do something, here, to give her a chance to...mm, maybe 'catch her breath' emotionally."

"What, you wish me to extend her medical leave?" Zarnix wondered, pulling his tablet in front of him.

"No, I want you to put me back on partial leave," Echo declared.

* * *

"I— what?" Zarnix said, glancing up in confusion.

"Okay, lemme explain my logic," Echo said with a sigh. "Meg is obviously still trying to get a grip on the whole PTSD

274

thing, and apparently I'm a big part of the core of that..."

"Well observed," Zz'r'p affirmed. "She still has trouble dealing with the fact that her body, under Azeln's programming, nearly killed you, early in your partnership. Her fears of you dying 'on her watch,' as she puts it to me, are great."

"Oooo," Echo hummed. "She's never said that to ME. That's telling."

"It is," Zarnix agreed.

"So she's afraid of something happening to me," Echo continued. "And right now, I AM coming off major injuries, just getting back in the saddle as it were, and honestly? I realized while I was out there—I NEED her with me right now. I need that backup. Hell, I'd need that even if I was fully up to speed—I needed that before the Cortians' torture, before the space plane accident. In Alpha Line, there's a reason we have partnerships. Shit, the standard field agents work partnerships, too. This job can be damn dangerous. We. Need. Backup. And Meg's my partner, not 'merely' a wife—as if having her for a wife was 'merely' anything; as if having a wife, period, was no big wup, when it IS, it's a big deal, she's the other half of me and I know it—but you know what I mean. There's so much to our relationship, I can't begin to name all she is to me. But one thing she IS—she IS my backup, and I'm hers. So..."

"Ah, I understand now," Zarnix said, his eyebrows shooting upward. "Since she is not ready, you cannot be ready. Even though you are physically and mentally better, you are only half a partnership. And the other half of that partnership...is not yet ready."

"Exactly!" Echo exclaimed. "Rather than sending me back into the field full-time before my partner and backup is ready to go, let's work on coordinating this—both of us go online at the same rate, if you understand what I'm trying to say."

"I do, and it makes sense," Zarnix determined. "Zz'r'p, my friend? What is your professional opinion?"

"I agree," the Deltiri counselor and ambassador said. "It makes excellent sense, and is, I think, precisely what we should do." He paused, then added, "More, I think that this is a good way to do it. Else Omega will be upset because she is the cause of Alpha One being 'off-line,' as they sometimes say, and it will hinder things, for she will try to rush through it, instead of taking matters at the pace her mind and emotions require."

"Yeah," Echo agreed. "Use me for the obvious reason for keeping Alpha One part-time. I don't even care if you indicate, at least to her, that, say, my muscles show signs of fatigue at all the strenuous activity, so you wanna slow things down." He paused, then admitted, "Because frankly, after THAT little game of chase, I AM tired."

"I think anyone would be," Zz'r'p noted, "no matter their medical condition."

"Yes, they would. And an excellent notion, that. So I should modify the orders in the computer," Zarnix said, "and pretend, at least to Omega, that they were always like that. That way, we do not give her feelings of guilt or discouragement over the matter."

"Bingo," Echo averred.

"This can be done," Zarnix said, pulling up the pertinent entries on his tablet and modifying them as he had just recommended. "And I will see to it that Zee, Whiskey, and Rglfrz, as well as Fox, all know about it...and know not to say anything to her."

"That'll work," Echo decided. "Thanks, guys, for understanding."

"No understanding is needed; it was a good thought, Echo," Zarnix said. "If her reaction was that strong...well. You did not need to be out there without backup, but if Fox was not even able to shake loose someone to accompany you, and there was a pressing need..."

"According to what Meg told me over our breakfast this morning, it's only a matter of time before the damn giant cootie hits something vital and sends up half of Manhattan," Echo pointed out. "At least, if she's right about what it's doing. Which, based on what I saw, I'm convinced she is."

"Oh damnation," Zarnix breathed in horror, and even Zz'r'p turned a paler shade of blue. "All right. It was a calculated risk. One which you survived."

"Exactly."

Zarnix hit a few more keys on his tablet, then glanced up at the other two males.

"There," he said. "It is done. The two of you are firmly tied together in the medical system, at least for this little session. Neither may return to full-time field work until BOTH of you do. I will discuss it with Zebra; we may make that permanent."

"That works," Echo noted.

"Now, I know you need to return to the chemical lab," Zarnix said, "but under the circumstances, I should like to perform a brief examination to verify your condition."

"I can understand why, and Whiskey wanted you to, anyhow, just to cover our bases," Echo capitulated instantly. "Zz'r'p? How am I from your perspective?"

"Doing quite well, under the circumstances," the Deltiri said. "I am really very surprised at just how well, considering all of the doubts you had during your recovery."

"I think part of that doubt was the enforced inactivity," Echo pointed out. "I'm more a man of action type, I think; I've thought of myself that way for a few years, now. Meg's made that kind of observation about me, too. And when I can't do ANYthing, well...I start getting wrapped around the axle in my head. Or...my head gets wrapped around the axle, or...however you wanna put it."

"Excellent point...wherever that axle is! And one I believe Zarnix and I should both remember, for the future. Now, I think we still have a few things to cover in our counseling," Zz'r'p decided, "but you have made very, VERY good progress. I am quite pleased."

"Good. And I agree about the 'man of action' consideration, and will enter it in his medical records. All right then, Zz'r'p, I shall see you later, for our evening drink, my friend," Zarnix said. "We can compare notes more then, if you like. Echo, if you would come with me, I will have this done in about five minutes."

* * *

"So has there been any word about Crutch?" Echo wondered, as he doffed his Suit jacket, holsters, tie, and shirt, while Zarnix set up several items of medical equipment he would use to scan Echo for internal or external injury.

"Not really," Zarnix sighed. "She is in the regeneration pod, and seems to be coming along slowly. Decently, but slowly.

277

But given her age and the severity of her injuries, I do not know how well it will turn out, when she is decanted."

"But she's in great shape," Echo pointed out.

"She is, and that is definitely in her favor," Zarnix agreed, as he began scanning Echo. "But most sentients' ability to heal slows as they grow older, no matter how well they maintain their stamina and strength. It is just something that tends to happen as the tissue structures age."

"Mm. Well, shit," Echo grumbled. "Listen, what with Crutch being an almost-Original, and Fox an' me BEING Originals, um..."

"You are worried about your old friend," Zarnix said. "Should I call Fox and discuss her condition with him, as well, do you think?"

"I think it'd be a good idea, yeah," Echo conceded.

"Very well. I will try to take care of that when I have the time," Zarnix agreed. "Now let us see to you."

* * *

"So I really DO have some muscular issues," Echo said five minutes later, as he slipped back into his shirt.

"You do, and that is not surprising," Zarnix explained. "You were running for your life. Virtually any agent, field or Alpha Line, would have something similar. Especially coming off an extended leave, such as you have had. You are in excellent shape, but there is only so much preparation for an active mission that can be accomplished in the gymnasium."

"True. So you need to slow me down anyway," Echo asked, though he couched it as a statement.

"I think that would be wise," Zarnix said. "Oh, you are still cleared for field duty, but only part-time. I would like to see that build back up a bit more slowly than the last couple of days has done. Of course," he sighed, "until this damned Zheen exoheteroc is captured or killed, that could end up being somewhat moot."

"I'll do my best, Zarnix," Echo offered. "I will NOT be going back out there solo, I can tell you that much. There's need, and then there's foolhardy. That almost crossed the line. And I'd have bitten it, as a result."

"This is, frankly, rather more to my taste than telling Omega a falsehood, or trying to tiptoe around the truth, to make one thing appear another," Zarnix admitted then. "I want you to know, Echo, that I do not lie to my patients, no matter what. If the news is harsh, I do try to gentle my telling of it, but tell them I do. I know you had your moments of doubt, back when you were confined to your antigrav chair; we—the 'family,' I mean—could all read it in your face, your posture...and we understood. We know you too well for you to fully hide it from us. I cannot blame you in the least, but..." he shook his head. "None of us here would do that to you...or to any other of our patients. But especially not to our 'family.'"

"I know—now," Echo told him, laying a hand on the other male's shoulder. "There were a couple of things going on in my head, according to both Meg and Zz'r'p, that were messing with it, and with my perspective on things."

"Oh? What?"

"Well, the basic trauma and subsequent PTSD, for one thing," Echo explained. "I didn't expect to get off the Cortian ship alive, and even when I did, I thought I'd be maimed for life." He paused, then shook his head. "I try hard not to think about having those injuries inflicted on me..."

"I can imagine, my human nephew," Zarnix said softly. "Do not try, on my account. Just continue on, enumerating the things."

"Just two things," Echo said. "The other was that it hadn't been that long since the mental integration, after the mostly-dead thing. Apparently the part of me that went through the regen an' shit after the space plane incident...that was the part that was anxious about getting back to normal, because it was still lacking in experience with what y'all can truly do, medically. Let alone what I can do, when I'm really determined."

"Ah," Zarnix said in understanding. "That makes a great deal of sense."

"But I watched all of you at Thanksgiving," Echo continued. "It was the first time I had ALL of you together, to watch, to see you interact. And I realized then that none of you were lying to me. And that none of you WOULD. And I already knew that; I just kept getting...obsessed isn't quite the right word; maybe fixated? About being permanently disabled. You know." He shook his head. "So then it was just a matter of reminding myself of that, or getting Meg to help me remember, whenever the anxiety would crop up again."

"Understood, my friend," Zarnix said, nodding. "And now?"

"And now, after all that's happened since we got dragged in on the mega moth incident, I think my confidence in my abilities is back up to snuff," Echo declared. "And I'll do what y'all say needs doing. And glad of it."

"Excellent," Zarnix said with a smile. "Then, for now...go find your partner."

* * *

"THERE you are! Where'd you go?" Omega wondered, glancing up from her work as Echo came back into the lab.

"Oh, when Alpha Two dropped me off at the staging area, Whiskey did a quick scan on me to make sure nothing was immediately wrong, then told me to run by and see Zarnix, when I arrived back at Headquarters," Echo told her; it wasn't a lie, for Whiskey really had recommended it, but he was still careful to maintain a rudimentary block around the entire event; he wanted to relieve her mind, not worry her. "So once you two got going, I ran over to let him give me a quick once-over. I'm fine."

"He said so?"

"He said so. He even brought in Zz'r'p to check me mentally," Echo added. "Not even any spit spatters." He paused, then added, "He did think I needed to take it easy, though; evidently the kinds of strains I've had to put my muscles through—gettin' chased by giant bugs, jumpin' off buildings, ridin' on the back of an airskimmer, that sorta shit—are a bit much for my first day or two back in the field. I'm okay, he just wants to make sure I STAY okay. So," he concluded, "I'm supposed to stay in the background as much as I can get away with, in a Level 3 Facility Alert, anyway. I'm still cleared for field duty, but preferably part-time, for a while yet."

"Oh, good," Omega said with a barely-audible sigh. "That makes me feel much better. ALL of that."

"I knew it would," Echo said. "How's the analysis going?"

"Quite promising," Item interjected. "I really think Omega

has determined the answer. In fact, once this last test runs and gives me a readout," she gestured at the computer screen, "I think that will be all we need to give the 'yea, verily' to Fox."

Just then, the computer dinged, and a table popped up on the indicated computer screen. Item and Omega bent their heads over it for long moments, studying the readout.

"And that does it," Omega determined.

"It does, indeed," Item agreed. "Your hypothesis is verified. The exoheteroc has a very different biochemistry from what any of us expected, and it IS a predator. More, its salivary digestive juices do seem to rely on some kind of organolithium reagent to break down its prey."

"Okay," Echo said. "So the 'melted' bodies, the fact that they were pretty much all patients taking lithium, and the attacks on lithium-battery-powered vehicles of various sorts, are all part and parcel of that, aren't they?"

"They are," Item confirmed. "Judging by this, our 'giant cootie,' as Omega likes to put it, is sating its appetite on the local people and their pets, sating a lithium craving by selective choice of source—though as yet we don't know how it's able to sense the lithium—and is possibly very thirsty. It doesn't seem to drink water, which is understandable, as water would cause it to combust from within once the water contacted the lithium. But...Omega, do you see the ether in the...?"

"Yeah, I noticed that, Item," Omega replied. "And yeah, I'm thinking maybe, where Earth animals use water as a universal solvent in their bodies, the cootie uses an ether. Given what I saw in the chromatography readout, and what I know of exometeorology and interstellar abundances, I'm fully expecting that ethyl methyl ether is the solvent in question. Not to mention adding to the overall flammability of the digestive juices." She paused, then added, "But given the boiling point of methoxyethane, I—"

"You said ethyl methyl ether," Echo pointed out. "Oh wait. Damn, my chemistry courses were a long time ago! But that's..."

"Right," Omega clarified. "Another name for ethyl methyl ether. And given its relatively low boiling point, I think the ONLY time of year this thing could survive in the Big Apple is the dead of winter...and an unusually cold, dry one, at that."

"What's the boiling point?" Echo asked.

"About 45 degrees Fahrenheit," Item answered. "So yes, Omega is right; since blood plasma is usually composed principally of the main solvent used to dissolve and transport the needed body chemicals, this poor creature's blood would boil by the time we reached spring. It likely dwells principally in a polar region of its homeworld, I should think."

"Bingo," Omega said. "And if we'd had our usual amount of precipitation, whether rain or snow, the giant cootie would probably have combusted from within."

"Damn. Really?" Echo wondered, eyebrows climbing his forehead.

"Oh hell yeah," Omega confirmed. "So much of what it's got inside is flammable on contact with water, you can't imagine, Ace."

"I believe I am in agreement with my esteemed colleague," Item said with a chuckle. "This has been a fascinating study."

"Once we have all this mess tidied away," Omega suggested, "would you like to co-author a paper with me about the thing's biochem?"

"I most certainly would," Item agreed. "Oh, and Echo, the analysis you requested on your cold case came back from Forensics a bit ago; I only glanced over it, but if memory serves, and given it was an older sample, it resembles the results here rather well." She tapped the computer screen.

"Oh. So our missing Yelfflani, Julian Thompson, was a victim of the mega moth, too," Echo said, and he and Omega both sighed.

"It looks that way," Item agreed. "But..."

"Yeah," Echo continued. "Now that we have that information, what do we do with it? How do we use it to take the thing down?"

"That's gonna take some thought," Omega decided.

* * *

"...So its saliva is what's causing the fires?" Fox verified on the video link from his cell phone. "I know Echo gave me a heads-up about that earlier, but you've confirmed it?"

"Without doubt, Fox," Omega determined. "There's a

282

certain multi-step reaction involved, in that it has to combine with some other constituents in the saliva, then contact air and water vapor, which then has to reach a certain threshold value for the combustive reactions to take over. But that's why it doesn't immediately combust, and why we had such a hard time connecting the fires to the exoheteroc in any sort of cause-and-effect way."

"Yes," Item agreed. "The combustion wouldn't take place for...well, it would depend upon how much of the saliva and digested fluids were left, but our estimate is a minimum of five minutes after it was excreted. Possibly as long as half an hour."

"So the more fluid, the faster it combusted?" Fox wondered.

"Actually, the inverse," Item explained. "According to Echo and Omega, the saliva is quite viscous in order to maintain a cohesive, spherical shape through the air, which results in it retaining a fairly rounded shape even after impact. Therefore, the more fluid, the less relative surface area it exposed to the air, and the SLOWER it would take to react to flash point."

"Based on what I've seen," Echo interjected, "the saliva is really thick, like she said, and worse than hockin' a loogie, Fox. It tends to want to form a ball, even when it's hit something."

"That's probably in order to concentrate the digestive juices on the prey," Omega noted.

"Mmm, interesting," Fox hummed. "But...so it sounds like our missing persons are more apt to be 'missing, presumed dead, search and recovery' rather than 'search and rescue.'"

"Unfortunately, that's our assessment, Fox," Echo agreed. "Meg, Item, and I have discussed it at length, just before we called you. It's possible we may find someone still alive, but chances are, they died within seconds when the exoheteroc spat on 'em."

"And the mega moth then proceeded to dissolve them and consume the fluids," Omega added. "Either on site, or after taking them off to someplace it deemed safe to feed. Depending on how long the mega moth spent feeding, and the fact that the digestive fluids were capable of dissolving even the bone, there may be little left to find."

"Maybe a few personal artifacts, shreds of clothing, or whatnot," Echo continued. "But that'd be about it."

"And those would be hard to locate," Fox sighed.

"Yup," Omega said, echoing his sigh. "I really hate that we might not be able to close all those missing-persons cases, though."

"Well, it is what it is, I suppose," Fox said. "We'll still try. Meanwhile, do you have a way to stop it?"

"Not yet," Echo said. "We're working on that. This was just the start. But it explains how the second fire started BELOW Meg, before she could get the day care group out of that building. Right before she went in, the mega moth tried to attack a civilian in the street, and when I shot at it and it dodged, the blob of spit it had intended to hit its victim flew off to the side instead. I vaguely remember seeing it fly through a busted second- or maybe third-floor window, out of the corner of my eye."

"Oh wow," Omega said, blue eyes wide with surprise. "That DOES explain it."

"Yes, it does," Fox agreed. "Do you have ANYthing I can work with?"

"Yes, Fox," Item said. "We are working with Madrid on a system that can detect the chemicals in the saliva and perhaps even neutralize them before they have a chance to ignite. Even if your field agents cannot find it in time to neutralize it, they should be able to extinguish the fires before they have a chance to become established and start to spread to the local combustibles. We expect to have it in production within the hour."

"That's a good start," Fox decided.

"And once we figure out how to stop it," Omega added, "I know what to use as a lure."

"What?"

"We'll have to be awfully careful, 'cause we don't need people passing out or something, but I'm betting a nice kiddie pool full of ethyl methyl ether would draw it in like a bird to a birdbath."

"Mmm, that does sound promising," Fox said. "I take it, that's what it drinks?"

"We're pretty sure, Fox, yeah," Echo confirmed.

"All right; the lot of you, get back to it, and get me that fire detection and prevention kit," Fox ordered, "and a way to stop the thing as soon as you can."

"All over it, Boss," Echo averred. "Echo—and others—out."

"Fox out."

* * *

The three looked at each other after Echo closed the comm.

"Now what?" Item wondered. "We need to figure out a weakness in the exoheteroc that we can exploit, based on this information, but...I don't even know where to start. Even with all this information we now have."

"Well, I think the best thing is gonna be to contact Kydeen again," Omega decided. "Madrid is already working on the 'fire detection kit' and we can go help him in a little bit, but... Echo?"

"Yeah, baby?"

"Don't you think the Assistant Director needs to place an off-world call?"

"Hm," Echo grunted, thoughtful. "That...actually sounds like a damn good plan, Meg."

* * *

"...Yes, so we were hoping you might have someone who was your go-to expert on Zheen biology," Echo said from behind Fox's desk, as Omega sat beside him in her antigrav chair.

Alpha One was in the Director's office with the bay window opaqued, while Echo contacted the PGLEIA lead on Kydeen via vidcomm. The big wall screen depicted an older Kydeen, his fur lightly frosted with white, a thoughtful expression on his face.

"Yes, we do," Iziguzeer Takul, the Division Four PGLEIA chief on Kydeen, responded. "In fact, after Director Fox contacted us the first time, to ask for information, I dug deeper into the situation and uncovered exactly the beings I believe you will need, and they have agreed to assist. They are already en route, with their equipment; they are traveling at emergency speeds, per my authorization."

"Now THAT is some really damn good news, and thank you!" Omega decided. "We're working hard on things from our end, but we're starting off three steps behind, with almost no familiarity with this...creature."

"It is an animal, but a fairly intelligent one by our reckoning, and it is always hard to predict animal behavior, especially if one is unfamiliar with the animal," Iziguzeer agreed. "Which is why, as soon as I determined we do have some relative experts with the beast, and that they were more than willing to help, I sent them at once. They are on board a special spacecraft of their own, on an emergency run to Earth, and should arrive within..." Iziguzeer glanced to one side, apparently consulting a clock, "...no more than two of your hours, perhaps less."

"'Relative' experts?" Omega queried. "What does that mean?"

"Well, Agent Omega, I am certain you know that our moon, Zheen, has never been fully explored," Iziguzeer elaborated. "Its environment is not hospitable to life forms such as yourself, or even to the Kydeen. We are only just beginning to discover what Zheen has in store for us, so there are no experts of long standing. However, the experts I am sending you are on the forefront of the explorations, and are scientists—biologists, biochemists, behavioral experts, and such. More, they have successfully handled such creatures several times before."

"That's even better news," Echo said. "I'll have my people check to get an estimated arrival time for the spacecraft, and do what I can to have us ready for them, and whatever they need to do."

"This works well, then," Iziguzeer affirmed. "I am glad I was able to assist."

"Very much so," Echo averred. "Thank you deeply."

"Is there anything else I may do to assist?"

"I don't know of anything at this time, Chief," Echo concluded. "May we call you if need be?"

"Absolutely. Before you end the communiqué, however, let me ask—is Director Fox all right? You call, rather than he..." Iziguzeer gave the Kydeen equivalent of a shrug. "I grew concerned. He is a good being, and very knowledgeable, skilled, and wily; I should hate to lose him to injury...or worse."

"No, no, he's all right," Echo explained, "just extremely busy. The exoheteroc is causing so many problems in the downtown area of the major city where we headquarter the division that we've had to call in hundreds of agents from other Offices on the planet just to try to keep everything under control. He's been in the field for hours, and the field agents from Headquarters are about to drop in their tracks from the heavy load. Meanwhile, I'm coming off medical leave, and so I'm trying hard to hold down the fort for him, here in his office."

"Though we've been out in the field some, too," Omega added, "trying to help gather information on the exoheteroc, as well as rescue a few civilians."

"Ah. And is this why you are in a medical chair, Agent Omega?"

"It is," Omega confirmed with a sigh. "I got hurt in the process. The exoheteroc is setting accidental fires when its digestive juices contact our moist air—New York City is an ocean harbor city, complete with several rivers, so it's humid, even now, in our winter—and I was trying to help a small group of human children—uh, younglings—and their caretakers get out of a burning building..." She shrugged. "Part of the building came down on me."

"Oh great Maker! Will you be well?"

"She will be, provided she rests and lets everything heal," Echo noted. "She has some broken bones and torn tendons in her foot and lower leg, but as long as she stays off that foot and doesn't make things worse, the physicians say it'll heal up fine."

"Oh, that is very good, then," Iziguzeer said, obviously relieved. "And now I understand why you are there with your partner, Omega, and have been conveying the scientific information to me—as a scientist yourself, this is what you are doing to help, since you cannot walk at the moment."

"Exactly," Omega said with a nod. "I do whatever I can, when I can. We both do."

"Very well. Let me stop rambling and allow you to return to that work," Iziguzeer said. "Do please call me if you need anything, and update me on matters as you are able. I should like to see your after-action report; if you would not mind copying me on it when you send it to Chief Wuxullian, it would be appreciated. Given it was one of our people who brought it to Earth, and the creature is from our system, there are certain responsibilities here, you know."

"That won't be a problem, sir," Echo agreed. "If I'm the one that puts it together, I'll see to it, and I'll ensure Fox knows to do it, otherwise."

"Very good, then. Iziguzeer out."

"Alpha One out," Echo said. The wall screen went dark as he killed the vidcall. He and Omega sat there for long moments, silent.

"Time to determine some ETAs," Echo said then.

"Alla that," Omega agreed.

* * *

Just then, Echo's cell phone rang. He pulled it from his pocket and activated it, holding it to his ear.

"Echo here."

Omega watched as he listened, then straightened up.

"Oh really?" he said into the phone. "Well, that's not surprising...no, no, I've already been doing a few things as it is, what with him out in the field. No, I don't have a problem with it, though it might be a little while before I can get out there. No, Kydeen is sending us a team of experts to help with the sitch, and I probably need to be here when they arrive. No, that'll work. Yeah, I'm on it. Yeah. Echo out."

He hung up, and slipped the phone back into his pocket.

"What's up?" Omega wondered.

"Oh, Medical is about to come down on somebody's ass," Echo noted, "and for once, it ain't you OR me."

"Hmm," Omega hummed, intrigued.

Chapter 11

The cell phone in Fox's pocket rang, and he instantly and instinctively grabbed for it, extracting and activating it in one move. "Fox here."

"It's Zee, honey."

"Ah! Hello, bubeleh. What is the word?"

"The word is that Zar and I have both decided that you've been at it plenty long enough," his wife told him. "And as the Chief of Staff of Medical, and the Assistant Chief of Staff, we're pulling rank on you. Come home and rest."

"Zebra, my dear, you know I cannot."

"I know you WILL, or we will declare you medically incapacitated," she retorted. "You've been at this at least as long as Alpha One was when you sent THEM home to rest."

"Bubeleh, I—"

"Fox, please look up and notice who is standing there, waiting for your decision."

Fox looked up. Lima and Bravo were both standing there, accompanied by Alpha Two, Alpha Four, the chief of Security Agent Uncle, and Nab, Crutch's second in command of the Field Agents department. All eight agents stood with arms folded, wearing stern expressions.

"Ah," Fox said then, nonplussed.

"I expected your reluctance, honey," Zebra said, "and Zarnix made the decision to call in backup to reinforce our orders. You either stand down and come home to rest willingly, or it will be enforced. You HAVE to rest."

"But who is going to run the operation in my stead?" Fox wondered.

"You have a perfectly good Assistant Director who is now back on semi-active duty, but whose partner is OFF field duty due to injury," Zebra noted. "Echo can run it, and Romeo, Alpha Four, and the Boys can manage until he gets there."

"Right," Fox said with a sigh, defeated. "Very well. I'll be home as soon as I can get there, Zebra. Where are you?"

"Waiting for you at home," she responded with her own sigh, as the waiting agents stood down their alert status and relaxed. "Zar and I went off duty about an hour ago, and Whiskey and Rglfrz are running things for a few hours. And we called in additional medical staff from Atlanta and Chicago, at which time even those two will stand down for a rest break." She paused, then added, "The cycle should be delivered to you any moment, if it's not there already."

"Your motorcycle is here, sir," Lima announced then, pointing to the vehicle. "Complete with helmet. You can leave right now."

"Oh, and don't you dare go by the office first," Zebra added. "Echo's been notified, and he'll go by the office, then head for the staging area, shortly."

"Is he all right after all his little adventures?"

"He's fine. That man is amazingly cool under pressure. Like somebody else I know of."

"All right," Fox said, capitulating, as he headed for the motorcycle. "On my way."

* * *

"Oh yes, Assistant Director," the captain of the *Arkeed* confirmed on the vidcomm. "We have already entered your system, and are establishing cloaked orbit now. Our excursion team should be arriving at Pennsylvania Station within half of one of your hours, and taking the connecting train to Grand Central Station."

"That sounds excellent, Captain," Echo replied. "I'll see to it that someone from Diplomacy escorts the team you have aboard, straight from their gate in Grand Central to the Director's office, and—"

"Fox is already inbound," Omega reported, looking up from her cell phone. "The medlab pulled rank on him, all right. But under the circumstances, I've gotten permission for him to swing by here before he goes home to crash."

"Right," Echo said. "Captain, I'll see to it that the team is introduced to Director Fox as well, and we get his approval for whatever is needed. He's on the way now, in fact."

"I will make certain they know, then," the captain said. "*KNS Arkeed* out."

"Assistant Director Echo out."

Echo and Omega looked at each other.

"This...might just work," Omega decided.

"I sure hope so," Echo agreed.

* * *

Echo met Fox at the vehicle hangar.

"Hey, Boss," he murmured, as Fox secured the bike and removed his helmet. "You need to come with me."

"I'm on medical orders to report directly to my quarters, zun," Fox informed him.

"I know. But not now. Meg contacted all four Headquarters staff doctors—Zarnix, Zebra, Whiskey, and Rglfrz," Echo told him. "We have a bit of a situation, and I wanted you in the loop before we did this. It shouldn't take long, so they all okayed it, provided you go straight home after."

"All right. What's up?"

"Kydeen sent us some help. Meg's waiting in your office with them."

"Oh REALLY?" Fox said, both eyebrows going up. "That's interesting. Lead on, then."

* * *

Five Kydeen were waiting with Omega in her antigrav chair in the Director's office when Echo led Fox into it. As usual, they looked like nothing so much as giant koalas; muscular, furry, and roughly human-height, they appeared cuddly...unless they scowled and bared teeth. Offworlders on Kydeen very quickly realized then that these were fierce, highly intelligent warriors and hunters.

"Fox, I'd like you to meet Kir Agrumbib Ozir and her team," Echo said. "Guys, this is Director Fox. He'll be going off-duty as soon as we're finished here, and you'll be working with me, but I felt he needed to be in on this."

"Understood, and that is wise," Agrumbib noted, stepping forward and shaking Fox's hand with her paw. "We have heard much of the esteemed Lord Franz Levy; we are very pleased to make your acquaintance, Director Fox. Assistant Director Echo and his highly intelligent partner and mate, Agent Omega, have been so kind as to fill us in on the situation and what has been happening, as well as what Omega and Echo have deduced."

"Mostly Meg," Echo said modestly.

"Nuh-uh," Omega piped up. "It was both of us, Echo."

"Indeed. The way I understood it, you were the one who filled her in on exoheterocs to begin with, zun," Fox said, "because you were present for the dissection of the first one ever found."

"Well..." Echo said, flushing, and fell silent. The Kydeen all smiled.

"We are here to help, as best we can," Agrumbib declared then. "I and my team are exobiologists, specializing in the life forms of our moon, Zheen; we have made some breakthroughs in recent months, as we have been working with the commercial exploration teams to determine precisely 'what' lives there. The egg that wound up here was, we think, supposed to come to our team, as we were just beginning to work with the companies doing the exploration, and a clutch of eggs was indeed delivered to us. However, evidently a rather precocious and promising juvenile Kydeen got her paws on one of those eggs instead...just before her family left on vacation to Earth."

"That latter is correct, in as far as I know the story," Fox confirmed. "I talked with her and her family, though I think they went back to Kydeen shortly afterward..."

"Yes, and I have spoken with her and her family, not long before we left Kydeen to come here," Agrumbib informed them. "I made sure to impress upon her the seriousness of what she did, and she was duly well-chastened by that information. It seems she had no idea that it would be so big, nor so dangerous; she has not yet studied chemistry—let alone exobiology—at her school."

"Aha," Omega said. "THAT sure explains a lot."

"Doesn't it?" Echo said, shaking his head.

"It does," Fox agreed.

"We have considered proper punishment," Agrumbib continued, "but I, personally, felt that she needed mentorship more than punishing, in some respects—though she will not be walking away from this without consequences; that is one reason why Echo wanted you 'in the loop,' as he put it, Director Fox. You, personally, will be responsible for providing feedback as to the magnitude of destruction on Earth, and the appropriate level of punishment she is due. But she is very young, not even pre-adolescent, and very immature in most ways save intellect. I will be mentoring her, and helping to guide her studies, from now on; I hope to have a new team member there, in a dodecade or so."

"That seems reasonable," Fox agreed. "I'll be happy to work with your people on the matter. She's definitely a juvenile, so I don't see doing something that will ruin her future, especially since it seems so promising. But this was a major mistake, and many humans have died. She needs to learn from it."

"She already is learning from it," one of the other Kydeen observed. "She is extremely upset, and very frightened. She cried a great deal, and our people—even our younglings—do not cry often. She said she never meant anyone to be hurt, and did not realize the exoheteroc would be so big, so powerful, or so dangerous. SHE could have died, with her entire family, had they not come to Earth and the egg become lost...and she knows this now."

"Director, this is my second, Stregenar Wenk," Agrumbib introduced the other Kydeen. "Like myself, all of my team have kir degrees—what you would term a Ph.D."

"Aha. Pleased to meet you, Kir Stregenar. Well, there's a good start on the child, then," Fox decided. "Not even pre-adolescent, you say? Then, precocious though she may be intellectually, she likely didn't have the emotional development to understand the seriousness of what she did."

"No, not at all," Agrumbib confirmed. "Her parents, who are extremely upset about this, told us that they keep trying to impress upon her to think through the consequences of her actions before she makes them, but as yet, she has not understood the necessity."

"We believe that will change now," Stregenar said, voice dry with irony.

"I'll bet," Omega opined.

"At any rate, we are now here to assist you and your people as best we are able," Agrumbib explained. "In the last few months we have been learning to negotiate the Zheen landscape, mostly via small remotes..."

"What?!" Echo exclaimed. "But how do you keep them

going in the noxious atmosphere on Zheen?"

"Force fields," Stregenar said. "Our technicians have had a breakthrough in the power supply technology. It is not sufficient as yet for personal fields, else we should likely be exploring first-paw, but it is enough to protect our remote units, which are moderately large."

"And it is also enough to enable us to capture large quantities of the atmosphere, and to 'bottle' it to transport to Wheen, our other moon, where we have created a fully enclosed habitat for direct study," Agrumbib continued. "We have five other exoheterocs, two hatched from eggs found at the same time as the one on Earth—likely from the same clutch—one captured in its larval form, and two that we captured as adults. We have also been able to capture and breed several of its preferred prey animals, insofar as we can tell, as well as a handful of other species we found on Zheen...and some plant life, to ensure a functional ecosystem within the habitat. We are gradually creating a complete, contained ecosystem for study."

"So...you now have some experience wrangling these creatures," Fox realized.

"Exactly. And the equipment to do so," another Kydeen averred.

"Gentlebeings, this is Kir Barog Enweek," Agrumbib said. "He is our equipment developer."

"You propose to capture the thing, then?" Fox asked.

"Yes, if at all possible, without causing further damage to your city or your people," Barog confirmed. "And take it back with us to the habitat for breeding purposes. As nearly as we can determine, they are relatively rare even on Zheen, and we would like to study the species with an eye toward preserving it; they seem to have some level of intelligence, though whether they are sentients as such has yet to be determined. This particular specimen is likely ill after so long on Earth, eating and drinking substances poorly suited to its systems. From our initial research, Zheen life is not oxygen-and water-based."

"I'm not surprised, all things considered," Omega observed. "Once I started thinking in terms of organolithium reagents in its digestive juices, I began realizing just how different its biochemistry was likely to be."

"Exactly," Stregenar agreed. "If this were to keep up, it would likely eventually die, poisoned by too many chemicals its body cannot process...but the question is, would this happen before it had destroyed half of your city?"

"If I may be allowed to kydomorphize for a moment, I suspect it will be glad to be placed in a habitat that is more suited to it, where it can find sustenance more to its taste and its needs," Agrumbib said. "Let alone being tended for its illness in consuming what, to it, consisted of as much poison as nutrient."

"No offense, but we won't mind seeing the back of it, either," Echo admitted. "It's been a damn lotta trouble for us, and nearly killed my partner and myself, in separate incidents... and DID seriously injure one of our colleagues, the head of the Field Agents department. But how do you propose to capture it?"

"We have designed and manufactured a net that will hold, even against the exoheteroc's saliva," Barog said. "Its fibers are composed of an organosilicon polymer ceramic that is impervious both to the organolithium reagent in its saliva, as well as the more corrosive components of Zheen's atmosphere. And the mesh is extremely strong. More, the net's structure is such that it neither harms, nor can be easily broken by, the exoheteroc, though we have the means to cut it in an emergency. So we draw it in with an ethyl methyl ether pool as bait, perhaps with the addition of some lithium oxide bars such as may be found in the more basic technology of rechargeable batteries, should it be convenient to do so—much as your partner proposed. Then we enmesh it in the organosilicon ceramic net , then tranquilize it with a dart filled with a variant on the same drug used to sedate gurfdins."

"And will you use remotes to do this?" Omega wondered. "Our several efforts with some remote drones were, um, less than successful."

"No, we will have to...what is the word humans use? Oh yes—wrangle. We will have to wrangle it ourselves," Barog said. "Given the atmospheric components on Zheen, we MUST use remotes, but that same atmosphere also tends to hide the remote's presence from our quarry. The atmosphere here is rather too transparent for that tactic to be successful. It also likely slows the exoheteroc, as the lesser air density on Earth means its wingbeats do not displace as much atmosphere."

"SLOWS it?!" Echo exclaimed. "Shit."

"...Do not fear, however; we brought what is sometimes termed 'hazmat suits' for the purpose. And the slower motions will work to our advantage."

"Do you require any of our people for assistance?" Fox wondered.

"That remains to be seen," Agrumbib replied. "We need to be briefed about the location and the environment, and then we can begin to plan how to do it."

"That, Meg and I can do," Echo noted. "Fox, are you good with all of this?"

"As long as it's no longer on Earth, and nobody else gets injured or killed, I'm for whatever works," Fox vouched. "And once I've had a bit of rest, I can start working on the matter of the Kydeen child. That's going to require subtlety, understanding, and fair-handedness, and I think I need to be better rested than I am now to handle it properly."

"Good," Echo said. "Then I've got this. You head on off home and crash. Zebra said to tell you she'd have a nice hot dinner waiting—it'll be take-out from the deli down the street, 'cause she's too tired herself to cook, but that's still gonna be good—and the bed's already turned down."

"She also said that, as tired as she is, it might be dinner in bed," Omega added. "With trays and disposable plates an' shit."

"Any of that is fine," Fox said, as his own shoulders began to slump. "I...damnation..."

"Somebody's adrenaline just evaporated," Omega observed.

"Well, it did," Fox sighed.

"C'mon, Abba Fox," Omega said, directing her antigrav chair to his side and taking his hand. "Lemme escort you home, so you don't keel over on the way, and Echo can work out the details with the capture team, here. Then I can come back and do what I can to help 'em."

"That will work, tekhter," Fox agreed, gently squeezing

her hand. "Though it is a bit backwards from how we usually do such things, you and I."

"Well, I figure it's about time I paid you back for all the times you've been there for me an' Echo," Omega murmured with a smile that Fox answered.

"See you later, hon," Echo said, leaning over to kiss his wife and partner. "Fox, take it easy and get some rest."

"Thank you, zun."

And the pair were gone.

* * *

Omega delivered Fox to his door, where Zebra, wrapped in a robe, awaited. The younger woman hugged both adoptive 'parents,' then turned her antigrav chair and headed back for the Core.

There, she found that Echo had been busy. Alpha Two waited inside the Alpha Line Room, with Alpha Four and Five; the Kydeen biological team was quickly briefing them, while Echo worked on the computer at his desk.

"There," he said, moments later. "We'll have the supplies waiting for us at the staging area just off Central Park."

"What supplies?" Omega wondered, maneuvering the hoverchair to his side as he pushed his office chair away from his desk.

"A big feeder full of syrup to lure the giant hummingbird in," Echo explained.

"Ah! Gotcha," Omega said with a wry grin. "Based on what Item and I turned up, that oughta work nicely."

"Then let's go," Romeo declared.

"Consider it done, junior," Echo agreed. "Let's head for the vehicle hangar."

* * *

Once they had worked out the distribution of the Kydeen scientists among the four airskimmers, it was a simple matter to get them to the staging area, where Echo exited the *Schmaltzblitz* long enough to set up orders with Bravo—he wanted everyone but the agents working fire suppression and perimeter guard recalled, and kept out of a two-block radius around 63 West 67th Street.

"Because this could get tricky, and I don't want anyone

getting their wires crossed and getting hurt as a result," Echo pointed out.

"Is that with Assistant Director authority, sir?" Bravo asked.

"It is."

"Very good, then." He entered something on his electronic tablet, then hit the <enter> key. "There. Done. Which airskimmer do you want us to load the bait onto?"

"Put it on the *Schmaltzblitz*; it was Meg's original idea, and she and I will see it handled," Echo ordered.

"Copy that, sir."

* * *

Five minutes later, the four craft were in the air, headed for the chosen target area.

"I'm thinking it needs to go on the roof, guys," Omega recommended. "The exoheteroc seems to rarely come down to street level."

"And that, only over in Central Park, among the trees," Echo added. "Which would make for poor lines of sight for targeting. So...yeah, the rooftop is probably best."

"That sounds like an excellent plan," Stregenar agreed. "The two of you have watched the exoheteroc closely, then?"

"And interacted with it a couple times," Echo confirmed, voice dry and ironic.

"Aha. Which was likely unpleasant," Stregenar observed, a hint of bleak amusement in his own voice. "I gather these craft have some sort of cloaking or disguise capability?"

"They do," Echo agreed, as he sat in the pilot's seat of the *Schmaltzblitz*. "We've mostly been using it to prevent the civilians from recognizing the tech, but...what? You want to use it as camo against the exoheteroc spotting us?"

"Precisely," Stregenar confirmed. "Can you do this?"

"We can," Omega averred. "Ace, you want me to handle the camo, and pass on the details to the others?"

"You have the best eye for it, baby," he pointed out. "Go for it."

"All over it, then. I'll work something out, then ping it to the other skimmers."

"Fantastic. So let's make sure we have this plan straight,"

Echo said, addressing Stregenar. "We put out the bait, then we station the four airskimmers in a perimeter, camouflaging ourselves, and wait for the exoheteroc to take the bait."

"Correct. Then one of your crafts fires a net—whoever is in best position to do so—and I will stand at the hatch of your vessel and fire the tranquilizer gun at the body, just behind the head—what you would term 'between the shoulders.' We have found that to be the most vulnerable part, and the easiest area into which to place a dart. Also, being close to the brain, the sedation takes effect more swiftly."

"That's interesting info," Omega murmured, setting up the camo and relaying it to the other craft. "Good to know."

"Yes. And once the tranquilizer has taken effect, we can pick it up using the tractor beams on your craft, and carry it to the floating container our spaceship's crew is setting up, right off the shoreline of your city."

"And once it's in there, you take it aboard your ship, and head back for the Kydeen system," Echo finished.

"Precisely."

"Why are you the one shooting the tranq gun?"

"Because I am the most highly trained and most accurate shooter on our team."

"Okay, that works. We're coming up on the rooftop Meg and I chose," Echo said then. "Meg, send the word: everybody, get ready."

"All over it, Ace."

* * *

It took about ten minutes to extract the bait: one basic kiddie pool, small, made of fiberglass so the ether wouldn't melt it, filled with forty gallons of ethyl methyl ether, with all personnel involved in filling it—including Echo, India, Uniform, and Easy—equipped with oxygen masks, to avoid the traditional general-anesthetic effect of the ether. While those four, plus two more Kydeen, formed a kind of bucket brigade between the kiddie pool and the *Schmaltzblitz*, passing gallon jugs of ether between them, the others kept careful watch for the mega moth; it would not do to have it show up unexpectedly, with so many of their people vulnerable.

The airskimmers then lifted back off from the roof

designated as the 'trap.' The *Schmaltzblitz* simply moved to the far end of that rooftop; given the dart-gun sniper was in their airskimmer, they wanted to be as close as possible, to allow for the best shot. The other three skimmers moved nearby, where they hovered mere inches off several neighboring rooftops; Omega had chosen an overall solid hologram camo that made each airskimmer resemble a large air conditioning unit.

Then they waited.

* * *

It only took about a quarter of an hour for the mega moth to detect the scent of the ether. Even inside the airskimmers, the swift beat of its wings could dimly be heard.

"It is coming," Stregenar noted, hefting his tranquilizer rifle and doing one last swift check. "Be ready."

"Get in the airlock and hook off your tether now," Omega recommended. "We'll lift off and move upward a short distance to give you a good angle for the shot. I'll see about remotely opening the outer hatch for you, once we're fully airborne."

"Done," Stregenar agreed, opening the inner hatch and leaving it open as he stepped into the airlock and used the carabiner-style clip to hook his body harness and reel tether—provided by Alpha One—to the anchor ring inside it. He peeled off his special chemical-resistant gauntlets to give himself a finer control of the dart gun, hooking them to a clip at his waist. "There. I am ready."

"Here it comes," Echo said, as he spotted the creature flying up the cross street. "Alpha Four, you're in the best position to fire the net; you're up."

"On it," Easy replied on the comm.

Moments later, the mega moth hovered over the rooftop containing the pool of ether. It let out a squealing sound—to both members of Alpha One, it sounded like happiness—and settled down onto the rooftop, where it immediately moved to the side of the kiddie pool, inserted its proboscis, and began to drink.

Maintaining its camouflage, Alpha Four's airskimmer, the *High Flight*, eased up from the adjacent roof and floated slowly toward the mega moth from behind and to its left.

Echo, at the controls of the *Schmaltzblitz*, followed suit,

300

letting the airskimmer drift closer, even as Omega hit the buttons to drop their force field and remotely open the outer hatch. Stregenar swung his rifle around and tracked his quarry; Echo turned the *Schmaltzblitz* broadside, to give Stregenar the best angle possible.

* * *

But the mega moth's antennae twitched, apparently detecting the air currents produced by the airskimmers' movements, even as slow as they were moving; suddenly it leaped into the air and spun fully one hundred eighty degrees, then jerked to its left...

...Just as the *High Flight* fired its special net.

The net settled near the corner of the rooftop, empty.

"Grrf!" Stregenar cursed in his native language, and fired the tranquilizer dart...

...As the mega moth dodged, spun, and unleashed a blob of saliva, directly at him.

The dart clattered to the rooftop, broken and bent by the high-speed impact with concrete.

Startled, Stregenar jumped back, tossing the dart gun onto the deck behind him, as he instinctively flung up his hand to protect himself from the viscous projectile. The blob of sputum engulfed his hand and wrist to halfway up his forearm.

Stregenar screamed, falling to the decking within the airlock, then beginning to slide out of the hatch.

Ardennek, his colleague, leaped forward, grabbed the tether and pulled Stregenar back into the hatch before producing a huge knife from somewhere. With all his strength, the Kydeen brought the knife blade down on Stregenar's arm a few inches below the elbow. What was left of the dissolving hand, along with the blob of caustic mega moth spit, fell from the airskimmer toward the ground, as a gout of blood sprayed the inside of the airlock. Within moments, Ardennek had the stub of Stregenar's arm encased in a special compression bandage.

"Back off! BACK OFF!" Echo cried through the comm, even as he pulled the *Schmaltzblitz* away from the mega moth, turning the hatch away, while Omega hit the controls, closing the outer hatch and erecting the force field. "We have a casualty! Everyone back off! Retreat to the staging area! I'm calling Alpha-One-Purple-One! Ally down! Medical, stand by for an emergency transport to the medlab at Headquarters!"

"No! NO!" Stregenar gasped through his pain. "N-no! We need t-to get..."

"For all this time," Omega told the two Kydeen scientists, holding up her hands to stay their protests, "the thing hasn't gone off Manhattan Island, nor even left this vicinity. I don't think it's gonna go anywhere now."

"She's right," Echo said. "We need to get you to medical help, fast."

"He will not bleed out," Ardennek noted, "not with this bandage. The hand is gone, and that is extremely regrettable, but it cannot be helped."

"Yes, it can," Echo said, pulling back the left sleeve of his shirt and Suit jacket. Then he fingered his wrist. "See this scar? I was captured and tortured by Cortian slavers. They whacked off my left hand, my right leg just below the knee, and gouged out my left eye. And as you can see, it's all back, as good as ever. We have a process to grow it back, taught to our medics by the famous Edeptan healer, Doron. But without the 'scaffolding' of the bone structure, we need to get you into the regeneration pod as soon as possible."

"Ooo," Omega murmured. "So THAT'S why they needed the bones for you, but not so much for me..."

"Right," Echo confirmed. "I talked to 'em about it a little bit, there, during some of my therapy. The longer you wait to be 'dunked,' as Whiskey likes to put it, the harder it is to regenerate a missing limb without something more to go on than the stump...though I have to admit, I didn't understand the medical science behind WHY. They had you in the regeneration pod within a couple days. But since you had to find me, then go in and rescue me from the Cortian ship, THEN bring me to Earth, it was several days, nearly a week, after the injuries were inflicted before they could put me in the solution, so they needed the extra 'scaffolding' to make it all turn out right." He shrugged. "They can grow it back without it, but there's a lot less guarantee that it'll be like the original."

"Echo, Romeo," the comm annunciated just then. "You got

th' mic stuck open, an' we can hear th' debate. Y'all got th' tranq gun, but th' rest of us can stay here an' watch; it was only the *Schmaltzblitz* an' the *High Flight* that got revealed to it. Y'all back off, an' it'll settle down. Me 'n India think we can prob'ly trail it while you guys take Doc Stregenar t' th' medics."

"They'll have help, too," Uniform added. "Love an' I are in the *Take Five*, still camouflaged, and we'll be right there, backing up Alpha Two. Alpha One, I vote you guys take the casualty back to the medics, then ease back in; Alpha Four, I'm thinkin' you need to back off the *High Flight* a little, too, and hand off with us. You can both ease back into the formation later, once the beastie has settled down. Two and Five can take the point in the meantime, just to keep up with what it does."

"I'm betting, if it drinks ether and hasn't had any this whole time," India's voice came over the speaker, "it's probably horribly thirsty, and will come back to the pool to drink once it calms down a little, and doesn't feel threatened. And it didn't look to be able to drink it in THAT fast...and it won't evaporate that fast. So forty gallons is gonna last us a while. If the two perceived threats 'go away,' and the rest of us sit tight, this will still work."

"They have a point, y'all," Omega said, turning to the two Kydeen. "If we take you to medical help fast, they can most likely regrow that hand, and after some therapy, you'll never know you lost it. And the rest of us can cover things," she added. "We got this for ya. And the other skimmers have your teammates aboard."

"But Stregenar was our sniper," Ardennek said, speaking for his colleague; within moments after his protest, Stregenar all but collapsed on the deck in a near-stupor, in terrible pain... that Echo understood all too well.

"Neither member of Alpha One is any slouch in that department, ourselves," Echo pointed out. "Meg can't stand, but I can, and she's as good a pilot as I am. She can fly the airskimmer, and I can snipe with the dart gun out the hatch."

"But you have not the special protective suit."

"Stregenar did, but he took off the gauntlets to shoot," Echo noted, "and now see where he is. If the protective gauntlets get in the way of shooting the gun, it doesn't matter anyhow."

After a moment to consider, Ardennek nodded.

"Go," he said, waving at Echo. "Let us take Wenk to medical help."

"Gone," Echo agreed, turning back to the flight console.

* * *

The Alpha Line emergency call had been relayed appropriately, and Whiskey's team was waiting for them at the staging area. They eased Stregenar onto an antigrav stretcher so they could easily whisk him into a waiting medical skimmer.

"No, it's okay," a soothing Whiskey told the other Kydeen, as his team transferred the injured Kydeen onto the stretcher. "We can return his hand to him. We had plenty of experience on Echo, and this is a fresh wound."

"How much do you know of Kydeen physiology?" a worried Ardennek asked. "Do I need to come along and provide...?"

"Oh, chief of staff Dr. Zarnix Chifejuz was stationed on Kydeen for his residency," Whiskey explained. "He was off-duty, but we've called him back in expressly for this, and he'll be waiting. You're welcome to come along, especially if you're close to Kir Stregenar, but if you think you need to stay here and help your team catch this thing, I promise you, your friend and colleague will be fine. We'll take very good care of him, I swear."

Ardennek met Whiskey's eyes, searching; finally he nodded.

"Good, then. You will keep him free of pain?"

"As much as we can, yes. I've already run a medscan, and as soon as we get him into the medical skimmer, where I can access my supplies, I'll administer appropriate pain medication."

"Then I will stay here with Alpha One and assist them. Should he wake, tell him Onglo will be there soon, but is helping Alpha Line capture the exoheteroc. Um...Wenk and I are, are, I think you call them 'best friends'?"

"Ah. I understand," Whiskey said, laying a hand on the other male's shoulder. "I'll make sure he knows you wanted to come, but felt your duty was here."

"Oh good, you do understand," Ardennek sighed.

"Sure I do," Whiskey averred. "Dr. Rglfrz is my best buddy, being from Kardor notwithstanding; we look really different, but we're the same where it counts. I'd feel the same way, in your shoes."

And Whiskey, with his patient and his team, were off.

* * *

Moments later, the *Schmaltzblitz* was airborne and headed back toward the ether pool on the roof. Omega pondered the settings on the solid hologram system, then turned to Ardennek.

"Kir Ardennek?"

"Yes?"

"The exoheteroc's eyesight is going to be optimized for the Zheen atmosphere, right...?"

"Yes," Ardennek confirmed. "I am surprised it sees as well as it does in Earth's much thinner atmosphere, frankly. I expect most of its sensory work is being performed by its antennae."

"Great; this might just work, then," Omega decided, punching in a selection. "All right, Ace, put 'er in hover mode, then help me swap places with you."

"Okay, baby," Echo agreed, as he eased the *Schmaltzblitz* to a stop, then unstrapped from the pilot's seat. "You've obviously got something in mind..."

"Yeah," she averred. "You know how there's a cloud sequence in the hologram settings, but it's not really that good..."

"Aha," Echo said, as he helped her transfer from the co-pilot's seat into the pilot's seat without putting weight on her injured foot. "Except if the mega moth's eyesight isn't that keen in our atmosphere, it won't be able to TELL that it's not that good."

"Right. Especially if we ease along, like a cloud, and take our time getting there. But here's the thing; like Kir Ardennek said, its eyes aren't its only sensors."

"No," Ardennek verified. "Its antennae detect movement, especially involving airflow, fairly readily. This is likely how it sensed the aircraft, how it avoided the net, and how it detected Wenk."

"That's what I thought," Omega said, nodding. "Okay, then let's rearrange things a little bit, here."

"What did you have in mind?" Ardennek asked.

"Ohhh, I get it," Echo said then, and Omega realized he had been piggybacking her ponderings through their bond. "Yeah, baby, go for it, but then I got an elaboration I wanna try."

"Okay," Omega said. "What I was thinking was that we'll use the other airskimmers simply to help lift once we capture it, but we'll use the *Schmaltzblitz* to sneak up on the exoheteroc. We'll tranq it first, THEN, once the tranquilizer is starting to take effect, we'll fire the net. That should minimize the possibility of missing it with the net. Then we bring in the other skimmers to lift and transport it once it's unconscious. The whole rearranged sequence of events should also minimize the movement that it could detect, and let us get closer than we might, otherwise."

"And I want to add to that," Echo reminded. "I want to keep the force field up and the hatch closed until I'm lined up on the mega moth by looking through the hatch port, then I want you to only open the hatch just enough for me to stick the muzzle through, drop the force field, I fire, you bring up the force field, and if I miss, we'll drop it again long enough to fire again. Lather, rinse, repeat, as often as it takes, and sooner or later we'll nail this sucker, then you can close the hatch completely and leave the force field up." *And if we use our bond for the timing of it all, the 'giant cootie' won't have a chance to spit at me, because you'll already have the force field back up before it can,* he added mentally.

"Ah. That...makes me a little happier about it," Omega admitted then. "Okay, I can deal with that." *Alla that,* she added through the nd't'lq.

That's my gal, Echo told her privately. *I picked up on your worry through the nd't'lq, but you kept it damped down. When I thought of that little addendum, I figured, it wasn't just a good strategic idea; it'd help you feel I was better protected, too. And it lets YOU be the one protecting me. Directly.*

Yeah, it does, on all counts. Thanks.

No prob, baby.

"If I understood you both correctly, I believe this will be an excellent plan," Ardennek said then, unaware of the private mental conversation, "and more likely to be successful than our first attempt was."

"Okay, then let me ping the other skimmers and let them know the new plan," Omega noted, "as well as fill in your colleagues on Kir Stregenar's condition, and exactly what happened, and we'll get with this. It's likely to take longer, 'cause we'll have to go slower, but if it works, hey."

"Exactly," Echo agreed.

* * *

The mega moth was, indeed, still drinking its fill at the children's pool full of ethyl methyl ether. The *High Flight* had backed off and disappeared behind a building, then changed its solid hologram to a brick 'pod,' and very slowly eased up to the top of said building, becoming a rooftop 'penthouse.' The *Crash Cart* and the *Take Five* were still in position, still disguised as air conditioning units, observing the mega moth at the 'water hole.'

While Omega allowed the *Schmaltzblitz*, disguised as a cloud, to drift gently toward the rooftop, Ardennek helped Echo shrug into a restraint holster, then tether himself inside the hatch airlock. He brought the tranquilizer rifle to Echo after a quick check-out to ensure that the darts within had not been damaged—the offworld device had a small magazine of darts, and Stregenar had loaded it up before they headed out—then showed him a few quirks in the weapon's usage. Echo nodded his understanding and took his station, weapon at the ready but not yet aimed, watching closely through the hatch port, as they eased up on the mega moth's position.

As they grew near the rooftop on which the mega moth rested and quenched its thirst, Omega slowly rotated the *Schmaltzblitz* until it was nearly broadside to their direction of motion, thankful for the magnetic levitation drive that enabled her to perform that maneuver and still maintain their motion in the desired direction.

When they were within easy range, Omega murmured, "Get ready, Ace."

"I'm ready." He raised the rifle to his shoulder and sighted along it. "Bring us full around," he ordered.

"Aye, sir," Omega said, as she brought the *Schmaltzblitz* to an orientation fully perpendicular to their direction of motion,

307

then slowed the craft to a hover. "In position."

Echo took the time to hone his aim, then ordered, "Now!"

Paying attention to his actions through the nd't'lq, Omega was already moving by the time he spoke. She hit two controls in sequence, and the force field around the *Schmaltzblitz* dropped, then the hatch opened about six inches.

Echo leaned forward slightly and depressed the trigger on the dart gun. There was a soft *fwip!* and he moved back, ordering, "Shield!"

Omega immediately raised the force field again, erecting it almost before Echo spoke the order, and they watched as the mega moth let out a shriek of startlement and pain as it whirled about, seeking the source of the attack.

"Damn," Echo muttered, "I hit it, but not in the right place. It's too far down the body, and sort of in the side."

"Yes, that is not optimal," Ardennek agreed. "There will not be a sufficient quantity of the drug in its circulatory system to render it unconscious."

"Doesn't look like it's recognized us, Ace," Omega pointed out. "So it doesn't know where the dart came from. Try again."

"Okay," he said, bringing the rifle to bear another time. "Drop field."

Omega hit the force field toggle, and Echo fired the dart gun once more.

"Raise field!" he cried, even as Omega did so. The mega moth let out another screech of pain, whirling about and trying to dislodge the dart implanted between its shoulders. "I got it this time! Dead on target!"

"Great! Closing hatch, too!" Omega said, suiting action to words. "Prepping to follow if it flees!"

"It most likely will," Ardennek noted, still watching beside Echo.

"Shall I fire the net and try to tangle it?" Omega asked.

"No, not the way it is thrashing about now," Ardennek said. "The net is more for the tractor beams at this point. We accidentally killed the first exoheteroc we attempted to capture in a tractor beam—we tore it apart. They are surprisingly fragile, for such powerful, dangerous creatures; we all felt terrible for submitting it to such a gruesome death. At least,"

Ardennek sighed, "it was unconscious and felt no pain. But no; the perimeter of the nets have special nodes in them to allow the tractor beams to lock on and simply lift the exoheteroc as if it were in a bag. That is why we instructed your people during the briefing to aim for the nodes on the nets."

"Aha," Echo murmured, handing the dart rifle to the Kydeen scientist and swiftly taking his seat in the co-pilot's chair, fastening the five-point straps around his body without bothering to take the time to remove the tether harness. "Well, grabbing a human in a tractor beam isn't that great for 'em, either, so I guess I'm not surprised. Some species, mostly from other planets, handle it better, but unless it's a flat-out emergency, we try not to do that."

"I understand," Ardennek agreed.

"And it's off," Echo observed, as the mega moth headed away at speed.

"And running away," Omega noted. "Flying, anyway. Hang on, guys; the chase is on."

* * *

The four airskimmers shifted their camouflage to one of the cloud options, varying their disguises slightly, and followed after the mega moth, allowing it some space, confident that the tranquilizer would knock it out sooner or later. In the meantime, it helped if the mega moth had no idea where its pursuers were, or even if it WAS being pursued, and in that regard, the 'cloud' camo kept it marginally calmer than it might otherwise have been.

But they had yet to net it; it was still thrashing and whirling about in mid-air, attempting to dislodge the tranquilizer dart. The consensus between the various crew members aboard the airskimmers—especially including the Kydeen scientists—was that it would be better for it to tire itself out before any attempt was made to ensnare it in a net.

Thus they spent the next forty-five minutes following it as it flew, increasingly erratically, from this rooftop to that building façade to the next penthouse.

"Echo, I don't like the direction it's heading," Omega noted, as they tracked the giant creature.

"Me too neither," Echo agreed. "It'll be just our luck if it lands there. It's slowing down a lot, too."

"Yeah, it is, and getting kinda loopier," Omega observed. "About like I was, the other night on the pain meds."

"Yup. All doped up. Aaaand, there it goes, landing on exactly the building roof we did NOT want to get anywhere near," Echo grumbled, watching as the legs of the mega moth wobbled, then collapsed.

"And it's down," Omega added.

"And not moving," Echo tag-teamed.

"Yes, it is likely unconscious now," Kir Agrumbib noted from the *Crash Cart*'s comm. "Is there a problem with its location?"

"Not if we move fast," Echo explained. "This is the building that's in danger of collapse, because of a fire in its core that the exoheteroc set...was it yesterday? Last night? We've been so busy, we're having trouble with time frames, guys. So basically, it isn't a problem IF we hurry and get it out of here."

"Right, then. Go," Agrumbib ordered.

"Done," Echo said, firing the net.

Just as it was supposed to do, the net expanded from a small, neat package into a full latticework, capable of completely surrounding the alien creature. It settled over the mega moth, then programmed actuators initiated, gently wrapping the net around the mega moth so that it was fully enclosed.

"And that should take care of matters," Kir Barog, the equipment designer, said on the comm link. "You may activate your tractor beams at your discretion, and we shall transport the exoheteroc to the designated coordinates where our spacecraft waits with the holding facility."

"You're in the pilot's seat of the lead craft, Meg," Echo said. "It's your call."

"All right. Airskimmers, call out."

"Alpha Two in th' *Crash Cart*. Ready," Romeo's voice replied.

"Alpha Four in the *High Flight*," Golf answered. "Ready."

"Alpha Five in the *Take Five*," Love said. "We are ready."

"Copy readiness," Omega said, nodding at Echo, whose hands hovered over the controls. "All airskimmers, activate tractors on my mark. And three...two...one...mark."

Four tractor beams locked onto the beacons on the net's periphery and began to lift.

Until they didn't.

* * *

"Oh DAMN!" Romeo exclaimed on the comm, as the net tugged against them in half a dozen locations. "How th' HELL did it manage to hang up all over?!"

"Because there's antennas an' air unit hardware an' shit all over this roof," Omega pointed out. "I guess our giant cootie picked it because it had tree-equivalents and whatnot."

"Yes," Agrumbib agreed. "It would feel safe, or at least safer."

"Deactivate tractors," Echo ordered. "This isn't gonna work quite as planned."

"But we need to go down there and free it," Barog noted. "The net is designed not to break, so we must either untangle it or use our special devices to cut it loose."

"I don't like that at all," Echo countered. "That building could go at any time. We have smoke pouring out the side, over here. And as Assistant Director an' with Fox off duty, I'm responsible for the lot of you."

"It's that, or lose the exoheteroc, Echo," India argued. "We gotta do SOMEthing."

"What if a couple of the airskimmers hover just off the roof and unload several people to go handle this," Love suggested, "while the rest of us stand ready in case something bad starts going down? That way, we can grab people off the roof if we have to. If nothing else, once they get the net free, they can bail onto the net with the mega moth, an' we pick 'em ALL up."

"An' the more folks we put there, the faster we can free it," Romeo reminded.

"I'm not keen on it," Echo countered. "We don't know how much weight the roof can hold, given the conditions..."

"C'mon, man, let us at least try," Romeo protested. Echo drew a deep breath as Omega watched him, sensing his internal turmoil and worry.

"All right," he finally capitulated. "We'll go down there and all of us not piloting will—"

"Nope," Omega decreed just then. "Because you ARE the

Assistant Director, you'll be parkin' your butt right there in that co-pilot's chair, sir."

"She's right, Echo," Golf agreed. "This is the time you need to delegate. You an' Meg sit tight and be the backup in case something goes wrong, while the rest of us deal with this one. It's not a hard thing to do, we just gotta be fast and tread lightly."

"...Point," Echo conceded with considerable reluctance. "All right. The *Schmaltzblitz* will remain airborne and alert, as backup, while the rest of you free the net...except for the skimmer pilots."

* * *

"...No, you need to fly th' *Crash Cart*, babe," Romeo told India. "You're as good a pilot o' this thing as I am, now."

"But I'm lighter! I'll put less weight on the roof!" India protested.

"Yeah, but I'm taller, with a longer reach an' stronger arms," Romeo responded. "I c'n run out there, whack through a few cords, an' come back, while you might still be sawin' on 'em."

"Well, true," India sighed. "Dammit, having so much smaller a stature and musculature can be a pain in the ass, some days."

"I still think ya need t' be workin' with Meg some more in th' gym," Romeo suggested. "I think it'd help ya a lot in that respect. She got tricks f'r buildin' 'er upper body strength, an' that's what ya need, honey."

"I guess I'll talk to her when this mess is all over and done, then," India finally relented. "Go. But YOU BE CAREFUL."

"You know it, babe. I always am."

"I know. I'm just...I'm like Meg, this time," India said, anxious. "I got a bad feeling about it."

"Ugh," Romeo grunted, pulling a face. "Awright. I'll make extra sure."

"Good."

* * *

"This is Agrumbib aboard *High Flight* for Ardennek aboard *Schmaltzblitz*, please," Agrumbib's voice came over the comm then.

"Go, Kir Agrumbib," Omega said, flipping a switch. "We have you on speaker now."

"I am here, Ozir," Ardennek said. "What are your orders?"

"Onglo, stay aboard the aircraft," Agrumbib commanded. "I am only taking three of our people, along with the three Division One Agents who will be assisting, and leaving the rest aboard the various craft. As Assistant Director Echo wisely points out, we do not want too much weight upon the roof, lest it prove disastrous, and I believe we have more than sufficient personnel as a result. And Wenk will appreciate seeing you at the bedside, not in the bed beside him."

"True, all of it, Ozir. I will do as you say, though I should prefer to help..."

"Then help Alpha One watch for danger."

"Ah. Very well. Be careful, all of you."

"We shall, my friend."

* * *

"All right," Echo determined, "there's really only one good place for debarkation—right there, between the mega moth and that big AC unit—and there's only room for one skimmer at a time. *Crash Cart*, you're up."

"*Crash Cart* moving into position," India replied. "Romeo's got this one, and he's taking the two Kydeen we've got aboard with him."

"Copy that," Omega murmured, moving the *Schmaltzblitz* into position to watch carefully—both the rooftop operation and the side of the building, which was starting to discolor with the thermal stresses within it. From time to time, great billows of smoke rose from several breaks in the sides of the structure, obscuring their view, but Omega kept the airskimmer moving in an attempt to ensure the best visibility possible in the circumstances. "Echo, this doesn't look good," she murmured, careful to mute the communications system. "This high-rise could go any minute."

"I know, an' I'm not happy either, baby," Echo agreed, "but we need to try, at least."

"We could lose somebody."

"I know. So do they."

"All right. Shuttin' up."

"*Crash Cart* debark complete," India's voice reported, as Alpha Two's airskimmer rose and moved away.

"*High Flight*, you're up next," Echo ordered.

"Copy, *High Flight* moving into position for crew debarkation."

* * *

Within five minutes, three Agents and four Kydeen scientists were on the roof, spreading out around the periphery of the net, working along it and finding the snared mesh. Then they either worked to free it, or simply cut it.

"But they do not want to cut it any more than they can help," Ardennek noted, as the three beings in the *Schmaltzblitz* watched. "It weakens the net, and should 'Dukeer,' as the youngling named it, awaken before we have it in its travel habitat, it could find a way to slip free."

"I can see that," Echo decided, watching. "If the mesh starts to unravel, the net loses its structure."

"Exactly."

Just then, they saw Romeo extract his cell phone and speak into it.

"Romeo t' Echo."

"Go, Romeo," Echo said immediately, hitting the mic.

"That oughta have it. An' Kir Agrumbib says it should only take a couple airskimmers t' pick up this puppy; it ain't that heavy, since it flies."

"Well, that's true," Omega agreed.

"Good," Echo decreed. "*Take Five*, y'all are gonna help the *Schmaltzblitz* lift the mega moth; *High Flight*, move to the station, hover, and take on roughly half the personnel; that's Easy, Love, and a couple of the Kydeen scientists. *Crash Cart*, you'll follow, and pick up whoever's left."

"And HURRY," Omega added on the comm. "I'm seeing an increase in smoke from this hole in the side, and it's starting to sag."

"On it," Romeo replied. "C'mon, guys, time t' go!"

* * *

Omega handled the tractor beam and the flight controls in tandem as Echo watched her skill, pleased. Within moments, the mega moth was suspended in a mesh hammock of sorts, slung between the *Schmaltzblitz* and the *Take Five*.

Ardennek was exultant.

* * *

Alpha One watched as two of the four Kydeen scientists boarded the *High Flight*, along with Easy—and Love, who normally would have boarded the *Take Five* to join her partner, except it was busy helping lift the mega moth. Then the *High Flight* pulled away from the rooftop, and the *Crash Cart* eased into position. Both pilots were careful not to let their craft contact the roof...but in the end, it didn't matter.

"Oh no!" Omega exclaimed, looking down the side of the building. "ECHO! The building's going! It's started to pancake, down at the fire level!"

"SHIT!" Echo exclaimed, keying the mic. "ROMEO! GO GO GO! You're outta time, buddy!"

* * *

"Oh shit! GO!" Romeo cried to Agrumbib and Barog, herding them in front of him. "Get on board! NOW!" he shouted...

...Even as the rooftop began to descend in height, and the far corner started to crumble.

Barog and Agrumbib made the hatch, and Romeo was right behind, a stalwart but frightened India holding the *Crash Cart* about a foot above what had been the level of the roof.

But when the roof started to drop, Romeo found the step was too high to make. He tried to jump the distance, but with the surface beneath his feet beginning to accelerate downward, he simply could not generate the force necessary to make the leap.

"ROMEO!" India screamed, as she saw her partner and husband disappear below the deck of the airlock as the building collapsed underneath him.

Chapter 12

"SHIT!" Echo cried, ripping off the seat's five-point straps and leaping to his feet. "MEG! Emergency hatch open! Kill the force field!"

Then he spun and ran for the hatch, as Omega scrambled to do as he ordered.

* * *

Echo darted completely through the airlock and leaped on the threshold of the hatch, searching the smoke and dust for his former partner as he dove downward, once more utilizing skydiving techniques, as well as some of the moves he had learned in the glide park on Emdali a few months earlier.

Streamlining his body as finely as he could, Echo shot downward toward a flailing Romeo, now in free-fall just above the top of a pancaking building.

"C'mon, c'mon," Echo muttered to himself, as he closed the gap. "I don't have that much length..."

Romeo, seeing his ex-partner flying toward him, flung out a hand, and Echo grabbed it, then yanked upward. Romeo's downward motion slowed from the force of the yank, and Echo wrapped both arms and both legs around Romeo's body as he slammed against it.

"Grab me and hold tight!" Echo commanded, and Romeo did as he said...

Just as the tether to which Echo was still harnessed, and which was still hooked to the anchor in the *Schmaltzblitz*'s airlock, snapped tight.

"Uuf!" Echo gasped, the harness knocking a significant amount of the wind out of him.

"Ugh!" Romeo grunted at the same time, as his downward acceleration abruptly halted. "Oh man," he murmured then, voice weak. "Oh man."

"Hang in there, little brother," Echo said then. "Don't let go, whatever you do."

"Dude, you gonna have to pry me offa you once we get on

th' ground," Romeo declared, his voice shaky. "Meg's gonna be jealous o' me, man. I am SO not lettin' go!"

* * *

"*High Five* to *Schmaltzblitz*," Uniform called. "Meg, he got 'im! Damn, I gotta catch my breath over here. But we need to get 'em onto a solid surface, so they can get aboard one of the other airskimmers; they can't hang on like that indefinitely. I'm popping you a little trajectory, so we can carry the mega moth and still get 'em onto that building adjacent. Then India can come in with the *Crash Cart* and pick 'em both up."

"I copy plan, and concur," Omega said. She had seen the tether flying through the cabin as Echo sprinted across the flight deck, then watched it unreel in the airlock, even as she tried to resist the temptation to try and watch, knowing any movement of the skimmer would throw off Echo's trajectory and doom Romeo. She had, however, piggybacked Echo's eyes through the nd't'lq, and knew that he had been successful...barely. "Awaiting trajectory transmission."

"Annnd...sent."

"Received," Omega confirmed. She opened the file and studied it briefly. "Yeah, that's good, Uniform. Execute on my mark. In three...two...one...mark."

The two airskimmers began to ease toward an adjacent building, with the *Crash Cart* and the *High Flight* paralleling.

* * *

As the two men dangling at the end of the tether felt the motion, they glanced up, then in the direction the two skimmers were moving.

"Oh good," Echo said. "They're gonna set us down on that roof over there."

"That's a plan," Romeo decided. "But dude, I'm still not gonna let go. My arms an' legs done turned t' stone, I think. Or cramped up solid, one. THANK you, man!"

Echo laughed.

* * *

Ten minutes later, both men were aboard the *Crash Cart*; Ardannek reeled the now-empty tether and harness back into the airlock, and Omega closed the hatch and raised the force field.

India unstrapped, leaped from the pilot's seat, and grabbed Romeo, hugging him and fighting to keep from crying. Echo quietly slipped into the pilot's seat and strapped into the chair.

"Y'all catch your breaths back there," he told them, his tone gentle. "I got this." He thumbed the mic. "*Crash Cart* to *Schmaltzblitz*. Do you copy?"

"Good to hear your voice, Ace," Omega responded. "Everybody okay over there?"

"Other than a little shaken up, I think everybody's fine," Echo averred, "and they got reason to be a little shaken up."

"No shit," came his mate's reply. "Okay, is everybody ready to transport the giant cootie to the interplanetary pet carrier?"

"More than! Amen! Let's get this show on the road," came back the responses.

"*Take Five*, like we discussed before," Omega said. "*High Flight, Crash Cart*, please shadow us and be prepared to assist as required."

"*Crash Cart* confirms," Echo replied.

"*High Flight* confirms," Golf said.

"On my mark, and three...two...one...mark," Omega counted down.

The airskimmers, and their unconscious quarry, began to move, headed across the East River and Brooklyn, to the open ocean beyond.

* * *

Since Brooklyn was heavily populated, and they were going to be flying directly over one of the densest population centers, Omega wisely ordered the solid hologram camouflage changed to the same VTOL craft imagery Echo had used in his rescue of the daycare group. She then projected an additional solid hologram around the mega moth in its net, to ensure that no one saw anything but a group of aircraft, likely military, flying in formation.

Well out of sight of shore, and out of the shipping lanes, the Kydeen spacecraft awaited. It had deployed an advanced version of pontoons, and floated comfortably on the surface, while its crew had set up a small, special enclosure, also floating on deployable pontoons. As the airskimmer flight approached with its special cargo, it dropped its own cloaking system, so the Division One craft could approach accurately.

"Agent Omega," Kir Agrumbib called from the *Crash Cart*, "I am informed by our crew that the top of the enclosure is wide open, and ready for the exoheteroc to be placed within. If you and your companion craft will lower it into the enclosure, net and all, they will close the top, then activate the retraction mode on the net actuators, and replace the Earth air within it with our artificial replica of Zheen's atmosphere. There are already a feeder and a drink container, suited to the creature, loaded and within the enclosure."

"I hope the habitat you're taking it to will be bigger than this enclosure," Omega noted, as the *Schmaltzblitz* and the *High Five* began maneuvering to lower the mega moth, in its sling, into the container.

"It is," Agrumbib confirmed. "It is quite large. They are flying creatures, after all, and require room to move. We simply need a smaller vessel to transport it, else it would not fit into our spaceship. Even with an internal warp, it becomes difficult to get in and out without structurally compromising our spacecraft."

"Ah. Understood," Omega replied, as the mega moth, still unconscious, settled onto the floor of the containment vessel. "And there we go. Disengage tractor beams."

The *High Five* dropped its beams at the same time as Omega deactivated the *Schmaltzblitz*' beams.

"Good. And there is the lid closure," Agrumbib noted, as the 'roof' of the container automatically folded across the opening. "There goes the net, and the exoheteroc is now properly enclosed. Captain Vwrenkerib, would you transfer the Zheen air from the reservoir?"

"Transferring now," an unknown voice responded from the Kydeen craft.

Within moments, a murky cloud filled the zoological container, and only a minute or two later, a squeal emerged from the enclosure.

"That sounded happy," Omega noted.

"Oh, I am quite certain it is, now," Agrumbib agreed. "It has what, to it, will feel like a normal and comfortable environment. Even though it has only known the Earth environ, its instinct will tell it that it belongs in this one."

"I guess it's a good thing we got it in there when we did," Golf said over the comm. "We barely got it in there and the thing closed before it woke up."

"Oh, no, no," Agrumbib corrected. "The atmosphere is only to be released once the exoheteroc is safely enclosed, so we place the counter-agent to the tranquilizer in its air."

"Ah," Golf said. "So it's not unconscious any longer than it needs to be."

"Exactly. I am certain your medical personnel will tell you that being anesthetized for longer than needed is not good for the organism."

"True," India's voice replied. "Especially if it's sick or injured, and this creature may well be both, after so long in an improper environment, eating and drinking all the wrong stuff."

"So," Echo declared. "That little matter is taken care of, and thank you, Kir Agrumbib and colleagues for your invaluable assistance in doing so. Now...I guess we have to deal with the subsequent cleanup, rebuilding, ensuring that nobody in the general population knows what REALLY happened, getting a few agents healed up alongside your colleague, and..." he paused, then drew a breath audible over the comm, "try to figure out what exactly happened to our missing persons, and provide closure for their loved ones."

"And those, unfortunately, are things we cannot help you with, Assistant Director," Agrumbib said with a sigh.

"Oh no, I didn't expect you to," Echo said. "I was mostly going over 'em in my head, and just verbalized 'em in case one of my people realized I was forgetting something."

"No, Ace, I think you covered it," Omega confirmed. "Kir Agrumbib, is there a good way to let y'all off here, at your ship, or shall we take you back to Headquarters so you can see to your comrade first, and catch a shuttle up?"

"I think the latter is more appropriate," Agrumbib said. "Our ship's crew will ensure the enclosure is taken into the hold, then the *Arkeed* will contact your ground control for permission to depart, and we will, as you say, catch a shuttle from one of your spaceports when our business is completed."

"All right, y'all, back to Headquarters," Echo ordered.

* * *

"There you are, Wenk," Ardennek said roughly an hour later, as he entered the hospital room where the injured Kydeen scientist was being kept. "How are you?"

"Mmh," the wounded Kydeen grunted. "About as well as can be expected. The medics here tell me that I will be placed in something called a 'regeneration pod' in a few hours. They claim they can regrow my hand, and with some therapy, I will likely be back to normal function in a couple of lunations."

"That is good news," Agrumbib, the Kydeen team lead, said, as she stood in the doorway behind Ardennek. "Your team has been very worried about you, Wenk."

"I am in no pain," Stregenar informed them. "The Division One medical personnel are taking very good care of me. Their chief of staff knows our people and has worked on Kydeen before. I think I am in good hands."

"Agent Echo said as much," Ardennek affirmed. "I do not know how much you recall after you were injured, Wenk, but it seems he recently lost his hand and the lower part of his leg...though he did not mention how; something about those grrf Cortians, I think...and this same 'regeneration' procedure regrew them. So yes, I think this place will do an excellent job in healing you."

"Ah. That is...good to know," Stregenar said with a sigh, settling back into his pillows. "I am sorry for the complication, Ozir."

"There is nothing to apologize for, Wenk," Agrumbib told her injured colleague. "You have the most dangerous job, in any case. I am simply glad you are alive to BE healed. I suppose," she added, "we seriously need to look at modifying the tranquilizer rifle so that you may be able to shoot it without removing your gauntlets."

"I think that would be wise," Ardennek agreed.

"I should not argue," Stregenar said. "What are you going to do now? Did you capture the exoheteroc?"

"We did, and it is already in the environmental containment vessel," Agrumbib confirmed. "What will happen next is that the rest of the team shall be flown to our spacecraft, and we will return to the Kydeen system to place our newest acquisition in the habitat. Onglo, here, is going to stay on Earth with you; Assistant Director Echo has already made temporary housing available to him. He will be your voice while you are healing in this 'pod,' and then provide any assistance needed while you are being rehabilitated. Then he will accompany you home; Echo has assured me that Division One will see to it you are returned safely."

"This...is good, then," Stregenar decided, seeming to relax still more, even as he cast a grateful glance at Ardennek. "They will be putting me in this pod shortly, I think. So do not let me keep the team from departing as needed for our new exoheteroc."

"Very good," Agrumbib said with the Kydeen equivalent of a smile. "Onglo, you have your personal gear kit?"

"I do," Ardennek said. "I gave it to Agent Echo, who said he would see to it that it was placed in the quarters assigned to me for the duration of Wenk's medical treatment."

"Excellent. Then I think we shall bid you both farewell for the time," Agrumbib said. "Wenk, try to relax and heal well. We will see you both very soon."

And she departed, as Ardennek settled down in the visitor's chair beside the bed.

* * *

"...So this...'exoheteroc'...is now safely contained and in the Kydeen spacecraft in orbit?" Fox wondered in surprise, as he and Echo handed back over in the Director's office.

"It is, Fox," Echo said. "Not only off the planet, but already headed out of the system. And I can confirm it personally: Meg was flying the *Schmaltzblitz*, and it was one of the two airskimmers towing the mega moth. Once I grabbed Romeo and the two of us boarded the *Crash Cart*, I spelled India in the pilot's seat and she tended Romeo—stopping the fall sprained a few joints, I think, especially his shoulder."

"Stopping the fall? I don't like the sound of THAT..."

"Oh," Echo said, smearing a hand across his face. "More details in the shift report, I promise. The abridged version—the mega moth landed on that building you were worrying about collapsing, and we had to land a team to untangle the net...and

322

they almost didn't get off the roof in time. Romeo DIDN'T, and I bailed outta the skimmer wearing a tether harness, doing some 'a those specialized skydiving techniques, on a successful fishing expedition."

"Farkakte!" Fox exclaimed in horror. "And that's all? He had a few sprains? What about you?"

"That's all he had, yeah, and India confirmed that nothing is too serious, though his shoulder was mildly dislocated," Echo said, "where I hadda yank on it. But I'm fine. I got a few harness bruises, but that's to be expected." He paused, then added, "We DO have an injured Kydeen in the medlab; the sniper with the dart gun took a hit from cootie spit, and lost a hand. But after working on me, Zarnix assures me he can dunk the guy and grow the hand back, good as new."

"This is as good as possible then, I think," Fox decided. "What about getting him home? If his team has left..."

"His best buddy stayed behind," Echo explained. "I assigned Kir Ardennek quarters in the temporary housing; they'll be fine, and he'll see to it that Kir Stregenar gets home safely. I, uh, I did promise I'd see to it they had means to get home..."

"Not a problem," Fox said, nodding. "I'll make sure that gets done."

"Thanks, Fox. Hey, what's gonna happen to the little Kydeen girl? I know Meg is gonna ask about that, and I kinda wanna know, too..."

"Ah. Well, I've already initiated a few things," Fox noted. "I called and talked to my equivalent over on Kydeen, and we had a long discussion about the situation. It seems the girl is only about equivalent to a six-year-old human, or thereabouts, in actual age and growth. But her intellect is well advanced beyond that; she's even in a special school on Kydeen for precocious intellects. I think it would be a case of, 'What if Omega got into this situation as a six-year-old?' kind of thing..."

"Ah," Echo said, understanding. "But...I dunno, I think Meg was more...with it, if you get me...at that age."

"Well, probably. Omega was a special case, even before she was kidnapped, zun."

"No argument at all."

"But at any rate, it seems that her emotional maturity is NOT at the same level as her intellect," Fox continued. "And she truly did not understand that what she did was wrong, or that it could all go south on her, very badly, very fast."

"Ooo."

"Exactly. So we decided that we want her to have some psychological testing, to see where she IS with all of that. You know, mental, emotional, intellectual...how well does it all line up?" Fox said, spreading his hands as if laying cards on a table. "And based on those results, we're going to have her placed with a counselor, then put in some special classes, to try to balance out those maturity levels. Then we're going to see to it that she's officially monitored and mentored, most likely by one of the exoheteroc wrangling team. That way, she might even get to see her 'little' pet, once in a while." Fox grinned.

"Nice," Echo decided. "She's taught that what she did was wrong, and why, but with an eye toward maturing her into what she needs to be, and teaching her how to handle things like that..."

"By the people who know how," Fox finished. "Exactly. I just don't see charging a six-year-old with multiple counts of..." He shrugged. "Murder, or manslaughter, or...whatever. Given this creature was so little known even by the principal authorities on Kydeen, she surely didn't know what she was getting into." He cocked his head. "BUT, she MUST have the coursework and counseling, and she must be monitored, to ensure that it all goes where it needs to go, and this sort of thing doesn't happen again."

"No, I can agree with that," Echo said, thoughtful. "Now, if she was older, and more mature, if we knew she understood the ramifications of what she did, it'd be different."

"Oh HELL yes," Fox confirmed. "A child in late adolescence is only marginally removed from an adult, if they have matured properly in all facets."

"So now..." Echo said, and sighed.

"Right," Fox agreed, sighing himself. "Now we pick up the pieces here on Earth."

* * *

In the end, Fox inserted a news story into the media

that indicated the mega moth was just an old urban legend derived from the Lenape people, who had originally inhabited Manhattan Island before the Europeans. This legend was taken advantage of by a group of terrorists attempting a 9-11 type attack, and all the damage resulted from their drone fleet. Any 'observations' of the so-called mega moth were merely sightings of one or more disguised drones the terrorists were using as a decoy.

"After all," Fox noted to Alpha One and Two, "look at the building that pancake-collapsed. Same concept, right?"

"Right," India said with a snort. "Hey, whatever works, right?"

"Exactly," Echo agreed. "I'm just thankful that THIS time, the collapsing building was empty."

"Amen to that," India agreed. "And that our brother was on top of things when Romeo started going down with it."

"LOTTA that!" Romeo declared.

"Amein. I cannot tell you how relieved I was, kinder, to wake up from my shift off-duty to discover that the 'giant cootie,' as Omega put it so aptly, was not only captured, but offworld," Fox admitted. "Now we need to make some efforts to locate all the missing persons."

"That's gonna be hard," Omega decided.

"Yes, it will," Fox agreed with a sigh. "I'll have Forensics get on it, and we'll see what we can turn up."

* * *

When all was said and done, enough evidence was found to enable body identification of all but one person—Joshua Kanapkey, the zookeeper who went missing after several animals were killed. He would remain a missing person even though Forensics was better than ninety-nine percent certain that Kanapkey was dead.

"If we coulda found some remains," Romeo noted in a team-leads tag-up after an Alpha Line department meeting, "India says we coulda made sure o' what happened to 'im."

"It's the right time frame, though," Golf pointed out. "At least for the early attacks, like, shortly after the thing hatched."

"But with no clues or actual, provable latents, we got nothing legal but assumptions," Easy said.

"Yeah. And that also means that my cold case, back in early December, was one of the early victims of the mega moth," Echo said.

"Sure looks like it, Ace," Omega agreed. "When you and I talked about that the other night over dinner, I pinged Item the next day and had her send some people out there to take some more samples, then work with Forensics on the analysis. There's been some degradation from the weather in the weeks since, but there was enough residue left there to confirm the initial findings Forensics sent to Item...it was the giant cootie, all right. Except I guess it was a...a caterpillar-thing, at the time?"

"I guess," Echo shrugged. "At least we've identified what happened to him."

"What cover are we using for the deaths?" Easy asked. "I mean, the people that the mega moth...ate."

"We talked it over with Fox," Omega answered, "and decided that they were, um, 'acid attacks' by the same terrorists that were buzzing those 'drones' around everywhere, maybe even made by the drones."

"Oh. Ew," Easy said, as the others pulled faces.

"Hey, it isn't any worse than what actually happened," Echo reminded. "And leaves out the 'getting eaten' part, at that."

They all sighed.

* * *

"...So that's that," Fox declared to a joint Headquarters Alpha Line/Field Agents meeting in the big auditorium. "Thank you all for your most excellent, and very hard, work, during the recent crisis."

"Fox?" Chi, Omega's old friend among the field agents, raised a hand.

"Yes, Chi?"

"Can you tell us what's going on with Crutch, sir?"

"I had a suspicion that question was coming, at some point," Fox said with a wry smile. "Why don't you just ask her yourself?" He waved at the door.

Crutch appeared in it. In a medical antigrav chair.

A cheer went up from the Field Agents and Alpha Line

combined, as she slowly navigated the chair to the front of the auditorium, and up the ramp to the podium. She turned the chair to face her audience as Fox stepped back, then raised a hand.

The room silenced almost immediately.

"Hi there," she said with a smile. "I survived Omega's 'giant cootie.'"

Another cheer. Another raised hand.

"Be patient with me, guys," Crutch continued. "I got pretty badly banged up; according to Echo's report, my hoverpod bounced down the street. And that was after bouncing off the side of a building. Not that I remember any of it." She paused. "There's a pretty good-sized hole in my memory, 'cause the last thing I remember before waking up from the regen pod is looking at the first video of the mega moth in Fox's office. But the medics tell me that's good, relative to what they were afraid of. So that's good news. The bad news is that not everything stayed in place like it was supposed to during the regeneration process, so some of it didn't heal back quite right. It looks like my days of personally going into the field are probably done, though the medlab isn't giving up quite that easily; they want me to come back for some surgery, followed by additional regen treatments, that they think ought to fix things...assuming I take 'em up on it. But for the foreseeable future, once I get outta this thing," she patted the arm of the antigrav chair, "I'm probably gonna be on a cane."

An unhappy murmur rippled through the room.

"So you guys might want Nab heading up the department, I dunno. If you do, I'll understand, and I might take a desk job someplace. But if you don't mind having a desk jockey for a department chief, I promise I'll look out for the department as well as I ever did...with the sole exception of not being able to do it PERSONALLY, any more."

One of the field agents popped to his feet.

"Permission to speak, ma'am?"

"Go ahead, son."

"Crutch, ma'am, I think I speak for most, probably all, of us in saying that, no disrespect intended to Nab, but you're the den mom for this bunch, and we'd be delighted to have you continue running the department, however you have to do it."

Nab stood.

"Go, Nab." Crutch nodded at her departmental second.

"No offense is taken, Xi, because I feel the same way," Nab declared. "I'll be happy, as the assistant chief, to do whatever Crutch can't manage to do herself, as long as she continues to run the department."

Fox stepped forward.

"Why don't we wait just a little while before we decide who gets what part of the job?" he suggested. "Being married to the assistant chief of staff of Medical has its advantages; I'm aware of what they have in mind for those future procedures on Crutch, and it sounds to me like a good plan. The only reason they didn't do 'em to begin with is because they wanted to get her 'dunked' before she expired on us. And once they get the skeletal structure corrected and everything running optimally, they plan on running what Zebra and I have been calling a 'de-aging' on her, too. You might just get back a spry and active twenty-something Crutch with her current levels of experience."

"Or they might not," Crutch pointed out.

"Or not," Fox agreed. "But I'd say the probabilities are in your favor, old friend. After all, look how well Echo and Omega both turned out. Meanwhile, don't worry about the future, and concentrate on your healing in the NOW. Nab and I have the department covered, for the time being."

Crutch stared at Fox for long moments, considering. Then she turned her attention back to their audience and held out a querying hand.

The room erupted again, in whoops and cheers and general good wishes.

"All right," Crutch capitulated. "I guess that's what we'll do, then."

Fox grinned, as the field agents celebrated.

* * *

"...So, with GALINT indicating that nothing much is coming down the pipe at us, for a change," Echo told the department in the next morning's Alpha Line meeting, "we're giving all the Headquarters Agents some down time, from both the Field department and from Alpha Line. I want volunteers by second lunch from the other Offices, willing to come in and give us some time off, guys. Skeleton staffing, per Fox's approval and recommendation, for the next two weeks."

"Woo," Romeo hooted, pleased. "Jus' in time f'r Valentine's Day, too!"

"Yeah, an' for the first time, Meg and I are gonna get to go out on a date for it," Echo averred, pleased. Omega grinned. "Is everybody good with that overall plan at Headquarters?"

A cheer went up.

"What about the rest of y'all?" he wondered, addressing the big video monitors along the side walls. "Are things too busy there to send a few Agent teams here to spell us for a bit?"

"Sure, man, we got you," Quebec replied on the video screens. "We're big enough now to fill in like that, provided you were serious about that skeleton staffing."

"I was," Echo confirmed. "If I get one or two teams per Office, I think we'd be good. Unless something big and unexpected goes down, in which case, it goes back to 'all hands on deck.' But," he added, "that doesn't look like happening."

"Well, we all know those kinda things never give you much, if any, warning, anyhow," Jack observed.

"Ain't it th' truth," Romeo agreed.

"Unless Meg's around an' has a 'feeling,'" Monkey noted with a grin. "Damn, can that be handy."

"No shit," Yankee agreed.

"Point," Echo said, raising a pleased eyebrow at Yankee's enthused concurrence. "Meg?"

"Nope. I got nothin', Ace," Omega said then. "I already thought about that when we were talking to Fox about it earlier, so I checked." She shrugged. "Not that it always works, but hey."

"Great. We're on track, in so far as we can tell," Echo decreed.

"Okay. The Office Alpha Line leads will get with you after the meeting, Echo, and work it all out," Quebec offered.

"That sounds good, then," Echo said. "In that case, the meeting is adj—"

"Hold on a sec, boss," Golf said, as he, Easy, Romeo, and

India stood and moved to the front of the room. All the other Alpha Line Agents, in the room and on the monitors, perked up. "Listen, um, we know that you and Meg are still on part-time…"

"Well, we're up to three-quarters time now," Omega pointed out, from her seat in the medical antigrav chair beside Echo. "And that's mostly on account of needing to ease back into the work, plus the medlab wants a little more counseling for both of us."

"You two have had a rough time of it lately," India agreed. "You need all of that."

"We know," a serious Echo said. "That's why we're not pushin' it."

"And Alpha One won't be goin' into the field on a full active status until I get this bum foot healed up, anyhow," Omega added. "Zebra says it's comin' along good, and to be patient, 'cause tendons heal slow, but…"

"Not as fast as Meg wants," Echo finished for her. "And damn, do I know about that!"

"Yeah, but you're back in the office and working now, both of you," Golf continued. "And…damn, guys, you two did some amazing work during the whole kaiju mess we just wound up. And that, with Meg having that busted foot, and Echo coming off major regen work after being tortured."

Echo and Omega both shrugged.

"We just did what we had to do, y'all," Omega murmured, and Echo nodded.

"Lotsa that," he said.

"We know, but your 'have to do' is, like, head an' shoulders above most people's. And, well, we just wanted to let you know how much we all appreciate you two," Easy declared, earnest. "I think Romeo is one of the biggest cheerleaders for that, especially after you pulled his ass outta the fire, pretty much literally, Echo."

"What he SAID, dude," Romeo averred with appreciation.

"Amen," India added.

"Anyway," Golf tag-teamed his partner, "the whole department put our heads and our wallets together an' got you two a…" He broke off, shaking his head. "Call it a combined wedding, housewarming, an' welcome-back gift." He waved a hand, then called, "Bring it to the door, guys!"

Four agents from Supplies trundled a tall object in a box, on a dolly, to the open door of the Alpha Line Room. India walked down the aisle between desks and pulled back a flap near the top of the box.

This revealed a clock face with gold scrollwork, Roman numerals, and mother-of-pearl inlay, encased in a decorative dark wood casing. Omega clapped her hands in delight.

"It's a grandfather clock!" she exclaimed. "Oh, my grandmama on Dad's side had one of those! I loved it! She was gonna will it to me. But it got destroyed in the tornado..."

"We thought it looked like you guys," India explained, "and it could go in the back of the den, beside the door into the dining room. It chimes the Westminster Quarters, but you can turn those off and on, AND adjust the volume, so it won't wake you in the middle of the night."

"We had one, too, when I was a kid," Echo admitted. "I think Mom took it with her after I joined the Agency, though. I'm not sure what ever happened to it." He pressed his lips together, trying to hide the emotion he felt, then said, "Thanks, y'all. That's...cool."

"I tolja they'd like it," Romeo said with a huge grin.

"Yeah, man, but you hadda do something to make up to Meg for hittin' all over her man," Easy teased. "You had him in such a clinch on that rooftop, I didn't think you were ever lettin' go. You put out the baby shower invitations yet?"

The whole room roared with laughter.

* * *

Fifteen minutes later, the meeting was adjourned, the replacement shift schedule was set, and Alpha One saw their new, heirloom grandfather clock set in place beside the dining room door. Echo wound up the chain, Omega set the clock hands, and a gentle tap by Echo to the pendulum set it going, with a soft, slow, *tick, tick, tick, tick.*

"Oh, that's nice," Omega sighed. "So soothing."

"Yeah. And the clock is gorgeous," Echo agreed. "Something else for us to enjoy."

"Yup."

"Now what?"

"I dunno, Ace. We got some more time off, here. What do you wanna do?"

"I vote for a nice long soak in the hot tub, with glasses of something, to start," Echo suggested. "I think we could both use it. We can figure out what else to do while we soak, maybe."

"Ooo. I could get behind that platform."

"Let's go, then."

* * *

"Well," Echo sighed several hours later, when the pair finally extracted themselves from the hot tub in the bathroom. He had placed several oversized bath towels within reach before they ever entered the tub, and now they dried wet bodies with them. "I guess these are about as good as they're gonna get, now." He fingered the scar just below his knee as he sat on the edge of the hot tub; the scar was still slightly depressed, and still a purplish-red. "Dammit."

"No, no, no, hon," Omega said, scooting over to sit next to him, careful to avoid using her injured foot. "First off, it's still only about a month and a half since you were decanted from the regen process. You've come an AMAZING way since then. So you need to remember that. And second off, see this color right here?" She fingered the scar. "See how it's kind of that odd bright pinkish shade, with some purple thrown in for good measure?"

"Yeah?"

"YOU know as well as I do, that's the sign of a FRESH scar. Over time, the color will change, will fade, will turn a lot closer to your normal skin color."

"Yeah, but they're usually paler than your skin. Given my Apache ancestry, I have a little more pigment to my skin than somebody who was full Caucasian. It'll show."

"Not as much as you think, I'd bet. Especially this leg, and between it and your wrist, the leg scar's bigger. But you mostly keep your legs covered in your Suit trousers except when we're at the beach house, so they're paler than, say, your arms."

"Well, true..."

"And three, have you stopped to think back and realize just how much they've filled out since you were first decanted?"

Omega wondered. "I'd estimate they're easily two-thirds of the way to filled out, relative to what they were."

"Huh," Echo said then, studying the scars closer, and trying to remember what they'd looked like before. "You know what? I think you might be right."

"Yeah, I AM right, Ace! So just be patient. I'd lay money that, as you continue to work out and build the muscle strength back an' stuff, it'll KEEP filling out, until it's pretty close to the same level as the rest of it. Besides, you don't want it to form a keloid. That's kinda goin' the other direction with it."

"Yeah, but..." He stopped, shrugged, and sighed again.

"What?"

He answered through the nd't'lq, apparently unable to voice it, or uncertain of the words.

You're stuck with damaged goods now, baby. This is permanent. So is the limp. An' I've studied my face while I'm shavin' an' shit, and I can see where the scar is around that eye.

You can? 'Cause I can't, and I look at you every day.

You're kidding.

Nope.

But it's...

Are you sure you're not seeing something you expect to see, honey? I swear to you, Omega told him, *I have studied you backwards, forwards, and sideways, including while you were sacked out in your recliner WITH THE LIGHTS ON, and there is nothing noticeable about that eye. If there IS scarring, it's hidden in the eyelid folds. But I don't think there's any at all.*

Echo just stared at her in surprise.

You don't believe me, she said.

No, I do, I just...I saw...

C'mere to the big mirror, then, and show me.

Omega tossed her towel over the seat of the vanity chair, then carefully transferred to the rolling seat, grabbed him by the hand, and towed him across the room to the mirror over the dual sinks, turning on all the bathroom lights. She pointed at his reflection.

There. Now show me.

I, um... He pulled his eyelids open with the fingers of one hand, then tried to point. *It's, uh, well, I think it's...no wait, I got that under the other eye, too. It's right...no, that's not it, either...*

Omega sat there, staring, arms folded across bare breasts, one eyebrow raised.

I'm waiting, she told him. *Where's the scar?*

I, um...I dunno, he admitted then, feeling sheepish. *I...maybe you're right. I'm seein' things that aren't really there, 'cause I'm lookin' for something.*

Exactly, hon. Her entire body language, including her expression, softened into affection, and she leaned up and deposited a kiss on his cheek. *You're bein' WAY the hell harder on yourself than anybody else is being, including me, including the docs. You're gorgeous, sweetheart. I have the most built, the most handsome man for a husband that I have ever seen.*

Echo flushed.

Seriously, Alex, she reiterated. *I mean it. When I look at you, especially if you're asleep or relaxed in the shower or something, it's like watching the statue of a Greek god come to life, sometimes. At least, I think so. You're a hunk. Hell, maybe the statue DOES have a couple of scratches to the finish, here an' there. It doesn't harm the structural integrity of the statue, an' he's still a looker.*

Whoa, waitaminit, Meg, that's kinda over the top, Echo protested.

Maybe YOU think so, but I don't! she told him with a lustful grin. *Look. When I say Greek statue, I'm talking about general shape and bodily proportions. Early on in our partnership, when we were in the gym, I remember tellin' you, you had great proportions and definition. That's what I meant, even back then.*

Yeah, I think I remember that, he said, thoughtful. Then he shot a smirk in her direction, and deliberately glanced down at his body. *But I think the family jewels are a little better than most o' the statues...*

Omega stifled a bark of laughter into a really loud snort, then grabbed her nose in both hands with a muffled, "Ow!"

Echo doubled over, laughing.

Omega shot him a dirty look, then, watching, grinned.

* * *

When he finally sobered, Echo teased her. *So you like the package, huh? Better than the statues?*

334

I won't argue that at all, she agreed. *I read somewhere that the ancient Greeks had some weird ideas about stuff like that, and were prone to NOT depictin' it to the proper proportions.*

A pleased Echo grinned, then grew serious.

So...you're not bothered by any of it? The scars, the...

* * *

Not one bit, Echo, she declared, calm. *Hon, back before Christmas, I think it was, I told you that, in a choice between having you here beside me with a few scars, versus not having you back at all, I'd take a few scars any day. And I haven't changed my mind. I'm angry that they were such sons o' bitches that they'd dare to harm your knockout of a body, and I'll always regret that they hurt you so badly and I couldn't stop or prevent it. But frankly, Ace, YOU notice it way the hell more than anybody else does, now. The scars aren't that noticeable any more unless you deliberately call attention to 'em, and the limp is the same way. That limp is so damn UNnoticeable, it's almost not there.*

He stared at her, considering, and she suddenly realized that consideration was as much mental as visual; he wanted to know if she really meant what she had said, really believed it. So she allowed her calm honesty to show in her mind as well as her face. Finally he nodded.

Something else I want you to realize, she told him, *is how little ANY of it affected your performance in the field. Oh, sure, you went from zero to Alcubierre warp in half a second, essentially, an' that prob'ly wasn't great on the muscles, but you were running, ducking, dodging, jumping, carryin' my ass all over, even jumping out of a building with me in your arms! Never mind skydiving to the rescue an' grabbing Romeo! All in do-or-die situations! And not only did you do it, you're here, unharmed, and everything's taken care of! We're BOTH here, ROMEO'S here, because you did it! It. Did. Not. Affect. You. In. The. Field. Not one little bit.*

Echo flatly gaped at her.

* * *

"You're right," he realized then, startled into speaking aloud. "I didn't even have time to think about any of that. I just had time to react. And I reacted the way I always have, with the same instincts and feel and muscle memory...and it all worked like it always has. Every time. And it was SO instinctive, I didn't even consider that until just now, when you pointed it out."

"Exactly," Omega said. "And I watched you, and shared a lot of the sensations with you, and you looked like the Echo I've always worked with. And I know it felt like your body was doing just what you expected and needed it to do. I could FEEL it, Ace. You're back. Nine hundred and ninety-eight percent, and then some." She paused, then added, "And as soon as my foot and ankle heal up, Alpha One is gonna be back *in toto*, at least physically."

"I guess so," Echo agreed. "We're still getting counseling, you an' me, and likely we'll continue to for the next few months, I suppose. But we're both getting better, even on that. Zz'r'p checked me out after the whole dodge-ball thing on the roof, and he was pleasantly surprised at how well I handled things mentally and emotionally."

"Why do you think you're handling it now?" Omega wondered, curious.

"I told him an' Zarnix that I thought it was 'cause I'm basically an action-oriented guy," Echo explained. "The forced inactivity caused by the healing and needing to re-strengthen everything left me antsy and prone to anxiety over how well that healing was going...because I COULDN'T act. At all. Even for day-to-day shit. Combine that with the PTSD an' the 'fragmentary me,' and it left me in a mess."

"Ooo," Omega said, suddenly understanding. "Yeah, that makes sense. Me, I just need to get used to the notion that we're a thing, an' the mere fact of you bein' so close to me is NOT gonna get you killed—I mean, I'm not some sort of a target where the near misses take out the people close to me, you know? All right, granted, Slug took out my parents an' grandmomma, but that's the ONLY thing, because..." she shrugged. "I guess he wanted me a free agent."

"That's what I always figured, yeah."

"And so that's all done, 'cause he's DEAD, and I'm pretty sure we came to the end of the booby traps he left, so we're good. And we have each other's backs."

"In spades, I think," Echo decided. "I mean, let's face it. With the nd't'lq link we have, we're hot shit, Meg. If not for that, I'd probably have died up on that roof the other day. Hell, if not for that, the Cortians and their 'customers' woulda killed me."

"I..." Omega began, doubtful.

"Hush, baby," he murmured, putting an arm around her. "I know. It's okay. But...I got a little secret. An' I think it's time to tell you about it."

"What?"

"I've been tryin' a few things, the last couple days, just little subtle stuff, piggybacking on your senses here and there. And it worked! Every single time. You're the one has the low-level telepathy, but with this link that Zz'r'p set up for us, I can run it the other way now. *I* can look out for YOU now, too." He shrugged. "You'll probably always be better at that than I am, but hey. I CAN help YOU now. So," he explained, "if, say, the tables get turned, and you're the one duckin' an' dodgin', I can help you watch out, can direct you where you need to go...just like you did, for me."

"Whoa," Omega said blankly. "That's...good."

"So we have an advantage that most of our perps won't have a clue about," Echo pointed out. "Yeah, you told me there's scuttlebutt. But even those who have heard it won't KNOW. And they sure as hell won't know we can do THIS."

"Cool," Omega decided, and Echo picked her up and carried her into the bedroom.

* * *

"Now," he said, sitting her on the side of the bed, then kneeling before her, "I'm betting you forgot all about what yesterday was."

"Ace, after everything that went down with that damn giant cootie, I don't even know what day of the WEEK yesterday was," Omega declared in mild exasperation, throwing up her hands. "Never mind calendar dates."

"I figured as much," he said with a grin. "Yesterday was two years exactly from the time me an' my perp ran over your telescope on the Ranch in Texas. For all intents and purposes, it was your anniversary of joining the Agency. Not the official date—which would be the day we got you into our computer system, which anniversary is in a couple more weeks, like, late February—but the date when we met, the date when, essentially, you became one of us."

"Oh!" Omega said, clapping her hands. "Yes! I'd forgotten all about that!"

"So," he added, "I haven't really looked through your closet or anything to know what you got in there, but is there any chance you have some sort of, you know, kinda sexy loungewear in there? Not flannel or sweatshirts or whatever, but..." He shrugged. "You know. Something...pretty."

"Huh?" Omega said, surprised by the question, and wondering what he had planned. "Um, yeah, I do, actually. I got a pair of silk lounging pajamas back when I hadda have all those evening gowns for the Broadway show. India spotted 'em when we were shopping, and told me I oughta grab 'em while I could, 'cause sooner or later they'd come in handy."

"Pajamas?" Echo looked askance.

"Well, that's what they're called; they're not really pajamas as such, in that they're not actually sleepwear, though I suppose you could use 'em for lingerie. They're considered a more casual eveningwear than a formal gown—think cocktail party or somethin'—and they're comfy."

"Perfect. Where are they?" Echo rose and slid open her closet door.

"Back of the closet, behind the evening gowns. I was gonna wear 'em for you back during the Broadway show case, but things didn't time out right."

He dug around for a few minutes, then came up with a couple of black garments on a hanger.

"This them?"

"Bingo."

"Okay, baby, you put that on. I got those silk lounge pants an' shit that you gave me for Christmas that I can wear. I didn't figure either of us was up for a night on the town, but now that things have settled, I did wanna celebrate the first of your two anniversaries with the Agency. So I called our restaurateur friend Gianna Ricci, and she's sending over a four-course meal for us. It oughta arrive in about half an hour, forty-five minutes, complete with candles, all ready to serve...and enjoy in private. Just you an' me."

"Aw, Ace," Omega said, smiling, as she reached for the silk pajamas. "You think of everything."

"I dunno about that," he said, modest, "but I try."

"You do great!"

"And I'll keep doin' my best to do that," he added, as he leaned over and kissed her.

"We're Alpha One, you an' me," Omega pointed out with a dimpling grin. "Nothing less than our best will do."

Author Notes

"Once more until the breach, dear friends..." It's book 12 of the series! I'm really excited about that! See, this series comes from a group of novellas I wrote a couple decades back, which I expanded and made novel-length, as well as (in my humble opinion) more exciting. Where my enthusiasm over THIS book comes in is that (other than book 2, *A Small Medium at Large*, which started out as a promotional short story and turned into a novel of its own), the original novella series stopped at *Head Games*, book 8. (There were 7 original novellas.) I did have a very few notes, and even a scene or two, for what became book 10, *Break, Break Houston*, but that only amounted to a few thousand words, not even ten thousand...when these novels are typically averaging 120 to 130 thousand words! That means that I'm already two additional novels (from scratch!) past that original novella series! With more planned!

I may have to slow down production a little bit; the *Displaced Detective* series looks like picking up again with its new publisher, and the publisher of that series is interested in a steampunk novel I have which would be the first in another series, *The Adventures of Aemelia Gearheart*. Plus I've agreed to write a trilogy in Richard Weyand's *Empire* universe. That means that my usual 4-5 books per year quota is likely to be spread out over several series! (I don't have THAT many spoons, folks!) But never fear, Echo and Omega and the rest of the 'family' will be back soon!

And to that end, I need to thank Mom & Dad aka Colene and Steve Gannaway; for those who always ask about Mom, she's doing pretty well after her strokes, and starting to get around the house a bit more. And my husband Darrell, of course, who not only helps me with the print layouts, but does such an AWESOME job on the cover art!

Beta reader Dr. James K. Woosley helped me do a lot of brainstorming on the mega moth, both from the physics of how it's so big, and the chemistry of how it does what it does, in addition to the beta reading. Beta reader Evelyn Zinn, along with fellow author Dan Hollifield, helped me figure out the offworld gift-giving! Randy Jones is one of the fastest beta readers I've ever seen, and quite accurate in picking up misspellings and typos!

There are several Tuckerizations in this particular tome. Paul Sparks, I hope you recognize Agent Prep! Not to mention Joanna and Dave Weiner, never mind Joshua Kanapkey, Julian Thompson, and Curtis Ackerman! A certain department head over the Field Agents is right in there, too! Thanks for letting me have some fun with your literary avatars!

This one was a little different, but I have to admit, I had as much fun with it as usual. I hope you do, too.

~Stephanie Osborn
March 2019
Huntsville, AL

About the Author

Stephanie Osborn is a former payload flight controller, a veteran of over twenty years of working in the civilian space program, as well as various military space defense programs. She has worked on numerous Space Shuttle flights and the International Space Station, and counts the training of astronauts on her resumé. Of those astronauts she trained, one was Kalpana Chawla, a member of the crew lost in the *Columbia* disaster.

She holds graduate and undergraduate degrees in four sciences: Astronomy, Physics, Chemistry, and Mathematics, and she is "fluent" in several more, including Geology and Anatomy. She obtained her various degrees from Austin Peay State University in Clarksville, TN and Vanderbilt University in Nashville, TN.

Stephanie is currently retired from space work. She now happily "passes it forward," teaching math and science via numerous media including radio, podcasting, and public speaking, as well as working with SIGMA, the science fiction think tank, while writing science fiction mysteries based on her knowledge, experience, and travels.

For more, or to subscribe to Stephanie's newsletter, go to her website, http://www.stephanie-osborn.com/.

Don't miss any of these highly entertaining SF/F books by Stephanie Osborn!

The *Division One* series by Stephanie Osborn (from Chromosphere Press):

Alpha and Omega
A Small Medium At Large
A Very UnCONventional Christmas
Tour de Force
Trojan Horse
Texas Rangers
Definition and Alignment
Phantoms
Head Games
Break, Break, Houston
Tourist Trap
Mega Moth

Coming soon:
Everywhere Signs
Diplomatic Catfight
Shake, Rattle and Roll
Die Glocke
Forming Terra
With more on the way!

* * *

The *Burnout* series by Stephanie Osborn (from Twilight Times Books and Chromosphere Press):
The Fetish
Burnout: The mystery of Space Shuttle STS-281
Coming soon:
Escape Velocity
* * *

Sherlock Holmes: Gentleman Aegis series by Stephanie Osborn (from Pro Se Productions):

Sherlock Holmes and the Mummy's Curse
Coming soon:
Sherlock Holmes in the Wild Hunt
Sherlock Holmes and the Tournament of Shadows

* * *

The *Displaced Detective* series by Stephanie Osborn (being rereleased by Enigma House Press, an imprint of Hydra Publications):
The Case of the Displaced Detective: The Arrival
The Case of the Displaced Detective: At Speed
The Case of the Cosmological Killer: The Rendlesham Incident
The Case of the Cosmological Killer: Endings and Beginnings
A Case of Spontaneous Combustion
Fear in the French Quarter

9 781950 633258